Revelat

Of the

True Ripper

By

Vanessa A Hayes

Paperback ISBN

Published by Lulu

www.lulu.com

Acknowledgements

My grateful thanks go to my husband and my daughters. There is no doubt I have bored them totally with the subject of the Ripper, and yet they endure my endless musings. Without their support and help I would have never written this book.

A big "thank you" goes to my friend Gina who now knows as much about the Ripper as I do. I would also like to thank Ivory Moon Literary Agents who have put up with this obsessed woman, who does nothing but talk about the Ripper.

To my many friends and to anyone who was willing to listen to my ideas and theories on the case: thank you for listening, or at least looking conscious.

Finally, I would like to thank all my neighbours whose computers I have ruined during the writing of this book.

I would like to dedicate this book to two very special people I lost during my research and writing: Morvyth Hayes and Thomas Atherton.

I hope you both approve.

Contents

Preface

Police Constable Robert Spicer 101 H Division.

Does this make you think?

On the 30th September, 1888, Police Constable Spicer was on duty at the time of the murders of both Elizabeth Stride and Catherine Eddowes. He wrote this report to the *Daily Express* in 1931:

I had worked my beat backwards, and had come to Heneage Street off Brick Lane. About fifty yards on the right down Heneage Street is Heneage Court. At the bottom of the court was a brick-built dustbin. Both Jack and a woman (possibly Rosy) were sitting on this. She had 2s in her hand, and she followed me when I took Jack on suspicion. He turned out to be a highly respected Doctor, and gave a Brixton address. His shirt cuffs still had blood on them. Jack had the proverbial bag with him (a brown one). This was not opened and he was allowed to go. I saw him several times after this at Liverpool Street Station accosting women, and I would remark to him, "Hello, Jack! Still after them?" He would immediately bolt. He was always dressed the same—high hat, black suit with silk facings, and a gold watch and chain. He was about 5 feet 8 or 9...and about 12 *stone, fair moustache, high forehead, and rosey cheeks.* (Spicer March 1931 *Daily Express.*)

In addition, an *Express* reporter interviewed Constable Spicer. Spicer told him that he was reprimanded on arrival at the police station for arresting the doctor and told that he could have no further role in any further investigations. He went on to say that there were at least eight or nine Inspectors working on the case, in the station, at that time. Spicer was amazed that no-one wanted to search the bag or question the blood-stained cuffs of the doctor.

Police Constable Spicer's family believe the suspect doctor was not a qualified doctor, but a medical student at the London Hospital.

What was it about this doctor that put him beyond the law?

Chapter 1

An Introduction to Whitechapel

Until 1888, Whitechapel's most infamous character was Dick Turpin. Born in Essex in 1705, Turpin went on to serve as an apprentice in a butcher's shop in Whitechapel. He was sacked because of the "brutality of his manners," according to Harrison Ainsworth in his book *Rockwood.* He turned to crime and teamed up with a man called Matthew King around 1735, the pair mainly operated around the East End. While drinking in the Old Red Lion public house on Whitechapel High Street, King was mortally wounded during an ambush. Turpin escaped only to be caught later in York.

On August 31st 1888, Britain's first serial killer would make his mark in history on the streets of London. He would stalk Whitechapel for ten dark weeks.

Today, "Jack the Ripper" might not be considered the most *evil* killer Britain has ever had, but he is certainly the most notorious. Since the 1880s, all other serial killers have been benchmarked against him.

The abhorrent crimes of Jack the Ripper first appeared on the 31st of August 1888, and disappeared after the 9th of November 1888. Many people were questioned, yet "Jack" was never caught. He chose the local prostitutes as his victims and went on to inflict extensive post-mortem mutilations, after silencing them by cutting their throats. So shocking were these murders in the 1880s that Jack the Ripper became infamous overnight. How many women he actually murdered is still not clear.

Many Ripper experts generally agree that there were only five victims. Other murders committed at the time were added to the list of "Whitechapel Murders," but there was no concrete evidence to prove that these other poor women were murdered by Jack the Ripper. Assistant commissioner Robert Anderson of the Metropolitan Police believed that Martha Tabram was the first victim during Jack the Ripper's reign, as do many authors. I disagree. Although this woman was murdered and stabbed, there appears to be no evidence to suggest it was by the same hand who committed the "Whitechapel Murders" as they were called by the Police. There are Authors who do not believe that Mary Kelly, Catharine Eddowes, or Elizabeth Stride were victims of the Ripper. In my opinion, if any of these women were not a Ripper victim, it would have to have been Elizabeth Stride, for reasons you will read later in this book.

The Victims

I have included all of the women who, over time, have been suggested as Ripper victims. The names in bold print are the five canonical victims.

26th December 1887

Fairy Fay was found in the Commercial Street area.

3rd April 1888

Emma Elizabeth Smith was found on Osborn Street.

7th August 1888

Martha Tabram was found at 39 George Yard.

31st August 1888

Mary Ann Nichols was found in Buck's Row.

8th September 1888

Annie Chapman was found at 29 Hanbury Street.

30th September 1888

Elizabeth Stride was found on Berner Street.

And

Catharine Eddowes was found in Mitre Square.

9th November 1888

Mary Jane Kelly was found at Millers Court off Dorset Street.

21st November 1888

Annie Farmer was found at 19 George Street; this was an *alleged* attempted murder by the Ripper.

20th December 1888

Rose Mylett was found in Clarke's Yard, Poplar High Street.

17th July 1889

Alice McKenzie was found in Castle Alley.

10th September 1889

Unidentified woman, possibly a local prostitute called Linda Hart, was found on Pinchin Street.

13th February 1891

Frances Cole was found in Swallow Gardens.

During my research for this book I visited Whitechapel. I found it is still very multicultural. The pubs looked shabby and neglected. I walked past *The Ten Bells*; it was rundown and scruffy looking. The area on the whole was bleak. There were some original Victorian buildings that had been left to ruin, seemingly just waiting to be destroyed. Many others had already been demolished with offices built in their place, or are now flats and shops. The building that was once *The Providence Row Refuge*, at the end of Millers Court, is being converted into office blocks.

Some areas of Whitechapel, it seems, have hardly changed since the Ripper ruled these streets, with little courts and dim street lighting. You can easily imagine one of the Ripper's victims walking these narrow, dark passages. Anyone interested in Victorian history should visit Whitechapel.

By 1800, London's population had topped one million. The cesspits, installed after the Great Fire in 1666 regularly overflowed onto the streets. The Thames became the main source of waste disposal. It was so foul by the middle of the century that it was generally described as a "stygian lake". The sewerage generated by 2.5 million Londoners was simply dumped in the streets and most of it found its way into the river. From 1847, the "nightsoil" men who used to collect excrement for use as fertiliser lost their jobs as *guano* was introduced from South America. The Whitechapel of 1888 was a filthy, dangerous place to live. Only those who worked in the area, ventured out. Whitechapel had no tourist attractions to speak of. An American author of the time called Whitechapel *"an abyss"* because of the dire conditions in which people lived. (Jack London 1903)

The first elections for the London County Council were about to begin and the Radical Party had every hope of winning the East End by attacking the Government. Their strategy was to state the obvious! They argued the Government at the time was not doing anything about the awful living conditions in the East End.

The Whitechapel parish church of St. Mary Matfellon stood on the south side of Whitechapel High Street, almost opposite the junction with Osborn Street. Unfortunately, it was destroyed by enemy action in 1941. Today, it is marked by a small park with the paved outlines of the old church.

When Oliver Cromwell permitted Jewish resettlement in 1652, the immigrants came to London and settled in and around Jewry Street. There were already some illegally settled Jews clandestinely worshipping in a building in Creechurch Lane. The Great Synagogue had been built by the eighteenth century; it was situated at the eastern edge of the city of London. This synagogue ensured the continued Jewish settlement centred on the adjacent parish of Whitechapel. The Jewish poor made a living buying and selling second-hand clothes. This, in turn, led to a growth of street markets including Royal Mint Street (Ragfair), Finsbury Square and the most famous one of all, Petticoat Lane, which is still running today. By 1888, Whitechapel was known as the principle Jewish settlement in England. This was a result of the increased immigration of Jews from the Russian Empire. There was an overflow of immigrants into the neighbouring parishes of Spitalfield, St. George in the East, Stepney, and Mile End.

With the great influx of people, in addition to the local residents of Whitechapel, the area quickly became over populated. In 1848 the great Potato Famine struck Ireland causing 100,000 impoverished Irish to settle in London. At one time, the Irish community comprised up to twenty percent of the total population of the city. London experienced many changes in the 1800s and here are just a few examples:

1829 - Sir Robert Peel founded the Metropolitan Police to handle law and order in areas outside the city. These officers became known as "Bobbies" after their founder.

1830 - The land east of Buckingham Palace that once housed the Royal stables was cleared and Trafalgar Square was created. This was followed two years later by the National Gallery.

1834 - The Houses of Parliament, at Westminster Palace, burned down. Charles Barry and A.W. Pugin designed the mock Gothic building that replaced it.

1836 – The first Railway in London was built. It was created to convey passengers from London Bridge to Greenwich. The Railway stations at Euston (1837), Paddington (1838), Fenchurch Street (1841), Waterloo (1848), and King's Cross (1850) followed.

1870 - The laws providing compulsory education for children between the ages of five and twelve came into effect.

In 1888, London was still the centre of the British Empire with more shipyards and docks than any other country. The Thames was always full of traffic from all over the world delivering and collecting their cargo. The railway had not yet evolved to any great extent in London to be a viable cargo carrier.

The Whitechapel of 1888, with its mixture of coal-fired stoves and no sanitation, smelled foul. Whitechapel was comprised of rundown tenement buildings and equally rundown public houses where the residents spent most of their days. Sanitation as we understand it today did not exist. There were no such things as public conveniences either! The only way of going to the toilet would have been a chamber pot that was used in the room. When the pot became full, one of the occupants would either empty the pot into the yard or straight onto the street. That there was no running water meant the pot would not get washed out when emptied. People who did not have the *luxury* of a room to live in would just urinate in the street, or in the Thames.

The typical rooms in these tenement houses where filthy, often with broken windows and damp floors and walls continually affected by the weather. Each room would house a family of as many as seven or eight people. A typical room would have one bed, usually occupied by the oldest member of the family. The rest of the occupants slept on the floor on either straw or rags. The broken windows would be stuffed with either paper or rags in an attempt to keep the cold at bay. The windows would never be opened because of the smell outside and because the wretches who lived inside wore only rags. The rent for one of these rooms was eight pence a night. Believe it or not, these people were the lucky ones. Andrew Mearns has written an excellent book called *The Bitter Cry of Outcast London*. In this book, he describes the housing in the East End as follows:

"Every room in these rotten and reeking tenements houses a family, often two. In one cellar a sanitary inspector reports finding a father, mother, three children, and four pigs! In another room a missionary found a man ill with small-pox, his wife just recovering from her eighth confinement, and the children running about half naked and covered with dirt. Here are seven people living in an underground kitchen, and a little dead child lying in the same room. Elsewhere is a poor widow, her three children, and a child who had been dead thirteen days. Her husband, who was a cabman, had shortly before committed suicide. Here lives a widow and her six children, two of them who are ill with scarlet fever. In another, nine brothers and sisters, from 29 years of age downwards, live, eat and sleep together. Here is a mother who turns her children into the street in the early evening because she lets her room for immoral purposes until long after midnight, when the poor little wretches creep back again if they have not found some miserable shelter elsewhere. Where there are beds they are simply heaps of dirty rags, shavings of straw, but for the most part these miserable beings find rest only upon the filthy boards. The tenant of this room is a widow, who herself occupies the only bed, and lets the floor to a married couple for 2s.6d per week. In many cases matters are made worse by the unhealthy occupation followed by those who dwell in these habitations. Here you are choked as you enter by the air laden with particles of the superfluous fur pulled from the skin of rabbits, rats, dogs and other animals in their preparation for the furrier. Here the smell of paste and of drying match-boxes, mingling with other sickly odours, overpowers you; or it may be the fragrance of stale fish or vegetables, not sold the previous day, and kept in the room overnight. A daily procession of carts taking their uncovered load through the streets to the dust destructor, filled the with a dust cloud". (Mearns 1896)

The Common Lodging House Act of 1851 was introduced to enable some control over the abundance of these houses. Approximately 9000 inhabitants would sleep in the more than 200 common lodging houses in Whitechapel on any given night. It was thought that under this new Act all the houses would be subject to police supervision. This meant that every room had to be inspected and that the maximum number of lodgers allotted to each room had to be displayed at each of the houses. The Act also stated that the rooms had to be aired out for two hours each day, and a fresh supply of linen was to be available weekly. In addition, there should be separate houses for men and women and there should be separate rooms set aside for married couples.

These laws did not work and were never upheld. The lodging house police sergeant visited once a week and always during the day, never at night when the rooms were overcrowded and there were mattresses laid between the beds on the floor. The owners of these lodging houses always lived elsewhere and the extra mattresses were stored at their homes until needed at night. His intended visit was always known in advance. These lodging houses were a profitable business and anyone who had the four pence for a bed could have one, but would have to share with whoever had paid for the other side. If a couple had eight pence, they could have a double bed to themselves to do what ever they wanted. The bed was not always in a separate room either. There could be anything from sixty to eighty beds all in one room. In some of the lodging houses there was a two penny rope lean-to. This consisted of a rope stretched across a room that the person could lean on to sleep as best they could. A magistrate named Montague Williams went to visit one of these lodging houses and wrote about his experience whilst in and around the East End of London in 1884 He described the lodging house: "You get a tolerably good clue to the character of these dens even from an external scrutiny. At the windows you see some hideous human heads, male and female, with blotched, bloated and bestial faces, matted and tangled hair, and hungry, desperate eyes".

In 1888, during Annie Chapman's inquest Montague Williams questioned a lodging house keeper about the running of the house it went as follows:

"*Williams: How many beds do you make up there?*
Witness: twenty eight singles and twenty eight doubles. (There were probably twice that amount actually in the house but the witness had to be careful about his facts as he did not want the Lodging House to be closed down.)
Williams: by "doubles" do you mean for a man and woman?
Witness: yes sir.
Williams: and does that mean that the woman can take any man she chooses? Do you know if the couple are married or not?
Witness: no sir, we do not ask them.
Williams: Precisely what I thought. The sooner these lodging houses are closed down the better. They are the haunt of the burglar, the home of a pickpocket and a hotbed of prostitution. I do not think that I can put in stronger words than that. It is time that the owners of these places, who reap large profits from them, were looked at."

The only running water available to the residents of the East End at this time was found in standpipes and these were only piped to the main roads. As a result, some people had to walk a few miles to get the water if and when they where healthy enough to carry it. This water was not safe to drink and regularly caused an outbreak of cholera. The problem with cholera was that despite the connection between drinking dirty water and the health issues, many reformers denied it. The theory of airborne infection still prevailed, with high-profile figures like Florence Nightingale believing that all diseases came from the atmosphere. So, the only alternative safe drink was alcohol, leading many residents of the East End to be drunk most of the time. Human waste was not the only thing that filled the streets. Many of the courts that ran off the main streets were full of rubbish and piles of rags that had accumulated. Of course, the raw sewage covering the ground gave a certain odour to the whole area.

Horse-drawn carriages were the mode of transport and, of course, the horses did their *business* in the street. The local slaughterhouses also contributed to the smell and filth. Cattle would be herded through the streets to the slaughterhouses in and around Aldgate. When they slaughtered an animal, the blood and waste from the carcass ran directly into the street.

At night, the streets and parks would be filled with people. As mentioned, there were 200 common lodging houses in Whitechapel alone, with each one renting out beds at four pence per bed per night. Yet there were still very poor people, including whole families, who could not afford this amount on a regular basis. No doubt these poor people sleeping in filthy streets, drinking unclean water, starving, must have had a unique aroma. The philanthropist Octavia Hill remarked about the conditions when she visited Christchurch Garden, Spitalfields. She wrote;

"There where dozens of men and women ranging from twenty to seventy, huddled up in their rags trying to sleep propped up against the wall for some shelter. The weather was "cold enough to chill to the bone" and he noted that a baby, no more than nine months old, slept on a hard bench with no cover or pillow. Other families huddled together with the baby asleep in its mother's arms."

You can only *try* to imagine the pitiful scene this man describes. When you read his account you cannot begin to understand how people managed to exist in the East End at the time.

More than half the children born in the East End in the 1800s died before the age of five. If they did survive, many where mentally and physically handicapped. People lived from day to day, a hand-to-mouth existence trying to earn money any way they could. Children as young as five where often sent begging or cleaning chimneys. This was probably the inspiration for *The Water Babies* written by Charles Kingsley in 1863.

Children were sent to the workhouses to earn their keep. They did very dangerous jobs and, as a result, were often killed or maimed. Women could sell matches, or work long hours for a pittance, in terrible conditions, in the workhouses. The Union Workhouses had been the home for many poor individual since they were set up in the 1600s. They were set up by church parishes and were not meant as a place of punishment. Instead, their main purpose was to bring some relief to the destitution. The Poor Law Amendment act of 1834 changed the admittance criteria from the undeserving poor to only the deserving poor. This Act made entering the workhouse so difficult, that only the really destitute would qualify and gain entry. Subsequently, any able-bodied men or women would search for alternative employment rather than going into a workhouse. Many people entered the workhouse because they were either too old or too ill to be able to do any other work to support them. The other regular inmates in these workhouses were unmarried pregnant women. These women would have been disowned by their family, and would have had nowhere else to go. Despite the awful conditions in these workhouses they were always full and would have queues of people waiting outside trying to get admitted. Before admittance, people were searched to see if they had any money on them, if so they were refused admittance. If a person was admitted, they had to stay the whole night and the next day and work hard in one of the many unpleasant jobs. If a person wanted to leave the workhouse they had to go and see those in charge of admission and give them three hours notice before they could actually leave the building. Jack London wrote about these workhouses and gives a vivid description of what it was like to be in one of these workhouses:

"I looked at the brick in my hand, and saw that by doing violence to the language it might be called "bread." The light was very dim down the cellar, and before I knew it some other man had thrust a pannikin (this was a small drinking vessel) into my other hand. Then I stumbled on to a still darker room, where there were tables and men... Most of the men were suffering from tired feet, and they prefaced the meal by removing their shoes and unbinding the filthy rags with which there feet were wrapped. The pannikin contained three quarters of a pint of skilly. This was a mixture of hot water and Indian corn. These men were dipping their bread into heaps of salt scattered over the dirty tables, I attempted the same, but the bread seem to stick in my mouth". (London 1903)

Jack London's night at the workhouse was not pleasant either. He recalls that at 7:00 p.m. the inmates were forced to bathe in pairs. Twenty-two men washed themselves in the same tub of water. One man's back was a mass of blood from the attacks of vermin and constant scratching. He then had his clothes taken away and was given a nightshirt to wear. He was also given a couple of blankets for sleeping. Once inside the dormitory, he saw lengths of canvas stretched between two iron rails on the ground. Each strip of canvas was six inches apart and only eight inches off the ground. One of these canvas strips was to be his bed for the night. He awoke to find a rat sitting on his chest. At 6:00 a.m. the day started again. After a breakfast of skilly, which he gave away, the men were given various jobs. Some had to pound stones into a fine dust that would be then sieved through a grill in the wall at the end of the room. London was then sent to the Whitechapel infirmary to do scavenger work. This work consisted of collecting waste food from the sick wards in sacks and emptying them into waste bins and then cleaning these bins immediately with disinfectant. When this job was finished, London was given tea and some scraps of food. London recalled this experience:

"...heaped high on a huge platter in an indescribable mess— pieces of bread, chunks of grease and fat pork, the burnt skin from the outside of roasted joints, bones, in short, all the leavings from the fingers and mouths of the sick ones suffering from all manners of disease. Into this mess the men plunged their hands, digging, pawing, turning over, examining, rejecting and scrambling for. It was not pretty. Pigs could not have done worse. But the poor devils were hungry, and they ate ravenously of the swill, and when they could eat no more they bundled what was left into their handkerchiefs and thrust it inside their shirts. This all proved too much and having only worked half of the day in the repulsive and dangerous working conditions he bolted over the fence into freedom." (London 1903)

Now that you understand the horrid conditions of the workhouse, you can see why the most common method of earning a few pence for women in the East End was to sell their best and only asset, themselves. It was estimated that in Whitechapel alone there were 1,200 prostitutes (or "Unfortunates" as Victorian society liked to call them) and an estimated 60 brothels. The women who resided in Whitechapel did not use brothels. They would ply their trade in the courts and alleyways; anywhere outside that was dark enough not to be caught by the local police.

Sometimes these women would use the lodging houses if they could get their punter to pay for a bed. Many young women could earn as much on a good day selling their body as they would earn in a full week in the workhouse. As they got older, however, clients were harder to find, unless they were drunk or only had a few pence to spare. This is where the term "the four penny knee trembler" came from, as it was the usual price for the services of one of these women. Payment could take the form of a loaf of stale bread for their services. If these poor women did not earn any money in a day, they could not afford anything to eat or drink, except the unclean water for sustenance and the cold street for a bed. Many women of the time were in danger of starving to death (of course some did) and catching venereal diseases. There was no protection in Victorian times. The more clients a woman had, the higher the risk she ran of being infected. In turn, a prostitute would often infect her next client who would then infect another woman and so on. Contraception of the day was most commonly the vaginal sponge, syringing, or "the safe period."

One can picture the scene: drunken women walking the streets trying to pick up willing clients and often failing. Also looking for clients would be girls as young as thirteen. Thirteen was the age of consent in 1888. Prior to 1875 it had been twelve. Unfortunates had to keep on walking when looking for a client as they could only be arrested if they where standing still in an attempt to solicit customers. A popular place for Unfortunates looking for clients was St Botolph's Church Aldgate; later known as the prostitutes' church. When London was a walled city (you can still see some of the original wall today), there where four sets of gates by which one could enter and depart. A St. Botolph Church stood at each set of gates. London has four such churches; one at Aldgate, Billingsgate, Aldersgate, and at Bishopgate.

St. Botolph was an English Catholic Abbot born in 610 C.E. He became the English version of St. Christopher, the patron saint of travellers. A St. Botolph Church was found at every gate so the travellers could pray for a safe journey or to be thankful for having arrived safely. The Unfortunates would walk around the church looking for willing clients who might have a little bit of money to spare. The other popular place for these Unfortunates securing clients would be one of the many public houses. The Unfortunates would walk from pub to pub plying their trade. They never stayed in one place, thus reducing the chances of being caught by the police. During my research for this book, I came upon an unknown author's description of a young girl in Whitechapel:

"It is an unfortunate young, and as well as we can see under the dirt and paint, pretty. She has boots and stockings on and an old silk skirt, with a torn velvet bodice showing the flesh through the rents. She smells strongly of spirits, and we hear her imploring the deputy to trust her for a night's shelter. She offers him anything only to let her rest there that night. He refuses; she catches him by the hand, she almost kneels to him, buy he is obdurate, shakes her from him and shuts the door on her."

This writer describes the young girl as an explorer might write about a strange animal. There is no compassion in his words for this young girl. Destitute boys would either take work in one of the many workhouses or do any job they could get, which usually meant very long hours and often dangerous work. The only alternative for these boys was to steal to live, as depicted in *Oliver Twist*, or sell their bodies. The whole subject of sexuality was taboo in Victorian London. However, because it was not talked about did not mean it did not happen; it was dealt with very discreetly and "business" was conducted in male brothels and not on the streets.

In the August thirty thousand London inhabitants went hop picking in Sussex and Kent. This would be the nearest thing these people would ever get to a holiday. Hop picking was family work. This meant that every member of the family that could walk would work including very young children. There were few other places the poor could find shelter, food, and warmth. And the places that did exist were often full. One such place was *The Providence Row Night Refuge*, founded in 1860 in London by Monsignor Daniel Gilbert.

Monsignor Gilbert was a young catholic priest who wanted to set up a charity in order to help the poor, regardless of religion, receive help. Monsignor Gilbert asked the Sisters of Mercy to help him establish the first non-sectarian shelter for the poor in London. In September 1858, five sisters travelled from Wexford to London after talks with the Monsignor. The sisters raised money and soon had enough to lease a house in Finsbury Square. There was a stable and a coach house at the rear of the property. It was used to shelter fourteen women and children. This house was situated near Providence Row and is how the refuge got its name.

By 1866, the sisters were overwhelmed with the sheer volume of people seeking help at Providence Row. They raised more funds and built a bigger refuge in Crispin Street. These extra funds allowed the sisters to build a convent and extend the refuge. The Providence Row Refuge opened in 1868 to help men and women. In 1871, Sister Ignatius was elected as Mother Superior at Crispin Street. She held the position for thirty-nine years. By 1877, the refuge could house three hundred men and women each night.

As all the *canonical* Ripper victims were from the same area, it is logical to presume that a number of them may have stayed at this refuge at one time or another. We know that Mary Kelly stayed here and went to live at Millers Court, across from the refuge.

Drunkenness and violence in Whitechapel was commonplace. Many women were brutally raped. Gangs roamed the streets demanding protection money from the poor Unfortunates. If they did not have the protection money they were attacked and often killed as an example to other Unfortunates who would not, or could not, pay. The "Nichols," from Old Nichol Street at the top of Brick Lane, was one such gang. Other gangs included the "Limehouse Forty Thieves" and the "Blind Beggar Gang" (this gang were race track pickpockets). Some Unfortunates would pay protection money to a local man who would promise to protect them from the gangs. Today, he would be called a "pimp" and he would not be patient if the Unfortunates did not pay on a regular basis.

George Hutchinson, the last person to see Mary Kelly alive on the night she was murdered, was probably her pimp. We know from his witness statement that Mary Kelly allegedly asked him for money, but it was probably the other way round. Why else would he have followed Mary Kelly and her "client" to Millers Court and wait outside the court for three quarters of an hour?

The middle-class residents of the East End did not care about the conditions the poor were living in. They desperately tried to move away from the filth that was not only covering the streets, but walking them. The upper classes were unaware, or did not care, about the conditions in the East End. Murders and attacks happened on a regular basis and were never reported in the papers. Newspaper reports were the only way the upper classes would have known about what was going on, as they would have no reason to ever visit the East End.

Why, then, did the press suddenly become interested when, in 1888, a series of murders began? What was it about the "Whitechapel Murders" that caught the public interest immediately?

It was not unusual for an East End "Unfortunate" to be found dead in the street with her throat cut; this was the most common form of murder at that time. So what was it that caused a media frenzy?

Could it have been a series of letters sent to both the press and the police at the time of the murders? Each letter was allegedly written by the murderer. A woman in Bradford, Maria Coroner, was even charged on the 21st of October 1888 for causing a breach of the peace. She had sent a letter signed "Jack the Ripper" to her local Chief Constable and a local newspaper. In the letter, she stated that the Ripper was "coming to Bradford to do a little business." Maria Coroner was the only author of a Ripper letter that has ever been positively identified. Whatever it was, the media frenzy reverberated in newspapers around the world. It has been alleged that the police initially thought a journalist could have been responsible for some of the letters to boost sales. If this is true, and a journalist was to blame, it worked.

So did sensational journalism make Jack the Ripper, or did Jack the Ripper make sensational journalism?

The most popular papers at that time were the *Morning Post*, the *Daily News*, the *Daily Telegraph*, and the *Daily Chronicle*. These papers were aimed at a middle/upper-class, primarily male readership. George Newnes who was a manager for a fancy good business realised that none of the penny dailies could be read easily by the slightly literate lower classes. In 1880, he decided to launch a weekly publication called *Tit-Bits*. This provided a voice for the common citizen. This publication reported the events as they unfolded in Whitechapel and started to criticise the way the police were handling the situation, calling them "inadequate." The problem the police had was a lack of experience; they had never had to deal with a serial killer before. The officers did not have the general and forensic knowledge that today's police officers rely on to help identify perpetrators of crime, so they had to do what they thought was right at the time. I honestly believe the police officers at the time of the murders did their best. However, I do not feel the same about the higher-ranking officers who thought they did not have to liaise with the rank and file policemen or even other high-ranking officers from other divisions. These people deserved all the bad press they received.

The police would not be the only ones the press would target; the vast population of Jews in Whitechapel was already an issue with the anti-Semitics. One witness described the man they saw as foreign looking, which led the press to throw accusations in the direction of the Jews. So much fear and frenzy had been generated by the press that vigilante groups started up in Whitechapel. The police issued leaflets to residents informing them to stay off the streets. This did not work because the women of the East End had to "work" the streets to survive. They lived and slept on the streets so how could they stay indoors?

The various press reports caused a new craze among the upper classes; it was called "slumming." This curious but appropriate term is used when the lady members of certain aristocratic families of Park Lane and Belgravia visited (during the day of course) many of the poorest localities and slums of London. The press described these mercy missions as "angels' visits" saying they undoubtedly saved many a poor wretch from starvation and possibly death. It was reported in the newspapers of the time that "These kind visitors have been very welcome. At one rundown tenement house, the "angel" visitors gave a few loaves of bread to a starving family and at another the angel ordered a hundred weight of coal, tea, sugar, flour or anything they thought could help their situation."

None of this good work would have been done if it were not for the press reporting the Ripper crimes, bringing to light the circumstances in the East End.

Of course, not all of the upper classes went "slumming" for the good of the poor. Some visited the East End just to see the inhabitants as if they were "freaks" in a Carnival show.

Nevertheless, there were many genuine people trying to help the poor. In July 1865, William Booth began the Salvation Army. It was not until 1878 that Booth adopted the name "Salvation Army" for his movement. He preached to a small street congregation in the slums of London. His undaunted spirit attracted loyal followers. The numbers continued to rise for thirteen years after its formation. The Salvation Army became a legal entity with a military structure. At first, church people persecuted the "army" because it was so unconventional. Despite this persecution, the army attacked the plight of hunger, homelessness, and poverty. This organisation is still today working for the plight of the homeless.

Another organisation was to be formed in 1888. Dr Barnardo Homes helped the poor and destitute children of the East End. This book is not saying that this organisation itself had anything to do with the murders in any way. In fact I do believe that even today the work this organisation does, is still as important as it was in 1888.

My theory is about the very calculating man who founded this organisation. He knew exactly what was needed to improve the East End's deprivation. He knew how to get the attention of the press and keep it by writing the Ripper letters. He knew he had to make certain people sit up and listen, but that he had to do it in a way that they could not just brush under the carpet. What better way than to get every British, Irish, and American Newspaper reporting on the murders in Whitechapel.

Now that the conditions of Whitechapel were widely known, something surely must be done?

Recently I came across this quote, which I feel describes my Jack the Ripper:

"Many famous people, who did good and great things which made a difference to people's lives, were not necessarily of good and great character themselves."

Chapter 2

Profile of a Killer.

Dr. Barnardo

Abigail Matilda O'Brien and John Michaelis Barnardo were allegedly married in the German Church in London on the 23rd of June 1837. I say allegedly because very little is known about Barnardo's parents and there are varying reports of their origins. John Michaelis Barnardo was thought to have arrived in Ireland some time during 1823. Jewish historians who have written about this period believed that the family was of Jewish extraction.

Dr. John Thomas Barnardo was born on the 4th of July 1845. The birth was a difficult one and he was not expected to live. He went on to have more than his fair share of childhood illnesses. Barnardo's mother was considerably weakened by the birth of her fifth child. So much so, that the little boy had to be placed in the care of a local wet nurse who lived in a suburb of Dublin. This fact (Barnardo not living at his parents' home from birth) was the main reason that he and his mother never really bonded in the normal way.

It is ironic that the very man who would later take every opportunity to attack Catholicism, was himself suckled by a Roman Catholic wet nurse. While Barnardo's mother stayed with relatives, his sister Sophie, aged seventeen, ran the family home. Sophie visited Barnardo constantly and it was while she was on one of her visits to the wet nurse that Barnardo was taken home. Sophie had arrived at the wet nurse's home unexpectedly. She found Barnardo lying in his cot under an open window, unattended. Angry at such a sight, she took Barnardo back to the Dame Street family home. When the wet nurse arrived at Dame Street, Sophie refused to let her take Barnardo away. She insisted that the nurse should live at the family home to care for the child. The wet nurse agreed and remained with the family until Barnardo was ten months old. Shortly after his birth, Barnardo's mother became pregnant again. She left to stay with relatives. Sadly, the baby girl who was born in May, died after just a few hours. A year later, his mother had another son, Henry Lionel, who was everything Barnardo was not. The new son was the apple of his mother's eye. While Barnardo was kept away upstairs, the new son was called down to his parents and shown to all. Barnardo would often take revenge on the young boy when he returned to the nursery. It is not surprising that Barnardo felt unloved and craved attention from his parents, which he managed by throwing tantrums. He would be emotionally scarred for the rest of his life by this lack of love and affection.

Case studies of serial killers have identified that many suffered from childhood abuse of one kind or another. Many felt isolated from their mothers who were cold, distant, and unloving towards them. Such emotional scarring remains and is manifest in various "unhealthy" ways later in life.

Barnardo's first school was St. Ann's Sunday school. At ten years old he went to St John's Parochial School on Fishamble Street. He followed his brothers to St. Patrick's Cathedral Grammar School.

At the time of Barnardo's birth, his father's company was in the midst of collapse and failure. His father allegedly lost a lot of money through bad investments. He applied for British citizenship in 1860. A certificate was granted in August while he was away on business, so he could not take the oath of allegiance within the time allowed. He had to reapply and became a British citizen in the November of the same year.

When he left school Barnardo started his working career as an apprentice for a local wine merchant. However, there is no actual record of what Barnardo did for the four years between leaving school and arriving in London. In trying to understand Barnardo and his early years, it is more important to recognize that at this time he was discovering Evangelism. This new religious belief was so resolute that within a few weeks he had joined the Open Plymouth Brethren. This was a young men's Christian Association. Barnardo became a Sunday school teacher at Merrion Hall. Here he met a man who would be associated with him for the rest of his life. This man was Robert Anderson, who would later become Assistant Commissioner of the Metropolitan Police Criminal Investigations Division (CID) and the man in charge of the Whitechapel murder investigations. Barnardo quickly grew restless with this position. He believed he could do much better. He wanted a room for himself to hold his own prayer meetings. These began in the summer of 1863 when a room in Augier Street became available. However, it soon became clear to Barnardo that the idea of holding his own prayer meetings was not as successful as he would have liked, as the meetings were not well attended. The only reason for his breaking away was his domineering nature and the desire for power rather than the needs of the people to whom he was preaching. Barnardo found it difficult to subdue his need to assert himself.

Serial killers, by their nature, need to dominate their victim in one way or another. The important issue for Barnardo was the power he felt he had over the victim; initially apparent, perhaps, in his approach to preaching and the thirst for power over the congregation.

The Move to London

In 1866, against his father wishes, Barnardo left Dublin bound for London to start his training as a missionary. Upon his arrival in London, Barnardo lodged at 30, Coburn Street in the East End. He was not in London long before Hudson Taylor, founder of the China Inland Mission, had doubts about him. In correspondence between W. T. Berger and Hudson Taylor, Barnardo was discussed. The word "peculiar" was used to describe his strong beliefs. Barnardo would not accept the necessity of "headship and government" within the China Mission and was one reason why he would not be considered an immediate candidate.

Barnardo was overbearing and superior in attitude. Believing he could do better, he openly criticised the way the mission was being run. When the time came for the missionaries to set sail for China in May, Barnardo was not among them. Barnardo was very disappointed; he left Coburn Street, found his own lodgings, and decided to study medicine. He thought that this would increase his chances of becoming a missionary.

Barnardo registered as a student at the London Hospital in Whitechapel in November of 1867. He became very interested in anatomy and spent most of his time in the dissecting room (morgue). In a letter he wrote to W.T. Berger (who was Hudson Taylor's Chief Administrator), Barnardo enthusiastically wrote that with God's help he had been able to dissect two complete subjects.

He was not popular with his fellow students at all. They thought he was a religious fanatic. During the cholera outbreak, when several thousand people lost their lives, he was seen preaching to the despondent masses, while having slops poured over his head. Barnardo later described how he once had a pellet of mud thrown at him by a young boy, which hit him opened mouthed.

This stopped any further preaching. Barnardo would use banners as a means of making his ideas known. He would carry goodies in his pockets, probably some form of sweets for the children, and he would try to tempt them to go with him and listen to God's word.

I know the offer of a cup of tea, today, does not sound too tempting, but if you had no shoes on your feet and your clothes were rags, you would be inclined to listen to anything just to have a warm drink.

Barnardo has been described as a real loner. Because of his superior attitude, the other students would have nothing to do with him and thought he was weird.

Barnardo started helping out at Ragged Schools teaching the word of God to the poor children.

If the children paid a penny a day they would get fed and educated in one of these Ragged Schools. This gave them an opportunity to learn to read and write. It was very hard for them to get this penny each day. While teaching at one of the Ragged Schools, Barnardo met a young boy called Jim Jarvis. This boy would earn the nickname "my first Arab" by Barnardo. One particularly cold night, Barnardo went to close the school and noticed a boy was still hanging about. Barnardo spoke to the boy about going home, to which he replied that he had no home to go to. He begged Barnardo to allow him to stay in the school for the night. It was about nine thirty in the evening and bitterly cold outside. Barnardo had asked the boy where he had slept the previous evening to which the boy answered that he had slept in one of the hay carts parked in Whitechapel. Barnardo could not see the boy thrown out in the cold to sleep on the streets, so he took the boy to his own room, fed him, allowing the boy respite from the cold. Barnardo seemed to have a split personality; he showed kindness and compassion to the children who were victims of circumstance, yet he abhorred the "Unfortunates "and blamed them for the children's misery.

At this first meeting, Barnardo asked Jim if he knew who Jesus was. To Barnardo's astonishment the boy replied, "He's the Pope of Rome." Barnardo explained to Jim, who was clearly Roman Catholic, his notion of who Jesus was. Jim, in turn, told Barnardo about the destitute children sleeping on the streets. That same night Jim took Barnardo to one of the "lays," a rooftop covered with boys fast asleep. These poor children wearing rags and having nothing to cover them had their heads resting on the higher part of the roof and their feet in the gutters. Lays were the secret hiding places for children at night. Jim went on to show Barnardo most of Whitechapel's "lays."

After this meeting, Barnardo decided that rescuing these poor children would be his calling. He reflected on his meeting with Jim Jarvis at a subsequent dinner party. The other guests did not believe a word of it! To prove his point, Barnardo took a number of the men to view one of the lays. The plight of these children touched the guests and money was provided to help Barnardo in his cause.

And so the work began. Barnardo started scouring the streets of Whitechapel looking for destitute children in their hideaways. He also spent time helping out at a rundown school in Earnest Street, where he took Bible classes. Barnardo's ability to keep order among the children impressed the school committee. He was soon promoted to Superintendent of the school. This gave him a seat on the board, but the committee retained full financial control. As Superintendent he helped out wherever required. His typical autocratic behaviour got him into trouble while helping in the Hertford Street Ragged School at Mile End Road.

Barnardo was asked to leave when the committee found out he was misleading people by using the school name to raise funds in the religious journal *The Revival*. He really wanted the money for himself in order to create a place for preaching in the West End. He actually wanted to "move up," so to speak, and preach in the West End. He did not want to stay in the deprived East End. Of course, he thought he would receive more contributions for his work in the West End.

He believed that those who devoted themselves to the work of the gospel should be supported by voluntary and unsolicited contributions. That he was living on the charitable donations from the Plymouth Brethren to help him during his training to be a doctor, did not bother him at all.

A main part of the Brethren belief was that they were living in an important age in history with a limited time in which to achieve their objectives. So, to them, their work had a definite urgency. This was the force that drove Barnardo. He could not wait fifty or even fifteen years for things to change, he had to make change right then. He understood what had to be done and felt the need to follow his calling through to the end. He was passionate in his belief of the Brethren doctrine.

He resigned from the school and decided he wanted to do work over which he would have complete control. He carried on raising funds until he reached £90. That was a large sum in the 1800s. Then, out of the blue, an offer came enabling him to use the assembly rooms at the *King's Arms*. The public house was situated at the corner of Mile End Road and Beaumont Square. Seeing this as a way to get ahead, he spent the £90 on a big party inviting all the poverty-stricken youths of Stepney and the surrounding areas. Unfortunately, this arrangement did not last long. The *King's Arms* was sold and the new owner did not agree to the previous arrangement. All of the raised money was essentially wasted and Barnardo hit rock bottom. He had a nervous breakdown, which would be the first of several. He was unable to work for a few months. During his recovery, he decided to give up on his dream of going to China. He began to concentrate on opening his own youth mission. He continued his training as a doctor.

Barnardo moved to 5 Bromley Place, the home of a Mrs. Johnson, whose husband was a sailor. In March 1868, the first Barnardo mission was established; it was called the East End Juvenile Mission. It consisted of two small houses, which Barnardo rented in Hope Place.

This Mission was very successful and Barnardo was soon managing it full time. In 1884, Barnardo visited Canada and America. In America, he spent a lot of time with detectives studying the roughest areas of New York, Boston, and Chicago. Barnardo described some of these areas as being "*as bad as the East End.*" The American word "boss" was used frequently while Barnardo was in the States, so he would have become accustomed to it. The word "boss" was not common in England in

1888. Of course, this word was used in the "Dear Boss" letter sent by Jack the Ripper, dated the 25th of September, 1888. The letter arrived at the Central News Agency on September 27, 1888, and was passed to Scotland Yard two days later. An important fact to note is that Barnardo's editorial office was close in proximity to the location from which the very first letter was posted. His offices were based at 279 the Strand. After meeting Dwight Moody a fellow philanthropist whilst visiting the States, Barnardo went on to use some of Moody's ideas. In 1869, Barnardo used one of Moody's ideas in particular; it was to take some photographs of the children in his care. These photographs would be in the format of 'before and after 'being "rescued by Barnardo. Barnardo decided he would sell the photographs to raise some much-needed funds. Barnardo was carefully warned to stop selling these pictures in 1877 after parents complained their children were not found in the condition he had photographed the child in.

With the plans of China far behind him, Barnardo decided to stop his training in medicine to concentrate on his mission, a decision he would later regret. Before he finished his medical examinations and just after he had bought the *Edinburgh Castle* (a public house) he had an announcement put in *The Christian* saying he was now to be known as Dr. Barnardo.

It is alleged that Barnardo claimed he obtained an M.D. from the University of Glessen in February 1872. The letter he produced to support his claim was alleged to be a forgery. It was purported to have been signed by the Dean of the Faculty, L.D. Wichen. Again, it is alleged that the records at Glessen University show that no such person existed either as Dean or as any member of the Faculty at that time. Although he had passed the first professional examinations in anatomy and physiology at the Royal College of Surgeons in England in 1869, he was not, as people at the time rightly pointed out, a fully qualified Doctor. Therefore, he was not legitimately entitled to call himself a doctor.

Realising that this situation would not go away, and not wanting to lose his title, he resumed his studies. He finally qualified as a licentiate of the Royal College of Surgeons in Edinburgh in 1876 and was elected a fellow of the Royal College of Surgeons in 1879. While finishing his studies, he also studied for a qualification in gynaecology or a certificate as an accredited *Accoucheur*, as it was then known. Studying gynaecology seemed an odd thing to do, as he never intended to use it. Once he had qualified as a doctor the contributions from the Plymouth Brethren stopped.

So, we may indeed wonder—why the interest in gynaecology? We may never really know why he was so interested in women's genitalia. It was, however, a factor in each murder. And, this specific

medical background reinforces Barnardo as a viable suspect as the Ripper.

The Coroner Wynne Baxter, when discussing the murder of Annie Chapman, said *"no mere slaughterer of animals could have carried out these operations. It must have been someone accustomed to the post-mortem room.*

Police Surgeon Dr. George Bagster Phillips Police surgeon of H division was of same opinion*:*

"Obviously the work was that of an expert or one, at least, who had such knowledge of pathological examinations as to be able to secure the pelvic organs with one sweep of the knife."

Of course, one can conclude from these official reports that the person who committed the murders had a good knowledge of female organs and was adept at using a knife or scalpel.

By the age of 27, Dr. Barnardo's increasing autocratic and domineering attitude made it very difficult for people to work closely with him. If he received any opposition he became more aggressive. This attitude alienated him from other adults. However, in his contact with children he was softer, more tempered. On the June 17, 1873, Dr. Barnardo married Syrie Elmslies. Barnardo wanted to be married in the East End so his congregation and helpers could be present. He publicized his status as a married man in an effort to legitimate his intention to open a home for destitute girls. Around 1874, Dr. Barnardo acquired a magazine called *Father William's Stories*. He changed the name to *The Children's Treasury*. In 1876, the sum of money entrusted to Dr. Barnardo through charitable donations was well over five figures. Marriage, however, had increased his financial needs. His wife was extravagant and could not make the housekeeping money he provided cover the costs she was accruing. As a Preacher and a Freelance Journalist, Barnardo did not earn enough. To improve their situation, Dr. Barnardo moved his family back to the East End to Newbury House, Bow.

The Charities Commission evolved in the 1800s with the sudden growth of charitable organisations. Prior to this, there was no control over their actions and the use of unsolicited contributions. It was believed that charities needed to be accountable. Dr. Barnardo's homes for destitute boys and girls were monitored by the commission. Because of his financial situation, Dr. Barnardo, for the first time in his life, was forced to ask the Trustees of his homes for a salary.

In 1882 Barnardo was to lose a son called Tom sadly the child only lived a few weeks. In 1883, the Trustees agreed and awarded Dr. Barnardo a salary of £600 a year. This must have affected the arrogant and domineering man greatly. It was, most likely, a shot to his ego having to ask them for a salary when, in his opinion, these were *his* missions, *his* homes. At this point, a great deal of the control and power he must have felt he had was being withdrawn. Dr. Barnardo suffered bouts of ill health and depression as a direct result.

In 1884 tragedy would hit Barnardo once again. This time his nine year old son Herbert died of diphtheria. Barnardo started suffering from bouts of depression and ill health.

If there was one person who had a good reason for disliking prostitutes, it was Dr. Barnardo. He thought that the battle against prostitution was a war against evil itself. He saw the Unfortunates as the embodiment of evil. Another part of the Plymouth Brethren's general belief was women of any class were second rate citizens and should be seen and not heard unless spoken to. It was also part of the class structure of Victorian England. Unfortunates often physically and verbally attacked him. They regularly undermined his attempts to save the young girls from a life of prostitution. To add insult to injury, his reputation was almost destroyed by an Unfortunate Barnardo had encountered in previous years.

As mentioned, Dr. Barnardo purchased a pub called the *Edinburgh Castle* on the Rhodeswell Road. Following the purchase, a nearby Reverend named George Reynolds (a Baptist Minister and a former railway porter) became very angry when his small congregation started to dwindle and move to Dr. Barnardo's meetings. The Reverend was dependent on his flock's donations to live. Facing ruin and starvation he sought to destroy Dr. Barnardo. He did not need to look very far. A neighbour of Barnardo's, Mrs. Johnson of 5, Bromley Street, gave the Reverend all the ammunition he needed. Mrs. Johnson told the Reverend that while Dr. Barnardo was a medical student he had lodged with her and that they had been lovers. With this information he started a whispering campaign in the East End.

Although Dr. Barnardo flatly denied these claims, the deacons at the People's Mission Church were forced to act. The deacons decided to interview Mrs. Johnson in the presence of her mother and her doctor. The outcome of the interview was that Mrs. Johnson was judged a rambling woman, who was suffering from a form of sexual hysteria. The findings of this hearing are not surprising, as the deacons certainly would not take the word of an Unfortunate over their pastor. Moreover, Reynolds solicited the help of Frederick Charrington who, at one time, had been a friend of Dr. Barnardo. The friendship was severed when they had a falling out over a plot of land in Mile End Road.

Charrington planned to build a mission church and coffee palace there. Through the grapevine, Charrington heard Dr. Barnardo had intended to build a second mission church in the same spot. Being a gentleman, Charrington asked for a meeting with Barnardo. At this meeting, Charrington asked him not to build his mission on the site. Barnardo replied that the construction of the mission had already started and he was under obligation to see the project through. This stubborn and selfish act by Dr. Barnardo was not taken well by Charrington. When Reynolds asked him for help he was only too pleased to oblige.

Their first plan of attack was in the form of a letter sent to Dr. Barnardo's wife telling her about the affair between him and Mrs. Johnson. The letter included allegations that since their marriage, Dr. Barnardo was seen on a regular basis walking the streets arm in arm with Unfortunates and had been seen entering their homes. Angered by these accusations, Dr. Barnardo wrote to Charrington demanding an apology. In reply, Charrington denied any involvement in the letter, but dared Dr. Barnardo to take him to court over the allegation knowing only too well that he could not because he was part of the Plymouth Brethren and was not permitted to enter into litigation. Their next tactic was to send regular articles to the letter columns of the local press. Charrington had written these articles using a pseudonym.

After three years of the continued campaign against Dr. Barnardo, Reynolds decided to reveal his identity and released a 62 page booklet called *Dr. Barnardo Homes: The Startling Revelations.* The booklets were snapped up by the public at a shilling a copy. This booklet not only brought up the affair between Mrs. Johnson and Dr. Barnardo, it went deeper into the treatment the children received in his care. These booklets alleged that children were punished by being locked in coal sheds for days for trivial offences. It also alleged that the medical facilities in the missions were non-existent and disease was rife. In short, the children were being physically abused and were malnourished.

The daily routine for the children in Dr. Barnardo's care in Victorian times was not an easy one, but it was better than sleeping on the streets and starving to death. The children woke at 5:30 a.m. and had breakfast at 6:00 a.m. The rest of the day consisted of doing chores, praying, and performing military drills. At 6:30 p.m. they sat down and ate their supper, followed by classes from 7:00 p.m. until 9:15 p.m. Then it was prayers and lights out by 10:00 p.m. It was alleged that Dr. Barnardo punished badly behaved boys by locking them in the coal cellar and by flogging them.

If Dr. Barnardo deemed a boy not likely to prosper in England, the boy was sent to Canada. This was done in the early years, with the help of a woman called Annie McPherson. Each year she took children to Canada if they were able to raise the ten pounds needed for their passage. The children were fostered out to families in Canada who could look after them. Many were used as an extra pair of hands to work on farms.

The arguing between these three men could not carry on, as they were all Evangelists. They were told to take the matter to court. Dr. Barnardo was cleared of all charges. However, his reputation was damaged and donations towards the upkeep and the growth of the homes started to fade. His health was also suffering and he was on his way to another nervous breakdown.

It is clear that Barnardo's hatred of prostitutes was encouraged by the role they played in some of the hardships he encountered. If we combine this with the maternal neglect he experienced and how he blamed the Unfortunates for the impoverished condition in which the East End children lived, a clear motivation for the Ripper murders begins to emerge. One could speculate that in those neglected children, Barnardo saw an image of himself; one that was strong enough for him to want to avenge such injustice.

In one of the Ripper letters received by the police was a sentence "I am down on whores." This Phrase would be a good way to describe how Dr. Barnardo felt about prostitutes and prostitution at that time. It was the word of one of these women that started the three-year campaign to ruin him. He must have felt a great anger towards this type of woman. In 1888, contraception was not readily available; many "Unfortunates" would try to get their clients to have anal sex as a form of contraception. If the client refused, the woman took the chance of getting pregnant. As a result, "Unfortunates" consistently had children that either died at birth, or only survived a couple of weeks. If the child survived, eventually they would be sent out on the streets to beg, borrow, or steal the money for their mothers and fathers to spend on food and drink. Many of these women were gin-sodden creatures, and if they had a daughter they would send the girl on the streets at a very young age to earn money the only way they could: by following their mothers' examples.

By the 1880s, Dr. Barnardo had a pathological hatred of prostitutes. When he tried to help these women by holding prayer meetings at night for them, they could not be bothered and carried on plying their trader right outside his establishments. He blamed these *"shameless women"* for the high level of child prostitution.

In 1884, the legal age of consent was thirteen. A Bill had been put through parliament to raise the age to sixteen, but the opposition was very strong. By today's standards, one would be termed a paedophile if one had sex with a thirteen year old. In the 1880s, a thirteen-year-old girl was seen as an asset to her mother as she would probably earn more. If the young girl was still a virgin at thirteen it was not unheard of for the mother to sell the daughter to a brothel; "gentlemen" would pay handsomely for sex with a virgin.

"In the vilest haunts of women of shameful lives, in 'furnished rooms' where decency and virtue are disregarded, if not mocked at, in those low lodging houses which are the hotbeds of immorality and vice, are to be found many virtually unshielded girls of tender years whose dangers cannot be thought of without a shudder." (Dr. Barnardo)

Reading these words, one can see Dr. Barnardo's caring side, his conception of the demise of the children of the East End and the hatred he felt for these women; women like Mary Ann Nichols, Annie Chapman, Elizabeth Stride, Catharine Eddowes, and Mary Kelly.

Dr. Barnardo seemed to be taking one step forward and two steps back. He knew that letter writing and the placing of innocent young children in homes was not really making any difference in the East End. He decided that something drastic had to be done. He wanted to show these women just what the bible thought of them and took it upon himself to be God's messenger. While campaigning to get the law for the custody of children changed, Dr. Barnardo wrote the following:

"Are we as Christian men, always under all circumstances to be governed by English law? Is judicial law always to be co-extensive with moral law? Does a period never arise when a higher law may compel a man to take a step, which the law of the land would possibly condemn?"
He lived by God's word, doing God's work, and he found it difficult to accept "man-made" rules, even more so when they conflicted with his conscience.

Now, reader, you are about to enter the world of the "Unfortunates". Here are their stories and how Dr. Barnardo became "Jack the Ripper," for the purpose of what he deemed his 'calling': to release the children of the East End from a life of destitution and depravity.

Chapter 3

Mary Ann Nichols

1845 -1888.

Mary Ann Nichols (also known as Polly) was an Unfortunate who lived in Whitechapel. She was the first victim of "Jack."

Polly stood 5 feet, 2 inches tall. She had brown hair that had started to turn grey at the top, brown eyes, high cheek bones, and a dark complexion. She was considered a little on the plump side and had a scar on her forehead that she had received as a child. A number of her front teeth were missing.

Polly was born Mary Ann Walker, the daughter of a locksmith and blacksmith called William Walker. The family lived on Dean Street. At nineteen, Polly married William Nichols; he was a printer from Bouverie Street. They were married in St Bride's Church, Fleet Street. It was called the "printers" church for obvious reasons. Polly and William lived at the Bouverie Street address. She also stayed with her father, from time to time, at 131, Trafalgar Street, Walworth. From 1874 to 1880, the couple lived at 6d in the Peabody Buildings, Stamford Street in Lambeth. During this time, Polly gave birth to her children: Edward John in 1866, Percy George in 1868, Alice Esther in 1870, Eliza Sarah in 1877, and Henry Alfred in 1879.

Around 1877 William Nichols briefly eloped with a woman who had helped Polly with the birth of Eliza Sarah. Shortly after this, Polly's eldest, Edward John, went to live with his grandfather. Edward John felt no connection with his father and only spoke to him after his mother's death. Polly probably started drinking around this time and left home five or six times.

The couple separated in 1880 and William Nichols retained custody of the children except Edward John who remained with his grandfather. William Nichols continued to pay 5 shillings (25p) per week allowance until 1882, when he learned that she was living on immoral earnings, possibly under the protection of a man called Thomas Drew. William Nichols was summoned by the Lambeth Union to pay Polly maintenance, but she lost the case when he proved that she was, in fact, living off immoral earnings. William Nichols explained how he proved his wife's immoral earnings at her inquest. He said, "I had her watched." The last time William Nichols saw his wife alive was in 1885.

Polly's life is quite well documented following the breakdown of her marriage:

6th Sept 1880-31st May 1881: Working and staying in the Lambeth Workhouse.

31st May 1881-24th April 1882: Residence not known, possibly sleeping on the streets.

24th April 1882-18th Jan 1883: Working and staying in the Lambeth Workhouse.

18th Jan 1883-20th Jan 1883: Admitted into the Lambeth Infirmary.

20th Jan 1883-24th March 1883: She was back working in and staying at the Lambeth Workhouse.

24th March 1883-21st May 1883: Polly went to live with her father. Because her habitual drinking became a problem, it caused many arguments between her and her father. It was after one of these many arguments that Polly decided to leave. At her inquest, her father said, "Well, at times she drank and that was why we did not agree."

21st May 1883-2nd June 1883: Returned to work and stayed in the Lambeth Workhouse.

2nd June 1883-25th Oct 1887: Polly started living a stable life with a man called Thomas Stuart Drew at 15 York Street, Walworth. This relationship would last four years. In June 1886, Polly attended her brother's funeral. Her brother had died tragically in an accident. Notably, at the funeral Polly's appearance was described as "respectably dressed. This was the last time Edward Walker would actually see his daughter alive.

25th October 1887: She spent one day at St. Giles Workhouse on Endell Street.

26th Oct 1887-2nd Dec 1887: She worked in the Strand Workhouse, Edmonton.

2nd Dec 1887-19th Dec 1887: It is alleged that Polly was probably sleeping rough [sleeping on the streets] in Trafalgar Square when the area was cleared. She was then readmitted into the Lambeth Workhouse.

19th Dec 1887-29th Dec 1887: Stayed and worked in the Lambeth Workhouse.

29th Dec 1887-4th Jan 1888: Residence not known, possibly sleeping on the streets.

4th Jan 1888-12th July 1888: Worked in the Mitcham Workhouse and was admitted to the Holborn Infirmary.

16th April 1888-30th Aug 1888: Dr. Barnardo may have introduced Polly to Samuel and Sarah Cowdry. He had connections with both the workhouses who tried to rehabilitate these women as he ran an employment agency, and, of course, the police. He would have met many "Unfortunates" on his forays into the workhouses looking for children to rescue.

Polly was then employed by Mr. and Mrs. Cowdry. The couple resided at Ingleside, Rose Hill, Wandsworth. They both worked as clerks in the police department. While Polly was still employed by the Cowdrys, she wrote a letter to her father. It read as follows:

"I just write to say you will be glad to know that I am settled in my new place, and going all right up to now. My people went out yesterday, and have not returned, so I am left in charge. It is a grand place inside, with trees and gardens back and front. All has been newly done up. They are teetotallers, and are very religious, so I ought to get on. They are very nice people, and I have much to do. I hope you are all right and the boy has work. So goodbye now for the present.

> *Yours truly,*
> *"Polly"*
> *Answer soon please, and let me know how you are."*

This was the last time Edward Walker heard from his daughter.

Polly's employment did not last very long before she decided to leave. When she left the couple's home, she stole some clothes worth £3.10.

12th July 1888-1st Aug 1888: Residence not known; again, possibly sleeping on the streets.

1st Aug 1888-2nd Aug 1888: Polly was at the Gray's Inn Temporary Workhouse. Temporary workhouses allowed occupants to stay on a day to day basis. Most workhouses in 1888 had a restriction on the amount of days in which the admitted person must stay.

2nd Aug 1888-24th Aug 1888: Polly then moved into 18 Thrawl Street. She shared this room with three other women. The women kept this room very clean and Polly actually shared a bed with a woman called Ellen Holland. Ellen Holland is also known as Emily or Nelly.

24th Aug 1888-30th Aug 1888: Polly stayed at the Whitehouse. It was situated at 56 Flower and Dean Street. The Whitehouse was a Lodging (Doss) house that allowed both men and women to sleep together. This may have been the reason Polly chose this particular Lodging House.

Thursday 31st August 1888

11:30 p.m. Polly was seen walking alone along the Whitechapel Road.

12:30 a.m. Polly was seen leaving the Frying Pan Public House in Brick Lane. It is believed that she then made her way to Thrawl Street.

1:20 a.m. Polly was seen in the Lodging House at 18 Thrawl Street. Polly gave the overall impression of being slightly tipsy. When asked for the 4d she needed to pay for a bed that night by the deputy, Polly explained to him that she did not have it, so the deputy turned her away.

As she was seen leaving the lodging house it is alleged that she laughed and said to the deputy,

"I'll soon get my doss money; see what a jolly bonnet I've got."
When questioned later, the deputy stated that Polly had been wearing a bonnet that he had not seen her wear before.

The question one should ask is where would an "Unfortunate" like Polly get a new hat from? This poor woman sold her body for a few pence, with which she would either spend on food, drink, or, perhaps, a bed for the night. She could not have earned enough money that day to buy a new hat and still have enough money left over to go and get tipsy. So where did that hat come from? Could Dr. Barnardo have given her the hat? I believe he did. During his daily visits to the Lodging houses I believe he met Polly. His plan was to lure her into a false sense of security and so ensure that she met him later that day.

2:30 a.m. Ellen (Emily) Hollands was returning from watching the Shadwell Dry Dock fire. The fire was so fierce that it had lit the sky above London that night. On her return she met Polly at the corner of Brick Lane and Whitechapel High Street. Polly told Ellen that she had earned her doss money three times that day but had spent it. Hollands said that Polly appeared to be very drunk and staggering against the wall. Ellen tried to persuade Polly to return to the Thrawl Street Lodging House with her but Polly refused, saying;

"After one more attempt to find trade, she would return to Flower and Dean Street where she could share a bed with a man."
When I read Ellen's statement I had to ask myself why Polly had changed her mind about where she was going to sleep that night. She was at the Lodging House in Thrawl Street and told the deputy that she would return. Then just over an hour later when Ellen spoke to Polly she had decided that she was going to spend the night at the Lodging House in Flower and Dean Street with a man. Who was this man? Had she met this man after leaving Thrawl Street and arranged to spend the night with him? In my opinion, while touring for business Polly had met Dr. Barnardo. He had promised her that they would meet up again later to spend the night at the Flower and Dean Street Lodging House. As he was no stranger to lodging houses and had by his own admission stayed in them, Polly would have believed him. When asked at Polly's inquest if she knew how Polly obtained her living Ellen replied that she did not. She also said that although Polly always gave the impression of being "weighed down by some trouble." Ellen also said that Polly was a quiet woman and that she had never seen her quarrel with anybody.

3:40 a.m. Charles Cross, a Carman was employed by the Pickfords in Broad Street. Charles Cross left his home in Bethnal Green at around 3:30 a.m. He entered Buck's Row and walked along the dimly lit cobbled street. On his way he noticed what he thought to be a tarpaulin laying on the opposite of the road. He crossed the road to investigate. Instead of finding a discarded tarpaulin, he found it was the dead body of Polly Nichols. He took a closer look and noticed that one of her hands was resting against the gateway and the other lay close to her new black bonnet, which was lying on the ground beside her. He noticed that Polly's skirts had been drawn up to the tops of her thighs. Cross immediately thought that she may have been raped and had fainted (swooned) and may not have recovered yet. Cross heard footsteps coming towards him and he called over to the man, Robert Paul, and said,

"Come and look over here, there's a woman."

Robert Paul went to investigate. The pair of men pulled down the woman's skirts to cover her. Both men were now late for work and decided they would tell a policeman about their discovery on the way to work.

Polly's body was found in Buck's Row across from Essex Wharf. The warehouse belonged to *Brown and Eagle Wool*. The body was almost directly underneath the window of Mrs. Green, whose house was called "New Cottage." Green was a widower who shared her home with her daughter and two sons. She claimed that she was a light sleeper, yet she had slept undisturbed and was woke by the police. Mrs. Green explained that between 9 p.m. and 11.00 p.m., when the family retired to bed, they heard nothing.

Living opposite "New Cottage" was the manager of Essex Wharf, a Mr. Walter Purkiss. He shared his home with his wife, children, and a servant. Mr. Purkiss said he and his wife both went to bed between 11 p.m. and 11.15 p.m. and that they had both been awake at various times during the night, but did not hear anything untoward.

Charles Cross's statement was as follows:

"At 3:45 am I saw a body lying opposite Essex Wharf Buck's Row. Thinking it was an abandoned tarpaulin I went to have a look. Robert Paul soon joined me. I decided the woman was dead as her hands and face was cold, but the arms above the elbows and legs were still warm."

Robert Paul's statement:

"I was on my way to work from home when at about 3:45am Charles Cross drew my attention to a body lying in Buck's Row. I felt her hands and face and thought I could hear a faint heartbeat. I said "I think she is still breathing, but it is very little if she is."

Robert Paul always seemed to be available to give interviews to the press, but the police took some time to identify him and actually find him. Robert Paul did not appear at Polly's inquest until it had been adjourned for two weeks. The police made repeated appeals for Paul to come forward but he did not. It could have been that Paul was being confused with an unidentified man seen in Buck's Row, a man Inspector Abberline was looking for at the time of the inquest. I believe that the unidentified man was Dr. Barnardo making his escape.

When Cross and Paul set off to find a policeman, Cross was puzzled at the sudden disappearance of Paul. He slipped into Corbett's Court and did not return. Cross found Police Constable Jonas Mizen at the corner of Hanbury Street and Bakers Row. Cross described the woman they had found as either drunk or dead. It was said that PC Mizen took his time getting to the deceased.

Police Constables Thain and Neil attended the scene while walking their beat. Later, PC Mizen joined them. Police Constable John Neil was on his beat and had been in Buck's Row half an hour earlier but had not seen a soul. He explained that when he returned to Buck's Row he noticed a body was lying in front of a gateway. Neil stated that the gateway was approximately nine or ten feet in height and was closed, and that they led to some stables. He inspected the body by the light of his lantern and immediately noticed blood seeping out of a wound from the neck. Polly was lying on her back with her clothes dishevelled. He felt her arm, which was warm to the touch. Her eyes were wide open and her bonnet was lying on the ground between her head and her left hand. Police Constable Thain reported that a large quantity of blood had come from the deceased, run across the pavement and into the gutter. Polly's clothing was saturated with blood, which seemed to have run from the back of the body. Neil instructed Thain to go and fetch the Doctor. He instructed Mizen to go and fetch the ambulance. An ambulance in 1888 consisted of a wooden-sided handcart that had a black leather bottom and had straps, which were used to tie the patient down. At the time, the ambulances were the police's responsibility.

When asked at the inquest whether Polly could have been killed elsewhere and her body moved to the place she was discovered, PC Neil replied that he had examined the area around the body thoroughly looking for any wheel marks on the road but did not find any. He also stated that if there had been an argument between Polly and a third party, the residents of Buck's Row would have heard it. Police Constable Neil described Whitechapel Road as a busy thoroughfare in the early part of the morning, and that anyone could escape easily without being noticed. Dr. Llewellyn corroborated the finding that Polly was murdered where she was found; he said at the inquest there were no blood stains that would have been consistent with the body being dragged.

4:00 a.m. Dr. Rees Ralph Llewellyn, who lived on Whitechapel Road, arrived at Buck's Row. He testified at Polly's inquest that the victim:

"Had severe injuries to the throat... Her hands and wrists were cold, but the body and lower extremities were warm." He went on to say that he examined the victim's chest and "felt her heart." One must assume that by "felt her heart," he meant he was trying to find a heartbeat. He estimated that Polly had not been dead for more than half an hour."

He never mentioned noticing the mutilations that Polly had suffered while examining the body at the murder scene. In his defence, he said at the inquest that it had been very dark at the time. Dr. Llewellyn pronounced the woman dead and noted that there was *"a wineglass-and-a-half of blood"* in the gutter at Polly's side. While Dr. Llewellyn was examining the dead woman's body an unidentified man walked along Buck's Row. Polly's body was then lifted into the ambulance and the doctor ordered the body to be moved to the mortuary shed at Old Montague Street Workhouse Infirmary.

Inspector John Spratling of J Division was in Hackney Road when he heard about the murder; he proceeded immediately to Buck's Row. He arrived after the body had been taken to the mortuary and found that James Green had already started clearing away the blood on the cobblestones. Inspector Spratling quickly made his way to the mortuary.

When Inspector Spratling arrived at the mortuary, Polly's body was still outside in the ambulance. This was because they were waiting for the "keeper of the dead house" to arrive with the keys. During the wait, Inspector Spratling took down the description of the deceased. Polly's mutilations were only noticed once she was inside the morgue and stripped. Following this discovery, Dr. Llewellyn was summoned again to do a further examination. Unfortunately, when he arrived at the mortuary the body had already been stripped and washed by Robert Mann and James Hatfield. The men said that there were many layers of clothing making it very difficult for them to remove them. In fact, Polly's clothes had been cut off and thrown in a heap in the yard outside. When asked about stripping the body, Hatfield said that the Ulster was the first item of clothing removed. They then removed Polly's jacket. The outside dress was loose so they did not need to cut it. He continued, explaining that the bands of the petticoats were cut and he then tore them with his bare hands. Lastly, he said that he tore her chemise down the front. Polly's body was then washed.

From the above reports, I think it is apparent how badly this investigation was carried out. Washing the body would have erased any evidence of sexual activity between the victim and the killer. Moreover, the ripping of Polly's clothing by hand and then throwing them outside in a dirty yard would have compromised any further findings. I think this conduct can be considered a "botched" investigation by the authorities.

The Police reported that they had left instructions for the body *not* to be touched until the Doctor arrived. The attendants at the mortuary indicated that they had not been given any instructions to leave the body alone.

Inspector Spratling cut out two labels from Polly's petticoats. They had the mark of the Lambeth Workhouse which they used to try to identify the woman.

Post-mortem by Dr. Reese Ralph Llewellyn

"Five of the teeth were missing and there was a slight laceration of the tongue. There was a bruise running along the lower part of the jaw on the right side of the face. A blow might have caused that from a fist or pressure from a thumb. There was a circular bruise on the left side of the face, which also might have been inflicted by the pressure of the fingers. On the left side of the neck, about 1 inch below the jaw there was an incision of about 4 inches in length and ran to the point directly under her ear. On the same side, but an inch below, and commencing an inch in front of it, was a circular incision, which terminated at a point about 3 inches below the right jaw. That incision completely severed all the tissues down to the vertebrae. The large vessels on both sides of the neck were severed. The incision was about 8 inches in length. The cuts must have been made by a long bladed knife, moderately sharp, and used with great violence. No blood was found on the breast, either of the body or the clothes. There were no injuries about the body until just about the lower part of the abdomen. Two or three inches from the left side was a wound running in a jagged manner. The wound was a very deep one, and the tissues were cut through. There were several incisions running across the abdomen. There were also three or four similar cuts running downwards, on the right side, a knife being used violently and in a downward manner caused all. The injuries were from left to right, and might have been done by a left-hand person. The same knife caused all the injuries".

Dr. Llewellyn noted the surprising cleanliness of the dead woman's thighs. Remembering that this woman could not simply take a bath, that her thighs were clean would be seen as a rare thing among women like her.

The description of the clothes Mary Ann Nichols was wearing is as follows:

- **Black Straw bonnet trimmed with black velvet**

- **Reddish brown Ulster with seven large brass buttons bearing the pattern of a woman on horseback accompanied by a man**
- **Brown Lindsey frock (apparently new, according to Sugden. Could this be a dress she stole from the Cowdrys?)**
- **White flannel chest cloth**
- **Black, ribbed, wool stockings**
- **Two petticoats, one grey wool, one flannel. Both stencilled on bands "Lambeth Workhouse"**
- **Brown stays (short)**
- **Flannel drawers**
- **Men's elastic (spring) sided boots with the uppers cut and steel tips on the heels.**

The following were listed as her possessions at the time of the Murder:

- **Comb**
- **White pocket handkerchief**
- **Broken piece of mirror (this was a prized possession in a lodging house).**

The occupants of the lodging houses frequented by Polly knew her as Polly Nichols. Mary Monk, a fellow Lambeth Workhouse inmate, identified the body as Mary Ann Nichols (Polly) after visiting the mortuary. Mary Monk was described as a young woman with "a haughty air and a flushed face." When asked at the inquest if she knew how Polly obtained her living, Mary replied, "No." William Nichols visited the mortuary on the evening of the September 1, 1888. He was respectably dressed and carried an umbrella. Once inside, he inspected the body of his ex-wife. Apparently, he said to the dead woman, *"Seeing you as you are now I forgive you for what you have done to me."* William Nichols emerged from the inspection visibly pale and remarked, *"Well, there is no mistake about it. It has come to a sad end"* (emphasis added)

The way William Nichols called poor Polly "it" is shocking. This poor woman was a victim of circumstance. She had been brutally murdered and he showed her no compassion; instead, he referred to her as "it." This remark provides good insight on the perception the middle and upper classes had of these poor Unfortunates.

Outside the mortuary, he met Polly's father and her son Edward John who was 21 years old and an Engineer. Mary Ann Nichols (Polly) was laid to rest on the afternoon of Thursday the 6th of September, 1888. The polished Elm coffin that carried Polly's remains was transported from the morgue to an undertaker on Hanbury Street. Her funeral cortege consisted of the hearse and two mourning coaches. These coaches carried her father, her son, and her ex-husband. As the Undertaker (Mr. Henry Smith) took the cortege down Hanbury Street, no one would have guessed that a little more than a day later that very street would be the location of Jack the Ripper's next murder. Polly's body was taken to The City of London Cemetery. She was placed in public grave number 210752, which is now situated on the edge of the memorial gardens. In late 1996, the Cemetery Authorities made a decision to mark Polly's grave with a plaque.

The Education Act of 1870 lead to an increase in the number of people who were able read. As the ability to read increased among common people, and with the removal of taxes on newspapers and advertising in 1885, the sales of newspapers increased. So, one can just imagine what the Jack the Ripper murders did for the press. By 1888, Britain had 180 "Penny Dailies." The murders caused a ratings war for circulation by these dailies. With the never-ending reports of the murders, many papers were calling for officials to offer a reward. The pleas were refused by the government and this caused the papers to criticise the police. Although Polly was the first canonical Ripper victim, she was one of two women that had been killed in a short space of time. Martha Tabram had been killed in 37 George Yard on August 7, 1888. She had been stabbed 39 times and the breasts, belly, and genitals had been the principle targets.

A foreman at Polly's inquest stated that the Government should offer "a substantial reward." He went on to say:

"if it had been a rich person that was murdered there would have been a reward of £1,000 offered, but as it was a poor Unfortunate hardly any notice was taken".

The coroner was not pleased with this remark and replied:

"I think that you are wrong altogether, and have no right to make such statements. For some time past the offering of rewards has been discontinued, no distinction being made between rich or poor."

The Foreman, however, responded, saying:

"nevertheless I maintain that if a large reward had been offered in the George Yard [Martha Tabram] murder the last horrible murder would not have been committed. I am glad to see inhabitants are themselves going to offer a reward, and I myself give £25."

Polly's inquest lasted for four days over a three-week period. Most of the inquiry was spent trying to piece together Polly's movements prior to her death. The inquest did not come to any conclusion as to who the killer was, based on the facts available to them. The only thing that came from this inquest was the idea that the killer could appear and disappear very quickly, and not be heard. Though the police talked to every resident in Buck's Row, the investigation did not seem to get very far.

The police officers of 1888 were not murder specialists. They did not have first-hand knowledge of investigative procedures. As mentioned, Polly was stripped and washed in the Infirmary, with no officer guarding the body. In their defence we have to remember that Jack the Ripper was Britain's first "serial killer"

If the police did have information they chose not to divulge to the world, I cannot see what it was.

I would like to include the Coroner's summation of the inquest as I think it gives a good outline of how inquests in 1888 were very important to murder cases. The reader should remember that when this inquest was conducted, Annie Chapman's body had been discovered and examined. There are references to the murders of both Polly and Annie in the coroner's summation.

The Coroner, Mr. Baxter gave the jury a brief outline of the lifestyle the deceased had been living since her separation from her husband.

"Polly was last seen alive at half-past two o'clock on Saturday morning, September 1, by Mrs Holland, who knew her well. At the time, Polly was most likely drunk and search of more alcohol. She was endeavouring to walk eastward down Whitechapel. What her exact movements were after this it was impossible to say. The discovery of the body was around 3:45a.m, and this time is fixed by independent reports The evidence indicated that the woman was killed exactly were her body was discovered. There was blood found at the scene of the murder, and it was only present in the area where the deceased's throat had been cut, nowhere else. That there was no blood around her legs suggested the abdominal injuries were inflicted while she was lying on the ground. The injury to the throat was also carried out while the woman was lying on the ground. The coroner then turned his attention to the perpetrator of the murder. It is astonishing that the murderer escaped detection. Surely there must have been blood stains on him. The many slaughter-houses in the neighbourhood would have allowed the killer to walk through the streets with blood on his person, either on his clothes or his hands, unnoticed. Whitechapel Road was busy at that time of the morning, which also helped the killer slip away unnoticed. The coroner explained that this killing was one of four that had happened in the space of five months."

The coroner described his opinion of the crimes further:

"All [occurred] within a very short distance of the place where we are sitting. All four victims were women of middle age, all were married, and had lived apart from their husbands in consequence of

intemperate habits, and were at the time of their death leading irregular lives, and eking out a miserable and precarious existence in common lodging houses. In each case there were abdominal as well as other injuries. In each case the injuries were inflicted after midnight, and in places of public resort, where it would appear impossible but that almost immediate detection should follow that crime, and in each case the inhuman and dastardly criminals are at large in society."

The coroner said *"the criminals are still at large,"* which leads you to believe that although these cases have similarities, the coroner did not believe that these murders were done by one person. He continued, saying,

"Emma Elizabeth Smith, who received her injuries in Osborn Street on the early morning of Easter Tuesday, April 7th 1888, survived in the London Hospital for upwards of twenty-four hours, and was able to state that she had been followed by some men, robbed and mutilated, and even to describe imperfectly one of them. Emma was probably killed by one of the many gangs that roamed the East End; she was robbed and was what we today would call sexually assaulted (forcing an instrument into her vagina) and not mutilation as was in the case in the Ripper killings."

He continued,

"Martha Tabram was found at 3 a.m. on Tuesday August 7th, on the first floor landing of George Yard buildings, Wentworth Street, with thirty-nine puncture wounds on her body. In addition to these, and the case under your consideration, there is the case of Annie Chapman, still in the hands of another jury. The instruments used in the two earlier cases are dissimilar. In the first it was a blunt instrument, such as a walking stick; in the second, some of the wounds were thought to have been made by a dagger; but in the two recent cases the instruments suggested by the medical witness are not so different."

The Coroner then explains the medical opinion of Dr. Llewellyn:

"He says that the injuries on Nichols could have been produced by a strong bladed instrument, moderately sharp. Dr. Phillips is of the opinion that the injuries inflicted on Chapman were also done by a very sharp knife, probably a thin, narrow blade, at least six to eight inches in length, probably longer. The similarity of the injuries in the two cases is considerable. There are bruises about the face; the head is nearly severed from the body in both cases; there are other dreadful injuries, again have in each case been performed with anatomical knowledge. Dr. Llewellyn seems to incline to the opinion that the abdominal injuries were first, and caused instantaneous death; but, if so, it seems difficult to understand the object of such desperate injuries to the throat, or how it comes about that there was so little bleeding from the several arteries,

and that the clothing on the upper surface was not stained, and, indeed, very much less bleeding from the abdomen than from the neck. Surely it may well be that, as in the case of Chapman, the dreadful wounds to the throat were inflicted first and the other injuries followed. This is a matter of some importance when we come to consider what possible motive there can be for all this ferocity. Robbery is out of the question; and there is nothing to suggest jealousy; there could not have been any quarrel between victim and her killer, or it would have been heard. I suggest to you as a possibility that these two women may have been murdered by the same man with the same object, and that in the case of Nichols the wretch was disturbed before he had accomplished his object, and having failed in the open street he tries again, within a week of his failure, in a more secluded place. If this should be correct, the audacity and daring is equal to its maniacal fanaticism and abhorrent wickedness. This surmise may or may not be correct, the suggested motive may be the wrong one; but the one thing that is clear is that a murder of a most atrocious character has been committed."

With the Coroner's summation finished, and after a short consultation, the jury delivered a verdict of wilful murder against a person or persons unknown. The coroner finished the proceedings by stating the need for a mortuary in Whitechapel.

Buck's Row, where the Ripper murders occurred, became known locally as "Killer's Row." This eventually became too much for the residents to bare and in 1892, after a petition, the name changed. Buck's Row and White's Row were joined together to become Durward Street.

The next few pages follow the Inquest into

The next few pages follow the Inquest into the death of Mary Ann Nichols   (also known as Polly), as recorded by the newspapers at the time, followed by a copy of the Death Certificate.

Inquests were very important in the 1800's and they give an insight into how people, spoke, behaved and thought.

The inquests make for great reading as part of the book or separately for research.

The way in which the print irregularity appears on the pages is due to the typesetting of the day

Day 1, Saturday, September 1, 1888
(As told by *The Daily Telegraph*, Monday, September 3, 1888, Page 3)

On Saturday [1 Sep] Mr. Wynne E. Baxter, the Coroner for Southeast Middlesex, opened an inquiry at the Working Lads' Institute, Whitechapel Road, into the circumstances attending the death of a woman supposed to be Mary Ann Nicholls, who was discovered lying dead on the pavement in Buck's Row, Baker's Row, Whitechapel, early on Friday morning. Her throat was cut, and she had other terrible injuries.

Inspector Helston, who has the case in hand, attended, with other officers, on behalf of the Criminal Investigation Department.

Edward Walker deposed: I live at 15, Maidwell Street, Albany Road, Camberwell, and have no occupation. I was a smith when I was at work, but I am not now. I have seen the body in the mortuary, and to the best of my belief it is my daughter; but I have not seen her for three years. I recognise her by her general appearance and by a little mark she has had on her forehead since she was a child. She also had either one or two teeth out, the same as the woman I have just seen. My daughter's name was Mary Ann Nicholls, and she had been married twenty-two years. Her husband's name is William Nicholls, and he is alive. He is a machinist. They have been living apart about seven or eight years. I last heard of her before Easter. She was forty-two years of age.
Coroner: How did you see her?
Witness: She wrote to me.
Coroner: Is this letter in her handwriting?
Witness: Yes that is her writing. The letter, which was dated April 17, 1888, was read by the Coroner, and referred to a place, which the deceased had gone to at Wandsworth.
Coroner: When did you last see her alive?
Witness: Two years ago last June.
Coroner: Was she then in a good situation?
Witness: I don't know. I was not on speaking terms with her. She had been living with me three or four years previously, but thought she could better herself, so I let her go.
Coroner: What did she do after she left you?
Witness: I don't know.
Coroner: This letter seems to suggest that she was in a decent situation.

Witness: She had only just gone there.

Coroner: Was she a sober woman?

Witness: Well, at times she drank, and that was why we did not agree.

Coroner: Was she fast?

Witness: No; I never heard of anything of that sort. She used to go with some young women and men that she knew, but I never heard of anything improper.

Coroner: Have you any idea what she has been doing lately?

Witness: I have not the slightest idea.

Coroner: She must have drunk heavily for you to turn her out of doors?

Witness: I never turned her out. She had no need to be like this while I had a home for her.

Coroner: How is it that she and her husband were not living together?

Witness: When she was confined her husband took on with the young woman who came to nurse her, and they parted, he living with the nurse, by whom he has another family.

Coroner: Have you any reasonable doubt that this is your daughter?

Witness: No, I have not. I know nothing about her acquaintances, or what she had been doing for a living. I had no idea she was over here in this part of the town. She has had five children, the eldest being twenty-one years old and the youngest eight or nine years. One of them lives with me, and the other four are with their father.

Coroner: Has she ever lived with anybody since she left her husband?

Witness: I believe she was once stopping with a man in York Street, Walworth. His name was Drew, and he was a smith by trade. He is living there now, I believe. The parish of Lambeth summoned her husband for the keep of the children, but the summons was dismissed, as it was proved that she was then living with another man. I don't know who that man was.

Coroner: Was she ever in the workhouse?

Witness: Yes, sir; Lambeth Workhouse, in April last, and went from there to a situation at Wandsworth.

By the Jury: The husband resides at Coburg Road, Old Kent Road. I don't know if he knows of her death.

Coroner: Is there anything you know of likely to throw any light upon this affair?

Witness: No; I don't think she had any enemies, she was too good for that.

John Neil, police constable, 97J, said: Yesterday morning I was proceeding down Buck's Row, Whitechapel, going towards Brady Street. There was not a soul about. I had been round there half an hour previously, and I saw no one then. I was on the right-hand side of the street, when I noticed a figure lying in the street. It was dark at the time, though there was a street lamp shining at the end of the row. I went across and found deceased lying outside a gateway, her head towards the east. The gateway was closed. It was about nine or ten feet high and led to some stables. There were houses from the gateway eastward, and the School Board school occupies the westward. On the opposite side of the road is Essex Wharf. Deceased was lying lengthways along the street, her left hand touching the gate. I examined the body by the aid of my lamp, and noticed blood oozing from a wound in the throat. She was lying on her back, with her clothes disarranged. I felt her arm, which was quite warm from the joints upwards. Her eyes were wide open. Her bonnet was off and lying at her side, close to the left hand. I heard a constable passing Brady Street, so I called him. I did not whistle. I said to him, "Run at once for Dr. Llewellyn," and, seeing another constable in Baker's Row, I sent him for the ambulance. The doctor arrived in a very short time. I had, in the meantime, rung the bell at Essex Wharf, and asked if any disturbance had been heard. The reply was "No." Sergeant Kirby came after, and he knocked. The doctor looked at the woman and then said, "Move her to the mortuary. She is dead, and I will make a further examination of her." We placed her on the ambulance, and moved her there. Inspector Spratley came to the mortuary, and while taking a description of the deceased turned up her clothes, and found that she was disemboweled. This had not been noticed by any of them before. On the body was found a piece of comb and a bit of looking glass. No money was found, but an unmarked white handkerchief was found in her pocket.

Coroner: Did you notice any blood where she was found?
Witness: There was a pool of blood just where her neck was lying. It was running from the wound in her neck.
Coroner: Did you hear any noise that night?
Witness: No; I heard nothing. The farthest I had been that night was just through the Whitechapel Road and up Baker's Row. I was never far away from the spot.
Coroner: Whitechapel Road is busy in the early morning, I believe. Could anybody have escaped that way?
Witness: Oh yes, sir. I saw a number of women in the main road going home. At that time any one could have got away.
Coroner: Some one searched the ground, I believe?
Witness: Yes; I examined it while the doctor was being sent for.

Inspector Spratley: I examined the road, sir, in daylight.
A Juryman (to witness): Did you see a trap in the road at all?

Witness: No.

A Juryman: Knowing that the body was warm, did it not strike you that it might just have been laid there, and that the woman was killed elsewhere? **Witness:** I examined the road, but did not see the mark of wheels. The first to arrive on the scene after I had discovered the body were two men, who work at a slaughterhouse opposite. They said they knew nothing of the affair, and that they had not heard any screams. I had previously seen the men at work. That would be about a quarter-past three or half an hour before I found the body.

Henry Llewellyn, surgeon, said: On Friday morning I was called to Buck's Row about four o'clock. The constable told me what I was wanted for. On reaching Buck's Row I found the deceased woman lying flat on her back in the pathway, her legs extended. I found she was dead, and that she had severe injuries to her throat. Her hands and wrists were cold, but the body and lower extremities were warm. I examined her chest and felt the heart. It was dark at the time. I believe she had not been dead more than half-an-hour. I am quite certain that the injuries to her neck were not self-inflicted. There was very little blood round the neck. There were no marks of any struggle or of blood, as if the body had been dragged. I told the police to take her to the mortuary, and I would make another examination. About an hour later I was sent for by the Inspector to see the injuries he had discovered on the body. I went, and saw that the abdomen was cut very extensively. I have this morning made a post-mortem examination of the body. I found it to be that of a female about forty or forty-five years. Five of the teeth are missing, and there is a slight laceration of the tongue. On the right side of the face there is a bruise running along the lower part of the jaw. It might have been caused by a blow with the fist or pressure by the thumb. On the left side of the face there was a circular bruise, which also might have been done by the pressure of the fingers. On the left side of the neck, about an inch below the jaw, there was an incision about four inches long and running from a point immediately below the ear. An inch below on the same side, and commencing about an inch in front of it, was a circular incision terminating at a point about three inches below the right jaw. This incision completely severs all the tissues down to the vertebrae. The large vessels of the neck on both sides were severed. The incision is about eight inches long. These cuts must have been caused with a long-bladed knife, moderately sharp, and used with great violence. No blood at all was found on the breast either of the body or clothes. There were no injuries about the body till just about the lower part of the abdomen. Two or three inches from the left side was a wound running in a jagged manner. It was a very deep wound, and the tissues were cut through. There were several incisions running across the abdomen. On the right side there were also three or four similar cuts running downwards. All these had been caused by a knife, which had been used violently and been used downwards. The wounds were from left to right, and might have been done by a left-handed person. All the injuries had been done by the same instrument.

The inquiry was adjourned till to-morrow [sic, ('today', 3 Sep)].

Day 2, Monday, September 3, 1888
(*The Daily Telegraph*, Tuesday, September 4, 1888, Page 2)

Mr. Wynne E. Baxter, the coroner for Southeast Middlesex, yesterday [3 Sep] resumed his inquiry at the Working Lads' Institute, Whitechapel Road, into the circumstances attending the death of the woman Mary Ann Nicholls, who was discovered lying dead on the pavement in Buck's Row, Baker's Row, Whitechapel, early on Friday morning last.

Inspectors Helston and Aberline attended for the police; whilst Detective- sergeant Enright, of Scotland Yard was also in attendance.

Inspector John Spratling, J Division, deposed that he first heard of the murder about half-past four on Friday morning, while he was in Hackney Road. He proceeded to Buck's Row, where he saw Police-constable Thain, who showed him the place where the deceased had been found. He noticed a blood stain on the footpath. The body of deceased had been removed to the mortuary in Old Montague- Street, where witness had an opportunity of preparing a description. The skin presented the appearance of not having been washed for some time previous to the murder. On his arrival Dr. Llewellyn made an examination of the body which lasted about ten minutes.
Witness said he next saw the body when it was stripped.
Detective-Sergeant Enright: That was done by two of the workhouse officials.
Coroner: Had they any authority to strip the body?
Witness: No, sir; I gave them no instructions to strip it. In fact, I told them to leave it as it was.
Coroner: I don't object to their stripping the body, but we ought to have evidence about the clothes.
Sergeant Enright, continuing, said the clothes, which were lying in a heap

in the yard, consisted of a reddish-brown ulster, with seven large brass buttons, and a brown dress, which looked new. There were also a woollen and a flannel petticoat, belonging to the workhouse. Inspector Helson had cut out pieces marked "P. R., Princes-road," with a view to tracing the body. There was also a pair of stays, in fairly good condition, but witness did not notice how they were adjusted.

Coroner said he considered it important to know the exact state in which the stays were found.

On the suggestion of Inspector Aberline, the clothes were sent for.

The Foreman of the jury asked whether the stays were fastened on the body.

Inspector Spratling replied that he could not say for certain. There was blood on the upper part of the dress body, and also on the ulster, but he only saw a little on the under-linen, and that might have happened after the removal of the body from Buck's Row. The clothes were fastened when he first saw the body. The stays did not fit very tightly, for he was able to see the wounds without unfastening them. About six o'clock that day he made an examination at Buck's Row and Brady Street, which ran across Baker's Row, but he failed to trace any marks of blood. He subsequently examined, in company with Sergeant Godley, the East London and District Railway lines and embankment, and also the Great Eastern Railway yard, without, however, finding any traces. A watchman of the Great Eastern Railway, whose box was fifty or sixty yards from the spot where the body was discovered, heard nothing particular on the night of the murder. **Witness** also visited half a dozen persons living in the same neighbourhood, none of whom had noticed anything at all suspicious. One of these, Mrs. Purkiss, had not gone to bed at the time the body of deceased was found, and her husband was of opinion that if there had been any screaming in Buck's Row they would have heard it. A Mrs. Green, whose window looked out upon the very spot where the body was discovered, said nothing had attracted her attention on the morning of Friday last.

Replying to a question from one of the jury, witness stated that Constable Neil was the only one whose duty it was to pass through Buck's Row, but another constable passing along Broad Street from time to time would be within hearing distance.

In reply to a juryman, witness said it was his firm belief that the woman had her clothes on at the time she was murdered.

Henry Tomkins, horse-slaughterer, 12, Coventry Street, Bethnal Green, was the next witness. He deposed that he was in the employ of Messrs. Barber, and was working in the slaughterhouse, Winthrop Street, from between eight and nine o'clock on Thursday evening till twenty minutes past four on Friday morning. He and his fellow workmen usually went home upon finishing their work, but on that morning they did not do so. They went to see the dead woman, Police-constable Thain having passed the slaughterhouse at about a quarter-past four, and told them that a murder had been committed in Buck's Row. Two other men, James Mumford and Charles Britten, had been working in the slaughterhouse. He (witness) and Britten left the slaughterhouse for one hour between midnight and one o'clock in the morning, but not afterwards till they went to see the body. The distance from Winthrop Street to Buck's Row was not great.

Coroner: Is your work noisy?
Witness: No, sir, very quiet.
Coroner: Was it quiet on Friday morning, say after two o'clock?
Witness: Yes, sir, quite quiet. The gates were open and we heard no cry.
Coroner: Did anybody come to the slaughterhouse that night?
Witness: Nobody passed except the policeman.
Coroner: Are there any women about there?
Witness: Oh! I know nothing about them, I don't like 'em.
Coroner: I did not ask you whether you like them; I ask you whether there were any about that night.
Witness: I did not see any.
Coroner: Not in Whitechapel Road?
Witness: Oh, yes, there, of all sorts and sizes; it's a rough neighbourhood, I can tell you.
Witness, in reply to further questions, said the slaughterhouse was too far away from the spot where deceased was found for him to have heard if anybody had called for assistance. When he arrived at Buck's Row the doctor and two or three policemen were there. He believed that two other men, whom he did not know, were also there. He waited till the body was taken away, previous to which about a dozen men came up. He heard no statement as to how the deceased came to be in Buck's Row.
Coroner: Have you read any statement in the newspapers that there were two people, besides the police and the doctor, in Buck's Row, when you arrived?
Witness: I cannot say, sir.
Coroner: Then you did not see a soul from one o'clock on Friday morning till a quarter-past four, when the policeman passed your slaughterhouse?
Witness: No, sir.
A Juryman: Did you hear any vehicle pass the slaughterhouse? No, sir.

Juryman Would you have heard it if there had been one? Yes, sir.
Juryman Where did you go between twenty minutes past twelve and one o'clock? I and my mate went to the front of the road.
Juryman is not your usual hour for leaving off work six o'clock in the morning, and not four? No; it is according to what we have to do. Sometimes it is one time and sometimes another.
Juryman what made the constable come and tell you about the murder? He called for his cape.

Inspector Jos. Helson deposed that he first received information about the murder at a quarter before seven on Friday morning. He afterwards went to the mortuary, where he saw the body with the clothes still on it. The dress was fastened in front, with the exception of a few buttons, the stays, which were attached with clasps, were also fastened. He noticed blood on the hair, and on the collars of the dress and ulster, but not on the back of the skirts. There were no cuts in the clothes, and no indications of any struggle having taken place. The only suspicious mark discovered in the neighbourhood of Buck's Row was in Broad Street, where there was a stain which might have been blood.
Witness was of opinion that the body had not been carried to Buck's Row, but that the murder was committed on the spot. **Police-Constable Mizen** said that at a quarter to four o'clock on Friday morning he was at the crossing, Hanbury Street, Baker's Row, when a carman who passed in company with another man informed him that he was wanted by a policeman in Buck's Row, where a woman was lying. When he arrived there Constable Neil sent him for the ambulance. At that time nobody but Neil was with the body.

Chas. Andrew Cross, Carmen, said he had been in the employment of Messrs. Pickford and Co. for over twenty years. About half-past three on Friday he left his home to go to work, and he passed through Buck's Row. He discerned on the opposite side something lying against the gateway, but he could not at once make out what it was. He thought it was a tarpaulin sheet. He walked into the middle of the road, and saw that it was the figure of a woman. He then heard the footsteps of a man going up Buck's Row, about forty yards away, in the direction that he himself had come from. When he came up witness said to him, "Come and look over here; there is a woman lying on the pavement." They both crossed over to the body, and witness took hold of the woman's hands, which were cold and limp. Witness said, "I believe she is dead." He touched her face, which felt warm. The other man, placing his hand on her heart, said, "I think she is breathing, but very little if she is." Witness suggested that they should give her a prop, but his companion refused to touch her. Just then they heard a policeman coming. Witness did not notice that her throat was cut, the night being very dark. He and the other man left the deceased, and in Baker's Row they met the last witness, whom they informed that they had seen a woman lying in Buck's Row. Witness said, "She looks to me to be either dead or drunk; but for my part I think she is dead." The policeman said, "All right," and then walked on. The other man left witness soon after. Witness had never seen him before.

Replying to the coroner, witness denied having seen Police-constable Neil in Buck's Row. There was nobody there when he and the other man left. In his opinion deceased looked as if she had been outraged and gone off in a swoon; but he had no idea that there were any serious injuries.

Coroner: Did the other man tell you who he was?

Witness: No, sir; he merely said that he would have fetched a policeman, only he was behind time. I was behind time myself.

A Juryman: Did you tell Constable Mizen that another constable wanted him in Buck's Row?

Witness: No, because I did not see a policeman in Buck's Row. **Wm. Nicholls** [Nichols], printer's machinist, Coburg Road, Old Kent Road, said deceased was his wife, but they had lived apart for eight years. He last saw her alive about three years ago, and had not heard from her since. He did not know what she had been doing in the meantime.

A Juryman: It is said that you were summoned by the Lambeth Union for her maintenance, and you pleaded that she was living with another man. Was he the blacksmith whom she had lived with?

Witness: No; it was not the same; it was another man. I had her watched. Witness further deposed that he did not leave his wife, but that she left him of her own accord. She had no occasion for so doing. If it had not been for her drinking habits they would have got on all right together.

Emily Holland, a married woman, living at 18, Thrawl Street, said deceased had stayed at her lodgings for about six weeks, but had not been there during the last ten days or so. About half-past two on Friday morning witness saw deceased walking down Osborne Street, Whitechapel Road. She was alone, and very much the worse for drink. She informed witness that where she had been living they would not allow her to return because she could not pay for her room. Witness persuaded her to go home. She refused, adding that she had earned her lodging money three times that day. She then went along the Whitechapel Road. Witness did not know in what way she obtained a living. She always seemed to her to be a quiet woman, and kept very much to herself.

In reply to further questions witness said she had never seen deceased quarrel with anybody. She gave her the impression of being weighed down by some trouble. When she left the witness at the corner of Osborne Street, she said she would soon be back.

Mary Ann Monk was the last witness examined. She deposed to having seen deceased about seven o'clock entering a public house in the New Kent Road. She had seen her before in the workhouse, and had no knowledge of her means of livelihood.

The inquiry was then adjourned until Sept. 17.

Day 3, Monday, September 17, 1888
(*The Daily Telegraph*, Tuesday, September 18, 1888, Page 2)

Yesterday [17 Sep], at the Working Lads' Institute, Whitechapel-road, Mr. Wynne Baxter, coroner for the north-eastern District of Middlesex, resumed his inquiry relative to the death of Mary Ann Nicholls, the victim of the Buck's Row tragedy, on Friday morning, Aug. 31.

Dr. Llewellyn, recalled, said he had re-examined the body and there was no part of the viscera missing.

Emma Green, who lives in the cottage next to the scene of the murder in Buck's Row, stated that she had heard no unusual sound during the night. **By the Jury:** Rough people often passed through the street, but she knew of no disorderly house in Buck's Row, all the houses being occupied by hardworking folk.

Thomas Ede, a signalman in the employ of the East London Railway Company, said he saw a man with a knife on the morning of the 8th. The coroner was of opinion that this incident could have no reference to the present inquiry, as the 8th was the day of the Hanbury Street murder. He would, however, accept the evidence.
Witness then said: On Saturday, the 8th inst., at noon, I was coming down the Cambridge Heath road, and when near the Forester's Arms I saw a man on the other side of the street. His peculiar appearance made me take notice of him. He seemed to have a wooden arm. I watched him until level with the Forester's Arms, and then he put his hand to his trousers pocket, and I saw about four inches of a knife. I followed him, but he quickened

his pace, and I lost sight of him.

Inspector Helson, in reply to the coroner, stated that the man had not been found.

Witness described the man as 5 ft. 8 in. high, about thirty-five years of age, with a dark moustache and whiskers. He wore a double-peaked cap, a short dark brown jacket, and a pair of clean white overalls over dark trousers. The man walked as though he had a stiff knee, and he had a fearful look about the eyes. He seemed to be a mechanic.

By the Jury: He was not a muscular man.

Walter Purkess [Purkiss], manager, residing at Essex Wharf, deposed that his house fronted Buck's Row, opposite the gates where deceased was discovered. He slept in the front room on the second floor and had heard no sound, neither had his wife.

Alfred Malshaw [Mulshaw], a night watchman in Winthorpe Street, had also heard no cries or noise. He admitted that he sometimes dozed.

Coroner: I suppose your watching is not up to much?

Witness: I don't know. It is thirteen long hours for 3s and find your own coke (Laughter.)

By the Jury: In a straight line I was about thirty yards from the spot where the deceased was found.

Police-constable John Thail [Thain] stated that the nearest point on his beat to Buck's Row was Brady Street. He passed the end every thirty minutes on the Thursday night, and nothing attracted his attention until 3.45 a.m., when he was signalled by the flash of the lantern of another constable (Neale). He went to him, and found Neale standing by the body of the deceased, and witness was despatched for a doctor. About ten minutes after he had fetched the surgeon he saw two workmen standing with Neale. He did not know who they were. The body was taken to the mortuary, and witnessed remained on the spot. Witness searched Essex Wharf, the Great Eastern Railway arches, the East London Railway line, and the District Railway as far as Thames Street, and detected no marks of blood or anything of a suspicious character.

When I went to the horse-slaughterer's for my cape I did not say that I was going to fetch a doctor, as a murder had been committed. Another constable had taken my cape there.

By the Coroner: There were one or two working men going down Brady Street shortly before I was called by Neale.

Robert Baul [Paul], 30, Forster Street, Whitechapel, Carman, said as he was going to work at Cobbett's Court, Spitalfields, he saw in Buck's Row a man standing in the middle of the road. As witness drew closer he walked towards the pavement, and he (Baul) stepped in the roadway to pass him. The man touched witness on the shoulder and asked him to look at the woman, who was lying across the gateway. He felt her hands and face, and they were cold. The clothes were disarranged, and he helped to pull them down. Before he did so he detected a slight movement as of breathing, but very faint. The man walked with him to Montague Street, and there they saw a policeman. Not more than four minutes had elapsed from the time he first saw the woman. Before he reached Buck's Row he had seen no one running away.

Robert Mann, the keeper of the mortuary, said the police came to the workhouse, of which he was an inmate. He went, in consequence, to the mortuary at five a.m. He saw the body placed there, and then locked the place up and kept the keys. After breakfast witness and Hatfield, another inmate of the workhouse, undressed the woman.
Coroner the police were not present? No; there was no one present. Inspector Helson was not there.
Coroner Had you been told not to touch it? No.
Coroner Did you see Inspector Helson? I can't say.
Coroner was he present? I can't say.
Coroner I suppose you do not recollect whether the clothes were torn? They were not torn or cut.
Coroner you cannot describe where the blood was? No, sir; I cannot.
Coroner how did you get the clothes off? Hatfield had to cut them down the front.
A Juryman: Was the body undressed in the mortuary or in the yard? In the mortuary.
Coroner: It appears the mortuary-keeper is subject to fits, and neither his memory nor statements are reliable.

James Hatfield, an inmate of the Whitechapel Workhouse, said he accompanied Mann, the last witness, to the mortuary, and undressed the deceased. Inspector Helson was not there.
Coroner who was there? Only me and my mate.
Coroner What did you take off first? An ulster, which I put aside on the ground. We then took the jacket off, and put it in the same place. The outside dress was loose, and we did not cut it. The bands of the petticoats were cut, and I then tore them down with my hand. I tore the chemise down the front. There were no stays.

Coroner who gave you instructions to do all this? No one gave us any. We did it to have the body ready for the doctor.

Coroner who told you a doctor was coming?I heard someone speak about it.

Coroner Was any one present whilst you were undressing the body? Not as I was aware of.

Coroner having finished, did you make the post-mortem examination? No, the police came.

Coroner Oh, it was not necessary for you to go on with it! The police came? Yes, they examined the petticoats, and found the words "Lambeth Workhouse" on the bands.

Coroner it was cut out? I cut it out.

Coroner who told you to do it? Inspector Helson.

Coroner is that the first time you saw Inspector Helson on that morning? Yes; I arrived at about half-past six.

Coroner Would you be surprised to find that there were stays? No.

Coroner A juryman: Did not you try the stays on in the afternoon to show me how short they were. I forgot it.

Coroner: He admits that his memory is bad.

Witness: Yes. **The Coroner**: We cannot do more. (To the police): There was a man who passed down Buck's Row when the doctor was examining the body. Have you heard anything of him?

Inspector Abberline: We have not been able to find him. Inspector Spratley, J Division, stated he had made inquiries in Buck's- Row, but not at all of the houses.

Coroner: Then that will have to be done.

Witness added [Spratling] that he made inquiries at Green's, the wharf, Snider's factory, and also at the Great Eastern wharf, and no one had heard anything unusual on the morning of the murder. He had not called at any of the houses in Buck's Row, excepting at Mrs. Green's. He had seen the Board School keeper.

Coroner: Is there not a gentleman at the G.E. Railway? I thought we should have had him here.

Witness: I saw him that morning, but he said he had heard nothing. The witness added that when at the mortuary he had given instructions that the body was not to be touched.

Coroner: Is there any other evidence?

Inspector Helson: No, not at present.

The Foreman thought that, had a reward been offered by the Government after the murder in George Yard, very probably the two later murders would not have been perpetrated. It mattered little into whose hands the money went so long as they could find out the monster in there midst, who was terrorising everybody and making people ill. There were four horrible murders remaining undiscovered.

Coroner considered that the first one was the worst, and it had attracted the least attention.

The Foreman intimated that he would be willing to give £25 himself, and he hoped that the Government would offer a reward. These poor people had souls like anybody else.

Coroner understood that no rewards were now offered in any case. It mattered not whether the victims were rich or poor. There was no surety that a rich person would not be the next.

The Foreman: If that should be, then there will be a large reward.

Inspector Helson, in reply to the coroner, said rewards had been discontinued for years.

The inquiry was then adjourned until Saturday.

Day 4, Saturday, September 22, 1888
(*The Daily Telegraph*, Monday, September 24, 1888, Page 3)

On Saturday [22 Sep] Mr. Wynne E. Baxter resumed the inquest upon the body of Mary Ann Nicholls, aged forty-seven, the victim in the Buck's Row murder, one of the series of Whitechapel tragedies. The inquiry was held at the Working Lads' Institute.

Signalman Eades was recalled to supplement his previous evidence to the effect that he had seen a man named John James carrying a knife near the scene of the murder. It transpired, however, that this man is a harmless lunatic who is well known in the neighbourhood.

The Coroner then summed up. Having reviewed the career of the deceased from the time she left her husband, and reminded the jury of the irregular life she had led for the last two years, Mr. Baxter proceeded to point out that the unfortunate woman was last seen alive at half-past two o'clock on Saturday morning, Sept 1, by Mrs. Holland, who knew her well. Deceased was at that time much the worse for drink, and was endeavouring to walk eastward down Whitechapel. What her exact movements were after this it was impossible to say; but in less than an hour and a quarter her dead body was discovered at a spot rather under three-quarters of a mile distant. The time at which the body was found cannot have been far from 3.45 am, as it is fixed by so many independent data. The condition of the body appeared to prove conclusively that the deceased was killed on the exact spot in which she was found. There was not a trace of blood anywhere, except at the spot where her neck was lying, this circumstance being sufficient to justify the assumption that the injuries to the throat were committed when the woman was on the ground, whilst the state of her clothing and the absence of any blood about her legs suggested that the abdominal injuries were inflicted whilst she was still in the same position. Coming to a consideration of the perpetrator of the murder, the Coroner said: It seems astonishing at first thought that the culprit should have escaped detection, for there must surely have been marks of blood about his person. If, however, blood was principally on his hands, the presence of so many slaughter-houses in the neighbourhood would make the frequenters of this spot familiar with blood- stained clothes and hands, and his appearance might in that way have failed to attract attention while he passed from Buck's Row in the twilight into Whitechapel-road, and was lost sight of in the morning's market traffic. We cannot altogether leave unnoticed the fact that the death that you have been investigating is one of four presenting many points of similarity, all of which have occurred within the space of about five months, and all within a very short distance of the place where we are sitting. All four victims were women of middle age, all were married, and had lived apart from their husbands in consequence of intemperate habits, and were at the time of their death leading an irregular life, and eeking out a miserable and precarious existence in common lodging-houses. In each case there were abdominal as well as other injuries. In each case the injuries were inflicted after midnight, and in places of public resort, where it would appear impossible but that almost immediate detection should follow the crime, and in each case the inhuman and dastardly criminals are at large in society. Emma Elizabeth Smith, who received her injuries in Osborn Street on the early morning of Easter Tuesday, April 3, survived in the London Hospital for upwards of twenty four hours, and was able to state that she had been followed by some men, robbed and mutilated, and even to describe imperfectly one of them. Martha Tabram was found at three a.m. on Tuesday, Aug. 7, on the first floor landing of George yard buildings, Wentworth Street, with thirty-nine punctured wounds on her body. In addition to these, and the case under your consideration, there is the case of Annie Chapman, still in the hands of another jury. The instruments used in the two earlier cases are dissimilar. In the first it was a blunt instrument, such as a walking-stick; in the second, some of the wounds were thought to have been made by a dagger; but in the two recent cases the instruments suggested by the medical witnesses are not so different. Dr. Llewellyn says the injuries on Nicholls could have been produced by a strong bladed instrument, moderately sharp. Dr. Phillips is of opinion that those on

Chapman were by a very sharp knife, probably with a thin, narrow blade, at least six to eight inches in length, probably longer. The similarity of the injuries in the two cases is considerable. There are bruises about the face in both cases; the head is nearly severed from the body in both cases; there are other dreadful injuries in both cases; and those injuries, again, have in each case been performed with anatomical knowledge. Dr. Llewellyn seems to incline to the opinion that the abdominal injuries were first, and caused instantaneous death; but, if so, it seems difficult to understand the object of such desperate injuries to the throat, or how it comes about that there was so little bleeding from the several arteries, that the clothing on the upper surface was not stained, and, indeed, very much less bleeding from the abdomen than from the neck. Surely it may well be that, as in the case of Chapman, the dreadful wounds to the throat were inflicted first and the others afterwards. This is a matter of some importance when we come to consider what possible motive there can be for all this ferocity. Robbery is out of the question; and there is nothing to suggest jealousy; there could not have been any quarrel, or it would have been heard. I suggest to you as a possibility that these two women may have been murdered by the same man with the same object, and that in the case of Nicholls the wretch was disturbed before he had accomplished his object, and having failed in the open street he tries again, within a week of his failure, in a more secluded place. If this should be correct, the audacity and daring is equal to its maniacal fanaticism and abhorrent wickedness. But this surmise may or may not be correct, the suggested motive may be the wrong one; but one thing is very clear - that a murder of a most atrocious character has been committed.

The jury, after a short consultation, returned a verdict of willful murder against some person or persons unknown.

A rider was added expressing the full coincidence of the jury with some remarks made by the coroner as to the need of a mortuary for Whitechapel.

This is a *copy* of the Death Certificate for Mary Ann Nichols (Polly). This indicates the violence she suffered.

	Registration District Whitechapel							
1888. Death in the Sub-district of Whitechapel Church in the County of Middlesex								
No.	When and where died	Name and surname	Sex	Age	Occupation	Cause of death	Signature, description, and residence of informant	When registered	Signature of registrar
370	Thirty First August 1888 in the Street in Bucks Row	Mary Ann NICHOLS	Female	44 years	Wife of William Nichols Printers Machinist lodging house 25 Dorset Street Spitalfields	Violent Syncope from loss of blood from wounds in neck and abdomen inflicted by some sharp instrument, Wilful murder against some person or persons unknown Post mortem	Certificate received from Wynne Baxter Coroner for Middlesex Inquest held 23 rd day of September 1888	Twenty first September 1888	John Hall Registrar

Certified to be a true copy of an entry in a register in my custody.

Superintendent Registrar.

Chapter 4

Annie Chapman

1841-1888

Annie Chapman was also known as "Dark Annie" or Annie Siffey (Sievey or Sivvy). She was a stout woman, 47 years old, and was only five feet tall. She had a fair complexion and a large thick nose. She had dark brown wavy hair and blue eyes; she was well proportioned but had two teeth missing from her lower jaw. Annie Chapman started life as Eliza Ann Smith in 1841. She was born in Paddington. Her mother was Ruth Chapman of Market Street and her father was George Smith. On his marriage certificate he was registered as a Private of the 2nd Battalion of Lifeguards.

The couple married six months after Annie was born and the family moved to Windsor in 1856. Annie had a brother called Fontain and either one or two sisters, one of which lived with her mother in Brompton. It seemed they did not get along with Annie.

Annie got married at the age of twenty eight to a relative from her mother's side called John Chapman. In the Victorian era, twenty eight was considered quite old to be single. The wedding took place at All Saints Church in Knightsbridge on the 1st of May 1869. On the marriage certificate the couple's address was 29, Montpelier Place Brompton. This was Annie's mother's address and remained so until her death in 1893.

The couple went to live in West London until 1881 when they moved back to Windsor. John took a job as a domestic coachman working for a Josiah Weeks. The couple had three children: Emily Ruth, born in 1870; Annie Georgina, born in 1873; and John, born in 1881. John junior was disabled and was sent to a home. Emily Ruth died of meningitis at the age of twelve. Some reports have Annie Georgina travelling with a circus in France at the time of her mother's death.

Annie and John separated by mutual consent in 1884 or 1885. The reason for the split is uncertain. A police report indicates it was because of her "drunken and immoral ways." She had been arrested several times in Windsor for drunkenness. It was alleged that her husband was also a heavy drinker.

John Chapman paid his wife 10 shillings per week by Post Office Order until his death on Christmas day in 1886. He died of cirrhosis of the liver and dropsy. This corroborates the statement that he was a heavy drinker. Annie found out about his death through her brother-in-law.

Annie was very upset at the passing of her husband even though they were not together at the time. When Annie spoke about his death to

Amelia Palmer she got very upset and cried. Amelia Palmer remarked that even two years later Annie was very downcast when speaking of her children. Palmer said that

"since the death of her husband she seemed to have given away all together."

Sometime during 1886 she was living with a sieve maker named John Sivvey at the common lodging house at number 30 Dorset Street, Spitalfields. The name Sivvey could be a nickname and apparently was also used by Annie. John Sivvey left her soon after her husband's death. This was probably because of Annie's sudden lack of funds following her husband's death.

From May to June 1888 Annie lived consistently at Crossingham's Lodging House on Dorset Street in Spitalfields. The lodging house slept approximately 300 people. The deputy of this lodging house was Timothy Donovan.

Dorset Street was an infamous road in Spitalfields, running east to west between Commercial Street and Crispin Street. The Commercial Street end (east) faced Christ's Church burial ground; the other end faced the Providence Road Night Refuge and Convent on Crispin Street. There were three public houses on Dorset Street. At the corner of Commercial Street was *the Britannia*, also known as "the Ringer's." *The Horn of Plenty* was at the corner of Crispin Street, and, in the centre, was *the Blue Coat Boy*. *The Blue Coat Boy* was directly across the street from Crossingham's Lodging House. About one third of the way down Dorset Street from Commercial Street was a narrow brick archway and the entrance to Miller's Court, which would later lead to the Ripper's fifth murder site. To the left of this entrance was number 27, McCarthy's Chandler shop. Dorset Street was known locally as "Dosset" Street because of the number of common lodging houses located there.

It is alleged that Annie had been having a relationship with Edward Stanley, a bricklayer's mate known locally as "the Pensioner". At the time of Annie's murder, Stanley lived at 1 Osborne Street, Whitechapel. He claimed to be a member of the military and was receiving a pension from them. He later changed his story and admitted that he had never been a military man and was not drawing a pension.

Edward Stanley and Annie spent weekends together at Crossingham's. Stanley instructed Timothy Donovan to turn Annie away if she tried to enter with another man. Stanley regularly paid for Annie's bed as well as that of Eliza Cooper. The couple spent Saturdays and Sundays together, parting between 1:00 and 3:00 a.m. Stanley alleged that he had not known Annie prior to this.

Annie resorted to prostitution after the death of her husband. Before his death, Annie had lived off the allowance her husband had sent her. She also earned money by doing crochet work and selling flowers.

Between mid to late August of 1888, Annie met her brother Fontain in Commercial Road. Annie told him that she had fallen on hard times, but refused to tell him where she was living. Her brother gave her 2 shillings, and then left.

Saturday 1st September 1888

Edward Stanley returns to Whitechapel after having been away since August 6th. He met Annie on the corner of Brushfield Street. Around the same time, Annie had a fight with Eliza Cooper over him; Eliza was a rival for Stanley's affections. The argument and subsequent fight broke out in the *Britannia* Public House, in the company of Stanley and Harry the Hawker. Eliza struck Annie, giving her a black eye and bruising her breast.

Different reasons have been given as to why this fight broke out between the two women. One story is that Annie had noticed Eliza "palming" a florin belonging to the Pensioner and replacing it with a penny. Annie mentioned Eliza's deceit to Harry the Hawker. Amelia Palmer recalled that Annie told her the argument took place at the pub but the actual fight did not occur until the two women had returned to the lodging house.

Eliza Cooper said the fight had broken out in the *Britannia* and that she struck Annie on September 2nd. John Evans, the night watchman at the lodging house, said a fight broke out between the two women in the lodging house on September 6th.

There are different versions of the story that circulate. One is that Annie threw a halfpenny at Eliza Cooper and slapped her in the face saying *"Think yourself lucky I did not do more."* Timothy Donovan stated that on August 30th he had noticed Annie had a black eye. Annie is alleged to have said to him *"Tim, this is lovely, ain't it."* Stanley noticed that Annie had a black eye on the evening of September 2 and again on September 3. Annie had shown her bruises to Amelia Palmer.

Donovan told the inquest that Annie had not been at the lodging house during the week prior to her death. From the available evidence we can assume that the fight took place in the last few days of August at the lodging house. Some witnesses remembered Annie saying she was going to the infirmary, but there is no record of any woman being admitted to either Whitechapel or Spitalfields workhouse infirmaries.

Could Annie have picked up medication from somewhere else? I believe Dr. Barnardo was supplying Annie with medication, as a bottle of medicine was found in her room after her death. When her body was discovered she was in possession of two tablets. Sadly, we do not know what the medication was or what it was used for. No one at this time would have known how ill she was. Dr. Barnardo would have been able to prescribe and provide Annie with various types of medication. Annie would have first met him on one of his many visits to the lodging houses in the area.

Monday 3ʳᵈ September 1888

Annie met Amelia Palmer on Dorset Street. Amelia asked her

"How did you get that?"

referring the bruise she had on her right temple. Annie opened her dress and replied, *"Look at my chest,"* showing the further bruises on her breast, from the fight. Annie complained that she was feeling unwell and that she was contemplating visiting her sister. Annie said, "If I can get a pair of boots from my sister I may go hop picking."*

Tuesday 4ᵗʰ September 1888

The next day Amelia saw Annie again near Spitalfields Church. Annie was still not feeling well. She told Amelia that she had nothing to eat or drink all day. Annie told Palmer that she intended on going to the casual ward for a day or two. Amelia gave Annie 2d for tea and told her not to spend it on rum. It was a large sum for one Unfortunate to give to another. She must have cared about Annie's welfare.

Wednesday 5ᵗʰ & Thursday 6ᵗʰ September

Annie was not seen by anyone for these two days. She could have been sleeping rough as she had no money and was not well enough to earn any.

Friday 7ᵗʰ & Saturday 8th September

5:00 p.m. Amelia Palmer saw Annie in Dorset Street. She noted that Annie was sober and asked her if she was going to Stratford. Stratford was where Annie mainly worked as a prostitute; today it would be called her "patch." Annie replied that she was too ill to do anything. Amelia left her where she was and returned a few minutes later to find that she had not moved. *"It's no use my giving way,"* Annie said. *"I must pull myself together and go out and get some money or I shall have no lodgings."*

11:30 p.m. Annie returned to Crossingham's Lodging House and asked for permission to go into the kitchen.

12:10 a.m. Frederick Stevens, a fellow lodger, said he drank a pint of beer with Annie who seemed already slightly inebriated. Stevens stated that Annie did not leave the lodging house until 1:00 a.m.

12:12 a.m. William Stevens, another lodger, saw Annie in the kitchen. Annie told him she had been to Vauxhall to see her sister to get some money and that her family had given her 5d.

Stevens saw her take a box of pills from her pocket. The box broke and Annie took a torn piece of envelope from the mantelpiece and put the pills in it. He watched Annie leave the kitchen. Stevens thought that Annie had gone to bed.

1:35 a.m. Annie returned to the lodging house and was seen eating a baked potato. John Evans, the night watchman, asked Annie for her bed money. She went upstairs to see Donovan in his office. Annie said to Donovan "I haven't sufficient money for my bed, but don't let it. I shall not be long before I'm in." Donovan chastised her saying, *"You can find money for your beer and you can't find money for your bed."* Annie was unperturbed by his words and stood in the office doorway for two or three minutes. *"Never mind, Tim,"* she replied. *"I'll soon be back."* On the way out Annie saw Evans and said to him, *"I won't be long, Brummy* [possibly a nickname for where he had come from]. *See that Tim keeps the bed for me."* Annie's regular bed in Crossingham's was number 29. Evans saw Annie leave the lodging house. She left via the exit onto Little Paternoster Row, went in the direction of Brushfield Street, and turned towards the Spitalfields Market.

4:45 a.m. Mr. John Richardson entered the backyard of 29 Hanbury Street on his way to work. He sat down on the steps of the building to cut off a piece of leather that was protruding from his boot. Although it was quite dark in the yard at the time, he was sitting no more than a yard from where Annie Chapman's head was when the body was found. Richardson testified that he had not seen or heard anything out of the ordinary.

5:30 a.m. Elizabeth Long claimed she saw Annie with a man, leaning against the shutters of 29 Hanbury Street. The two of them were talking. Long overheard the man asking *"Will you?"* Annie replied, *"Yes."* Long was certain of the time—the clock on the *Black Eagle Brewery*, Brick Lane, struck the half-hour just as she turned into Hanbury Street. Annie had her back to Spitalfields Market, her face towards Long. As Long passed the couple, the man had his back to her. The description Long gave of the man at the inquest is as follows:

"...Dark complexion, and was wearing a brown deerstalker hat. I think he was wearing a dark overcoat but cannot be sure. He was a man over forty, as far as I can tell. He seemed a little taller than the deceased, and he looked to me like a foreigner, as well as I could make out. He looked what I should call shabby genteel".

5:30 a.m. Albert Cadoche (You will see this name spelt differently throughout the book because the actual spelling of this surname is unknown.) a young carpenter who resided at 27 Hanbury Street, walked into his back yard, next door to the murder site. While he was standing in his yard, he heard a woman's voice next door (number 29) say *"No."* The wooden fence between the two yards was five feet tall and he heard something fall against it. He stated that he did not hear anything else. He left for work passing Spitalfields Church at 5:32 a.m. On his way down Hanbury Street he saw no one!

Dr. Barnardo would not have been seen on Hanbury Street at 5:32 a.m. because he was "busy" in the seclusion of the back yard, disembowelling Annie.

6:00 a.m. Saturday is market day. Mrs. Richardson's son, John Richardson, had entered the yard of 29 Hanbury Street between the hours of 4:45 a.m and 4:50 a.m. to check the cellar as there had been a recent break in. At the inquest, he reflected on that morning:

"The yard door was shut, I opened it and sat on the doorstep and cut a piece of leather off my boot with an old table knife. The sky was beginning to lighten and he noticed nothing amiss. He could see the padlock on the cellar was secure and then he left, the door closed behind him."

John Davis, a resident of 29 Hanbury Street had been restless during the hours of 3:00 and 5:00 a.m. After falling asleep again, he awoke to hear the Spitalfieds clock strike 5:45 a.m. He then got up, had a cup of tea with his wife, and then went into the back yard to relieve him self. As soon as the door swung open he found Annie's body lying on its back. It was parallel to the fence, which was on her left-hand side. Her head was close to the steps of the yard. Her dress had been lifted above her knees exposing her lower half, and her intestines lay across her left shoulder. Attempting to compose himself after seeing this horrid sight, he quickly ran back through the passage and into the street to get help. Once in the street, Davis saw two men standing outside their workshop a few doors away. James Green and James Kent saw Davis running towards them shouting *"men, come here!"* Also walking down Hanbury Street at the same time was Henry John Holland on his way to work. He heard Davis's pleas and joined the three men in returning to number 29. Kent recalled the scene:

"I could see the woman was dead. The face and hands were besmeared with blood, as if she had struggled. She appeared to have been on her back and fought with her hands to free herself. The hands were turned to the throat."

Kent was so shaken by the sight that when he went in search of a policeman, he had to go to his workshop to have a brandy. While there he looked for a piece of canvas to cover the poor women. He then went back to the house and arrived shortly after Inspector Chandler. Inspector Chandler recalled that he was standing on the corner of Hanbury and Commercial Streets when some men ran toward him shouting, *"Another woman has been murdered!"* A small crowd had already started to gather in the passage that ran from the front door of 29 Hanbury Street to the back yard. No one actually entered the yard. Shortly after 6 a.m. Inspector Chandler took charge of the murder scene and sent for a doctor. During a routine examination of the murder site, the Police found the torn envelope Annie had with the two pills still inside. In the yard the police also found a soaked leather apron folded neatly. This is where the "Leather Apron" rumour in the press originated. John Pizer a boot finisher, who lived at 22 Mulberry Street, went around Whitechapel demanding money with menaces (violence) from the Unfortunates. Because of his trade he would have wore a leather apron hence the local nick name.

6:30 a.m. Dr. George Bagster Phillips, the divisional surgeon of police, arrived at the murder scene. After a quick examination of the body, he ordered it to be taken to the Whitechapel Workhouse Infirmary Mortuary in Eagle Street. The word of the murder spread very quickly and a large crowd congregated outside number 29 by the time the ambulance arrived. There was also a crowd of several hundred people waiting outside the mortuary for the body to arrive.

According to press reports, Dr. Phillips discovered the contents of Annie's torn pocket lying neatly on the floor. The contents of the pocket were a piece of coarse muslin, two combs (only one was stated in the inquest reports) and two farthings that may have been polished (these were not mentioned in the inquest reports).

Two weeks later, Annie's possessions were mentioned again but this time the press said that Annie's rings were found on the floor. She was known to wear three brass rings, but these rings were not on her body upon arrival at the mortuary.

The mortuary that Annie's body was taken to was the same one as Polly's body was taken to and, again, the same problem arose. Annie's body had already been stripped and partly washed by Frances Wright and Mary Simond before Dr. Phillips could do a further examination. These two women carried out this task on the orders of the Clerk to the Parish Guardians. The police had *not* asked the women to attend to Annie. When Dr. Phillips arrived to do the post-mortem examination, he was furious that Annie had been attended to and that valuable evidence was lost. When the inquest heard about this, the coroner for the inquests in both Polly's and Annie's murders spoke up immediately saying

"The place is not a mortuary at all. We have no right to take a body there. It is simply a shed belonging to the workhouse officials. Juries have over and over again reported the matter to the District Board of Works. The East end, which requires mortuaries, more than anywhere else, is most deficient, a workhouse inmate is not the proper man to take care of a body in such an important matter as this."

Inspector Chandler arrived at the mortuary while Annie's body was still in the ambulance outside. He wrote a description of Annie's clothing:

- **Long, black, figured coat that came down to her knees**
- **A black skirt**
- **A brown bodice**
- **Another bodice**
- **2 petticoats**
- **A large empty pocket worn under the skirt and tied about the waist with strings**
- **Pair of Lace up boots**
- **Red and white striped woollen stockings**
- **Neckerchief, white with a wide red border folded and knotted at the front of her neck. She was seen wearing this scarf in this manner when she left Crossingham's lodging house.**
- **A scrap of muslin**
- **One small tooth comb**
- **One comb in a paper case**
- **A torn part of an envelope, which she had taken from the mantelpiece in the kitchen and in it had placed the two pills from the broken box. The envelope bore the seal of the Sussex Regiment. The postal stamp was "London, 28, Aug. 1888." A partial address was written on the envelope consisting of the letter "M," the number 2, and an "S." These numbers and initials could have been the beginning of an address.**

At some point, *The Star* newspaper photographed Annie's eyes in a vain hope that the murderer's image may have been seared on her retina. In 1888, it was thought that the image a victim saw immediately prior to death was somehow recorded on their retina. What ever happened to these photographs is unknown.

11:30 a.m. Mary Simmons identifies Annie's body after seeing it in the mortuary.

Timothy Donovan and a lodger at Crossingham's Lodging house went to the mortuary to view Annie's body. Annie was in the same roughly made temporary coffin (shell as it was known then) that had housed poor Polly's remains. The demand for the evening papers on the 8th of September was so immense that people waited in the shops until the next batch arrived. Five police officers were stationed in Hanbury Street preventing people from entering except those who actually lived there. A crowd of people congregated outside number 29 and, as *The Times* reported,

"The neighbours on either side did much business by making a small charge to persons who were willing to pay it to view from the windows the yard in which the murder was committed"

The Manchester Guardian reported:

"In the street half a dozen costermongers took up their stand and did a brisk business in fruit and refreshments. Thousands of respectably dressed persons visited the scene and occasionally the road became so crowded that the constables had to clear it by making a series of raids upon the spectators. All day nothing else was talked of, even by men who are hardened to seeing a great deal that is brutal. Strong, buxom and muscular women seemed to move in fear and trembling, declaring that they would not dare venture in the streets unaccompanied by the husbands."

The Star newspaper sensationalized the events saying;

"Hideous malice, deadly cunning, insatiable thirst for blood—all these are marks of the mad homicide. London lies today under the spell of a great terror. A nameless reprobate—half beast, half man—is at large, who is daily gratifying his murderous instincts on the most miserable and defenceless classes of the community."

Dr. Phillip's report of his crime scene findings were as follows:

"The left arm was placed across the left breast. The legs were drawn up, the feet resting on the ground, and the knees turned outwards. The face was swollen and turned on the right side. The tongue protruded between the front teeth, but not beyond the lips. The tongue was evidently much swollen. The front teeth were perfect as far as the first molar, top and bottom and very fine teeth they were. The body was terribly mutilated. The stiffness of the limbs was not marked, but was evidently commencing. He noticed that the throat was dissevered deeply; that the incision through the skin were jagged and reached right round the neck. On the wooden paling between the yard in question and the next, smears of blood, corresponding to where the head of the deceased lay, were to be seen. These were about 14 inches from the ground, and immediately above the part where the blood lay and that had flowed from the neck.

He should have indicated that the instrument used at the throat and abdomen was the same. It must have been a very sharp knife with a thin, narrow blade, and must have been at least 6 inches to 8 inches in length, or even longer. He also should have indicated that the injuries could not have been inflicted by a bayonet or a sword bayonet. Most interestingly, I am suggesting the wounds could have been inflicted by such an instrument as a medical man might use for post-mortem purposes, but that ordinary surgical cases might not contain such an instrument. The instruments used by the slaughter men, ground down, might have caused them. Dr. Phillips thought the knives used by those in the leather trade would not be long enough in the blade. Of course, there were indications of anatomical knowledge which were only less indicated in consequence of haste. The whole body was not present, the absent portions being from the abdomen. The mode in which these portions were extracted showed anatomical knowledge. Dr. Phillips should have explained that the deceased had been dead for at least two hours, probably more, when he first saw her. It was correct to mention that it was a fairly cool morning and that the body would be more apt to cool rapidly from having lost a great quantity of blood. There was no evidence of a struggle having taken place. He was positive the deceased entered the yard alive.

A handkerchief was around the throat of the deceased when he saw it early in the morning. He should say it was not tied on after the throat was cut."

On Saturday afternoon, Dr. Phillips made his post-mortem examination at the Whitechapel Workhouse infirmary Mortuary. Dr. Phillips protested about doing the examination in the inadequate and unhygienic run down shed.

Dr Phillips noticed that there was a bruise over the right temple. On the upper eyelid there was a bruise, and there were two distinct bruises, each the size of a man's thumb, on the forepart of the top of the chest."

In the 1800s midwifes and doctors used pressure points to render a patient unconscious, could Dr. Barnardo have done this to Annie before killing her? If so this was a humane act and not the act of a madman. The bruising about the face would be seen again in his killings

Dr. Phillips's post-mortem report is as follows:

"The stiffness of the limbs was now well marked. There was a bruise over the middle part of the bone of the right hand. There was an old scar on the left of the frontal bone. The stiffness was more noticeable on the left side, especially in the fingers, which were partly closed. There was an abrasion over the ring finger, with distinct markings of a ring or rings. The throat had been severed as before described. The incisions into the skin indicated that they had been made from the left side of the neck. There were two distinct clean cuts on the left side of the spine. They were parallel with each other and separated by about half an inch. The muscular structures appeared as though an attempt had made to separate the bones of the neck. There were various other mutilations to

the body, but he was of the opinion that they occurred subsequent to the death of the woman, and to the large escape of blood from the division of the neck.

The deceased was far advanced in disease of the lungs and membranes of the brain, but they had nothing to do with the cause of death. The stomach contained very little food, but there was no sign of fluid. There was no appearance of the deceased having taken alcohol, but there were signs of great deprivation. Dr. Phillips should have indicated that she was malnourished. He was convinced she had not taken any strong alcohol for some hours before her death. The injuries were certainly not self-inflicted. The bruises on the face were evidently recent, especially the trauma to the chin and the side of the jaw, but the bruises in front of the chest and temple were probably there for days prior to her death. Dr. Phillips's opinion was that the person who cut the throat of the deceased throat took hold of her by the chin and then commenced the incision from left to right. He thought it was highly probable that a person could call out, but with regard to an idea that she might have been gagged he could only point to the swollen face and the protruding tongue, both of which were signs of suffocation."

The killer had opened the abdomen entirely. The intestines, severed from their mesenteric attachments, had been lifted out of the body and placed on the shoulder of the corpse. In the pelvic region, the uterus and its appendages with the upper portion of the vagina and the posterior two thirds of the bladder had been entirely removed. No trace of these parts could be found and the incisions were made cleanly, avoiding the rectum and dividing the vagina low enough to avoid injury to the cervix uteri. Obviously the work was that of an expert; someone, at least, who had such knowledge of anatomical or pathological examinations as to be able to secure the pelvic organs with one sweep of the knife, which therefore must have been at least 5 or 6 inches in length, probably more. The appearance of the cuts confirmed Dr. Phillips's opinion that the instrument, like the one which divided the neck, had been very sharp. The mode in which the knife had been used seemed to indicate great anatomical knowledge.

Indeed, Dr. Phillips believed that he himself could not have performed all the injuries he described, even without a struggle, under a quarter of an hour. If he had done it in a deliberate way such as would fall to the duties of a surgeon it probably would have taken him the best part of an hour."

This is the first staunch statement made by any Doctor implying that the Ripper had some surgical expertise. The lower cut in the removal of the uterus was characterized as **"impressive."**

At Annie's post-mortem, Dr. Baxter said *"the uterus was removed by someone used to the post-mortem room"*

It has been rumoured that three brass rings were removed from Annie's body after her murder. In fact, Dr. Phillips commented on the ring marks on her fingers; Annie was allegedly wearing the rings when she left the lodging house. We cannot be certain that these rings were not pawned or sold by Annie earlier in the day, or even stolen from her fingers whilst she was lying in the mortuary. Whatever happened to them is a mystery—they were never found.

Hanbury Street residences like most of the properties around the East End were built for the Spitalfield weavers. The properties went into disrepair when the hand looms were replaced by machines using steam and power. Then the residences were used for housing the poor. Twenty-nine Hanbury Street was not used as a lodging house. It was slightly above the lodging houses in status and was a place that rented out furnished rooms to the poor. It was not used by Unfortunates for their trade at all.

Number 29 was situated just three or four hundred yards from Crossingham's Lodging House. The building was largely a wooden structure. It had four floors and consisted of eight rooms. At least seventeen people lived in these rooms. There are two front doors to the building. The first door on the right led into a shop, while the door on the left led into a passageway. The passageway ran the length of the building and included the cellar door and a set of stairs to the upper floors of the structure. The passageway also led to a door that opened into the backyard, the murder site of Annie Chapman. The door to the backyard swung from right to left and when open, covered a small recess of the yard. It has been described as a self-closing door. The Coroner Wynne Edwin Baxter referred to this door as a *"swinging door."* Two steps led down into the yard. The backyard was separated from the adjoining yards by a five-foot high wooden fence. From the top of the steps there is a small woodshed to the left; Annie's feet pointed towards this woodshed, her head towards the doorsteps. The yard itself was a patchwork of stone, grass, and dirt.

Mrs. Annie (Harriet) Hardyman and her sixteen-year-old son occupied the ground floor front room. Both of them slept in the front room, which doubled as a cat meat shop. The rear room was used as a kitchen.

Residing in the first floor front room was Mrs. Amelia Richardson and her fourteen-year-old grandson. She had lived at 29 Hanbury Street for fifteen years. She owned her own business making packing cases. She employed her son, John, who did not live with her and a man named John Tyler. She also rented the cellar, which she used for manufacturing the packing cases. Mrs. Richardson used one of her rooms for regular weekly prayer meetings. In the first floor back room resided Mr. Walker who made tennis shoes. He shared this room with his disabled adult son.

On the second floor in the front room, lived a family consisting of a Carman named Thompson who was employed by Goodson's of Brick Lane. He lived there with his wife and her daughter. Mr Thompson stated that he left for work on the morning of the murder at 3:30 a.m. He did not go into the yard and heard nothing out of the ordinary. Mr. and Mrs. Copsey both worked in a cigar factory and shared the room at the back of this floor.

The third floor front room was occupied by an elderly man named John Davis, who was also a Carman. He shared this room with his wife and his three sons. Sarah Cox occupied the third floor back room. She was an elderly woman who was allowed to live there by the charitable Mrs. Richardson.

The passageway and the yard were not a regular spot for Unfortunates to carry out their work. Dr. Barnardo must have taken Annie there. He obviously knew that the yard was a fairly safe place to do his deed. Barnardo was familiar with the yard and the cover it provided because he sometimes attended the weekly prayer meetings held there.

Annie Chapman was laid to rest on Friday, the 14th September 1888.

7 a.m. The hearse, supplied by a Hanbury Street Undertaker, went to the Whitechapel Mortuary to collect Annie's remains. The body was placed in a black-draped elm coffin. The coffin bore the words "Annie Chapman, died Sept. 8, 1888, aged 48 years." It was then driven to Harry Hawes, Undertakers, on Hunt Street in Spitalfields.

9 a.m. The hearse without any mourning coaches took Annie's body to the City of London Cemetery. Here she was placed in a public grave number 78, square 148. Annie Chapman's grave no longer exists; it has since been reused.

Mr. Smith and Annie's relatives, who paid for the funeral, met the hearse at the cemetery and at their request the funeral was kept a secret. The family were the only people in attendance. In a book entitled *I Caught Crippen* by Chief Inspector Walter Drew, the inspector stated;

"He was amazed that the prostitutes of Whitechapel area, even after the horrific murder of Annie Chapman proved to be such easy targets for the killer.

He also posed the question:

"is it feasible that there was something about him (Jack the Ripper) which placed him above suspicion?"

The inquest into Annie's murder started on the 10th of September 1888. It took place over five separate days until September 26. Most of the inquest time was spent trying to piece together the movements of Annie before her death and examining the medical evidence. This medical evidence presented a very clear conclusion. According to Dr. Baxter, there were *"no meaningless cuts, the uterus has been taken by one who knew where to find it, what difficulties he would have to contend against, and how he could use his knife so as to abstract the organ without injury to it. No unskilled person could have known where to find it or could have recognised it when it was found."*

False reports of arrests were rampant. Even people arrested on unrelated charges were almost lynched by angry crowds believing that the police had caught the Ripper. Undoubtedly, the police wished they were able to catch and identify the Ripper because public opinion about their ineptitude and criticism of them not catching the killer became monumental.

On the September 9, 1888, *The New York Times* opined *"the London Police and detective force is probably the stupidest in the world."* *The Weekly Herald* reported how *"the general feeling of dissatisfaction about the police is loudly expressed. He is by no means satisfied yet and it is gruesome to note the settled expectancy with which the people generally speak of 'the next murder."* The Manchester *Guardian* reported the following:

"Last night the police were posted in strong force throughout the neighbourhood. Their precautions are such that they consider it impossible that any further outrage can be perpetrated."

At the inquest, Amelia Palmer stated that she knew Annie and stated that she had seen the deceased two or three times during the week prior to her death. On the Monday Annie stood on the opposite side of the road from 35 Dorset Street. She had no bonnet on and had a bruise on one of her temples, possibly the right. Amelia asked *Annie "how did you get that?"* Annie's response was *"look at my chest."* Annie then opened her dress and showed Amelia bruising on her chest. Annie went on to explain how she acquired these bruises. Annie looked very pale and when Amelia asked her if she had eaten Annie told her that she had not even had a cup of tea. Amelia said she then gave Annie two pence to get some nourishment and told Annie not to buy rum. When asked by the coroner what Annie did for a living, Amelia replied that Annie did crochet work and sold flowers. Amelia testified that Annie had been ill and was hoping to get a pair of boots from her sister and go hop picking. Amelia described Annie as a respectable woman who never used bad language, but was forced to stay out in the streets at night. By staying out in the streets at night Amelia probably meant that because Annie had not earned her "doss" money for her bed, she had no choice but to sleep on the streets.

Amelia was asked if she knew of anybody that might have wanted to injure Annie. Her response was *"no."* Annie's brother was also at the inquest and said that he knew nothing of his sister's earnings and that she had asked him for some money for lodgings. James Kent, another witness at the inquest, described his experience at the murder scene. He mentioned hearing a man shout for help and that he then he went into 29 Hanbury Street. He described walking through the passage leading to the yard at the back of the house and standing on the top of the back door step. He explained how;

> *"He saw a woman lying in the yard between the yard and the next. Her head was near the house, but no part of the body was against the wall. The feet were lying towards the back. The deceased woman's clothes were disarranged and her apron was thrown over them. I did not go down the steps, but went outside and returned after Inspector Chandler had arrived. I could see the woman was dead. She had some kind of handkerchief around her throat, which seemed soaked in blood. The face and hands were besmeared with blood. The legs were wide apart and had marks of blood on them. The entrails were protruding."*

James Green told pretty much the same story but also added that no one touched the body. Amelia Richardson also saw Annie's body before the police arrived. She described how she heard a lot of noise in the passage and sent her grandson to investigate. Her grandson told her that there had been another woman killed and immediately went downstairs and saw the deceased. She claimed there was no one in the yard, but that there were people in the passage. Asked if she heard any cries that night, she answered *"no."*

At the inquest, John Richardson stated that when he checked it, the door to the passage was closed. He then went to the yard door and opened it, but did not go into the yard. Instead, he sat on the middle step. He then explained that he needed to cut a bit of leather off his boot and used a table knife that was five inches long. He explained that he had the knife on him because he had been feeding a rabbit and had used the knife to cut up a carrot. After cutting the leather and tying up his boot, he then left the yard closing the yard door behind him and going through the passage to the front door, which he closed behind him. He stated that if the woman's body had been in the yard at the same time as he was he could not have missed it as his feet were on the flags of the yard. Richardson was then dispatched by the coroner to fetch his knife. When he returned with the knife it was retained.

Although the police still had many questions, the main suspect was a man named John Pizer, or "Leather Apron" as he was commonly known. He was arrested on Monday September 10 in the early morning by

Sergeant William Thick and another officer at 22 Mulberry Street. As he answered the front door, Pizer heard Sergeant Thick say *"You're just the man I want."* Pizer turned pale and started to tremble. The police also took into custody some of his leather working knives and some of his hats. He was taken to lemon street police station where he was put into a police line-up for Mrs. Fiddymont and Emmanuel Violenia. Mrs. Fiddymont was unable to identify him, but Violenia recognised him as a man who had talked angrily with a woman outside 29 Hanbury Street. Emmanuel also said that he knew that Pizer was known as "Leather Apron." On Wednesday October 11, he was summoned to Annie's inquest to be cleared of suspicion of murder. At the inquest, Pizer said he was known as "Leather Apron" but was cleared of killing Annie and was asked to leave because the man had an alibi. Pizer may have received sums of money as compensation because various newspapers said damaging and hurtful things against him. The amount he received from Harry Dam for the *Star's* overenthusiastic vilification of "Leather Apron has not been disclosed."
Inspector Joseph Chandlers gave his evidence of the events;

"On Saturday morning, at ten past six, I was on duty in Commercial street. On the corner of Hanbury Street I saw several men running. I beckoned to them. One of them said, "Another woman has been murdered." I at once went with him to 29 Hanbury Street and through the passage into the yard. There was no one in the yard. I saw the body of a woman lying on her back. Her head was towards the back wall of the house, nearly two feet from the wall, at the bottom of the steps, but six or nine inches away from them. The face was turned to the right side, and the left arm was resting on the left breast. The right arm was lying down the right side. Deceased's legs were drawn up, and the clothing was above the knees. A portion of the intestines, still connected with the body, were lying above the right shoulder, with some pieces of skin. There were some pieces of skin on the left shoulder. The body was lying parallel with the fencing dividing the two yards. I remained there and sent for the divisional surgeon, Mr. Phillips, and to the police station for the ambulance and for further assistance. When the constables arrived I cleared the passage of people, and saw that no one touched the body until the doctor arrived. I obtained some sacking to cover it before the arrival of the surgeon, who came at about half-past six o'clock, and he, having examined the body, directed that it should be removed to the mortuary. After the body had been taken away I examined the yard, and found a piece of coarse muslin, a small toothcomb, and a pocket hair comb in a case. They were lying near the feet of the woman. A portion of an envelope was found near her head, which contained two pills

When asked by the coroner if there were any blood stains on the fence (palings), Inspector Chandler mentioned that there were stains near the body and there was a stain on the wall near the head of the deceased; no further blood stains were found anywhere else either in the yard or outside the yard. After giving a detailed autopsy report Dr Phillips asked that other details of the case be kept hidden from public knowledge. The coroner asked if these details had been recorded in case the killer was caught and these details needed to be used. Dr Phillips assured the coroner that these details had been recorded. The coroner then asked if the injuries could have been caused by a bayonet; Dr. Phillips replied, *"No."* The coroner repeated the question but this time asked if the knife used was an instrument normally used for medical purposes. The doctor replied that the knife would not be found in an ordinary post-mortem case. He agreed that some anatomical knowledge was shown in this case*: "I think the mode in which they were extracted did show anatomical knowledge"*

The Coroner then asked about the missing parts of the body to which Dr Phillips. Replied that the parts missing were from the abdomen and could not say if they had been lost during the transporting of the body to the mortuary. The doctor did speak about fresh bruising on Annie's face. The bruising was consistent with the killer holding his victim's chin before cutting her throat. Eliza Cooper was called as a witness at the inquest and described a fight she had with Annie and the bruises she gave her. She also recalled that the last time she saw Annie alive was the Thursday night in the Ringers. She said that Annie was wearing three rings on the middle finger of her left hand. Next to testify at the inquest was Mrs. Elizabeth Long. She confirmed she had seen Annie at 5:30 a.m. talking to a man outside 29 Hanbury Street. The man had his back was towards her, she saw Annie's face. The description Mrs. Long gave of the man even though she did not see his face was as follows;

"He was dark. He was wearing a brown low-crowned felt hat. I think he had on a dark coat, though I am not certain. By the look of him he seemed to me a man over forty years of age. He appeared to me little taller than the deceased. Asked whether he looked like a working man her response was "he looked like a foreigner"

The Coroner repeated his question of whether the man looked like a dock labourer or a workman. She then replied, "I should say he looked like what I would call shabby-genteel. Mrs. Long then said she heard the man ask Annie *"Will you?"* and Annie replied *"Yes."* Next up at the inquest was Edward Stanley who was shown to be nothing but a lair and a fraud as he had never received a pension from anyone and was just a builder's labourer. Albert Cadosch was the next witness called. This man is probably the only person ever to have heard the Ripper during his work.

He said that at a quarter past five on September 8, 1888, he entered the yard at 27 Hanbury Street, right next door to number 29. After being in the yard for about five minutes he was about to go inside. When he got to the back door he heard a voice say *"No."* He stated it came from number 29. He then went inside for three minutes or so. When he returned to the yard he heard a *"sort fall against the fence. It seemed as if something touched the fence suddenly"*

The coroner asked him if he took a look at what caused the noise and he answered that he did not. I honestly believe if he had looked over the fence, he would have seen the Ripper in the Act of disembowelling poor Annie.

I will finish this chapter with the coroner's summation of the inquest. It is important to the case because we can get a good idea of what he truly thought of the evidence that had been presented and his interpretation of that evidence. His summation is as follows:

"I congratulate you that your labours are now nearly completed. Although up to the present they have not resulted in the detection of any criminal, I have no doubt that if the perpetrator of this foul murder is eventually discovered, our efforts will not have been useless. The evidence is now on the records of this court, and could be used if the witnesses were not forthcoming; while the publicity given has already elicited further information, which I shall presently have to mention, and which, I hope I am not sanguine in believing, may perhaps be of the utmost importance. We shall do well to recall the important facts. The deceased was a widow, forty-seven years of age, named Annie Chapman. Her husband was a coachman living at Windsor. For three or four years before his death she had lived apart from her husband, who allowed her 10s a week until his death at Christmas, 1886. Evidently she had lived an immoral life for some time and her habits and surroundings had become worse since her means had failed. Her relations were no longer visited by her, and her brother had not seen her for five months, when she borrowed a small sum from him. She lived principally in the common lodging houses in the neighbourhood of Spitalfields, where such as she herd like cattle and she showed signs of great deprivation, as if she had been badly fed. The glimpses of life in these dens which the evidence in this case discloses is sufficient to make us feel that there is much in the nineteenth century civilisation of which we have a small reason to be proud; but you who are constantly called together to hear the sad tale of starvation, or semi-starvation, of misery, immorality, and wickedness which some of the occupants of the 5,000 beds in this district have every week to relate to the coroner's inquests, do not require to be reminded of what life in a Spitalfields lodging-house means. It was in one of these

that the older bruises found on the temple and in front of the chest of the deceased were received, in a trumpery quarrel, a week before her death. It was in one of these that she was seen a few hours before her mangled remains were discovered. On the afternoon and evening of Friday, September 7th 1888, she divided her time partly in such a place at 35 Dorset Street, and partly in the Ringers public-house, where she spent whatever money she had; so that between one and two on the morning of Saturday, when the money for her bed is demanded, she is obliged to admit that she is without means, and at once turns out into the street to find it. She leaves at 1:45 a.m., is seen off the premises by the night watchman, and is observed to turn down little Paternoster Row into Bushfield Street, and not in the more direct rout to Hanbury Street. On her wedding finger she was wearing two or three rings, which appear to have been palpably of base metal, as the witnesses are all clear about their material and value. We now lose sight of her for about four hours, but at half past five, Mrs. Long is in Hanbury Street on her way home in Church Street, Whitechapel, to Spitalfields Market. She walked on the northern side of the road going westwards, and remembers having seen a man and woman standing a few yards from the place where the deceased is afterwards found. And, although she did not know Annie Chapman, she is positive that that woman was the deceased. The two were talking loudly, but not sufficiently so to arouse her suspicions that there was anything wrong. Such words as she overheard were not calculated to do so. The laconic inquiry of the man, "Will you?" and the simple assent of the woman, viewed in the light of subsequent events, can be easily translated and explained. Mrs. Long passed on her way, and neither saw nor heard anything more of her, and this is the last time she is known to have been alive. There is some conflict in the evidence about the time at which the deceased was despatched (murdered.) It is not unusual to find inaccuracy in such details, but this variation is not very great or very important. She was found dead about six o'clock. She was not in the yard when Richardson was there at 4:50 a.m. She was talking outside the house at half past five when Mrs. Long passed them. Cadosh says it was about 5:20 a.m. when he was in the backyard of the adjoining house, and heard a voice say "No" and three or four minutes afterwards a fall against the fence; but if he is out of his reckoning but a quarter of an hour, the discrepancy in the evidence of fact vanishes, and he may be mistaken, for he admits that he did not get up till a quarter past five, and that it was after the half hour when he passed the Spitalfields clock. It is true that Dr. Phillips thinks that when he saw the body at 6:30 a.m. the deceased had been dead at least for two hours, but he admits that the coldness of the morning and the great loss of blood may affect his opinion; and if the evidence of the other witnesses be correct, Dr. Phillips has miscalculated the effect of those forces. But many minutes after Mrs Long passed the man and the woman cannot have elapsed before the deceased became a mutilated corpse in the yard of 29, Hanbury Street, close by where she was last seen by any witness. This place is a fair sample of a large number of houses in the neighbourhood. It was built, like hundred of others, for the Spitalfield weavers, and when handlooms were driven out by steam and power, these were converted into dwellings for the poor. Its size is about such, as a superior artisan would occupy in the country, but its condition such as would to a certainty leave it without a tenant. In this place seventeen persons were living, from a woman and her son sleeping in a cat's-meat shop on the ground floor to Davis and his wife and their three grown-up sons, all sleeping together in the attic. The street door and the yard door were never locked, and the passage and yard appear to have been constantly used by these people who had no legitimate business there. There is little doubt that the deceased knew the place, for it was only 300 or 400 yards from where she lodged. If so, it is quite unnecessary to assume that her companion had any knowledge—in fact, it is easier to believe that he was ignorant both of the nest of living beings by whom he was surrounded, and of their occupations and habits. Some were on the move late at night; some were up long before the sum. A Carman named Thompson left the house for his work as early as 3:50 a.m.; an hour later John Richardson was paying the house a visit of inspection; shortly after 5:15 a.m. Cadosh, who lived in the next house, was in the adjoining yard twice. Davis the Carman who occupied the third floor front room, heard the church clock strike quarter past six, got up, and had a cup of tea, and then went into the back yard, he was horrified to find the mangled body of the deceased. It was then a little after six a.m., and then Inspector Chandler had been informed of the discovery while on duty in Commercial Street. There is nothing to suggest that the deceased was not fully conscious of what she was doing. It is true that she had passed through some stages of intoxication, for although she appeared perfectly sober to her friend who met her in Dorset Street at five o'clock the previous evening; she had been drinking afterward, after she left the lodging house shortly before two o'clock the night watchman noticed that she was the worse for drink, but not badly so, while the deputy asserts that, though she had evidently been drinking, she could walk straight, and it was probably only malt liquor that she had taken, and its effects would pass off quicker than if she had taken spirits. "Consequently, is not surprising that Mrs. Long saw nothing to make her think that the deceased was worse for drink. Moreover, it is unlikely that she could have had the opportunity of getting intoxicants. Again the post-mortem examination shows that while the stomach contained a meal of food there was no sign of fluid and no appearance of her having taken alcohol for some time. The deceased, therefore, entered the yard in full possession of her faculties; although with a very different object from her companion. From the evidence, which the condition of the yard affords and the medical examination discloses, it appears that after the two had passed through the passage and opened the swing-door at the end, they descended the three steps into the yard. On their left hand side there was a recess between those steps and pailings. Here a few feet from the house and less distance from the pailing they must have stood. The wretch must have then seized the deceased, perhaps with Judas-like approaches. He seized her by the chin. He pressed her throat, and while thus preventing the slightest cry, he at the same time produced insensibility and suffocation. There is no evidence of any struggle. The clothes are not torn. Even in these preliminaries, the wretch seems to have known how to carry out efficiently his nefarious work. The deceased was then lowered to the ground, and laid on her back; and although in doing so she may have fallen slightly against the fence, this movement was probably effected with care. Her throat was then cut in two places with savage determination, and the injuries to the abdomen commenced. All was done with cool impudence and reckless daring; but, perhaps, nothing is more noticeable than the emptying of her pockets, and the arrangement of their contents with business-like precision in order near her feet. The murder seems, like the Buck's Row case, to have been carried out without any cry. Sixteen people were in the house. The partitions of the different rooms are of wood. Davis was not asleep after three a.m., except for three quarters of an hour, or less, between 5 a.m. and 5:45 a.m. Mrs. Richardson only dosed after 3 a.m., and heard no noise during the night. Mrs. Hardman, who occupies the front ground-floor room, did not awake until the noise succeeding the finding of the body had commenced, and none of the occupants of the houses by which the yard is surrounded heard anything suspicious. The brute who committed the offence did not even take the trouble to cover his ghastly work, but left the body exposed to the view of the first comer. This accords but little with the trouble taken with the rings, and suggest either that he had at length been disturbed, or that as the daylight broke a sudden fear suggested the danger of detection that he was running. There are two things missing. Her rings had been wrenched from her fingers and have not been found, and the uterus had been removed. The body has not been dissected, but the injuries have been made by someone who had considerable anatomical skill and knowledge. There are no meaningless cuts. It was done by one who knew where to find what he wanted, what difficulties he would have to contend against, and how he should use his knife, so as to abstract the organ without injury to it. No unskilled person could have known where to find it, or have recognised it when it was found. Foe instance, no mere slaughterer of animals could have carried out these operations. It must have been someone accustomed to the post-mortem room. The conclusion that the desire was to possess the missing part seems overwhelming. If the object were robbery, these injuries were meaningless, for death had previously resulted from the loss of blood at the neck. Moreover, when we find an easily accomplished theft of some paltry brass rings and such an operation, after, at least, a quarter of an hour's work, and by a skilled person, we are driven to the deduction that the mutilation was the object, and the theft of the rings was only a thin-veiled blind, an attempt to prevent the real intention from being discovered. Had not the medical examination been of a thorough and searching character, it might easily have been left unnoticed. The difficulty in believing that this was the real purport of the murderer is natural. It is abhorrent to our feelings to conclude that a life should be taken for so slight an object; but, when rightly considered, the reasons for most murders are altogether out of proportion to the guilt. It has been suggested that the criminal is a lunatic with morbid feelings. This may or may not be the case; but the object of the murderer appears palpably shown by the facts, and it is not necessary to assume lunacy, for it is clear that there is a market for the object of the murder. To show you this I must mention a fact which at the same time proves the assistance which publicity and the newspaper press afford in the detection of crime. Within a few hours of the issue of the morning papers, which contained reports of the medical evidence given at the last sitting of the court, I received a communication from an officer of one of our medical schools, that they had information which might or might not have a distinct bearing on our inquiry. I attended at the first opportunity, and was told by the sub-curator of the Pathological Museum that some months ago an American had called on him, and asked him to procure a number of specimens of the organ that was missing in the deceased. He stated his willingness to give money for each organ, and that his object was to issue an actual specimen with each copy of a publication on which he was then engaged. Although he was told that his wish was impossible to be complied with he still urged his request. He desired them preserved and not in spirits of wine, which is the usual medium, but in glycerine, in order to preserve them in a flaccid condition. He also asked for them to be sent to America direct. It is known that this request was repeated to another institution of a similar character. Now, it is not possible that the knowledge of this demand may have incited some abandoned wretch to possess himself of a specimen. It seems beyond belief that such inhuman wickedness could enter into the mind of any man. Unfortunately our criminal annals prove that every crime is possible. I need hardly say that I at once communicated my information to the Detective Department at Scotland Yard. Of course I do not know what use has been made of it, but I believe that publicity may possibly further elucidate this fact, and therefore, I have not withheld from you my knowledge. By means of the press some further explanation may be forthcoming from America if not from here. I have endeavoured to suggest to you the object with which this offence was committed, and the class of person who must have perpetrated it. The greatest deterrent from crime is the conviction that detection and punishment will follow with rapidity and certainty, and it may be that the impunity with which Mary Ann Smith and Anne Tabram (Two "Unfortunates" found before the Ripper killings started) were murdered suggested the possibility of such horrid crimes as those which you and another jury have been recently considering. It is, therefore, a great misfortune that nearly three weeks have elapsed without the chief actor in this awful tragedy having been discovered. Surely, it is not too much even yet to hope that the ingenuity of our detective force will succeed in unearthing this monster. It is not as if there were no clues to the character of the criminal or the cause of the crime. His object is clearly divulged. His anatomical skill carries him out of the category of a common criminal, for his knowledge could only have been obtained by assisting in post-mortems, or by frequenting the post-mortem room. Thus the class in which the search must be made, although a large one, is limited. Moreover it must have been a man who was away from home, if not all night. At least during the early hours of September 8th. His hands were undoubtedly bloodstained, for he did not stop to use the tap in the yard as the pan of clear water under it shows. If the theory of lunacy be correct—which I very much doubt the class is still further limited; while, if Mrs. Long's memory does not fail, and the assumption be correct that the man who was talking to the deceased at half past five was the culprit, he is even more clearly defined. In addition to his former description, we should know that he was a foreigner of dark complexion, over forty years of age, a little taller than the deceased, of shabby-genteel, with a brown dear stalker hat on his head, and a dark coat on his back. If your views accord with mine, you will be of the opinion that we are confronted with a murder of no ordinary character, committed not from jealousy, revenge, or robbery, but from motives less adequate than the many which still disgrace our civilisation, mar our progress, and blot the

85

pages of our Christianity. I cannot conclude my remarks without thanking you for the attention you have given this case and the assistance you have rendered me in our efforts to elucidate the truth of this horrible tragedy. (Emphasis added)"

After the Coroner's summation the Forman spoke: "We can only find one verdict—that of wilful murder against some person or persons unknown. We were about to add a rider with respect to the condition of the mortuary, but that having been done by a previous jury it is unnecessary."

After the murder of Annie Chapman Jack the Ripper sent a letter to the newspapers. This letter was tagged the "Dear Boss" letter. The letter was sent to the Central News Agency and not directly to the police. The letter was then sent to Scotland Yard on the 29th of September, 1888. The word "Boss" is an Americanism and was taken as a clue to the killer's nationality. Graphologists have studied these letters in an attempt to discover and profile the character of the murderer. There was a flood of hoax letters sent to both the press and the police. The original "Dear Boss" letter has all the hallmarks of a Dr. Barnardo letter. First, it was written in red ink, something he was known to do often. The underlining of certain words, again, was a feature Dr. Barnardo's correspondence. Another consideration is that the letter was posted near Dr. Barnardo's editorial offices.

Below is the "Dear Boss" letter dated September 25, 1888:

Dear Boss

I keep on hearing the police have caught me. But they wont fix me just yet. I have laughed when they look so clever and talk about being on the <u>right</u> track. That joke about Leather apron gave me real fits. I am down on whores and I shant quit ripping them till I do get buckled. Grand work the last job was. I gave the lady no time to squeal. How can they catch me now. I love my work and want to start again. You will soon hear of me with my funny little games. I saved some of the proper <u>red</u> stuff in a ginger beer bottle over the last job to write with but it went thick like glue and I cant use it. Red ink is fit enough I hope <u>ha.ha.</u> The next job I do I shall clip the ladys ears off and send to the police officers just for jolly wouldnt you. Keep this letter back till I do a bit more work. Then give it out straight my knife's so nice and sharp I want to get to work right away if I get a chance.

> *Good luck.*
> *Yours truly*
> *Jack the Ripper*

Don't mind me giving the trade name wasnt good enough to post this before I got all the red ink off my hands curse it no luck yet. They say I'm a doctor now <u>ha ha</u> "

Above is a copy of the Dear Boss letter taken from **www.casebook.org**

The next few pages follow the Inquest into the death of Annie Chapman, as recorded by the newspapers at the time, followed by a copy of the Death Certificate.

Inquests were very important in the 1800's and they give an insight into how people, spoke, behaved and thought.

The inquests make for great reading as part of the book or separately for research.

Day 1, Monday, September 10, 1888
(As told by *The Daily Telegraph*, Tuesday, September 11, 1888,)

At the Working Lads' Institute, Whitechapel Road, yesterday morning [10 Sep], Mr. Wynne Baxter opened an inquiry into the circumstances attending the death of Annie Chapman, a widow, whose body was found horribly mutilated in the back yard of 29, Hanbury Street, Spitalfields, early on Saturday morning. The jury viewed the corpse at the mortuary in Montague Street, but all evidences of the outrage to which the deceased had been subjected were concealed. The clothing was also inspected, and subsequently the following evidence was taken.

John Davies [Davis] deposed: I am a Carman employed at Leadenhall Market. I have lodged at 29, Hanbury Street for a fortnight, and I occupied the top front room on the third floor with my wife and three sons, who live with me. On Friday night I went to bed at eight o'clock, and my wife followed about half an hour later. My sons came to bed at different times, the last one at about a quarter to eleven. There is a weaving shed window or light across the room. It was not open during the night. I was awake from three a.m. to five a.m. on Saturday, and then fell asleep until a quarter to six, when the clock at Spitalfields Church struck. I had a cup of tea and went downstairs to the back yard. The house faces Hanbury Street, with one window on the ground floor and a front door at the side leading into a passage which runs through into the yard. There is a back door at the end of this passage opening into the yard. Neither of the doors could be locked, and I have never seen them locked. Any one who knows where the latch of the front door is could open it and go along the passage into the back yard.
Coroner when you went into the yard on Saturday morning was the yard door open or shut?

I found it shut. I cannot say whether it was latched - I cannot remember. I have been too much upset. The front street door was wide open and thrown against the wall. I was not surprised to find the front door open, as it was not unusual. I opened the back door, and stood in the yard entrance.

Coroner will you describe the yard?

It is a large yard. Facing the door, on the opposite side, on my left as I was standing, there is a shed, in which Mrs. Richardson keeps her wood. In the right-hand corner there is a closet. The yard is separated from the next premises on both sides by close wooden fencing, about 5 ft. 6 in. high.

Coroner: I hope the police will supply me with a plan. In the country, in cases of importance, I always have one. Inspector Helson:

Insp. Helson we shall have one at the adjourned hearing.

The Coroner: Yes, by that time we shall hardly require it.

Examination resumed: There was a little recess on the left. From the steps to the fence is about 3 ft. There are three stone steps, unprotected, leading from the door to the yard, which is at a lower level than that of the passage. Directly I opened the door I saw a woman lying down in the left-hand recess, between the stone steps and the fence. She was on her back, with her head towards the house and her legs towards the wood shed. The clothes were up to her groins. I did not go into the yard, but left the house by the front door, and called the attention of two men to the circumstances. They work at Mr. Bailey's, a packing-case maker, of Hanbury Street. I do not know their names, but I know them by sight.

Coroner: Have the names of these men been ascertained?

Inspector Chandler: I have made inquiries, but I cannot find the men.

Coroner: They must be found.

Davies: They work at Bailey's; but I could not find them on Saturday, as I had my work to do.

Coroner: Your work is of no consequence compared with this inquiry.

Davies: I am giving all the information I can.

Coroner (to witness): You must find these men out, either with the assistance of the police or of my officer.

Examination resumed: Mr Bailey's is three doors off 29, Hanbury Street, on the same side of the road. The two men were waiting outside the workshop. They came into the passage, and saw the sight. They did not go into the yard, but ran to find a policeman. We all came out of the house together. I went to the Commercial Street Police station to report the case. No one in the house was informed by me of what I had discovered. I told the inspector at the police station, and after a while I returned to Hanbury Street, but did not re-enter the house. As I passed I saw constables there.

Coroner Have you ever seen the deceased before? No.

Coroner Were you the first down in the house that morning? No; there was a lodger named Thompson, who was called at half-past three.

Coroner Have you ever seen women in the passage? - Mrs. Richardson has said there have been. I have not seen them myself. I have only been in the house a fortnight.

Coroner Did you hear any noise that Saturday morning? No, sir.

Amelia Palmer, examined, stated: I live at 35, Dorset Street, Spitalfields, a common lodging-house. Off and on I have stayed there three years. I am married to Henry Palmer, a dock labourer. He was foreman, but met with an accident at the beginning of the year. I go out charring. My husband gets a pension, having been in the Army Reserve. I knew the deceased very well, for quite five years. I saw the body on Saturday at the mortuary, and am quite sure that it is that of Annie Chapman. She was a widow, and her husband, Frederick Chapman, was a veterinary surgeon in Windsor. He died about eighteen months ago. Deceased had lived apart from him for about four years or more. She lived in various places, principally in common lodging-houses in Spitalfields. I never knew her to have a settled home.

Coroner Has she lived at 30, Dorset Street?

Yes, about two years ago, with a man who made wire sieves, and at that time she was receiving 10s a week from her husband by post-office order, payable to her at the Commercial Road. This payment stopped about eighteen months ago and she then found, on inquiry of some relative, that her husband was dead. I am under the impression that she ascertained this fact either from a brother or sister of her husband in Oxford Street, Whitechapel. She was nicknamed, "Mrs. Sivvy," because she lived with the sieve-maker. I know the man perfectly well, but don't know his name. I saw him last about eighteen months ago, in the City, and he told me that he was living at Notting Hill. I saw deceased two or three times last week. On Monday she was standing in the road opposite 35, Dorset Street. She had been staying there, and had no bonnet on. She had a bruise on one of her temples - I think the right. I said, "How did you get that?" She said, "Yes, look at my chest." Opening her dress, she showed me a bruise. She said, "Do you know the woman?" and gave some name, which I do not remember. She made me understand that it was a woman who goes about selling books. Both this woman and the deceased were acquainted with a man called "Harry the Hawker." Chapman told me that she was with some other man, Ted Stanley, on Saturday, Sept. 1. Stanley is a very respectable man. Deceased said she was with him at a beer-shop, 87, Commercial Street, at the corner of Dorset Street, where "Harry the Hawker" was with the woman. This man put down a two-shilling piece and the woman picked it up and put down a penny. There was some feeling in consequence and the same evening the book-selling woman met the deceased and injured her in the face and chest. When deceased told me this, she said she was living at 35, Dorset Street. On the Tuesday afternoon I saw Chapman again near to Spitalfields Church. She said she felt no better, and she should go into the casual ward for a day or two. I remarked that she looked very pale, and asked her if she had had anything to eat. She replied, "No, I have not had a cup of tea to-day." I gave her two-pence to get some, and told her not to get any rum, of which she was fond. I have seen her the worse for drink.

Coroner What did she do for a living?

She used to do crochet work, make antimacassars, and sell flowers. She was out late at night at times. On Fridays she used to go to Stratford to sell anything she had. I did not see her from the Tuesday to the Friday afternoon, 7th inst., when I met her about five o'clock in Dorset Street. She appeared to be perfectly sober. I said, "Are you going to Stratford to-day?" She answered, "I feel too ill to do anything." I left her immediately afterwards, and returned about ten minutes later, and found her in the same spot. She said, "It is of no use my going away. I shall have to go somewhere to get some money to pay my lodgings." She said no more, and that was the last time that I saw her. Deceased stated that she had been in the casual ward, but did not say which one. She did not say she had been refused admission. Deceased was a very industrious woman when she was sober. I have seen her often the worse for drink. She could not take much without making her drunk. She had been living a very irregular life during the whole time that I have known her. Since the death of her husband she has seemed to give way altogether. I understood that she had a sister and mother living at Brompton, but I do not think they were on friendly terms. I have never known her to stay with her relatives even for a night. On the Monday she observed: "If my sister will send me the boots, I shall go hopping." She had two children - a boy and a girl. They were at Windsor until her husband's death, and since then they have been in a school. Deceased was a very respectable woman, and never used bad language. She has stayed out in the streets all night.

Coroner Do you know of any one that would be likely to have injured her? No.
The Coroner (having read a communication handed to him by the police): It seems to be very doubtful whether the husband was a veterinary surgeon. He may have been a coachman.

Timothy Donovan, 35, Dorset Street, Spitalfields, said: I am the deputy of a common lodging house. I have seen the body of the deceased, and have identified it as that of a woman who stayed at my house for the last four months. She was not there last week until Friday afternoon, between two and three o'clock. I was coming out of the office after getting up, and she asked me if she could go down in the kitchen, and I said "Yes," and asked her where she had been all the week. She replied that she had been in the infirmary, but did not say which.

A police officer stated that the deceased had been in the casual ward.

Witness resumed: Deceased went down in the kitchen, and I did not see her again until half-past one or a quarter to two on Saturday morning. At that time I was sitting in the office, which faces the front door. She went into the kitchen. I sent the watchman's wife, who was in the office with me, downstairs to ask her husband about the bed. Deceased came upstairs to the office and said, "I have not sufficient money for my bed. Don't let it. I shan't be long before I am in."

Coroner How much was it?

Eight pence for the night. The bed she occupied, No. 29, was the one that she usually occupied. Deceased was then eating potatoes, and went out. She stood in the door two or three minutes, and then repeated, "Never mind, Tim; I shall soon be back. Don't let the bed." It was then about ten minutes to two a.m. She left the house, going in the direction of Brushfield Street. John Evans, the watchman, saw her leave the house. I did not see her again.

Coroner was she the worse for drink when you saw her last?

She had had enough; of that I am certain. She walked straight. Generally on Saturdays she was the worse for drink. She was very sociable in the kitchen. I said to her, "You can find money for your beer, and you can't find money for your bed." She said she had been only to the top of the street - where there is a public house.

Coroner Did you see her with any man that night? No, sir.
Coroner where did you think she was going to get the money from?

I did not know. She used to come and stay at the lodging-house on Saturdays with a man - a pensioner - of soldierly appearance, whose name I do not know.

Coroner Have you seen her with other men? At other times she has come with other men, and I have refused her.

Coroner you only allow the women at your place one husband?

The pensioner told me not to let her a bed if she came with any other man. She did not come with a man that night. I never saw her with any man that week.
In answer to the jury witness said the beds were double at 8d per night, and as a rule deceased occupied one of them by herself.

The Coroner: When was the pensioner last with deceased at the lodging-house?

On Sunday, Sept. 2. I cannot say whether they left together. I have heard the deceased say, "Tim, wait a minute. I am just going up the street to see if I can see him." She added that he was going to draw his pension. This occurred on Saturday, Aug. 25, at three a.m.
In reply to the Coroner, the police said nothing was known of the pensioner.
Examination continued: I never heard deceased call the man by any name. He was between forty and forty-five years of age, about 5 ft. 6 in. or 5 ft. 8 in. in height. Sometimes he would come dressed as a dock labourer; at other times he had a gentlemanly appearance. His hair was rather dark. I believe she always used to find him at the top of the street. Deceased was on good terms with the lodgers. About Tuesday, Aug. 28, she and another woman had a row in the kitchen. I saw them both outside. As far as I know she was not injured at that time. I heard from the watchman that she had had a clout. I noticed a day or two afterwards, on the Thursday, that she had a slight touch of a black eye. She said, "Tim, this is lovely," but did not explain how she got it. The bruise was to be seen on Friday last. I know the other woman, but not her name. Her husband hawks laces and other things.

John Evans testified: I am night watchman at 35, Dorset Street, and have identified the deceased as having lived at the lodging-house. I last saw her there on Saturday morning, and she left at about a quarter to two o'clock. I was sent down in the kitchen to see her, and she said she had not sufficient money. When she went upstairs I followed her, and as she left the house, I watched her go through a court called Paternoster Street, into Brushfield Street, and then turn towards Spitalfields Church. Deceased was the worse for drink, but not badly so. She came in soon after twelve (midnight), when she said she had been over to her sister's in Vauxhall. She sent one of the lodgers for a pint of beer, and then went out again, returning shortly before a quarter to two. I knew she had been living a rough nightlife. She associated with a man, a pensioner, every Saturday, and this individual called on Saturday at 2.30 p.m. and inquired for the deceased. He had heard something about her death, and came to see if it was true. I do not know his name or address. When I told him what had occurred he went straight out, without saying a word, towards Spitalfields Church. I did not see deceased and this man leave the house last Sunday week.

Coroner Did you see the deceased and another woman have a row in the kitchen?

Yes, on Thursday, Aug. 30. Deceased and a woman known as "Eliza," at 11.30 a.m., quarrelled about a piece of soap, and Chapman received a blow in the chest. I noticed that she had a slight black eye. There are marks on the body in a similar position.
I have never heard any one threaten her, nor express any fear of any one. I have never heard any one of the women in the lodging-house say that they had been threatened.

At this stage the inquiry was adjourned until tomorrow (Wednesday).

Day 2, Wednesday, September 12, 1888
(*The Daily Telegraph*, Thursday, September 13, 1888, Page 3)

Mr. Wynne Baxter yesterday [12 Sep] resumed the inquiry into the circumstances attending the death of Annie Chapman, whose body was found brutally mutilated in the back yard of 29, Hanbury Street, Spitalfields, at six o'clock on the morning of Saturday last.

The Police were represented by Inspector Abberline, of the Criminal Investigation Department, and Inspector Helson, J Division.

Fontain Smith, printer's warehouseman, stated: I have seen the body in the mortuary, and recognise it as that of my eldest sister, Annie, the widow of John Chapman, who lived at Windsor, a coachman. She had been separated from her husband for about three years. Her age was forty-seven. I last saw her alive a fortnight ago, in Commercial Street, where I met her promiscuously. Her husband died at Christmas, 1886. I gave her 2s; she did not say where she was living nor what she was doing. She said she wanted the money for lodging.

Coroner Did you know anything about her associates? No.

James Kent, 20, Drew's Blocks, Shadwell, a packing-case maker, said: I work for Mr. Bayley, 23A, Hanbury Street, and go there at six a.m. On Saturday I arrived about ten minutes past that hour. Our employer's gate was open, and there I waited for some other men. Davis, who lives two or three doors away, ran from his house into the road and cried, "Men, come here." James Green and I went together to 29, Hanbury Street, and on going through the passage, standing on the top of the back door steps, I saw a woman lying in the yard between the steps and the partition between the yard and the next. Her head was near the house, but no part of the body was against the wall. The feet were lying towards the back of Bayley's premises. (Witness indicated the precise position upon a plan produced by the police officers). Deceased's clothes were disarranged, and her apron was thrown over them. I did not go down the steps, but went outside and returned after Inspector Chandler had arrived. I could see that the woman was dead. She had some kind of handkerchief around her throat, which seemed soaked in blood. The face and hands were besmeared with blood, as if she had struggled. She appeared to have been on her back and fought with her hands to free herself. The hands were turned toward her throat. The legs were wide apart, and there were marks of blood upon them. The entrails were protruding, and were lying across her left side. I got a piece of canvass from the shop to throw over the body, and by that time a mob had assembled, and Inspector Chandler was in possession of the yard. The foreman gets to the shop at ten minutes to six every morning, and he was there before us.

James Green, of Ackland Street, Burdett Road, a packing-case maker, in the same employ as last witness, said: I arrived in Hanbury Street at ten minutes past six on Saturday morning, and accompanied Kent to the back door of No. 29. I left the premises with him. I saw no one touch the body. **Amelia Richardson**, 29, Hanbury Street, deposed: I am a widow, and occupy half of the house - i.e., the first floor, ground floor, and workshops in the cellar. I carry on the business of a packing-case maker there, and the shops are used by my son John, aged thirty-seven, and a man Francis Tyler, who have worked for me eighteen years. The latter ought to have come at six a.m., but he did not arrive until eight o'clock, when I sent for him. He is often late when we are slack. My son lives in John-street, Spitalfields, and he works also in the market on market mornings. At six a.m. my grandson, Thomas Richardson, aged fourteen, who lives with me, got up. I sent him down to see what was the matter, as there was so much noise in the passage. He came back and said, "Oh, grandmother, there is a woman murdered." I went down immediately, and saw the body of the deceased lying in the yard. There was no one there at the time, but there were people in the passage. Soon afterwards a constable came and took possession of the place. As far as I know the officer was the first to enter the yard.

Coroner Which room do you occupy?

The first floor front and my grandson slept in the same room on Friday night. I went to bed about half-past nine, and was very wakeful half the night. I was awake at three a.m., and only dozed after that.

Coroner Did you hear any noise during the night? No.

Coroner who occupies the first floor back?

Mr. Walker, a maker of lawn tennis boots. He is an old gentleman, and he sleeps there with his son, twenty-seven years of age. The son is weak-minded and inoffensive. On the ground floor there are two rooms. Mrs. Hardman occupies them with her son, aged sixteen. She uses the front room as a cat' meat shop. In the front room on the first floor on Friday night I had a prayer meeting, and before I went to bed I locked the door of this room, and took the key with me. It was still locked in the morning.

John Davies and his family tenant the third floor front, and Mrs. Sarah Cox has the back room on the same floor. She is an old lady I keep out of charity. Mr. Thompson and his wife, with an adopted little girl, have the front room on the second floor. On Saturday morning I called to Thompson at ten minutes to four o'clock. I heard him leave the house. He did not go into the back yard. Two unmarried sisters reside in the second floor back. They work at a cigar factory. When I went down all the tenants were in the house except Mr. Thompson and Mr. Davies. I am not the owner of the house.

Coroner Were the front and back doors always left open?

Yes, you can open the front and back doors of any of the houses about there. They are all let out in rooms. People are coming in or going out all the night.

Coroner Did you ever see anyone in the passage? Yes, about a month ago I heard a man on the stairs. I called Thompson, and the man said he was waiting for market.

Coroner At what time was this? Between half-past three and four o'clock. I could hear anyone going through the passage. I did not hear any one going through on Saturday morning.

Coroner you heard no cries? None.

Coroner Supposing a person had gone through at half-past three, would that have attracted your attention? Yes.

Coroner you always hear people going to the back yard? Yes; people frequently do go through.

Coroner People go there who have no business to do so? Yes; I daresay they do.

Coroner on Saturday morning you feel confident no one did go through? Yes; I should have heard the sound. They must have walked purposely

quietly? - Yes; or I should have heard them.
I should not allow any stranger to go through for an immoral purpose if I knew it.

Harriet Hardiman [Hardyman, Hardman], living at 29, Hanbury Street, catsmeat saleswoman, the occupier of the ground-floor front room, stated: I went to bed on Friday night at half-past ten. My son sleeps in the same room. I did not wake during the night. I was awakened by the trampling through the passage at about six o'clock. My son was asleep, and I told him to go to the back as I thought there was a fire. He returned and said that a woman had been killed in the yard. I did not go out of my room. I have often heard people going through the passage into the yard, but never got up to look who they were.

John Richardson, of John Street, Spitalfields, market porter, said: I assist my mother in her business. I went to 29, Hanbury Street, between 4,45 a.m. and 4.50 a.m. on Saturday last. I went to see if the cellar was all secure, as some while ago there was a robbery they're of some tools. I have been accustomed to go on market mornings since the time when the cellar was broken in.

Coroner was the front door open? No, it was closed. I lifted the latch and went through the passage to the **yard door.**

Coroner Did you go into the yard?

No, the yard door was shut. I opened it and sat on the doorstep, and cut a piece of leather off my boot with an old table-knife, about five inches long. I kept the knife upstairs at John-street. I had been feeding a rabbit with a carrot that I had cut up, and I put the knife in my pocket. I do not usually carry it there. After cutting the leather off my boot I tied my boot up, and went out of the house into the market. I did not close the back door. It closed itself. I shut the front door.

Coroner How long were you there? About two minutes at most.
Coroner was it light? It was getting light, but I could see all over the place.
Coroner Did you notice whether there was any object outside?

I could not have failed to notice the deceased had she been lying there then. I saw the body two or three minutes before the doctor came. I was then in the adjoining yard. Thomas Pierman had told me about the murder in the market. When I was on the doorstep I saw that the padlock on the cellar door was in its proper place.

Coroner Did you sit on the top step? No, on the middle step; my feet were on the flags of the yard.

Coroner you must have been quite close to where the deceased was found? Yes, I must have seen her.
Coroner you have been there at all hours of the night? Yes.

Coroner Have you ever seen any strangers there? Yes, plenty, at all hours - both men and women. I have often turned them out. We have had them on our first floor as well, on the landing.

Coroner Do you mean to say that they go there for an immoral purpose? Yes, they do.

At this stage witness was despatched by the coroner to fetch his knife.

Mrs. Richardson, recalled, said she had never missed anything, and had such confidence in her neighbours that she had left the doors of some rooms unlocked. A saw and a hammer had been taken from the cellar a long time ago. The padlock was broken open.
Coroner had you an idea at any time that a part of the house or yard was used for an immoral purpose?

Witness (emphatically): No, sir.
Coroner Did you say anything about a leather apron? Yes, my son wears one when he works in the cellar.
Coroner: It is rather a dangerous thing to wear, is it not?
Witness: Yes. On Thursday, Sept. 6, I found my son's leather apron in the cellar mildewed. He had not used it for a month. I took it and put it under the tap in the yard, and left it there. It was found there on Saturday

morning by the police, who took charge of it. The apron had remained there from Thursday to Saturday.

Coroner was this tap used?

Yes, by all of us in the house. The apron was on the stones. The police took away an empty box, used for nails, and the steel out of a boy's gaiter. There was a pan of clean water near to the tap when I went in the yard at six o'clock on Saturday. It was there on Friday night at eight o'clock, and it looked as if it had not been disturbed.

Coroner Did you ever know of strange women being found on the first-floor landing? No.
Coroner your son had never spoken to you about it? No.

John Piser [Pizer] was then called. He said: I live at 22, Mulberry Street, Commercial Road East. I am a shoemaker.

Coroner Are you known by the nickname of "Leather Apron?" Yes, sir.

Coroner Where were you on Friday night last? I was at 22, Mulberry-street. On Thursday, the 6th inst. I arrived there.

Coroner From where? From the West End of town.

Coroner: I am afraid we shall have to have a better address than that presently.
Coroner what time did you reach 22, Mulberry Street? Shortly before eleven p.m.

Coroner Who lives at 22, Mulberry Street? My brother and sister-in-law and my stepmother. I remained indoors there.

Coroner Until when? Until Sergeant Thicke arrested me, on Monday last at nine a.m.

Coroner you say you never left the house during that time? I never left the house.

Coroner why were you remaining indoors? Because my brother advised me.

Coroner you were the subject of suspicion? I was the object of a false suspicion.

Coroner you remained on the advice of your friends? Yes; I am telling you what I did.

Coroner: It was not the best advice that you could have had. You have been released, and are not now in custody? I am not.

Piser: I wish to vindicate my character to the world at large.

Coroner: I have called you in your own interests, partly with the object of giving you an opportunity of doing so.

Coroner Can you tell us where you were on Thursday, Aug. 30?

Witness (after considering): In the Holloway Road.

Coroner you had better say exactly where you were. It is important to account for your time from that Thursday to the Friday morning.

Pizer what time, may I ask?

The Coroner: It was the week before you came to Mulberry Street.

Witness: I was staying at a common lodging-house called the Roundhouse, in the Holloway Road.

Coroner Did you sleep the night there? Yes.

Coroner At what time did you go in? On the night of the London Dock fire I went in about two or a quarter-past. It was on the Friday morning.

Coroner when did you leave the lodging-house? At eleven a.m. on the same day. I saw on the placards, "Another Horrible Murder."

Coroner Where were you before two o'clock on Friday morning? At eleven p.m. on Thursday I had my supper at the RoundHouse.

Coroner Did you go out?

Yes, as far as the Seven Sisters Road, and then returned towards Highgate way, down the Holloway Road. Turning, I saw the reflection of a fire. Coming as far as the church in the Holloway Road I saw two constables and the lodging-housekeeper talking together. There might have been one or two constables, I cannot say which. I asked a constable where the fire was, and he said it was a long way off. I asked him where he thought it was, and he replied: "Down by the Albert Docks." It was then about half-past one, to the best of my recollection. I went as far as Highbury Railway Station on the same side of the way, returned, and then went into the lodging house.

Coroner Did any one speak to you about being so late?

No: I paid the night watchman. I asked him if my bed was let, and he said: "They are let by eleven o'clock. You don't think they are to let to this hour." I paid him 4d for another bed. I stayed up smoking on the form of the kitchen, on the right hand side near the fireplace, and then went to bed.

Coroner you got up at eleven o'clock? Yes. The day man came, and told us to get up, as he wanted to make the bed. I got up and dressed, and went down into the kitchen.

Coroner: is there anything else you want to say? Nothing.

Coroner: when you said the West-End of town did you mean Holloway? No; another lodging house in Peter Street, Westminster.

Coroner: It is only fair to say that the witness's statements can be corroborated.

William Thicke [Thick], detective sergeant, deposed: Knowing that "Leather Apron" was suspected of being concerned in the murder, on Monday morning I arrested Piser at 22, Mulberry Street. I have known him by the name of "Leather Apron" for many years.

Coroner: When people in the neighbourhood speak of the "Leather Apron" do they mean Piser? They do.

Coroner: He has been released from custody? He was released last night at 9.30.

John Richardson (recalled) produced the knife a much-worn dessert knife, with which he had cut his boot. He added that as it was not sharp enough he had borrowed another one at the market.
 My mother has heard me speak of people having been in the house. She has heard them herself.
Coroner: I think we will detain this knife for the present.

Henry John Holland, a boxmaker, stated as I was passing 29, Hanbury Street, on my way to work in Chiswell Street, at about eight minutes past six on Saturday. I spoke to two of Bayley's men. An elderly man came out of the house and asked us to have a look in his back yard. I went through the passage and saw the deceased lying in the yard by the back door. I did not touch the body. I then went for a policeman in Spitalfields Market. The officer told me he could not come. I went outside and could find no constable. Going back to the house I saw an inspector run up with a young man, at about twenty minutes past six o'clock. I had told the first policeman that it was a similar case to Buck's-row, and he referred me to two policemen outside the market, but I could not find them. I afterwards complained of the policeman's conduct at the Commercial Street police station the same afternoon.
Coroner: There does not seem to have been much delay. The inspector says there are certain spots where constables are stationed with instructions not to leave them. Their duty is to send some one else.
Foreman of the Jury: That is the explanation.
Coroner: The doctor will be here first thing tomorrow.

This afternoon the inquiry will be resumed.

Day 3, Thursday, September 13, 1888
(***The Daily Telegraph***, **Friday, September 14, 1888, Page 3**)

Yesterday [13 Sep] Mr. Wynne Baxter, coroner, resumed, at the Working Lads' Institute, Whitechapel Road, his adjourned inquiry relative to the death of Annie Chapman, who was murdered in the back yard of 29, Hanbury Street, on Saturday morning last.

Inspector's Abberline, Helson, and Chandler represented the police.

Joseph Chandler, Inspector H Division Metropolitan Police, deposed: On Saturday morning, at ten minutes past six, I was on duty in Commercial Street. At the corner of Hanbury Street I saw several men running. I beckoned to them. One of them said, "Another woman has been murdered." I at once went with him to 29, Hanbury Street and through the passage into the yard. There was no one in the yard. I saw the body of a woman lying on the ground on her back. Her head was towards the back wall of the house, nearly two feet from the wall, at the bottom of the steps, but six or nine inches away from them. The face was turned to the right side, and the left arm was resting on the left breast. The right hand was lying down the right side. Deceased's legs were drawn up, and the clothing was above the knees. A portion of the intestines, still connected with the body, were lying above the right shoulder, with some pieces of skin. There were also some pieces of skin on the left shoulder. The body was lying parallel with the fencing dividing the two yards. I remained there and sent for the divisional surgeon, Mr. Phillips, and to the police station for the ambulance and for further assistance. When the constables arrived I cleared the passage of people, and saw that no one touched the body until the doctor arrived. I obtained some sacking to cover it before the arrival of the surgeon, who came at about half-past six o'clock, and he, having examined the body, directed that it should be removed to the mortuary. After the body had been taken away I examined the yard, and found a piece of coarse muslin, a small toothcomb, and a pocket hair comb in a case. They were lying near the feet of the woman. A portion of an envelope was found near her head, which contained two pills.

Coroner what was on the envelope? On the back there was a seal with the words, embossed in blue, "Sussex Regiment." The other part was torn away. On the other side there was a letter "M" in writing.

Coroner A man's handwriting? I should imagine so.

Coroner: any postage stamp? No. There was a postal stamp "London, Aug. 3, 1888." That was in red. There was another black stamp, which was indistinct.

Coroner any other marks on the envelope? There were also the letters "SP" lower down, as if some one had written "Spitalfields." The other part was gone. There were no other marks.

Coroner Did you find anything else in the yard? There was a leather apron, lying in the yard, saturated with water. It was about two feet from the water tap.

Coroner was it shown to the doctor? Yes. There was also a box, such as is commonly used by casemakers for holding nails. It was empty. There was also a piece of steel, flat, which has since been identified by Mrs. Richardson as the spring of her son's leggings.

Coroner where was that found? It was close to where the body had been. The apron and nail box have also been identified by her as her property. The yard was paved roughly with stones in parts; in other places it was earth.

Coroner was there any appearance of a struggle there? No.
Coroner Are the palings strongly erected? No; to the contrary.
Coroner Could they support the weight of a man getting over them? No doubt they might.
Coroner is there any evidence of anybody having got over them? No. Some of them in the adjoining yard have been broken since. They were not broken then.

Coroner you have examined the adjoining yard? Yes.

Coroner was there any staining as of blood on any of the palings? Yes, near the body.

Coroner was it on any of the other yards? No.

Coroner Were there no other marks? There were marks discovered on the wall of No. 25. They were noticed on Tuesday afternoon. They have been seen by Dr. Phillips.

Coroner Were there any drops of blood outside the yard of No. 29?

No; every possible examination has been made, but we could find no trace of them. The bloodstains at No. 29 were in the immediate neighbourhood of the body only. There were also a few spots of blood on the back wall, near the head of the deceased, 2ft from the ground. The largest spot was of the size of a sixpence. They were all close together. I assisted in the preparation of the plan produced which is correct.

Coroner Did you search the body? I searched the clothing at the mortuary. The outside jacket - a long black one, which came down to the knees - had bloodstains round the neck, both upon the inside and out, and two or three spots on the left arm. The jacket was hooked at the top, and buttoned down the front. By the appearance of the garment there did not seem to have been any struggle. A large pocket was worn under the skirt (attached by strings), which I produce. It was torn down the front and also at the side, and it was empty. Deceased wore a black skirt. There was a little blood on the outside. The two petticoats were stained very little; the two bodices were stained with blood round the neck, but they had not been damaged. There was no cut in the clothing at all. The boots were on the feet of deceased. They were old. No part of the clothing was torn. The stockings were not bloodstained.

Coroner Did you see John Richardson?

Witness I saw him about a quarter to seven o'clock. He told me he had been to the house that morning about a quarter to five. He said he came to the back door and looked down to the cellar, to see if all was right, and then went away to his work.

Coroner Did he say anything about cutting his boot? No.

Coroner Did he say that he was sure the woman was not there at that time? Yes.

Coroner The back door opens outwards into the yard, and swung on the left hand to the palings where the body was. If Richardson were on the top of the steps he might not have seen the body.

Witness He told me he did not go down the steps.

Foreman of the Jury: Reference has been made to the Sussex Regiment and the pensioner. Are you going to produce the man Stanley?

Witness: We have not been able to find him as yet.

The Foreman: He is a very important witness. There is evidence that he has associated with the woman week after week. It is important that he should be found.

Witness: There is nobody that can give us the least idea where he is. The parties were requested to communicate with the police if he came back. Every inquiry has been made, but nobody seems to know anything about him.

Coroner: I should think if that pensioner knows his own business he will come forward himself.

Sergeant Baugham [Badham], 31 H, stated that he conveyed the body of the deceased to the mortuary on the ambulance.

Coroner Are you sure that you took every portion of the body away with you? Yes.

Coroner where did you deposit the body? In the shed, still on the ambulance. I remained with it until Inspector Chandler arrived. Detective-Sergeant Thicke viewed the body, and I took down the description. There were present two women, who came to identify the body, and they described the clothing. They came from 35, Dorset Street.

Coroner who touched the clothing?

Sergeant Thicke. I did not see the women touch the clothing nor the body. I did not see Sergeant Thicke touch the body.

Inspector Chandler, recalled, said he reached the mortuary a few minutes after seven. The body did not appear to have been disturbed. He did not stay until the doctor arrived. Police-constable 376 H was left in charge, with the mortuary keeper. Robert Marne, the mortuary keeper and an inmate of the Whitechapel Union Workhouse, said he received the body at seven o'clock on Saturday morning. He remained at the mortuary until Dr. Phillips came. The door of the mortuary was locked except when two nurses from an infirmary came and undressed the body. No one else touched the corpse. He gave the key into the hands of the police.

Coroner: The fact is that Whitechapel does not possess a mortuary. The place is not a mortuary at all. We have no right to take a body there. It is simply a shed belonging to the workhouse officials. Juries have over and over again reported the matter to the District Board of Works. The East-end, which requires mortuaries, more than anywhere else, is most deficient. Bodies drawn out of the river have to be put in boxes, and very often they are brought to this workhouse arrangement all the way from Wapping. A workhouse inmate is not the proper man to take care of a body in such an important matter as this.

Foreman of the jury called attention to the fact that a fund to provide a reward had been opened by residents in the neighbourhood, and that Mr. Montagu, MP, had offered a reward of £100. If the Government also offered a reward some information might be forthcoming.

Coroner: I do not speak with any real knowledge, but I am told that the Government have determined not to give any rewards in future, not with the idea to economise but because the money does not get into right channels. Were you present when the doctor was making his post-mortem? Yes.

Coroner Did you see the doctor find the handkerchief produced? It was taken off the body. I picked it up from off the clothing, which was in the corner of the room. I gave it to Dr. Phillips, and he asked me to put it in some water, which I did.

Coroner Did you see the handkerchief taken off the body? I did not. The nurses must have taken it off the throat.

Coroner how do you know? I don't know.

Coroner Then you are guessing? I am guessing.

Coroner: That is all wrong, you know. (To the jury). He is really not the proper man to have been left in charge.

Timothy Donovan, the deputy of the lodging-house, 35, Dorset Street was **Recalled.**

Coroner you have seen that handkerchief? I recognise it as one, which the deceased used to wear. She bought it of a lodger, and she was wearing it when she left the lodging-house. She was wearing it three-corner ways, placed round her neck, with a black woollen scarf underneath. It was tied in front with one knot.
Foreman of the Jury: Would you recognise Ted Stanley, the pensioner?
A Juryman: Stanley is not the pensioner.
Coroner (to witness): Do you know the name of Stanley?

Witness: No.
Foreman: He has been mentioned, and also "Harry the Hawker."
Witness: I know "Harry the Hawker."
The Coroner, having referred to the evidence, said: It may be an inference - there is no actual evidence - that the pensioner was called Ted Stanley.
Foreman said he referred to the man who came to see the deceased regularly. The man ought to be produced.

Coroner (to witness): Would you recognise the pensioner? Yes.
Coroner When did you see him last? On Saturday.
Coroner why did you not then send him to the police? Because he would not stop.
Foreman: What was he like? He had a soldierly appearance. He dressed differently at times - sometimes gentlemanly.

A Juror: He is not Ted Stanley.

Mr. George Baxter Phillips, divisional-surgeon of police, said: On Saturday last I was called by the police at 6.20 a.m. to 29, Hanbury Street, and arrived at half-past six. I found the body of the deceased lying in the yard on her back, on the left hand of the steps that lead from the passage. The head was about 6in in front of the level of the bottom step, and the feet were towards a shed at the end of the yard. The left arm was across the left breast, and the legs were drawn up, the feet resting on the ground, and the knees turned outwards. The face was swollen and turned on the right side, and the tongue protruded between the front teeth, but not beyond the lips; it was much swollen. The small intestines and other portions were lying on the right side of the body on the ground above the right shoulder, but attached. There was a large quantity of blood, with a part of the stomach above the left shoulder. I searched the yard and found a small piece of coarse muslin, a small-tooth comb, and a pocket-comb, in a paper case, near the railing. They had apparently been arranged there. I also discovered various other articles, which I handed to the police. The body was cold, except that there was a certain remaining heat, under the intestines, in the body. Stiffness of the limbs was not marked, but it was commencing. The throat was dissevered deeply. I noticed that the incision of the skin was jagged, and reached right round the neck. On the back wall of the house, between the steps and the palings, on the left side, about 18in from the ground, there were about six patches of blood, varying in size from a sixpenny piece to a small point, and on the wooden fence there were smears of blood, corresponding to where the head of the deceased laid, and immediately above the part where the blood had mainly flowed from the neck, which was well clotted. Having received instructions soon after two o'clock on Saturday afternoon, I went to the labour- yard of the Whitechapel Union for the purpose of further examining the body and making the usual post-mortem investigation. I was surprised to find that the body had been stripped and was lying ready on the table. It was under great disadvantage I made my examination. As on many occasions I have met with the same difficulty, I now raise my protest, as I have before, that members of my profession should be called upon to perform their duties under these inadequate circumstances.

Coroner: The mortuary is not fitted for a post-mortem examination. It is only a shed. There is no adequate convenience, and nothing fit, and at certain seasons of the year it is dangerous to the operator.
Foreman: I think we can all endorse the doctor's view of it.
Coroner: As a matter of fact there is no public mortuary from the City of London up to Bow. There is one at Mile-end, but it belongs to the workhouse, and is not used for general purposes.
Examination resumed: The body had been attended to since its removal to the mortuary, and probably partially washed. I noticed a bruise over the right temple. There was a bruise under the clavicle, and there were two distinct bruises, each the size of a man's thumb, on the fore part of the chest. The stiffness of the limbs was then well marked. The fingernails were turgid. There was an old scar of long standing on the left of the frontal bone. On the left side the stiffness was more noticeable, and especially in the fingers, which were partly closed. There was an abrasion

over the bend of the first joint of the ring finger, and there were distinct markings of a ring or rings - probably the latter. There were small sores on the fingers. The head being opened showed that the membranes of the brain were opaque and the veins loaded with blood of a dark character. There was a large quantity of fluid between the membranes and the substance of the brain. The brain substance was unusually firm, and its cavities also contained a large amount of fluid. The throat had been severed. The incisions of the skin indicated that they had been made from the left side of the neck on a line with the angle of the jaw, carried entirely round and again in front of the neck, and ending at a point about midway between the jaw and the sternum or breast bone on the right hand. There were two distinct clean cuts on the body of the vertebrae on the left side of the spine. They were parallel to each other, and separated by about half an inch. The muscular structures between the side processes of bone of the vertebrae had an appearance as if an attempt had been made to separate the bones of the neck. There are various other mutilations of the body, but I am of opinion that they occurred subsequently to the death of the woman and to the large escape of blood from the neck.

Witness, pausing, said: I am entirely in your hands, sir, but is it necessary that I should describe the further mutilations. From what I have said I can state the cause of death.

Coroner: The object of the inquiry is not only to ascertain the cause of death, but the means by which it occurred. Any mutilation which took place afterwards may suggest the character of the man who did it. Possibly you can give us the conclusions to which you have come respecting the instrument used.

Witness: You don't wish for details. I think if it is possible to escape the details it would be advisable. The cause of death is visible from injuries I have described.

Coroner: You have kept a record of them?

Witness: I have.

Coroner: Supposing any one is charged with the offence, they would have to come out then, and it might be a matter of comment that the same evidence was not given at the inquest.

Witness: I am entirely in your hands.

Coroner: We will postpone that for the present. You can give your opinion as to how the death was caused.

Witness: From these appearances I am of opinion that the breathing was interfered with previous to death, and that death arose from syncope, or failure of the heart's action, in consequence of the loss of blood caused by the severance of the throat.

Coroner was the instrument used at the throat the same as that used at the abdomen?

Witness: Very probably. It must have been a very sharp knife, probably with a thin, narrow blade, and at least six to eight inches in length, and perhaps longer.

Coroner is it possible that any instrument used by a military man, such as a bayonet, would have done it? No; it would not be a bayonet.

Coroner Would it have been such an instrument as a medical man uses for post-mortem examinations? The ordinary post-mortem case perhaps does not contain such a weapon.

Coroner would any instrument that slaughterers employ have caused the injuries? Yes; well ground down.

Coroner Would the knife of a cobbler or of any person in the leather trades have done? I think the knife used in those trades would not be long enough in the blade.

Coroner was there any anatomical knowledge displayed? I think there was. There were indications of it. My own impression is that that anatomical knowledge was only less displayed or indicated in consequence of haste. The person evidently was hindered from making a more complete dissection in consequence of the haste.

Coroner was the whole of the body there? No; the absent portions being from the abdomen.

Coroner Are those portions such as would require anatomical knowledge to extract? I think the mode in which they were extracted did show some anatomical knowledge.

Coroner you do not think they could have been lost accidentally in the transit of the body to the mortuary? I was not present at the transit. I carefully closed up the clothes of the woman. Some portions had been excised.

Coroner How long had the deceased been dead when you saw her? I should say at least two hours, and probably more; but it is right to say that it was a fairly cold morning, and that the body would be more apt to cool rapidly from its having lost the greater portion of its blood.

Coroner was there any evidence of any struggle? No; not about the body of the woman. You do not forget the smearing of blood about the palings.

Coroner In your opinion did she enter the yard alive? I am positive of it. I made a thorough search of the passage, and I saw no trace of blood, which must have been visible had she been taken into the yard.

Coroner you were shown the apron? I saw it myself. There was no blood upon it. It had the appearance of not having been unfolded recently.

Coroner you were shown some staining on the wall of No. 25, Hanbury Street? Yes; that was yesterday morning. To the eye of a novice I have no doubt it looks like blood. I have not been able to trace any signs of it. I have not been able to finish my investigation. I am almost convinced I shall not find any blood. We have not had any result of your examination of the internal organs.

Coroner was there any disease? Yes. It was not important as regards the cause of death. Disease of the lungs was of long standing, and there was disease of the membranes of the brain. The stomach contained a little food. **Coroner** was there any appearance of the deceased having taken much alcohol? No. There were probably signs of great privation. I am convinced she had not taken any strong alcohol for some hours before her death.

Coroner Were any of these injuries self-inflicted?

Witness: The injuries which were the immediate cause of death were not self-inflicted.
Coroner was the bruising you mentioned recent?

Witness: The marks on the face were recent, especially about the chin and sides of the jaw. The bruise upon the temple and the bruises in front of the chest were of longer standing, probably of days. I am of opinion that the person who cut the deceased's throat took hold of her by the chin, and then commenced the incision from left to right.

Coroner Could that be done so instantaneously that a person could not cry out? **Witness:** By pressure on the throat no doubt it would be possible.

Forman: There would probably be suffocation.

Coroner: The thickening of the tongue would be one of the signs of suffocation? **Witness:** Yes. My impression is that she was partially strangled. Witness added that the handkerchief produced was, when found amongst the clothing, saturated with blood. A similar article was round the throat of the deceased when he saw her early in the morning at Hanbury Street.

Coroner it had not the appearance of having been tied on afterwards?

Witness: No. Sarah Simonds, a resident nurse at the Whitechapel Infirmary, stated that, in company of the senior nurse, she went to the mortuary on Saturday, and found the body of the deceased on the ambulance in the yard. It was afterwards taken into the shed, and placed on the table. She was directed by Inspector Chandler to undress it, and she placed the clothes in a corner. She left the handkerchief round the neck. She was sure of this. They washed stains of blood from the body. It seemed to have run down from the throat. She found the pocket tied round the waist. The strings were not torn. There were no tears or cuts in the clothes.

Inspector Chandler: I did not instruct the nurses to undress the body and to wash it.

The inquiry was adjourned until Wednesday.

Day 4, Wednesday, September 19, 1888
(*The Daily Telegraph*, **Thursday, September 20, 1888, Page 2**)

In the Whitechapel Working Lads' Institute, yesterday [19 Sep] afternoon, Mr. Wynne E. Baxter, Coroner for East Middlesex, resumed his inquiry respecting the death of Mrs. Annie Chapman, who was found dead in the yard of the house 29, Hanbury Street, Whitechapel, her body dreadfully cut and mutilated, early on the morning of Saturday, the 8th inst. The following evidence was called:

Eliza Cooper: I am a hawker, and lodge in Dorset Street, Spitalfields. Have done so for the last five months. I knew the deceased, and had a quarrel with her on the Tuesday before she was murdered. The quarrel arose in this way: On the previous Saturday she brought Mr. Stanley into the house where I lodged in Dorset Street, and coming into the kitchen asked the people to give her some soap. They told her to ask "Liza" - meaning me. She came to me, and I opened the locker and gave her some. She gave it to Stanley, who went outside and washed himself in the lavatory. When she came back I asked for the soap, but she did not return it. She said, "I will see you by and bye." Mr. Stanley gave her two shillings, and paid for her bed for two nights. I saw no more of her that night. On the following Tuesday I saw her in the kitchen of the lodging-house. I said, "Perhaps you will return my soap." She threw a halfpenny on the table, and said, "Go and get a halfpennyworth of soap." We got quarrelling over this piece of soap, and we went out to the Ringers Public house and continued the quarrel. She slapped my face, and said, "Think yourself lucky I don't do more." I struck her in the left eye, I believe, and then in the chest. I afterwards saw that the blow I gave her had marked her face.

Coroner When was the last time you saw her alive? On the Thursday night, in the Ringers.

Coroner was she wearing rings? Yes, she was wearing three rings on the middle finger of the left hand. They were all brass.

Coroner Had she ever a gold wedding ring to your knowledge? No, not since I have known her. I have known her about fifteen months. I know she associated with Stanley, "Harry the Hawker," and several others.

Foreman: Are they're any of those with whom she associated missing? I could not tell.

A Juryman: Was she on the same relations with them as she was with Stanley? No, sir. She used to bring them casually into the lodging-house.

Dr. Phillips, divisional surgeon of the metropolitan police, was then **recalled**.

Coroner, before asking him to give evidence, said: Whatever may be your opinion and objections, it appears to me necessary that all the evidence that you ascertained from the post-mortem examination should be on the records of the Court for various reasons, which I need not enumerate. However painful it may be, it is necessary in the interests of justice.

Dr. Phillips: I have not had any notice of that. I should have been glad if notice had been given me, because I should have been better prepared to give the evidence; however, I will do my best.

Coroner: Would you like to postpone it?

Dr. Phillips: Oh, no. I will do my best. I still think that it is a very great pity to make this evidence public. Of course, I bow to your decision; but there are matters which have come to light now which show the wisdom of the course pursued on the last occasion, and I cannot help reiterating my regret that you have come to a different conclusion. On the last occasion, just before I left the court, I mentioned to you that there were reasons why I thought the perpetrator of the act upon the woman's throat had caught hold of her chin. These reasons were that just below the lobe of the left ear were three scratches, and there was also a bruise on the right cheek. When I come to speak of the wounds on the lower part of the body I must again repeat my opinion that it is highly injudicious to make the results of my examination public. These details are fit only for yourself, sir, and the jury, but to make them public would simply be disgusting.

Coroner: We are here in the interests of justice, and must have all the evidence before us. I see, however, that there are several ladies and boys in the room, and I think they might retire. (Two ladies and a number of newspaper messenger boys accordingly left the court.)

Dr. Phillips again raised an objection to the evidence, remarking in giving these details to the public I believe you are thwarting the ends of justice.

Coroner: We are bound to take all the evidence in the case, and whether it be made public or not is a matter for the responsibility of the press.

Foreman: We are of opinion that the evidence the doctor on the last occasion wished to keep back should be heard. (Several Jurymen: Hear, hear.)

Coroner: I have carefully considered the matter and have never before heard of any evidence requested being kept back.

Dr. Phillips: I have not kept it back; I have only suggested whether it should be given or not.

Coroner: We have delayed taking this evidence as long as possible, because you said the interests of justice might be served by keeping it back; but it is now a fortnight since this occurred, and I do not see why it should be kept back from the jury any longer.

Dr. Phillips: I am of opinion that what I am about to describe took place after death, so that it could not affect the cause of death, which you are inquiring into.

Coroner: That is only your opinion, and might be repudiated by other medical opinion.

Dr. Phillips: Very well. I will give you the results of my post-mortem examination. Witness then detailed the terrible wounds which had been inflicted upon the woman, and described the parts of the body which the perpetrator of the murder had carried away with him. He added: I am of opinion that the length of the weapon with which the incisions were inflicted was at least five to six inches in length - probably more - and must have been very sharp. The manner in which they had been done indicated a certain amount of anatomical knowledge.

Coroner: Can you give any idea how long it would take to perform the incisions found on the body?

Dr. Phillips: I think I can guide you by saying that I myself could not have performed all the injuries I saw on that woman, and effect them, even without a struggle, under a quarter of an hour. If I had done it in a deliberate way, such as would fall to the duties of a surgeon, it would probably have taken me the best part of an hour. The whole inference seems to me that the operation was performed to enable the perpetrator to obtain possession of these parts of the body.

Coroner: Have you anything further to add with reference to the stains on the wall?

Dr. Phillips: I have not been able to obtain any further traces of blood on the wall.

The Foreman: Is they're anything to indicate that the crime in the case of the woman Nicholls was perpetrated with the same object as this?

Coroner: There is a difference in this respect, at all events, that the medical expert is of opinion that, in the case of Nicholls, the mutilations were made first.

The Foreman: Was any photograph of the eyes of the deceased taken, in case they should retain any impression of the murderer.

Dr. Phillips: I have no particular opinion upon that point myself. I was asked about it very early in the inquiry, and I gave my opinion that the operation would be useless, especially in this case. The use of a bloodhound was also suggested. It may be my ignorance, but the blood around was that of the murdered woman, and it would be more likely to be traced than the murderer. These questions were submitted to me by the police very early. I think within twenty- four hours of the murder of the woman.

Coroner: Were the injuries to the face and neck such as might have produced insensibility?

Witness: Yes; they were consistent with partial suffocation.

Mrs. Elizabeth Long said: I live in Church Row, Whitechapel, and my husband, James Long, is a cart minder. On Saturday, Sept. 8, about half past five o'clock in the morning, I was passing down Hanbury Street, from home, on my way to Spitalfields Market. I knew the time, because I heard the brewer's clock strike half-past five just before I got to the street. I passed 29, Hanbury Street. On the right-hand side, the same side as the house, I saw a man and a woman standing on the pavement talking. The man's back was turned towards Brick Lane, and the woman's was towards the market. They were standing only a few yards nearer Brick Lane from 29, Hanbury Street. I saw the woman's face. Have seen the deceased in the mortuary, and I am sure the woman that I saw in Hanbury Street was the deceased. I did not see the man's face, but I noticed that he was dark. He was wearing a brown low-crowned felt hat. I think he had on a dark coat, though I am not certain. By the look of him he seemed to me a man over forty years of age. He appeared to me to be a little taller than the deceased.

Coroner Did he look like a working man, or what? He looked like a foreigner.

Coroner Did he look like a dock labourer, or a workman, or what? I should say he looked like what I should call shabby-genteel.

Coroner Were they talking loudly? They were talking pretty loudly. I overheard him say to her "Will you?" and she replied, "Yes." That is all I heard, and I heard this as I passed. I left them standing there, and I did not look back, so I cannot say where they went to.

Coroner Did they appear to be sober? I saw nothing to indicate that either of them was the worse for drink.

Coroner Was it not an unusual thing to see a man and a woman standing there talking? Oh no. I see lots of them standing there in the morning.

Coroner At that hour of the day? Yes; that is why I did not take much notice of them.

Coroner you are certain about the time? Quite.

Coroner what time did you leave home? I got out about five o'clock, and I reached the Spitalfields Market a few minutes after half-past five.

The Foreman of the jury: What brewer's clock did you hear strike half-past five? The brewer's in Brick Lane.

Edward Stanley, Osborn Place, Osborn Street, Spitalfields, deposed: I am a bricklayer's labourer.

Coroner: Are you known by the name of the Pensioner? Yes.

Coroner Did you know the deceased? I did.

Coroner And you sometimes visited her? Yes.

Coroner At 35, Dorset Street? About once there, or twice, something like that. Other times I have met her elsewhere.

Coroner When did you last see her alive? On Sunday, Sept. 2, between one and three o'clock in the afternoon.

Coroner was she wearing rings when you saw her? Yes, I believe two. I could not say on which finger, but they were on one of her fingers.

Coroner what sort of rings were they - what was the metal? Brass, I should think by the look of them.

Coroner Do you know any one she was on bad terms with? No one, so far as I know. The last time I saw her she had some bruises on her face - a slight black eye, which some other woman had given her. I did not take much notice of it. She told me something about having had a quarrel. It is possible that I may have seen deceased after Sept. 2, as I was doing nothing all that week. If I did see her I only casually met her, and we might have had a glass of beer together. My memory is rather confused about it.

Coroner: The deputy of the lodging-house said he was told not to let the bed to the deceased with any other man but you? It was not from me he received those orders. I have seen it described that the man used to come on the Saturday night, and remain until the Monday morning. I have never done so.

The Foreman: You were supposed to be the pensioner.

Coroner: It must be some other man?

Witness: I cannot say; I am only speaking for myself.

Coroner Are you a pensioner? Can I object to answer that question, sir? It does not touch on anything here.

Coroner: It was said the man was with her on one occasion when going to receive his pension?

Witness: Then it could not have been me. It has been stated all over Europe that it was me, but it was not.

Coroner: It will affect your financial position all over Europe when it is known that you are not a pensioner? It will affect my financial position in this way, sir, in that I am a loser by having to come here for nothing, and may get discharged for not being at my work.

Coroner Were you ever in the Royal Sussex Regiment? Never, sir. I am a law-abiding man, sir, and interfere with no person who does not interfere with me.

Coroner: Call the deputy. **Timothy Donovan**, deputy of the lodging-house, who gave evidence on a previous occasion, was then **recalled**.

Coroner: Did ever you see that man (pointing to Stanley) before? Yes.

Coroner is he the man you call "the pensioner"? Yes.

Coroner Was it he who used to come with the deceased on Saturday and stay till Monday? Yes.

Coroner Was it he who told you not to let the bed to the deceased with any other man? Yes; on the second Saturday he told me.

Coroner how many times have you seen him there? I should think five or six Saturdays.

Coroner When was he last there? On the Saturday before the woman's death. He stayed until Monday. He paid for one night, and the woman afterwards came down and paid for the other.

Coroner: What have you got to say to that, Mr. Stanley?

Stanley: You can cross it all out, sir.

Coroner Cross your evidence out, you mean?Oh, no; not mine, but his. It is all wrong. I went to Gosport on Aug. 6 and remained there until Sept. 1.

Coroner: Probably the deputy has made a mistake.

A Juror (to Stanley): Had you known deceased at Windsor at all? No; she told me she knew some one about Windsor, and that she once lived there.

Juror you did not know her there? No; I have only known her about two years. I have never been to Windsor.

Juror Did you call at Dorset Street on Saturday, the 8th, after the murder? Yes; I was told by a shoeblack it was she who was murdered, and I went to the lodging- house to ask if it was the fact. I was surprised, and went away.

Juror Did you not give any information to the police that you knew her? You might have volunteered evidence, you know? I did volunteer evidence. I went voluntarily to Commercial Street Police station, and told them what I knew.

Coroner: They did not tell you that the police wanted you? Not on the 8th, but afterwards. They told me the police wanted to see me after I had been to the police.

Albert Cadosch [Cadoche] deposed: I live at 27, Hanbury Street, and am a carpenter. 27 is next door to 29, Hanbury Street. On Saturday, Sept. 8, I got up about a quarter past five in the morning, and went into the yard. It was then about twenty minutes past five, I should think. As I returned towards the back door I heard a voice say "No" just as I was going through the door. It was not in our yard, but I should think it came from the yard of No. 29. I, however, cannot say on which side it came from. I went indoors, but returned to the yard about three or four minutes afterwards. While coming back I heard a sort of a fall against the fence which divides my yard from that of 29. It seemed as if something touched the fence suddenly.

Coroner: Did you look to see what it was? No.

Coroner Had you heard any noise while you were at the end of your yard? No.

Coroner Any rustling of clothes? No. I then went into the house and from there into the street to go to my work. It was about two minutes after half-past five as I passed Spitalfields Church.

Coroner Do you ever hear people in these yards? Now and then, but not often. I informed the police the same night after I returned from my work.

The Foreman: What height are the palings? About 5 ft. 6 in. to 6 ft. high.
Coroner And you had not the curiosity to look over? No, I had not.
Coroner it is not usual to hear thumps against the palings? They are packing-case makers, and now and then there is a great case goes up against the palings. I was thinking about my work, and not that there was anything the matter, otherwise most likely I would have been curious enough to look over.
Foreman of the Jury: It's a pity you did not.
Witness I did not see any man and woman in the street when I went out.
William Stevens, 35, Dorset Street, stated: I am a painter. I knew the deceased. I last saw her alive at twenty minutes past twelve on the morning of Saturday, Sept. 8. She was in the kitchen. She was not the worse for drink.

Coroner Had she got any rings on her fingers? Yes.
Witness was shown a piece of an envelope, witness said he believed it was the same as she picked up near the fireplace. Did not notice a crest, but it was about that size, and it had a red postmark on it. She left the kitchen, and witness thought she was going to bed. Never saw her again. Did not know any one that she was on bad terms with. This was all the evidence obtainable.

A Juryman: Is there any chance of a reward being offered by the Home Secretary?
Foreman: There is already a reward of £100 offered by Mr. Samuel Montagu, MP There is a committee getting up subscriptions, and they expect to get about £200. The coroner has already said that the Government are not prepared to offer a reward.
A Juror: There is more dignity about a Government reward, and I think one ought to be offered.
Foreman of the Jury: There are several ideas of rewards, and it is supposed that about £300 will be got up. It will all be done by private individuals.

Coroner: As far as we know, the case is complete.
Foreman of the Jury: It seems to be a case of murder against some person or persons unknown.

It was then agreed to adjourn the inquiry until next Wednesday before deciding upon the terms of the verdict.

Day 5, Wednesday, September 26, 1888
(*The Daily Telegraph*, Thursday, September 27, 1888, Page 2)

Yesterday [26 Sep] afternoon Mr. Wynne Baxter, coroner for East Middlesex, concluded his inquiry, at the Whitechapel Working Lads' Institute, relative to the death of Mrs. Annie Chapman, whose body was found dreadfully cut and mutilated in the yard of 29, Hanbury Street, Whitechapel, early on the morning of Saturday, the 8th inst.

The Coroner inquired if there was any further evidence to be adduced. Inspector Chandler replied in the negative.

*The Coroner **then addressed the jury. He said: I congratulate you that your labours are now nearly completed. Although up to the present they have not resulted in the detection of any criminal, I have no doubt that if the perpetrator of this foul murder is eventually discovered, our efforts will not have been useless. The evidence is now on the records of this court, and could be used even if the witnesses were not forthcoming; while the publicity given has already elicited further information, which I shall presently have to mention, and which, I hope I am not sanguine in believing, may perhaps be of the utmost importance. We shall do well to recall the important facts. The deceased was a widow, forty-seven years of age, named Annie Chapman. Her husband was a coachman living at Windsor. For three or four years before his death she had lived apart from her husband, who allowed her 10s a week until his death at Christmas, 1886. Evidently she had lived an immoral life for some time and her habits and surroundings had become worse since her means had failed. Her relations were no longer visited by her, and her brother had not seen her for five months, when she borrowed a small sum from him. She lived principally in the common lodging houses in the neighbourhood of Spitalfields, where such as she herd like cattle and she showed signs of great deprivation, as if she had been badly fed. The glimpses of life in these dens which the evidence in this case discloses is sufficient to make us feel that there is much in the nineteenth century civilisation of which we have small reason to be proud; but you who are constantly called together to hear the sad tale of starvation, or semi-starvation, of misery, immorality, and wickedness which some of the*** occupants of the 5,000 beds in this district have every week to relate to coroner's inquests, do not require to be reminded of what life in a Spitalfields lodging-house means. It was in one of these that the older bruises found on the temple and in front of the chest of the deceased were received, in a trumpery quarrel, a week before her death. It was in one of these that she was seen a few hours before her mangled remains were discovered. On the afternoon and evening of Friday, Sept. 7, she divided her time partly in such a place at 35, Dorset Street, and partly in the Ringers public-house, where she spent whatever money she had; so that between one and two on the morning of Saturday, when the money for her bed is demanded, she is obliged to admit that she is without means, and at once turns out into the street to find it. She leaves there at 1.45 a.m., is seen off the premises by the night watchman, and is observed to turn down Little Paternoster Row into Brushfield Street, and not in the more direct route to Hanbury Street. On her wedding finger she was wearing two or three rings, which appear to have been palpably of base metal, as the witnesses are all clear about their material and value. We now lose sight of her for about four hours, but at half-past five, Mrs. Long is in Hanbury Street on her way from home in Church-Street, Whitechapel, to Spitalfields Market. She walked on the northern side of the road going westward, and remembers having seen a man and woman standing a few yards from the place where the deceased is afterwards found. And, although she did not know Annie Chapman, she is positive that that woman was deceased. The two were talking loudly, but not sufficiently so to arouse her suspicions that there was anything wrong. Such words as she overheard were not calculated to do so. The laconic inquiry of the man, "Will you?" and the simple assent of the woman, viewed in the light of subsequent events, can be easily translated and explained. Mrs. Long passed on her way, and neither saw nor heard anything more of her, and this is the last time she is known to have been alive. There is some conflict in the evidence about the time at which the deceased was despatched. It is not unusual to find inaccuracy in such details, but this variation is not very great or very important. She was found dead about six o'clock. She was not in the yard when Richardson was there at 4.50 a.m. She was talking outside the house at half-past five when Mrs. Long passed them. Cadosh says it was about 5.20 when he was in the backyard of the adjoining house, and heard a voice say "No," and three or four minutes afterwards a fall against the fence; but if he is out of his reckoning but a quarter of an hour, the discrepancy in the evidence of fact vanishes, and he may be mistaken, for he admits that he did not get up till a quarter past five, and that it was after the half-hour when he passed Spitalfields clock. It is true that Dr. Phillips thinks that *when he saw the body at 6.30 the deceased had been dead at least two hours, but he admits that the coldness of the morning and the great loss of blood may affect his opinion; and if the evidence of the other witnesses be correct, Dr. Phillips has miscalculated the effect of those forces. But many minutes after Mrs. Long passed the man and woman cannot have elapsed before the deceased became a mutilated corpse in the yard of 29, Hanbury Street, close by where she was last seen by any witness. This place is a fair sample of a large number of houses in the neighbourhood. It was built, like hundreds of others, for the Spitalfields weavers, and when handlooms were driven out by steam and power, these were converted into dwellings for the poor. Its size is about such, as a superior artisan would occupy in the country, but its condition is such as would to a certainty leave it without a tenant. In this place seventeen persons were living, from a woman and her son sleeping in a cat's-meat shop on the ground floor to Davis and his wife and their three grown-up sons, all sleeping together in an attic. The street door and the yard door were never locked, and the passage and yard appear to have been constantly used by people who had no legitimate business there. There is little doubt that the deceased knew the place, for it was only 300 or 400 yards from where she lodged. If so, it is quite unnecessary to assume that her companion had any knowledge - in fact, it is easier to believe that he was ignorant both of the nest of living beings by whom he was surrounded, and of their occupations and habits. Some were on the move late at night, some were up long before the sun. A carman, named Thompson, left the house for his work as early as 3.50 a.m.; an hour later John Richardson was paying the house a visit of inspection; shortly after 5.15 Cadosh, who lived in the next house, was in the adjoining yard twice. Davis, the carman, who occupied the third floor front, heard the church clock strike a quarter to six, got up, had a cup of tea, and went into the back yard, and was horrified to find the mangled body of deceased. It was then a little after six a.m. - a very little, for at ten minutes past the hour Inspector Chandler had been informed of the discovery while on duty in Commercial Street. There is nothing to suggest that the deceased was not fully conscious of what she was doing. It is true that she had passed through some stages of intoxication, for although she appeared perfectly sober to her friend who met her in Dorset Street at five o'clock the previous evening, she had been drinking afterwards; and when she left the lodging-house shortly before two o'clock the night watchman noticed that she was the worse for drink, but not badly so, while the deputy asserts that, though she had evidently been drinking, she could walk straight, and it was probably only malt liquor that she had taken, and its effects would pass off quicker than if she had taken spirits. Consequently it is not surprising to find that Mrs. Long saw nothing to make her think that the deceased was the worse for drink. Moreover, it is unlikely that she could have had the opportunity of getting intoxicants. Again the post-mortem examination shows that while the stomach contained a meal of food there was no sign of fluid and no appearance of her having taken alcohol, and Dr. Phillips is convinced that she had not taken any alcohol for some time. The deceased, therefore, entered the yard in full possession of her faculties; although with a very different object from her companion. From the evidence, which the condition of the yard affords and the medical examination discloses, it appears that after the two had passed through the passage and opened the swing-door at the end, they descended the three steps into the yard. On their left hand side there was a recess between those steps and the palings. Here a few feet from the house and a less distance from the paling they must have stood. The wretch must have then seized the deceased, perhaps with Judas-like approaches. He seized her by the chin. He pressed her throat, and while thus preventing the slightest cry, he at the same time produced insensibility and suffocation. There is no evidence of any struggle. The clothes are not torn. Even in these preliminaries, the wretch seems to have known how to carry out efficiently his nefarious work. The deceased was then lowered to the ground, and laid on her back; and although in doing so she may have fallen slightly against the fence, this movement was probably effected with care. Her throat was then cut in two places with savage determination, and the injuries to the abdomen commenced. All was done with cool impudence and reckless daring; but, perhaps, nothing is more noticeable than the emptying of her pockets, and the arrangement of their contents with business-like precision in order near her feet. The murder seems, like the Buck's Row case, to have been carried out without any cry. Sixteen people were in the house. The partitions of the different rooms are of wood. Davis was not asleep after three a.m., except for three-quarters of an hour, or less, between five and 5.45. Mrs. Richardson only dosed after three a.m., and heard no noise during the night. Mrs. Hardman, who occupies the front ground-floor room, did not awake until the noise succeeding the finding of the body had commenced, and none of the occupants of the houses by which the yard is surrounded heard anything suspicious. The brute who committed the offence did not even take the trouble to cover up his ghastly work, but left the body exposed to the view of the first comer. This accords but little with the trouble taken with the rings, and suggests either that he had at length been disturbed, or that as the daylight broke a sudden fear suggested the danger of detection that he was running. There are two* things missing. Her rings had been wrenched from her fingers and have not been found, and the uterus has been removed. The body has not been dissected, but the injuries have been made by some one who had considerable anatomical skill and knowledge. There are no meaningless cuts. It was done by one who knew where to find what he wanted, what difficulties he would have to contend against, and how he should use his knife, so as to abstract the organ without injury to it. No unskilled person could have known where to find it, or have recognised it when it was found. For instance, no mere slaughterer of animals could have carried out these operations. It must have been some one accustomed to the post-mortem room. The conclusion that the desire was to possess the missing part seems overwhelming. If the object were robbery, these injuries were meaningless, for death had previously resulted from the loss of blood at the neck. Moreover, when we find an easily accomplished theft of some paltry brass rings and such an operation, after, at least, a quarter of an hour's work, and by a skilled person, we are driven to the deduction that the mutilation was the object, and the theft of the rings was only a thin-veiled blind, an attempt to prevent the real intention being discovered. Had not the medical examination been of a thorough and searching character, it might easily have been left unnoticed. The difficulty in believing that this was the real purport of the murderer is natural. It is abhorrent to our feelings to conclude that a life should be taken for so slight an object; but, when rightly considered, the reasons for most murders are altogether out of proportion to the guilt. It has been suggested that the criminal is a lunatic with morbid feelings. This may or may not be the case; but the object of the murderer appears palpably shown by the facts, and it is not necessary to assume lunacy, for it is clear that there is a market for the object of the murder. To show you this, I must mention a fact which at the same time proves the assistance which publicity and the newspaper press afford in the detection of crime. Within a few hours of the issue of the morning papers containing a report of the medical evidence given at the last sitting of the Court, I received a communication from an officer of one of our great medical schools, that they had information which might or might not have a distinct bearing on our inquiry. I attended at the first opportunity, and was told by the sub-curator of the Pathological Museum that some months ago an American had called on him, and asked him to procure a number of specimens of the organ that was missing in the deceased. He stated his willingness to give? For each, and explained that his object was to issue an actual specimen with each copy of a publication on which he was then engaged. Although he was told that his wish was impossible to be complied with, he still urged his *request. He desired them preserved, not in spirits of wine, the usual medium, but in glycerine, in order to preserve them in a flaccid condition, and he wished them sent to America direct. It is known that this request was repeated to another institution of a similar character. Now, is it not possible that the knowledge of this demand may have incited some abandoned wretch to possess himself of a specimen. It seems beyond belief that such inhuman wickedness could enter into the mind of any man, but unfortunately our criminal annals prove that every crime is possible. I need hardly say that I at once communicated my information to the Detective Department at Scotland- yard. Of course I do not know what use has been made of it, but I believe that publicity may possibly further elucidate this fact, and, therefore, I have not withheld from you my knowledge. By means of the press some further explanation may be forthcoming from America if not from here. I have endeavoured to suggest to you the object with which this offence was committed, and the class of person who must have perpetrated it. The greatest deterrent from crime is the conviction that detection and punishment will follow with rapidity and certainty, and it may be that the impunity with which Mary Ann Smith and Anne Tabram were murdered suggested the possibility of such horrid crimes as those which you and another jury have been recently considering. It is, therefore, a great misfortune that nearly three weeks have elapsed without the chief actor in this awful tragedy having been discovered. Surely, it is not too much even yet to hope that the ingenuity of our detective force will succeed in unearthing this monster. It is not as if there were no clues to the character of the criminal or the cause of his crime. His object is clearly divulged. His anatomical skill carries him out of the category of a common criminal, for his knowledge could only have been obtained by assisting at post-mortems, or by frequenting the post-mortem room. Thus the class in which search must be made, although a large one, is limited. Moreover it must have been a man who was from home, if not all night, at least during the early hours of Sept. 8. His hands were undoubtedly bloodstained, for he did not stop to use the tap in the yard as the pan of clean water under it shows. If the theory of lunacy be correct - which I very much doubt - the class is still further limited; while, if Mrs. Long's memory does not fail, and the assumption be correct that the man who was talking to the deceased at half-past five was the culprit, he is even more clearly defined. In addition to his former description, we should know that he was a foreigner of dark complexion, over forty years of age, a little taller than the deceased, of shabby-genteel appearance, with a brown dear-stalker hat on his head, and a dark coat on his back. If your views accord with mine, you will be of opinion that we are confronted with a murder of no ordinary character, committed not from jealousy, revenge, or robbery, but from motives less adequate than the many which still disgrace our civilisation, mar our progress, and blot the pages of our Christianity. I cannot conclude my remarks without thanking you for the attention you have given to the case and the assistance you have rendered me in our efforts to elucidate the truth of this horrible tragedy. The Foreman: We can only find one verdict - that of wilful murder against some person or persons unknown. We were about to add a rider with respect to the condition of the mortuary, but that having been done by a previous jury it is unnecessary.*

A verdict of willful murder against a person or persons unknown was then entered.

This is a copy of the death certificate for Annie Chapman.

Chapter 5

Ripper Victim or Not?

Elizabeth Stride

Elizabeth Stride eventually became known as the first victim of what has been termed the "double event," which occurred on September 30th, 1888. Elizabeth Stride was forty-two years of age, stood 5 ft. 5 in. tall. She had a pale complexion and light grey eyes. Elizabeth had a good head of dark brown curly hair. She also had all her lower teeth missing. In the mortuary photograph that was discovered in 1988, it looks as though Elizabeth had some swelling to her lower lip. Chief Inspector Walter Dew remarked that there were traces of prettiness in Elizabeth's face, and there must have been a time when Elizabeth would have been extremely proud of her curly black hair. Inspector Dew was twenty years younger than the deceased when he made this remark. This leads one to believe that Elizabeth may have been better looking than the prematurely aged hags people most often associate with the Ripper victims.

Elizabeth was born in 1843 in Gothenburg, Sweden. Her maiden name was Gustafsdotter. In 1860 she moved to Carl Johan Parish, Gothenburg, and worked as a domestic servant to a workman named Lars Fredrick Olofsson. In 1862 she moved to Cathedral Parish, still in domestic service. By 1865 she was registered as a prostitute and had twice been in the hospital suffering from venereal diseases. It is alleged that at this time she gave birth to a stillborn daughter.

By 1866 she moved again and exactly how or why she came to be in London is unknown. She often told two different stories about why she went to London. One such story was she was in domestic service for a foreign gentleman who lived near Hyde Park. The other version was that she had some family living in London and she came to see the country . At Elizabeth's inquest, a man named Michael Kidney said it was around this time (1866 in London) that Elizabeth courted a police officer, which also happened to be around the same time that she started courting John Stride. In 1869 she married John Thomas Stride, at St. Giles in the Fields Church. She gave her name as Elizabeth Gustifson and her address as 67 Gower Street. Stride later told friends that she and her husband had kept a coffee shop on Chrisp Street Poplar.

In 1869 there was a John Thomas Stride entered in the trade directories as the owner of a coffee shop in Poplar. In 1878 the *Princess Alice* steamer sank off Woolwich, and soon after Elizabeth started telling tall stories about how she had lost both her husband and two children in the tragedy. The marriage had already come to a natural end by 1882. Elizabeth periodically lived in a lodging house on Flower and Dean Street. In reality, John Stride died in 1884 in the Bromley Sick Asylum of heart failure.

By 1885 Elizabeth was living with a man named Michael Kidney at 33 Dorset Street. Elizabeth would periodically leave Kidney for short lengths of time during the remainder of her life. One time, Elizabeth accused Kidney of assaulting her, but Elizabeth never turned up to prosecute him.

In 1886 Elizabeth asked the Swedish Church (just off the Ratcliff Highway) for financial help on two occasions, and received it both times. Sven Olsson, a fellow member of the church, stated that although he knew Elizabeth, he never knew of her having any children. Later at Elizabeth's inquest, Mr. Sven Olsson from the same church stated that he had known Elizabeth for seventeen years, and that she was a Swede. He claimed there were records kept at his church of people who enter Britain bringing a certificate and desiring to be registered, and that Elizabeth was registered on the 20th July 1866 as an unmarried woman. A later, undated memorandum was filed stating that Elizabeth had married an Englishman called John Stride.

During 1887 and 1888, Elizabeth appeared before the Thames Magistrate Court eight times for drunkenness. She mostly appeared under her own name, but perhaps once on June 10th appeared under the name of Fitzgerald. Many Unfortunates often used other false names regularly when arrested for either drunkenness or soliciting so they would not go to prison for having too many offences against them. Everyone who knew Elizabeth and gave evidence at her inquest thought of her as Swedish; although they did comment that she spoke English without a foreign accent. Michael Kidney assumed Elizabeth was from a superior background. He also said that she was able to speak fluent Yiddish. Yiddish was not a language that was taught in schools. Yiddish is usually spoken by the Jewish community.

September 25, 1888

This was the last day that Michael Kidney saw Elizabeth alive. He saw Elizabeth between the hours of nine and ten that evening on Commercial Street. He said that they parted on friendly terms and that he expected her to follow him home a little later. He then said she did go home but then left again. He claimed that on the Monday night following Elizabeth's murder he had entered Leman Street police station and asked to see a detective because he had information that he wanted to give. After being asked to divulge this information to the inquest jury, Kidney refused. The coroner then asked Kidney would he then divulge his information to him directly, but again he declined. Kidney, however, seemed very certain he had information that would lead to the capture of the Ripper. He had asked for a young detective who was a stranger to the people of the area; he also said that he had received information from parties that knew him, but he was obviously worried about what he said in public concerning this information. It is a shame that even today we do not know what it was that Kidney knew, or thought he knew, about the killer. Elizabeth moved back into the lodging house at Flower and Dean Street. While at the lodging house Elizabeth told some of the residents that she had moved back into the lodging house because she had had words with her man.

September 30, 1888

The first sighting of Elizabeth Stride was early in the morning when Dr. Barnardo visited the lodging house at 32 Flower and Dean Street. In his own words, Dr. Barnardo said he had spoken with Stride that morning. He added that he had spoken to Elizabeth about the murders. In a letter Dr. Barnardo wrote to the *Times* newspaper on October 6th 1888, he stated,

"I had been examining many of the common lodging houses in Bethnal-green that night. The company [Unfortunates] soon recognised me, and the conversation turned upon the previous murders. The female inmates of the kitchen seemed thoroughly frightened at the dangers to which they were presumably exposed"

He then went on to say that he told the Unfortunates of his ideas for rescuing the children from these lodging houses. He wrote,

"Children at all events could be saved from the contamination of the common lodging houses and the streets. My remarks were manifestly followed with deep interest by the women. One poor creature, who had evidently been drinking exclaimed somewhat bitterly to the following effect: 'we're all up to no good, and no one cares what becomes of us. If anybody had helped the likes of us long ago we would never have come to this!"

6:30 p.m. Saturday was the busiest night in Whitechapel. Saturday was pay day and many of the local men as well as the passing tradesmen sometimes had spare cash to spend. As a result, the Unfortunates were out in force, walking the streets and wandering in and out of the public houses. Elizabeth Stride was no exception. Elizabeth Tanner had seen Elizabeth Stride in the Queen's Head public house. They sat down and had a drink together, they both then returned to the lodging house. Elizabeth Tanner, at the inquest, described Elizabeth as a quiet sober woman.

7:00 p.m. – 8:00 p.m. Elizabeth was seen by two people leaving the lodging house that night. Charles Preston remembers Elizabeth asking him if she could borrow his clothes brush, but he had lost it. The other person was a woman named Catherine Lane. Lane agreed to look after a piece of green velvet for Elizabeth until she returned to the lodging house that night. At Elizabeth's inquest, Lane said she did not understand why Elizabeth had asked her to look after the piece of velvet, which was produced at the inquest, as the deputy would have taken good care of it until Elizabeth returned again that night. This is the last time either of these people saw Elizabeth alive. In *Jack the Myth* by A.P. Wolf, it is suggested that Elizabeth was all dressed up in order to meet an admirer. This same admirer had given Elizabeth the piece of velvet material as a gift. I agree with Wolf's statement; I also believe the piece of velvet was a gift. I believe the gift was given to Elizabeth by the Ripper. Further, I think the "gift" was an enticement, which ensured that Elizabeth would meet her admirer (the Ripper) later that evening.

Thomas Bates was on duty as watchman at the lodging house that night. As she left, Elizabeth flashed the 6d at him she had earned for cleaning two rooms in the lodging house that day.

11:00 p.m. It was raining very hard. And J. Best and John Gardner from Chapman Street were on their way to the Bricklayer's Arms, on Settles Street for a drink when they saw Elizabeth Stride. They both stated that Elizabeth was with a short man who was respectably dressed and wearing a *BillyCock* hat. The couple were seeking shelter from the rain in the doorway of the pub. The man had a dark moustache and sandy eyelashes. The two men recounted that they were shocked by the man's conduct towards Elizabeth; the man was hugging and kissing her. The two men then asked him to join them for a drink, which he refused. The men called teasingly to Elizabeth, *"That's Leather Apron getting around you."* I believe that the man with Elizabeth at this time was Dr. Barnardo.

The physical description given by Gardner and Best fitted the appearance of Dr Barnardo. Also the fact that they stated that the man was wearing a Billycock hat also fits in with what Dr Barnardo wore when he was prowling Whitechapel in the course of his work.

Just after 11:00 p.m. Elizabeth and the man left the pub and made their way towards Commercial Road and Berner Street.

11:45 p.m. William Marshal, a labourer, saw Stride in Berner Street. He stood in the doorway of number 64, which is situated on the West Side of the street between Fairclough and Boyd Street. Marshal saw Stride with a man outside number 63 Berner Street. The man had a clerkly appearance, middle-aged, and was 5 ft., 6 in. tall. He was stout and was decently dressed and was wearing a short black cutaway coat, dark trousers, and a peaked sailor-type cap. When asked by the coroner if he thought the man he saw with Elizabeth was a sailor, Marshall replied *"No."* He also said he did not think that this man did any manual labour as a living. Marshall stated they were kissing and carrying on. He later heard the man say *"you would say anything except your prayers"* Elizabeth laughed after the man made this observation. Mr. Marshall said the man had a mild voice and spoke with an English accent. Marshall also thought the man spoke like an educated man. Thus, there is good reason to believe Elizabeth was still with Dr. Barnardo at that point.

12:00 a.m. A shopkeeper named Mathew Packer, who was a fruiterer from Berner Street, claimed that Elizabeth and a man had entered his shop and bought half a pound of black grapes. The couple then separated. This was in order for Dr Barnardo to go and meet his next victim as arranged, Catharine Eddowes.

12:35 a.m. PC William Smith saw Elizabeth and a young man in Berner Street, opposite the International Workers Club. The club was an old wooden house converted to be used as a social club. The building had a capacity of two hundred people. The club was used mainly by Jews of various nationalities as well as Russians and Poles. PC Smith described the man as 28 years old, wearing a dark coat and a *deerstalker* hat, carrying a parcel that was approximately six-inches high and eighteen-inches long. The parcel was wrapped in newspaper.

12:40 a.m. The last official sighting of Elizabeth alive according to the Home Office files was by Israel Schwartz of 22 Helen Street, Backchurch Lane. Schwartz had just turned the corner into Berner Street; he had gone as far as the gateway to the International Worker's Club. Schwartz claimed he saw a man stop and talk to a woman who was standing there. According to Schwartz the woman was Elizabeth Stride and the man tried to pull her into the street. When she resisted, the man turned her around and threw her to the ground. The woman cried aloud at the mistreatment.

Schwartz crossed to the opposite side of the street and, at that point, noticed another man standing close by, lighting his pipe. Schwartz remembered that the first man called the second man *"Lipsky"* loudly at him. A man named Israel Lipsky had been found guilty of forcibly poisoning a young girl and consequently was hanged. This murder caused a wave of anti-Semitism against the Jews. And the term "Lipsky" was used throughout the East End to insult anyone who looked Jewish. Because of this insult Schwartz quickened his pace, but soon realised that the second man was following him. Feeling rather afraid, Schwartz ran as far as the Railway Arch, the man did not follow him that far. Schwartz could not be certain that the two men were together, but said it sounded as though they were. When Schwartz visited the mortuary he identified the woman's body as the woman he had seen in Berner Street that night. Many have wondered why Schwartz was not called as a witness at Elizabeth's inquest. There never has been an explanation as to why he was not called.

1:00 a.m. A jewellery salesman (Hawker) named Louis Diemschutz was returning home from a long day at the market in Westow Hill, Sydenham. He was also the Steward of the club. He was just pulling into the court (passageway) that led to Dutfield Yard on Berner Street with his pony and cart. He intended to leave his wares with his wife, who was inside the club, while he stabled his pony in George Yard. As he turned into the court (passageway) from the street, he was met by immediate darkness. For a distance of about eighteen to twenty feet there was a wall surrounding the court. After sunset the only light the court received was the dim light coming out of the dirty windows of the club, which is situated on the right side of the court. Still, this was very little lighting and the rest of the court was in total darkness. Upon entering the yard, the pony shied and refused to go any further. Diemschutz used his long handled whip to feel around to see what was causing the problem; he felt something soft behind the gates. Getting down from the cart, Diemschutz struck a match and saw what looked like an unconscious woman lying on the ground. Thinking that the woman was either drunk or asleep, he went into the Workingman's Club to get help to rouse her. Diemschutz, at
At Elizabeth's inquest, Diemschutz recalled this event:

"All at once my pony shied at some object on the right. I looked to see what the object was, and observed that there was something unusual, but could not tell what. It was a dark object. I put my whip handle to it, and tried to lift it up, but as I did not succeed I jumped down from my barrow and struck a match. It was very windy, but in the brief light from the flame before it was extinguished, he saw a figure lying there. I could tell from the dress it was a woman."

Isaac Kozebrodsky and Morris Eagle were persuaded to help Diemschutz move the woman. Taking a candle with them, the men noticed that there was blood on the floor of the court before they reached the body. When they stood next to the victim, the three men soon realised the woman's throat had been cut.

Diemschutz and another club member ran out of the yard searching for a police officer; they were unable to find one. They did meet Edward Spooner standing outside the Bee-hive Public house with a young woman. At the inquests he said that he saw two men running towards him shouting *"murder"* and *"Police."* Why the three men chose to return to the crime scene and not continue to search for a policeman will never be known. When they did return to the crime scene, Spooner said he saw that Elizabeth's throat had been cut. Soon after, Police Constable Lamb and Police Constable Collins arrived at the scene. By the time the officers had arrived, a crowd of people had started to form. Constable Henry Lamb then went into the club to inspect the premises and the members for traces of blood. Unfortunately, he did not find any blood evidence, not on any of the member's nor anywhere in the club itself.

1:00 a.m. A few minutes after one o'clock, Edward Johnson, an assistant to Dr. Kaye and Dr. Blackwell, was informed of the murder. He immediately went to wake Dr. Blackwell. Johnson then went with Constable Smith to the crime scene, before the doctor arrived. At the inquest, when asked by the coroner if there was there anyone in the yard when Johnson arrived, he recalled that there was a "crowd" of people there. He then said that by the light of the policeman's lantern he examined the victim and saw the incision to the throat. The wound to the throat had stopped bleeding. He also said that he undid Elizabeth's dress to check if the chest was still warm, but that he left the body undisturbed. Whist this examination was being done Constable William Smith left the crime scene to fetch an ambulance. Constable Smith said at the inquest that he saw Elizabeth and a man talking together in Berner Street earlier that night. He stated the couple seemed sober and the description he gave of the man was that he was wearing a dark cut-away coat and a dark felt deerstalker's hat. The man was about five-foot-seven in height and was carrying a parcel wrapped in newspaper that was about eighteen-inches long and six to eight-inches broad.

1:16 a.m. Dr. Frederick William Blackwell arrived at the scene. He testified that the victim had only been dead for about twenty to thirty minutes. Dr. Blackwell recalled that the neck and chest were quite warm, as were the legs. The face was slightly warm. The hands were cold. The right hand was open and smeared with blood. It was on the deceased's chest. The left hand was on the ground and was partially closed and in that hand was a small packet of cachous wrapped in tissue paper (cachous were small lozenges that were sucked by smokers to freshen their breath). The incision on the neck began on the left side and severed the vessels there. It cut the windpipe completely in two and terminated on the opposite side about one and a half inches below the angle of the right side of the jaw, but without severing the vessels on the same side. At the inquest, Dr. Blackwell stated he thought that Elizabeth would have bled to death relatively slowly as only the vessels on one side of the neck were cut; the artery on the other side was not completely severed. He also stated that he thought the killer had got hold of the handkerchief Elizabeth was wearing around her neck and pulled her backwards while slitting her throat as she was falling, or even when she was on the ground.

1:25 a.m. Detective Inspector Reid received a telegram at the Commercial Street Police Station. He then set off to number 40 Berner Street. On his arrival, he noticed there were already a number of officers at the scene, as well as residents of the area. Dr. Phillips and Dr. Blackwell were also present. As Inspector Reid arrived, the doctors were examining the victim's throat. A thorough search of the yard was conducted and the houses therein. Unfortunately, this did not lead to any clues about who may have committed the murder. After the search was finished, the members of the club and the people who had entered the yard were questioned, with officers recording their names and addresses. They then had their pockets searched by the police and their hands and clothes searched by the doctors. There were twenty-eight people recorded and each one had an alibi. The houses were searched again, but the search was as fruitless as the first attempt. A description of the body was circulated by wire around all the police stations in London. None of the local residents heard anything unusual the night of the murder. Inspector Reid examined the wall near to where the body was found, but discovered no traces of blood evidence.

4:30 a.m. Elizabeth's body was removed, by ambulance, from the yard to the mortuary. Inspector Reid returned to the yard for a further examination of the murder scene only to find that the yard had already been washed. He then re-examined the wall and again could not see any blood spots or any sign that a person might have climbed over the wall. He returned to the mortuary to record a description of the victim. Here is his description:

Clothes Elizabeth was wearing at Time of Death

- **A long black cloth jacket with fur trimming at the bottom of the coat. Pinned to the coat was a small posy containing a red rose and white maidenhair fern, Stride was not wearing this posy when she left the lodging house earlier in the evening**
- **A black skirt**
- **A black crepe bonnet**
- **A checked neck scarf knotted on left side**
- **A dark brown velveteen bodice**
- **2 light serge petticoats**
- **1 white chemise**
- **White stockings**
- **A pair of spring sided boots**
- **2 handkerchiefs, one was larger than the other was and it was noted at the time of the post mortem to have had fruit stains on it**
- **A thimble**
- **A piece of wool wound around a piece of card.**

Items found in the Pocket of Stride's Underskirt
- **A key, the type of key used for a padlock**
- **A small piece of lead pencil**
- **Six large and one small button**
- **A comb**
- **A broken piece of comb**
- **A metal spoon**
- **A hook, the type of hook used on dresses**
- **A piece of muslin**
- **One or two small pieces of paper (whether anything was written on these bits of paper has not been noted).**

2:00 a.m. Dr. George Bagster Phillips was summoned to Leman Street Police Station where he was then directed to Berner Street. At Elizabeth's inquest on October 3, 1888, Dr. Phillips recalled;

"The body was found in the yard with the face turned towards the wall. The feet were towards the street. The left arm was extended and there was a packet of cachous in the left hand. The right arm lay over the belly. The back of the right hand and wrist had clotted blood on it. The legs were drawn up with the feet close to the wall. The legs were quite warm. The deceased had a silk handkerchief round the neck, and it appeared to be slightly torn. I have since ascertained that it was cut. This corresponded with the right angle of the jaw. The throat was deeply gashed, and there was an abrasion of the skin pf about one and a half inches in diameter, apparently stained with blood, under the right brow."

The police, not wanting any further criticism, decided to send Elizabeth's body to the mortuary in St. George in the East.

In a letter to the *Times* newspaper, Dr. Barnardo wrote,

"I have since visited the mortuary in which were lying the remains of the poor woman Stride, and I at once recognised her as one of those who stood around me in the kitchen of the common lodging house on the occasion of my visit last Wednesday week."

Why did Dr. Barnardo visit Elizabeth's body at the mortuary? He had nothing to do with the case and he was never asked to identify the deceased woman. In fact he never revealed the fact that he knew who the deceased woman was till after her inquest had started. This action seems strange because when the inquest did start the deceased woman had not been officially identified, and in fact a lot of time was wasted by a woman who wrongly identified the victim.

3:00 p.m. The following Monday, Dr. Phillips and Dr. Blackwell went to St. George's Mortuary and conducted a post-mortem examination. Here are the results:

"The body was laying on the near side, with the face turned towards the wall, the head up the yard and the feet towards the street. The left arm was extended and there was a packet of cachous in the left hand. The right arm was over the belly. The back of the hand and the wrist had on it clotted blood. The legs were drawn up with the feet close to the wall. The body and face were warm and the hands were cold. The legs were quite warm. The deceased had a silk handkerchief round her neck, which had been cut. This corresponded with the right angle of the jaw. It was decided that the victim was seized by the shoulders, pressed to the ground, and the murderer was on the victims left side when he cut her throat. The throat was cut from left to right. It was not decided how the victim's right hand became covered in blood, this is still unsolved. The victim had died within an hour of Dr. Phillips examining her. It is believed that the victim was lying on the ground when the wounds were inflicted. Rigor Mortis was still thoroughly marked. There was mud on the left-hand side of her face and it was matted in the head [sic]. Decomposition had commenced on the skin, and dark brown spots (probably lividity) were on the anterior surface of the left chin. Post-mortem lividity also known as hypostasis and livor mortis begins immediately after a person dies. The condition is not usually apparent till three to four hours, but is fully evident after around twelve hours. The blood inside the body coagulates in the vessels, giving rise to staining of the skin or lividity patches. The characteristic sites for lividity are the thighs, the small of the back and the back of the neck. The internal organs are also affected and the blood sinks by gravity to the lowest parts. There were small amounts of mud on the right side of her jacket; the left side was plastered with mud. All the teeth on the left lower jaw were missing. The body was fairly nourished. The stomach contained partly digested food, apparently consisting of cheeses, potato and farinaceous powder. Over both shoulders, especially the right and under the collar bone and also in front of the chest was present a bluish discoloration, which I have watched and have seen on two occasions since. There was a clean-cut incision on the neck. It was 6in. in length and commenced 2 1/2in. in a straight line below the angle of the jaw, 1/2in. Over an undivided muscle, and then becoming deeper, dividing the sheath. The cut was very clean and deviated downwards. The artery and other of the vessels contained in the sheath had all been cut through. The cut through the tissues on the right side was more superficial and tailed off to about 2in. below the right angle of the jaw. All the deep

vessels on that side were uninjured. From this the conclusion was arrived that the haemorrhage was caused through the partial severance of the left carotid artery. There was a deformity in the bones of the right leg, which was not straight and bowed forwards. There was no other recent external injury except the neck. After the body had been washed thoroughly Phillips noted some healing sores. The lobe of the left ear was torn as from the wearing through or pulling off an earring this had since healed. On the removal of the scalp there were no signs of bruising or extravasation of blood. The heart was small and the left ventricle firmly contracted and the right slightly so. There were no clots in the pulmonary artery, but the right ventricle was full of dark clot. The stomach was large and the mucous membrane only congested."

The Coroner asked Dr. Phillips about his findings regarding the cause of death. The doctor responded that the cause of death was *"undoubtedly from the loss of blood from the left carotid artery and the division of the windpipe."* Dr. Phillips also stated that the blood had run down the waterway to within a few inches of the side entrance of the club. He roughly estimated that there was an unusual flow of blood considering the stature and nourishment of the body.

On October 2, 1888, two private detectives, Mr. Grand and J.H. Batchelor recovered a grape stalk from the rubbish that was lying in the drain after the police had washed the yard. The two men asked the fruiterer Matthew Packer (who claimed to see Elizabeth on the day she died) to accompany them to the City Mortuary in Golden Lane. When they arrived, the two men showed Packer the body of the other victim that night, Catharine Eddowes, who had died in Mitre Square. Packer informed the private detectives rightly that he had never seen the deceased before. On October 4, the headline in the *News* was that Packer had spoken to Jack the Ripper. This statement I believe was true and that Dr Barnardo did accompany Elizabeth to the shop and buy her the grapes.

The reporter for the paper asked Packer if any policeman or detective had spoken to him. The journalist also asked if he had sold any grapes on the night of the murders. Packer was urged to be careful when answering; his response could have been harmful for the police. Packer responded to the questions: "except for a gentleman who is a private detective, no official detective or policeman has ever asked me a single question. Nor have they come near my shop to find out if I knew anything about the grapes the murdered woman had been eating before her throat was cut. That same afternoon, Batchelor and Grand went back to Packer's shop and took him this time to St. George in the East mortuary. Once at the mortuary, Packer identified Elizabeth as the woman who had been in his shop the night of her murder. At four o'clock, the men then took Packer in a hansom cab to

Scotland Yard to see Sir Charles Warren. **The question you have to ask yourself here is why did Sir Charles warren use two private detectives to take Packer to the mortuaries? Why did he not just send some police officers?**

Sir Warren then personally took down Packer's statement. **Again you have to ask why did warren do this, why not get a detective to do it if it was important? What could Packer have known that worried Warren that much that he did not want to go through the usual channels of investigation?**

If Packers statement was considered important enough to be handled by such a high ranking officer of Scotland Yard, why, then, was he not called as a witness at Elizabeth's inquest?

The statement written in Warren's own handwriting follows:

Mathew Packer

"Keeps a small shop in Berner St. has a few grapes in the window. Black and white. On Sat. night about 11 p.m. a young man from 25-30 about five foot seven inches with a long black coat buttoned up, soft felt hat, kind of hunter hat rather broad shoulders—rather quick in speaking. Rough voice. I sold him half a pound of grapes costing 3d. A woman came up with him from Back Church end (The lower part of the street). She was dressed in a black frock and jacket, fur round the bottom of jacket. A crape bonnet and she was playing with a flower that looked like a geranium that was white outside and red inside. I identified the woman at the St. George mortuary as the same one as I saw that night. They passed by as though they were going up Commercial Road, but instead of going up they crossed to the other side of the road to the board school, and were there for about half an hour till one should say 11.30 p.m. They were talking to one another. I then shut up my shutters. After they passed over opposite to my shop, they went near to the club for a few minutes apparently listening to the music. I saw no more of them after I shut up my shutters. I put the man down as a young clerk. He had a frock coat on and no gloves. He was about one and a half inches or two or three inches a little bit higher than she was."

This statement was then initialled "CW" and was dated 4.10.1888.

This evidence has not been taken very seriously by a lot of Ripperologists. Though there was no mention of grape skins found in Elizabeth's stomach, among Elizabeth's belongings was a large handkerchief which had fruit stains on it. This, perhaps, validates Packer's statement. Although Elizabeth may have not eaten the grapes herself, she may have let her companion use her handkerchief.

The police, in response to Packer's statement in the *Evening News*, made a statement trying to play down the importance of Packers statement by saying that Packer had contradicted himself and was therefore unreliable. The Police also said that there was no evidence that there were any grapes in Elizabeth Stride's hands. **Why did the police feel the need to answer to the press about this seemingly unimportant statement?**

Packer then gave another statement to the press at the end on October saying;

"That on October 27, 1888, he had seen the man that accompanied Elizabeth in his shop the night she was killed. Packer said he saw the man jump on a tram. Apparently, Packer called a shoeblack's attention to him. He also said that he had seen the same man several times since the murder".

This means the man seen earlier by Packer felt comfortable enough to walk around the area without fear of being questioned. I believe that this man was Dr Barnardo and of course he was still roaming Whitechapel after the murders, and yes he could do this without worrying about the police.

October 5, 1888 The inquest resumed. Dr. Phillips was questioned further. Dr. Phillips executed a re-examination with regard to the missing palate of the victim and, from very careful examination of the roof of the mouth, found that there was no injury to either the hard or the soft palate. This is because Elizabeth had told associates that she had been kicked in the mouth losing her lower teeth and damaging her hard palate, whilst escaping from the Princess Alice disaster. Dr. Phillips also testified that he carefully examined the handkerchiefs and decided that the source of the stains on the larger handkerchief was fruit, but he was convinced the victim had not eaten the skin or the inside of a grape within many hours of her death. Dr. Phillips was questioned about the possibility of the victim eating fruit because of Matthew Packer's statement on October 4 wherein he claimed he had sold the victim grapes between 11:00 p.m. and midnight on the day she died. Dr. Phillips explained more of his findings at the inquest: *"On washing the flesh of the victim the apparent abrasion which was found was not an abrasion after all because the skin was entire underneath."*

The doctor believed the victim was seized by the shoulders and pressed to the ground. The murderer was on her left when he inflicted the fatal wound. Dr. Phillips believed the fatal cut was administered from left to right and it was unlikely that a long knife inflicted the wound on the neck. The knife would not have been sharp and pointed. The evidence showed the weapon was probably round and only an inch across. There were no signs in the cut to indicate an incision by the point of a knife. The injuries would have taken only a few seconds to inflict.

When asked about the victim's hand lying across the body, Dr. Phillips stated that he could not form any reason for the hand being there, except that it was where the hand had fallen. Dr. Phillips stated that Elizabeth had not been dead longer than an hour when he first saw her at the murder scene.

After I did a lot of research in what we call today forensic pathology. It was obvious that because of the sudden the fatal act Elizabeth was clutching the cachous tightly in her hand at the point of death. She had suffered a cadaveric spasm, also known as the "death grasp" or "dead man's grip." This is an unusual condition that only happens to a person at the moment of sudden death. Cadaveric spasm or instantaneous rigor is usually associated with a violent death. This condition should not be confused with rigor mortis. It is a condition that cannot be produced by any means after the time of death. Dead man's grip can often offer clues about the murderer, where the victim met their fate, or if the body had been moved. We know that Dr. Blackwell stated at the inquest that Elizabeth had the *cachous "lodged between the thumb and first finger, and partially hidden from view."* He also stated that the hand was nearly open and it was him that scattered some of the cachous trying to remove it from the deceased's hand.

There were only a few mourners who attended Elizabeth's funeral. She was laid to rest in a pauper's grave, number 15509, in the East London Cemetery. The expense was covered by the parish and by the undertaker Mr. Hawkes (possibly the same Mr. Hawkes who arranged Catharine Eddowes's funeral.)

Many authors have argued as to whether Elizabeth Stride was a Ripper victim or not. A main reason for this debate is the differences in *modus operandi* (MO) that exists between Elizabeth Stride's case and the other Ripper cases. I agree with their conclusions that Elizabeth Stride was not a victim of the Ripper based on the differences outlined below

1. The position of the body, indicating it fell on its left side, rather than on its back as in the other Ripper cases.

2. Schwartz witnessed the assault. Not only did Schwartz witness the attack, there was another man standing right across the road. Having witnesses was not the normal MO of a serial killer. If the man Schwartz had seen was not the killer, then Stride was attacked twice in ten minutes—although this is not impossible, it is very unlikely.

3. No abdominal mutilations had been carried out on the body. This could have been because Diemschutz had disturbed the killer.

4. The injuries were made by a short, broad, and possibly a blunt knife. The knife could have had a bevelled end. In other Ripper cases, the knife used was a narrow-bladed long knife that had been sharpened to a point.

5. There was no extravasation of blood in the neck and head region. This could indicate that the victim had suffered asphyxiation before her throat was cut.

6. Elizabeth's body was found at 1:00 a.m. in Berner Street and forty-five minutes later, Catharine Eddowes body was discovered in Mitre Square.

Dr. Phillips confirmed Elizabeth had not eaten grapes before her death, but that the stains in her handkerchief were most likely from fruit juice. As mentioned earlier, this statement contradicts Packer's testimony. It should be noted that Packer's statement was backed by two witness accounts. These accounts are from Walter Dew, who said that detectives searching the area found grape skins and seeds, and another witness, unnamed but also in the same area, who said that a grape stalk fell out of the victim's hand when the body was removed.

Dr. Phillips was asked by the coroner at the inquest if there were any similarities between Elizabeth's murder and the murder of Annie Chapman. He replied,

"There is very great dissimilarity between the two. In Annie Chapman's case the neck was severed all around down to the vertebral column, leaving the vertebral bones being marked with two sharp cuts. There had been an evident attempt to separate the bones."

The Coroner then asked Dr. Phillips if there had been any evidence of chloroform. The doctor also indicated that there was no evidence of any narcotic or anaesthetic having been used.

Thomas Coram, who lived at 67 Plummer's Road, was called as a witness to Elizabeth's inquest. He recalled some specific events on the night of the murder. He said that he was walking home from a friend's house in Bath Gardens, Brady Street, shortly after midnight. He walked straight down Brady Street into Whitechapel Road towards Aldgate. He said that on the front steps of number 253 he saw a knife. This knife was produced at the inquest. The knife was the sort that was typically used by bakers in their work. It was flat at the top, about an inch broad, at least a foot long, and was riveted in three places. The blade was discoloured with something that resembled blood. It was not pointed as a butcher's knife would have been. The handle had a handkerchief wrapped around it. After Coram saw the knife, he saw a policeman heading towards him. He drew the officer's attention to the knife. The officer picked up the knife and he and Coram proceeded to the Leman Street police station.

Constable Joseph Drage

This officer was on duty at a fixed point opposite Brady Street, Whitechapel Road. He said that he saw a man he identified as Coram bend down as if he was going to pick something up. As he walked toward Coram he saw the man beckon him with his finger saying, *"Policeman, there is a knife lying here."* The officer saw a long-bladed knife on the step that appeared to be covered in blood. When asked whether the blood was wet or dry, he answered it was dry and there was a handkerchief bound around the handle tied with string. The boy that found it was sober and his behaviour was natural. The boy said that the discovery had made his blood run cold. The police officer said that he had passed the same steps a quarter of an hour before and had not noticed the knife there at that time. The police officer then stated he handed the knife to Dr. Phillips on Monday afternoon. Dr. Phillips confirmed this at the inquest. Dr. Phillips examined the knife and thought it be the type used in a Chandler's shop. At one time, it may have been a very sharp knife, but it had been blunted. Dr. Phillips did not think this was the knife used on Elizabeth. Dr. Blackwell agreed with Dr. Phillips on this issue.

October 6, 1888 Elizabeth's remains were taken to the East London cemetery. There were only a few mourners at the funeral. Elizabeth was laid to rest in grave number 15509. The expense was met by the parish and the undertaker Hawkes. This could be the same Mr. Hawkes who would go on to arrange Catharine Eddowes's funeral.

I will finish this chapter as I did in the case before with the coroner's summation of the inquest. Although some the facts may be repeated it is important to the case, as you can get a good idea of what the coroner truly thought of the evidence that had been told and his interpretation of that evidence. His summing up goes as follows:

"The first difficulty which presented itself was the identification of the deceased. This was an important matter. A main source of difficulty was Mrs. Malcolm who, after some hesitation and after having had two opportunities to view the body, positively swore the deceased was her sister—Mrs. Elizabeth Watts, of Bath. It was clear she was mistaken, notwithstanding the visions which were simultaneously vouchsafed at the hour of the death to her and her husband. If her evidence was correct, there were points of resemblance between the deceased and Elizabeth Watts which almost reminds one of Shakespeare's Comedy of Errors: both women had been courted by policemen; both bore the same Christian name, and were of the same age; both lived with sailors; both, at one time, kept coffee houses at Poplar; both were nicknamed "Long Liz"; both were said to have had children in charge of their husband's friends; both were given to drink; both lived in East End common lodging-houses; both had been charged at the Thames Police court; both had escaped punishment on the ground that they were subject to epileptic fits, although the friends of both were certain that this was a fraud; both had lost their front teeth; and both had been leading very questionable lives. Whatever might be the true explanation of these

marvellous similarities, it was established that the deceased was Elizabeth Stride and around the year 1869 she married a carpenter named John Thomas Stride. Unlike the other victims in the series of crimes in this neighbourhood—a district teeming with representatives of all nations—she was not an Englishwoman. She was born in Sweden in the year 1843, but, having resided in this country for upwards of 22 years, she could speak English fluently and without much foreign accent. At one time the deceased and her husband kept a coffee house in Poplar. At another time, she was staying in Devonshire Street, Commercial Road, supporting her self, it was said, by sewing and charring. On and off for the last six years she lived in a common lodging-house in the notorious lane called Flower and Dean Street. She was known there only by the nickname of "Long Liz," and often told a tale, which might have been apocryphal, of her husband and children having gone down with the Princess Alice. The deputy of the lodging-house stated that while Elizabeth was with her she was a quiet and sober woman, although at times she used to stay out late at night—an offence very venial, he suspected, among those who frequented the establishment. For the last two years, the deceased had been living at a common lodging-house in Dorset Street, Spitalfields, with Michael Kidney, a waterside labourer, belonging to the Army Reserve. However, intermittently during that period, she left him without any apparent reason, except a desire to be free from the restraint of that connection and to obtain greater opportunity for indulging her drinking habits. She was last seen alive by Kidney in Commercial Street on the evening of Tuesday, September 25. She was sober, but did not return home. She alleged that she had some words with her paramour, but this he denied. The next day she called during his absence. She took away some things, but with this exception they did not know what became of her until the following Thursday when she made her appearance at her old quarters in Flower and Dean Street. There she remained until Saturday, September 29. On that day, she cleaned the deputy's rooms and received a small remuneration for her trouble. Between six and seven o'clock on that evening she was in the kitchen wearing the jacket, bonnet, and striped silk neckerchief which were afterwards found on her. She had at least 6d in her possession, which was possibly spent during the evening. Before leaving she gave a piece of velvet to a friend to take care of until her return, but she said neither where she was going nor when she would return. She had not paid for her lodgings, although she was in a position to do so. They knew nothing of her movements during the next four or five hours at least—possibly not until the finding of her lifeless body. But three witnesses claimed having seen a woman that they identified as the deceased with more or less certainty, and at times within an hour and fifteen minutes of the period when, and at places within a hundred yards of the spot where she was ultimately found. William Marshall, who lived at 64 Berner Street, was standing at his doorway from half past eleven until midnight. About a quarter to twelve o'clock he saw the deceased talking to a man between Fairclough Street and Boyd Street. There was every demonstration of affection by the man during the ten minutes they stood together, and when last seen strolling down the road towards Ellen Street, his arms were round her neck. At 12:30 p.m. the constable on the beat (William Smith) saw the deceased in Berner Street standing on the pavement a few yards from Commercial Street and he observed she was wearing a flower in her dress. A quarter of an hour afterwards, James Brown of Fairclough Street passed the deceased close to the Board school. A man was at her side leaning against the wall, and the deceased was heard to say, "Not tonight, but some other night." Now, if this evidence was to be relied on, it would appear that the deceased was in the company of a man for upwards of an hour immediately before her death, and that within a quarter of an hour of her being found dead she was refusing her companion somewhere in the immediate neighbourhood of where she met her death. But was this the deceased? Even if it was the deceased, was it the same man who was seen in her company on three different occasions? With regard to the identity of the woman, Marshall had the opportunity of watching her for ten minutes while standing talking in the street at a short distance from him, and afterwards she passed close to him. The constable was certain that the woman he observed was the deceased, and when he was called to the scene of the crime he recognized her at once and made a statement. Brown was almost certain that the deceased was the woman to whom his attention was attracted. It might be thought that the frequency of the occurrence of men and women being seen together under similar circumstances might have led to mistaken identity; but the police stated, and several of the witnesses corroborated the statement, that although many couples are to be seen at night in the Commercial Road, it was exceptional to meet them in Berner Street. With regard to the man seen, there were many points of similarity, but some of dissimilarity, in the descriptions of the three witnesses. These discrepancies did not conclusively prove that there was more than one man in the company of the deceased, for every day's experience showed how facts were differently observed and differently described by honest and intelligent witnesses. Brown, who saw least because of the darkness of the spot at which the two were standing, agreed with Smith that his clothes were dark and that his height was about 5ft. 7in., but the man appeared to him to be wearing an overcoat nearly down to his heels. Marshall's description accorded with Smith's description in every respect but two. They agreed that he was respectably dressed in a black cut-away coat and dark trousers, and that he was middle-aged and without whiskers. On the other hand, they differed with regard to what he was wearing on his head. Smith stated he wore a hard felt deer stalker of dark colour. Marshall thought the man was wearing a round cap with a small peak, like a sailor's. They also differed as to whether he had anything in his hand. Marshall stated that he observed nothing. Smith was very precise, and stated that he was carrying a parcel, wrapped in a newspaper, about 18in. in length and 6in. to 8in. in width. These differences suggested either that the woman was, during the evening, in the company of more than one man—a not very improbable supposition—or that the witness had been mistaken in detail. If they were correct in assuming that the man seen in the company of deceased by was one and the same person, it follows that he must have spent much time and trouble to induce her to place herself in his diabolical clutches. They last saw her alive at the corner of Fairclough Street and Berner Street, saying "Not tonight, but some other night." Within a quarter of an hour her lifeless body was found at a spot only a few yards from where she was last seen alive. It was late, and there were few people about, but the place to which the two repaired could not have been selected on account of its being quiet or unfrequented. It had only the merit of darkness. It was the passageway leading into a court in which several families resided. Adjoining the passage and court there was a club of Socialists, who, having finished their debate, were singing and making merry. The deceased and her companion must have seen the lights of the clubroom, the kitchen, and the printing office. They must have heard the music and dancing, for the windows were open. There were people in the yard just before their arrival. At forty minutes past twelve o'clock, one of the members of the club, named Morris Eagle, passed the spot where the deceased drew her last breath, passing through the gateway to the back door, which opened into the yard. At one o'clock the body was found by the manager of the club. He had been out all day. He was in a two-wheeled barrow drawn by a pony, and as he entered the gateway his pony shied at some object on his right. There was no lamp in the yard, and having just come out of the street it was too dark to see what the object was and he passed on further down the yard. He returned on foot, and on searching found the body of the deceased with her throat cut. If he had not actually disturbed the wretch in the very act, at least he must have been close on his heels; possibly the man was alarmed by the sound of the approaching cart, for the death had only just taken place. He did not inspect the body himself *with any care, but blood was flowing from the throat, even when Spooner reached the spot some few minutes afterwards. Although the bleeding had stopped when Dr. Blackwell's assistant arrived, the whole of her body and the limbs, except her hands, were warm. Even at sixteen minutes past 1:00 a.m. Dr. Blackwell found her face slightly warm, and her chest and legs quite warm. In this case, as in other similar cases which had occurred in this neighbourhood, no call for assistance was noticed. Although there might have been some noise in the club, it seemed very unlikely that any cry could have been raised without being heard by someone near. The editor of a Socialist paper was quietly at work in a shed down the yard, which was used as a printing office. There were several families in the cottages in the court only a few yards distant, and there were 20 persons in the different rooms of the club. But if there was no cry, how did the deceased meet with her death? The appearance of the injury to her throat was not in itself inconsistent with that of a self-inflicted wound. Both Dr. Phillips and Dr. Blackwell have seen self-inflicted wounds more extensive and severe, but those have not usually involved the carotid artery. Had some sharp instrument been found near the right hand of the deceased this case might have had very much the appearance of a determined suicide. But no such instrument was found, and its absence made suicide an impossibility. The death was, therefore, one by homicide, and it seemed impossible to imagine circumstances which would fit in with the known facts of the case, and which would reduce the crime to manslaughter. There were no signs of any struggle; the clothes were neither torn nor disturbed. It was true that there were marks over both shoulders, produced by pressure of two hands, but the position of the body suggested either that she was willingly placed or placed herself where she was found. Only the soles of her boots were visible. She was still holding in her left hand a packet of cachous, and there was a bunch of flowers still pinned to her dress front. If she had been forcibly placed on the ground, as Dr. Phillips opines, it was difficult to understand how she failed to attract attention, as it was clear from the appearance of the blood on the ground that the throat was not cut until after she was actually on her back. There were no marks of gagging, no bruises on the face, and no trace of any anaesthetic or narcotic in the stomach; while the presence of the cachous in her hand showed that she did not make use of it in self-defence. Possibly the pressure marks may have had a less tragical origin, as Dr. Blackwell says it was difficult to say how recently they were produced. There was one particular which was not easy to explain. When seen by Dr. Blackwell her right hand was lying on the chest, smeared inside and out with blood. Dr. Phillips was unable to make any suggestion how the hand became soiled. There was* no injury to the hand, such as they would expect if it had been raised in self-defence while her throat was being cut. Was it done intentionally by her assassin, or accidentally by those who were early on the spot? The evidence afforded no clue. Unfortunately the murderer had disappeared without leaving the slightest trace. Even the cachous were wrapped up in unmarked paper, so that there was nothing to show where they were bought. The cut in the throat might have been affected in such a manner that bloodstains on the hands and clothes of the operator were avoided, while the domestic history of the deed suggested the strong probability that her destroyer was a stranger to her. There was no one among her associates to whom any suspicion had attached. They had not heard that she had had a quarrel with any one - unless they magnified the fact that she had recently left the man with whom she generally cohabited; but this diversion was of so frequent an occurrence that neither a breach of the peace ensued, nor, so far as they knew, even hard words. There was therefore in the evidence no clue to the murderer and no suggested motive for the murder. The deceased was not in possession of any valuables. She was only known to have had a few pence in her pocket at the beginning of the evening. Those who knew her best were unaware of any one likely to injure her. She never accused any one of having threatened her. She never expressed any fear of anyone, and, although she had outbursts of drunkenness, she was generally a quiet woman. The ordinary motives of murder - revenge, jealousy, theft, and passion - appeared, therefore, to be absent from this case; while it was clear from the accounts of all who saw her that night, as well as from the post-mortem examination, that she was not otherwise than sober at the time of her death. In the absence of motive, the age and class of woman selected as victim, and the place and time of the crime, there was a similarity between this case and those mysteries which had recently occurred in that neighbourhood. There had been no skilful mutilation as in the cases of Nichols and Chapman, and no unskilful injuries as in the case in Mitre Square - possibly the work of an imitator; but there had been the same skill exhibited in the way in which the victim had been entrapped, and the injuries inflicted, so as to cause instant death and prevent blood from soiling the operator, and the same daring defiance of immediate detection, which, unfortunately for the peace of the inhabitants and trade of the neighbourhood, had hitherto been only too successful. He himself was sorry that the time and attention which the jury had given to the case had not produced a result that would be a perceptible relief to the metropolis - the detection of the criminal; but he was sure that all had used their utmost effort to accomplish this object, and while he desired to thank the gentlemen of the jury for their kind *assistance, he was bound to acknowledge the great attention which Inspector Reid and the police had given to the case. He left it to the jury to say, how, when, and by what means the deceased came by her death."*

The jury, after a short deliberation, returned a verdict of "Wilful murder against some person or persons unknown."

The next few pages follow the Inquest into the death of Elizabeth Stride, as recorded by the newspapers at the time, followed by a copy of the Death Certificate.

Inquests were very important in the 1800's and they give an insight into how people, spoke, behaved and thought.

The inquests make for great reading as part of the book or separately for research.

The way in which the print irregularity appears on the pages is due to the typesetting of the day

Day 1, Monday, October 1, 1888
(As told by *The Daily Telegraph*, Tuesday, October 2, 1888, Page 3)

Yesterday [1 Oct], at the Vestry Hall in Cable Street, St. George in the East, Mr. Wynne E. Baxter, coroner for East Middlesex, opened an inquest on the body of the woman who was found dead, with her throat cut, at one o'clock on Sunday morning, in Berner Street, Commercial Road East. At the outset of the inquiry the deceased was described as Elizabeth Stride, but it subsequently transpired that she had not yet been really identified. A jury of twenty-four having been empanelled, they proceeded to view the body at the St. George's Mortuary.

Detective-Inspector Reid, H Division, watched the case on behalf of the police.

William Wess [West]: who affirmed instead of being sworn was the first witness examined. In reply to the coroner, he said: I reside at No. 2, William Street, Cannon Street Road. I am overseer in the printing office attached to No. 40, Berner Street, Commercial Road, which premises are in the occupation of the International Working Men's Education Society, whose club is carried on there. On the ground floor of the club is a room, the door and window of which face the street. At the rear of this is the kitchen, whilst the first floor consists of a large room which is used for our meetings and entertainment's, I being a member of the club. At the south side of the premises is a courtyard, to which entrance can be obtained through a double door, in one section of which is a smaller one, which is used when the larger barriers are closed. The large doors are generally closed at night, but sometimes remain open. On the left side of the yard is a house, which is divided into three tenements, and occupied, I believe, by that number of families. At the end is a store or workshop belonging to Messrs. Hindley and Co., sack manufacturers. I do not know that a way out exists there. The club premises and the printing office occupy the entire length of the yard on the right side. Returning to the clubhouse, the front room on the ground floor is used for meals. In the kitchen is a window, which faces the door, opening into the yard. The intervening passage is illuminated by means of a fanlight over the door. The printing office, which does not communicate with the club, consists of two rooms, one for compositors and the other for the editor. On Saturday the compositors finished their labours at two o'clock in the afternoon. The editor concluded earlier, but remained at the place until the discovery of the murder.

Coroner: How many members are there in the club? From seventy-five to eighty. Working men of any nationality can join.

Coroner: Is any political qualification required of members? It is a political - a Socialist - club.

Coroner: Do the members have to agree with any particular principles?

A candidate is proposed by one member and seconded by another, and a member would not nominate a candidate unless he knew that he was a supporter of Socialist principles. On Saturday last I was in the printing office during the day and in the club during the evening. From nine to half-past ten at night I was away seeing an English friend home, but I was in the club again till a quarter-past midnight. A discussion was proceeding in the lecture-room, which has three windows overlooking the courtyard. From ninety to 100 persons attended the discussion, which terminated soon after half-past eleven, when the bulk of the members left, using the street door, the most convenient exit. From twenty to thirty members remained some staying in the lecture-room and the others going downstairs. Of those upstairs a few continued the discussion, while the rest were singing. The windows of the lecture-room were partly open.

Coroner: How do you know that you finally left at a quarter-past twelve o'clock?

Because of the time when I reached my lodgings. Before leaving I went into the yard, and thence to the printing office, in order to leave some literature there, and on returning to the yard I observed that the double door at the entrance was open. There is no lamp in the yard, and none of the street lamps light it, so that the yard is only lit by the lights through the windows at the side of the club and of the tenements opposite. As to the tenements, I only observed lights in two first-floor windows. There was also a light in the printing office, the editor being in his room reading.

Coroner: Was there much noise in the club? Not exactly much noise; but I could hear the singing when I was in the yard.

Coroner: Did you look towards the yard gates? Not so much to the gates as to the ground, but nothing unusual attracted my attention.

Coroner: Can you say that there was no object on the ground? I could not say that.

Coroner: Do you think it possible that anything can have been there without your observing it? It was dark, and I am a little short sighted, so that it is possible. The distance from the gates to the kitchen door is 18 ft.

Coroner: what made you look towards the gates at all? - Simply because they were open. I went into the club, and called my brother, and we left together by the front door.

Coroner: On leaving did you see anybody as you Not that I recollect. I generally go home between twelve and one o'clock.
Coroner: Do low women frequent Berner Street? I have seen men and women standing about and talking to each other in Fairclough Street.
Coroner: But have you observed them nearer the club? No.

Coroner: Or in the club yard? I did once, at eleven o'clock at night, about a year ago. They were chatting near the gates. That is the only time I have noticed such a thing, nor have I heard of it.

Morris Eagle: who also affirmed, said: I live at No. 4, New Road, Commercial Road, and travel in jewellery. I am a member of the International Workmen's Club, which meets at 40, Berner Street. I was there on Saturday, several times during the day, and was in the chair during the discussion in the evening. After the discussion, between half-past eleven and a quarter to twelve o'clock, I left the club to take my young lady home, going out through the front door. I returned about twenty minutes to one. I tried the front door, but, finding it closed, I went through the gateway into the yard, reaching the club in that way.

Coroner: Did you notice anything lying on the ground near the gates? I did not.

Coroner: Did you pass in the middle of the gateway? I think so. The gateway is 9 ft. 2 in. wide. I naturally walked on the right side, that being the side on which the club door was.

Coroner: Do you think you are able to say that the deceased was not lying there then? I do not know I am sure, because it was rather dark. There was a light from the upper part of the club, but that would not throw any illumination upon the ground. It was dark near the gates.

Coroner: you have formed no opinion, I take it, then, as to whether there was anything there? No.
Coroner: Did you see anyone about in Berner Street?

Witness: I dare say I did, but I do not remember them.

Coroner: Did you observe any one in the yard?

Witness: I do not remember that I did.

Coroner: If there had been a man and woman there you would have remembered the circumstance?

Witness: Yes; I am sure of that.

Coroner: Did you notice whether there were any lights in the tenements opposite the club? I do not recollect.

Coroner: Are you often at the club late at night? Yes, very often.

Coroner: In the yard, too? No, not in the yard.

Coroner: And you have never seen a man and woman there?

Witness: No, not in the yard; but I have close by, outside the beershop, at the corner of Fairclough Street. As soon as I entered the gateway on Saturday night I could hear a friend of mine singing in the upstairs room of the club. I went up to him. He was singing in the Russian language, and we sang together. I had been there twenty minutes when a member named Gidleman came upstairs, and said, "there is a woman dead in the yard." I went down in a second and struck a match, when I saw a woman lying on the ground in a pool of blood, near the gates. Her feet were towards the gates, about six or seven feet from them. She was lying by the side of and facing the club wall. When I reached the body and struck the match another member was present.

Coroner Did you touch the body? No. As soon as I struck the match I perceived a lot of blood, and I ran away and called the police.
Coroner Were the clothes of the deceased disturbed?

Witness: I cannot say. I ran towards the Commercial Road, Dienishitz, the club steward, and another member going in the opposite direction down Fairclough Street. In Commercial Road I found two constables at the corner of Grove Street. I told them that a woman had been murdered in Berner Street, and they returned with me.

Coroner was any one in the yard then?

Witness: Yes, a few persons some members of the club and some strangers. One of the policemen turned his lamp on the deceased and sent me to the station for the inspector, at the same time telling his comrade to fetch a doctor. The onlookers seemed afraid to go near and touch the body. The constable, however, felt it.
Coroner Can you fix the time when the discovery was first made?

Witness: It must have been about one o'clock. On Saturday nights there is free discussion at the club, and among those present last Saturday were about half a dozen women, but they were those we knew not strangers. It was not a dancing night, but a few members may have danced after the discussion.
Coroner If there was dancing and singing in the club you would not hear the cry of a woman in the yard?

Witness: It would depend upon the cry.
Coroner The cry of a woman in great distress a cry of "Murder"?

Witness: Yes, I should have heard that.

Lewis Dienishitz [Diemschutz], having affirmed, deposed: I reside at No. 40 Berner Street, and am steward of the International Workmen's Club. I am married, and my wife lives at the club too, and assists in the management. On Saturday I left home about half-past eleven in the morning, and returned exactly at one o'clock on Sunday morning. I noticed the time at the baker's shop at the corner of Berner Street. I had been to the market near the Crystal Palace, and had a barrow like a costermonger's drawn by a pony, which I keep in George Yard Cable Street. I drove home to leave my goods. I drove into the yard; both gates being wide open. It was rather dark there. All at once my pony shied at some object on the right. I looked to see what the object was, and observed that there was something unusual, but could not tell what. It was a dark object. I put my whip handle to it, and tried to lift it up, but as I did not succeed I jumped down from my barrow and struck a match. It was rather windy, and I could only get sufficient light to see that there was some figure there. I could tell from the dress that it was the figure of a woman.

Coroner you did not disturb it?

Witness: No. I went into the club and asked where my wife was. I found her in the front room on the ground floor.

Coroner What did you do with the pony?

Witness: I left it in the yard by itself, just outside the club door. There were several members in the front room of the club, and I told them all that there was a woman lying in the yard, though I could not say whether she was drunk or dead. I then got a candle and went into the yard, where I could see blood before I reached the body.

Coroner Did you touch the body?

Witness: No, I ran off at once for the police. I could not find a constable in the direction which I took, so I shouted out "Police!" as loudly as I could. A man whom I met in Grove Street returned with me, and when we reached the yard he took hold of the head of the deceased. As he lifted it up I saw the wound in the throat.

Coroner Had the constables arrived then?

Witness: At the very same moment Eagle and the constables arrived.

Coroner Did you notice anything unusual when you were approaching the club? No.

Coroner you saw nothing suspicious? Not at all.

Coroner how soon afterwards did a doctor arrive? About twenty minutes after the constables came up. The police allowed no one to leave the club until they were searched, and then they had to give their names and addresses.

Coroner Did you notice whether the clothes of the deceased were in order? They were in perfect order.

Coroner how was she lying? On her left side, with her face towards the club wall.

Coroner was the whole of the body resting on the side?

Witness: No, I should say only her face. I cannot say how much of the body was sideways. I did not notice what position her hands were in, but when the police came I observed that her bodice was unbuttoned near the neck. The doctor said the body was quite warm.

Coroner What quantity of blood should you think had flowed from the body?

Witness: I should say quite two quarts.

Coroner In what direction had it run?

Witness: Up the yard from the street. The body was about one foot from the club wall. The gutter of the yard is paved with large stones, and the centre with smaller irregular stones.

Coroner Have you ever seen men and women together in the yard? Never.

Coroner Nor heard of such a thing? No.

A Juror: Could you in going up the yard have passed the body without touching it? Oh, yes.

Coroner any person going up the centre of the yard might have passed without noticing it? **Witness:** I, perhaps, should not have noticed it if my pony had not shied. I had passed it when I got down from my barrow.

Coroner How far did the blood run? **Witness:** As far as the kitchen door of the club.

Coroner was any person left with the body while you ran for the police?
Witness: Some members of the club remained; at all events, when I came back they were there. I cannot say whether any of them touched the body.

Inspector Reid (interposing): When the murder was discovered the members of the club were detained on the premises, and I searched them, whilst Dr. Phillips examined them.
A Juror; Was it possible for anybody to leave the yard between the discovery of the body and the arrival of the police?
Witness: Oh, yes or, rather, it would have been possible before I informed the members of the club, not afterwards.

Coroner when you entered the yard, if any person had run out you would have seen them in the dark?

Witness: Oh, yes, it was light enough for that. It was dark in the gateway, but not so dark further in the yard.

Coroner: The body has not yet been identified? Not yet.

The Foreman: I do not quite understand that. I thought the inquest had been opened on the body of one Elizabeth Stride.

Coroner: That was a mistake. Something is known of the deceased, but she has not been fully identified. It would be better at present to describe her as a woman unknown. She has been partially identified. It is known where she lived. It was thought at the beginning of the inquest that a relative had identified her, but that turns out to have been a mistake.

The inquiry was then adjourned till this (Tuesday) afternoon, at two o'clock.

Day 2, Tuesday, October 2, 1888
(*The Daily Telegraph*, Wednesday, October 3, 1888, Page 3)

Yesterday afternoon [2 Oct.], in the Vestry Hall of St. George in the East, Cable Street. Mr. Wynne E. Baxter, coroner for East Middlesex, resumed the inquiry into the circumstances attending the death of the woman who was found, with her throat cut, in a yard adjoining the clubhouse of the International Working Men's Education Society, No. 40, Berner-street, Commercial Road East, at one o'clock on Sunday morning last.

Constable Henry Lamb, 252 H division, examined by the coroner, said: Last Sunday morning, shortly before one o'clock, I was on duty in Commercial Road, between Christian Street and Batty Street, when two men came running towards me and shouting. I went to meet them, and they called out, "Come on, there has been another murder." I asked where, and as they got to the corner of Berner Street they pointed down and said, "There." I saw people moving some distance down the street. I ran, followed by another constable 426 H. Arriving at the gateway of No. 40 I observed something dark lying on the ground on the right hand side. I turned my light on, when I found that the object was a woman, with her throat cut and apparently dead. I sent the other constable for the nearest doctor, and a young man who was standing by I despatched to the police station to inform the inspector what had occurred. On my arrival there were about thirty people in the yard, and others followed me in. No one was nearer than a yard to the body. As I was examining the deceased the crowd gathered round, but I begged them to keep back, otherwise they might have their clothes soiled with blood, and thus get into trouble.
Coroner Up to this time had you touched the body?I had put my hand on the face.
Coroner was it warm? Slightly. I felt the wrist, but could not discern any movement of the pulse. I then blew my whistle for assistance.

Coroner Did you observe how the deceased was lying? She was lying on her left side, with her left hand on the ground.
Coroner was they're anything in that hand? I did not notice anything. The right arm was across the breast. Her face was not more than five or six inches away from the club wall.
Coroner Were her clothes disturbed? No.
Coroner Only her boots visible? Yes, and only the soles of them. There were no signs of a struggle. Some of the blood was in a liquid state, and had run towards the kitchen door of the club. A little that nearest to her on the ground was slightly congealed. I can hardly say whether any was still flowing from the throat. Dr. Blackwell was the first doctor to arrive; he came ten or twelve minutes after myself, but I had no watch with me.

Coroner did any one of the crowd say whether the body had been touched before your arrival?

No. Dr. Blackwell examined the body and its surroundings. Dr. Phillips came ten minutes later. Inspector Pinhorn arrived directly after Dr. Blackwell. When I blew my whistle other constables came, and I had the entrance of the yard closed. This was while Dr. Blackwell was looking at the body. Before that the doors were wide open. The feet of the deceased extended just to the swing of the gate, so that the barrier could be closed without disturbing the body. I entered the club and left a constable at the gate to prevent any one passing in or out. I examined the hands and clothes of all the members of the club. There were from fifteen to twenty present, and they were on the ground floor.

Coroner Did you discover traces of blood anywhere in the club? No.

Coroner was the steward present? Yes.

Coroner Did you ask him to lock the front door?

Witness: I did not. There was a great deal of commotion. That was done afterwards.

Coroner: But time is the essence of the thing.

Witness: I did not see any person leave. I did not try the front door of the club to see if it was locked. I afterwards went over the cottages, the occupants of which were in bed. I was admitted by men, who came down partly dressed; all the other people were undressed. As to the waterclosets in the yard, one was locked and the other unlocked, but no one was there. There is a recess near the dustbin.

Coroner Did you go there? Yes, afterwards, with Dr. Phillips.

Coroner: But I am speaking of at the time.

Witness: I did it subsequently. I do not recollect looking over the wooden partition. I, however, examined the store belonging to Messrs. Hindley, sack manufacturers, but I saw nothing there.

Coroner: How long were the cottagers in opening their doors? Only a few minutes and they seemed frightened. When I returned Dr. Phillips and Chief Inspector West had arrived.

Coroner: was there anything to prevent a man escaping while you was examining the body? Several people were inside and outside the gates, and I should think that they would be sure to observe a man who had marks of blood.

Coroner: But supposing he had no marks of blood? It was quite possible, of course, for a person to escape while I was examining the corpse. Every one was more or less looking towards the body. There was much confusion.

Coroner: Do you think that a person might have got away before you arrived? I think he is more likely to have escaped before than after.

Detective-Inspector Reid: How long before had you passed this place?

Witness: I am not on the Berner Street beat, but I passed the end of the street in Commercial Road six or seven minutes before.

Coroner: when you were found what direction were you going in?

Witness: I was coming towards Berner Street. A constable named Smith was on the Berner Street beat. He did not accompany me, but the constable who was on fixed-point duty between Grove Street and Christian Street in Commercial Road. Constables at fixed points leave duty at one in the morning. I believe that is the practice nearly all over London.

Coroner: I think this is important. The Hanbury Street murder was discovered just as the night police were going off duty. **(To witness):** Did you see anything suspicious? I did not at any time. There were squabbles and rows in the streets, but nothing more.

Foreman: Was there light sufficient to enable you to see, as you were going down Berner Street, whether any person was running away from No. 40? - It was rather dark, but I think there was light enough for that, though the person would be somewhat indistinct from Commercial Road.

Foreman: Some of the papers state that Berner Street is badly lighted; but there are six lamps within 700 feet, and I do not think that is very bad.

Coroner: The parish plan shows that there are four lamps within 350 feet, from Commercial Road to Fairclough Street.

Witness: There are three, if not four, lamps in Berner Street between Commercial Road and Fairclough Street. Berner Street is about as well lighted as other side streets. Most of them are rather dark, but more lamps have been erected lately.

Coroner: I do not think that London altogether is as well lighted as some capitals are.

Witness: There are no public-house lights in Berner Street. I was engaged in the yard and at the mortuary all the night afterwards.

Edward Spooner, in reply to the coroner, said: I live at No. 26, Fairclough Street, and am a horse keeper with Messrs. Meredith, biscuit bakers. On Sunday morning, between half past twelve and one o'clock, I was standing outside the Beehive Public house, at the corner of Christian Street, with my young woman. We had left a public house in Commercial Road at closing time, midnight, and walked quietly to the point named. We stood outside the Beehive about twenty five minutes, when two Jews came running along, calling out "Murder" and "Police." They ran as far as Grove Street, and then turned back. I stopped them and asked what was the matter, and they replied that a woman had been murdered. I thereupon proceeded down Berner Street and into Dutfield's Yard, adjoining the International Workmen's Clubhouse, and there saw a woman lying just inside the gate.

Coroner was any one with her? There were about fifteen people in the yard.

Coroner was any one near her? They were all standing round.

Coroner Were they touching her? No. One man struck a match, but I could see the woman before the match was struck. I put my hand under her chin when the match was alight.

Coroner was the chin warm? Slightly.

Coroner was any blood coming from the throat?

Witness: Yes; it was still flowing. I noticed that she had a piece of paper doubled up in her right hand, and some red and white flowers pinned on her breast. I did not feel the body, nor did I alter the position of the head. I am sure of that. Her face was turned towards the club wall.

Coroner Did you notice whether the blood was still moving on the ground? It was running down the gutter. I stood by the side of the body for four or five minutes, until the last witness arrived.

Coroner Did you notice any one leave the yard while you were there? No.

Coroner Could any one have left without your observing it? I cannot say, but I think there were too many people about. I believe it was twenty-five minutes to one o'clock when I arrived in the yard.

Coroner Have you formed any opinion as to whether the people had moved the body before you came? No.

Foreman: As a rule, Jews do not care to touch dead bodies.

Witness: The legs of the deceased were drawn up, but her clothes were not disturbed. When Police-constable Lamb came I helped him to close the gates of the yard, and I left through the club.

Inspector Reid: I believe that was after you had given your name and address to the police? Yes.

Coroner And had been searched? Yes.

Coroner And examined by Dr. Phillips? Yes.

Coroner: Was there no blood on your hands? No.

Coroner then there was no blood on the chin of the deceased? No.

Jury: I did not meet any one as I was hastening through Berner Street.

Mary Malcolm was the next witness, and she was deeply affected while giving her evidence. In answer to the coroner she said: I live at No. 50, Eagle Street, Red Lion Square, Holborn. I am married. My husband, Andrew Malcolm, is a tailor. I have seen the body at the mortuary. I saw it once on Sunday and twice yesterday.

Coroner who is it? It is the body of my sister, Elizabeth Watts.
Coroner you have no doubt about that? Not the slightest.
Coroner you did have some doubts about it at one time? I had at first.
Coroner when did you last see your sister alive? Last Thursday, about a quarter to seven in the evening.
Coroner Where? She came to see me at No. 59, Red Lion Street, where I work as a trousermaker.

Coroner What did she come to you for? To ask me for a little assistance. I have been in the habit of assisting her for five years.

Coroner Did you give her anything? I gave her a shilling and a short jacket not the jacket which is now on the body.

Coroner How long was she with you? Only a few moments.
Coroner Did she say where she was going? No.
Coroner where was she living? I do not know. I know it was somewhere in the neighbourhood of the tailoring Jews Commercial Road or Commercial Street or somewhere at the East End.
Coroner Did you understand that she was living in lodging-houses? Yes.
Coroner Did you know what she was doing for a livelihood? I had my doubts.
Coroner was she the worse for drink when she came to you on Thursday? No, sober.
Coroner But she was sometimes the worse for drink, was she not? That was, unfortunately, a failing with her. She was thirty-seven years of age last March.
Coroner Had she ever been married? Yes.
Coroner is her husband alive? Yes, so far as I know. She married the son of Mr. Watts, wine and spirit merchant, of Walcot Street, Bath. I think her husband's Christian name was Edward. I believe he is now in America.
Coroner Did he get into trouble? No.
Coroner why did he go away? Because my sister brought trouble upon him.
Coroner When did she leave him? About eight years ago, but I cannot be

quite certain as to the time. She had two children. Her husband caught her with a porter, and there was a quarrel.**Coroner** Did the husband turn her out of doors? No, he sent her to my poor mother, with the two children.
Coroner Where does your mother live? She is dead. She died in the year 1883.
Coroner Where are the children now? The girl is dead, but the boy is at a boarding school kept by his aunt.
Coroner was the deceased subject to epileptic fits? **Witness** (sobbing bitterly): No, she only had drunken fits.
Coroner Was she ever before the Thames police magistrate? I believe so.
Coroner charged with drunkenness? Yes.
Coroner Are you aware that she has been let off on the supposition that she was subject to epileptic fits? I believe that is so, but she was not subject to epileptic fits.
Coroner Has she ever told you of troubles she was in with any man? Oh yes; she lived with a man.
Coroner Do you know his name? I do not remember now, but I shall be able to tell you to- morrow. I believe she lived with a man who kept a coffee-house at Poplar.
Inspector Reid: Was his name Stride? No; I think it was Dent, but I can find out for certain by to-morrow.

Coroner: How long had she ceased to live with that man? Oh, some time. He went away to sea, and was wrecked on the Isle of St. Paul, I believe.
Coroner How long ago should you think that was? It must be three years and a half; but I could tell you all about it by to-morrow, even the name of the vessel that was wrecked.
Coroner Had the deceased lived with any man since then? Not to my knowledge, but there is some man who says that he has lived with her.

Coroner Have you ever heard of her getting into trouble with this man? No, but at times she got locked up for drunkenness. She always brought her trouble to me.
Coroner you never heard of any one threatening her? No, she was too good for that.
Coroner Did you ever hear her say that she was afraid of any one? No.
Coroner Did you know of no man with whom she had relations? No.
Inspector Reid: Did you ever visit her in Flower and Dean Street? No.
Coroner Did you ever hear her called "Long Liz"? That was generally her nickname, I believe.
Coroner Have you ever heard of the name of Stride? She never

mentioned such a name to me. I think that if she had lived with any one of that name she would have told me. I have heard what the man Stride has said, but I think he is mistaken.

Coroner: How often did your sister come to you? Every Saturday, and I always gave her 2s. That was for her lodgings.

Coroner Did she come to you at all last Saturday? No, I did not see her on that day.

Coroner the Thursday visit was an unusual one, I suppose? Yes.

Coroner Did you think it strange that she did not come on the Saturday? I did.

Coroner Had she ever missed a Saturday before? Not for nearly three years.

Coroner what time in the day did she usually come to you? At four o'clock in the afternoon.

Coroner Where? At the corner of Chancery Lane. I was there last Saturday afternoon from half-past three till five, but she did not turn up.

Coroner Did you think there was something the matter with her? On the Sunday morning when I read the accounts in the newspapers I thought it might be my sister who had been murdered. I had a presentiment that that was so. I came down to Whitechapel and was directed to the mortuary; but when I saw the body I did not recognise it as that of my sister.

Coroner how was that? Why did you not recognise it in the first instance? I do not know, except that I saw it in the gaslight, between nine and ten at night. But I recognised her the next day.

Coroner Did you not have some special presentiment that this was your sister? Yes.

Coroner Tell the jury what it was? I was in bed, and about twenty minutes past one on Sunday morning I felt a pressure on my breast and heard three distinct kisses. It was that which made me afterwards suspect that the woman who had been murdered was my sister.

Coroner (to the jury): The only reason why I allow this evidence is that the witness has been doubtful about her identification. (To witness) Did your sister ever break a limb? No. Never? - Not to my knowledge.

The Foreman: Had she any special marks upon her? Yes, on her right leg there was a small black mark.

Coroner: Have you seen that mark on the deceased? Yes.

Coroner when did you see it? Yesterday morning.

Coroner But when, before death, did you see it on your sister? Oh not for years. It was the size of a pea. I have not seen it for 20 years.

Coroner Did you mention the mark before you saw the body? I said that I could recognise my sister by this particular mark.

Coroner What was the mark? It was from the bite of an adder. One day, when children, we were rolling down a hill together, and we came across an adder. The thing bit me first and my sister afterwards. I have still the mark of the bite on my left hand.

Coroner (examining the mark): Oh that is only a scar. Are you sure that your sister, in her youth, never broke a limb? Not to my knowledge.

Coroner Has your husband seen your sister? Yes.

Coroner Has he been to the mortuary? No; he will not go.

Coroner Have you any brothers and sisters alive? Yes, a brother and a sister, but they have not seen her for years. My brother might recognise her. He lives near Bath. My sister resides at Folkestone. My sister (the deceased) had hollowness in her right foot, caused by some sort of accident. It was the absence of this hollowness that made me doubt whether the deceased was really my sister. Perhaps it passed away in death. But the adder mark removed all doubt.

Coroner Did you recognise the clothes of the deceased at all?

Witness: No. (Bursting into tears). Indeed, I have had trouble with her. On one occasion she left a naked baby outside my door.

Coroner One of her babies? **Witness:** One of her own.

Coroner One of the two children by her husband? **Witness:** No, another one; one she had by a policeman, I believe. She left it with me, and I had to keep it until she fetched it away.

Inspector Reid: Is that child alive, do you know? **Witness:** I believe it died in Bath.

Coroner: It is important that the evidence of identification should be unmistakable, and I think that the witness should go to the same spot in Chancery Lane on Saturday next, in order to see if her sister comes.

Witness: I have no doubt.

Coroner: Still, it is better that the matter should be tested.

Witness (in reply to the jury): I did not think it strange that my sister came to me last Thursday instead of the Saturday, because she has done it before. But on previous occasions she has come on the Saturday as well.

When she came last Thursday she asked me for money, stating that she had not enough to pay for her lodgings, and I said, "Elizabeth, you are a pest to me."

Coroner: Has your sister been in prison? **Witness:** Yes.

Coroner Has she never been in prison on a Saturday? No, she has only been locked up for the night.

Coroner Never more? No, she has been fined.

A Juror: You say that before when she has come on the Thursday she has also come on the Saturday as well? Always.

Coroner: So that the Thursday was an extra. You are quite confident now about the identity? I have not a shadow of doubt.

Mr. Frederick William Blackwell deposed: I reside at No. 100, Commercial Road, and am a physician and surgeon. On Sunday morning last, at ten minutes past one o'clock, I was called to Berner Street by a policeman. My assistant, Mr. Johnston, went back with the constable, and I followed immediately I was dressed. I consulted my watch on my arrival, and it was 1.16 a.m. The deceased was lying on her left side obliquely across the passage, her face looking towards the right wall. Her legs were drawn up, her feet close against the wall of the right side of the passage. Her head was resting beyond the carriage-wheel rut, the neck lying over the rut. Her feet were three yards from the gateway. Her dress was unfastened at the neck. The neck and chest were quite warm, as were also the legs, and the face was slightly warm. The hands were cold. The right hand was open and on the chest, and was smeared with blood. The left hand, lying on the ground, was partially closed, and contained a small packet of cachous wrapped in tissue paper. There were no rings, nor marks of rings, on her hands. The appearance of the face was quite placid. The mouth was slightly open. The deceased had round her neck a check silk scarf, the bow of which was turned to the left and pulled very tight. In the neck there was a long incision which exactly corresponded with the lower border of the scarf. The border was slightly frayed, as if by a sharp knife. The incision in the neck commenced on the left side, 2 inches below the angle of the jaw. Almost in a direct line with it, nearly severing the vessels on that side, cutting the windpipe completely in two, and terminating on the opposite side 1 inch below the angle of the right jaw, but without severing the vessels on that side. I could not ascertain whether the bloody hand had been moved. The blood was running down the gutter into the drain in the opposite direction from the feet. There was about 1lb of clotted blood close by the body and a stream all the way from there to the back door of the club.

Coroner Were there no spots of blood about? No; only some marks of blood which had been trodden in.

Coroner was there any blood on the soles of the deceased's boots? No.

Coroner No splashing of blood on the wall? No, it was very dark, and what I saw was by the aid of a policeman's lantern. I have not examined the place since. I examined the clothes, but found no blood on any part of them. The bonnet of the deceased was lying on the ground a few inches from the head. Her dress was unbuttoned at the top.

Coroner Can you say whether the injuries could have been self-inflicted? It is impossible that they could have been.

Coroner Did you form any opinion as to how long the deceased had been dead? From twenty minutes to half an hour when I arrived. The clothes were not wet with rain. She would have bled to death comparatively slowly on account of vessels on one side only of the neck being cut and the artery not completely severed.

Coroner After the infliction of the injuries was there any possibility of any cry being uttered by the deceased? None whatever. Dr. Phillips came about twenty minutes to half an hour after my arrival. The double doors of the yard were closed when I arrived, so that the previous witness must have made a mistake on that point.

A Juror: Can you say whether the throat was cut before or after the deceased fell to the ground? I formed the opinion that the murderer probably caught hold of the silk scarf, which was tight and knotted, and pulled the deceased backwards, cutting her throat in that way. The throat might have been cut as she was falling, or when she was on the ground. The blood would have spurted about if the act had been committed while she was standing up.

Coroner: Was the silk scarf tight enough to prevent her calling out? I could not say that.

Coroner A hand might have been put on her nose and mouth? Yes, and the cut on the throat was probably instantaneous.

The inquest was then adjourned till one o'clock today.

Day 3, Monday, October 3, 1888
(The Daily Telegraph, Thursday, October 4, 1888, page 5)

Yesterday [3 Oct], at St. George's Vestry Hall, Cable Street. Mr. Wynne E. Baxter, coroner for East Middlesex, again resumed the inquiry into the circumstances attending the death of the woman who was found with her throat cut at one o'clock on Sunday morning last in a yard adjoining the International Working Men's Club, Berner Street, Commercial Road East.

Elizabeth Tanner. examined by the Coroner, said: I am deputy of the common lodging-house, No. 32, Flower and Dean Street, and am a widow. I have seen the body of the deceased at St. George's Mortuary, and recognise it as that of a woman who has lodged in our house, on and off, for the last six years.
Coroner who is she? She was known by the nickname of "Long Liz."
Coroner Do you know her right name? No.
Coroner Was she an English woman? She used to say that she was a Swedish woman. She never told me where she was born. She said that she was married, and that her husband and children were drowned in the Princess Alice.
Coroner When did you last see her alive? Last Saturday evening, at half-past six o'clock.
Coroner Where was she then? With me in a public house, called the Queen's Head, in Commercial Street.

Coroner Did she leave you there? She went back with me to the lodging-house. At that time she had no bonnet or cloak on. She never told me what her husband was.
Coroner where did you actually leave her? She went into the kitchen, and I went to another part of the building.
Coroner Did you see her again? No, until I saw the body in the mortuary to day.
Coroner you are quite certain it is the body of the same woman? Quite sure. I recognise, beside the features that the roof of her mouth is missing. Deceased accounted for this by stating that she was in the Princess Alice when it went down, and that her mouth was injured.

Coroner How long had she been staying at the lodging-house? She was there last week only on Thursday and Friday nights.
Coroner Had she paid for her bed on Saturday night? No.

Coroner Do you know any of her male acquaintances? Only of one.
Coroner who is he? She was living with him. She left him on Thursday to come and stay at our house, so she told me.
Coroner Have you seen this man? I saw him last Sunday.
Detective-Inspector Reid: He is present to day.
Witness: I do not know that she was ever up at the Thames Police court, or that she suffered from epileptic fits. I am aware that she lived in Fashion Street, but not that she has ever resided at Poplar. I never heard of a sister at Red Lion Square. I never heard of any relative except her late husband and children.
Coroner What sort of a woman was she? Very quiet.
Coroner A sober woman? Yes.
Coroner Did she use to stop out late at night? Sometimes.
Coroner Do you know if she had any money? She cleaned two rooms for me on Saturday, and I paid her 6d for doing it. I do not know whether she had any other money.
Coroner Are you able to say whether the two handkerchiefs now at the mortuary belonged to the deceased? No.
Coroner Do you recognise her clothes? Yes. I recognise the long cloak, which is hanging up in the mortuary. The other clothes she had on last Saturday.
Coroner Did she ever tell you that she was afraid of any one? No.
Coroner Or that any one had ever threatened to injure her? No.
Coroner The fact of her not coming back on Saturday did not surprise you, I suppose? We took no notice of it.
Coroner what made you go to the mortuary, then? Because I was sent for. I do not recollect at what hour she came to the lodging-house last Thursday. She was wearing the long cloak then. She did not bring any parcel with her.
I do not know of any one else of the name of Long Liz. I never heard of her sister allowing her any money, nor have I heard the name of Stride mentioned in connection with her. Before last Thursday she had been away from my house about three months.
Coroner: Did you see her during that three months? Yes, frequently; sometimes once a week, and at other times almost every other day.
Coroner Did you understand what she was doing? She told me that she was at work among the Jews, and was living with a man in Fashion Street.
Coroner Could she speak English well? Yes, but she spoke Swedish also.

Coroner when she spoke English could you detect that she was a foreigner? She spoke English as well as an English woman. She did not associate much with Swedish people. I never heard of her having hurt her foot, nor of her having broken a limb in childhood. I had no doubt that she was what she represented herself to be, a Swede.

Catherine Lane: I live in Flower and Dean Street, and am a charwoman and married. My husband is a dock labourer, and is living with me at the lodging house of which the last witness is deputy. I have been there since last February. I have seen the body of the deceased at the mortuary.
Coroner: Did you recognise it? Yes, as the body of Long Liz, who lived occasionally in the lodging-house. She came there last Thursday.
Coroner Had you ever seen her before? I have known her for six or seven months. I used to see her frequently in Fashion Street, where she lived, and I have seen her at our lodging-house.

Coroner Did you speak to her last week? On Thursday and Saturday.
Coroner At what time did you see her first on Thursday? Between ten and eleven o'clock.
Coroner Did she explain why she was coming back? She said she had had a few words with the man she was living with.

Coroner when did you see her on Saturday? When she was cleaning the deputy's room.
Coroner And after that? I last saw her in the kitchen, between six and seven in the evening. She then had on a long cloak and a black bonnet.
Coroner Did she say where she was going? No. I first saw the body in the mortuary on Sunday afternoon, and I recognised it then.
Coroner Did you see her leave the lodging-house? Yes; she gave me a piece of velvet as she left, and asked me to mind it until she came back. (The velvet was produced, and proved to be a large piece, green in colour.)

Coroner Had she no place to leave it? I do not know why she asked me, as the deputy would take charge of anything. I know deceased had sixpence when she left; she showed it to me, stating that the deputy had given it to her.
Coroner Had she been drinking then? Not that I am aware of.
Coroner Do you know of any one who was likely to have injured her? No one.
Coroner Have you heard her mention any person but this man she was living with? No. I have heard her say she was a Swede, and that at one time she lived in Devonshire Street, Commercial Road never in Poplar.
Coroner Did you ever hear her speak of her husband? She said he was dead. She never said that she was afraid, or that any one had threatened her

life. I am satisfied the deceased is the same woman.
I could tell by her accent that she was a foreigner. She did not bring all her words out plainly.
Coroner Have you ever heard of her speaking to any one in her own language? Yes; with women for whom she worked. I never heard of her having a sister, or of her having left a child at her sister's door.

Charles Preston deposed: I live at No. 32, Flower and Dean Street, and I am a barber. I have been lodging at my present address for eighteen months, and have seen the deceased there. I saw the body on Sunday last, and am quite sure it is that of Long Liz.
Coroner: When did you last see her alive? On Saturday morning between six and seven o'clock.
Coroner Where was she then? In the kitchen of the lodging-house.
Coroner was she dressed to go out? Yes, and asked me for a brush to brush her clothes with, but I did not let her have one.
Coroner What was she wearing? The jacket I have seen at the mortuary, but no flowers in the breast. She had the striped silk handkerchief round her neck.
Coroner Do you happen to have seen her pocket-handkerchiefs? No.
Coroner you cannot say whether she had two? No.
Coroner Do you know anything about her? I always understood that she was born at Stockholm, and came to England in the service of a gentleman.
Coroner Did she ever tell you her age? She said once that she was thirty-five.
Coroner Did she ever tell you that she was married? Yes, and that her husband and children went down in the Princess Alice - that she had been saved while they were lost.
Coroner Did she ever state what her husband was? I have some recollection that she said he was a seafaring man, and that he had kept a coffee-house in Chrisp Street, Poplar.
Coroner Did she ever tell you that she was taken to the Thames Police court? I only remember her having been taken into custody for being drunk and disorderly at the Ten Bells public-house, Commercial- Street, one Sunday morning from four to five months ago.
Coroner Do you know of any one who was likely to have injured her? No.
Coroner Did she ever state that she was afraid of any one? Never.
Coroner Did she say where she was going on Saturday? No.
Coroner or when she was coming back? No.
Coroner Did she say whether she was coming back? She never said anything about it. She always gave me to understand that her name was

Elizabeth Stride. She never mentioned any sister. She stated that her mother was still alive in Sweden. She apparently spoke Swedish fluently to people who came into the lodging-house.

Michael Kidney I live at No. 38, Dorset Street, Spitalfields, and am a waterside labourer. I have seen the body of the deceased at the mortuary.

Coroner: Is it the woman you have been living with? Yes.
Coroner you have no doubt about it? No doubt whatever.
Coroner What was her name? Elizabeth Stride.
Coroner How long have you known her? About three years.
Coroner How long has she been living with you? Nearly all that time.
Coroner what was her age? Between thirty-six and thirty-eight years.
Coroner Was she a Swede? She told me that she was a Swede, and I have no doubt she was. She said she was born three miles from Stockholm, that her father was a farmer, and that she first came to England for the purpose of seeing the country; but I have grave doubts about that. She afterwards told me that she came to England in a situation with a family.

Coroner Had she got any relatives in England? When I met her she told me she was a widow, and that her husband had been a ship's carpenter at Sheerness.

Coroner Did he ever keep a coffee-house? She told me that he had.
Coroner Where? In Chrisp Street, Poplar.
Coroner Did she say when he died? She informed me that he was drowned in the Princess Alice disaster.

Coroner was the roof of her mouth defective? Yes.
Coroner you had a quarrel with her on Thursday? I did not see her on Thursday.

Coroner when did you last see her? On the Tuesday, and I then left her on friendly terms in Commercial- Street. That was between nine and ten o'clock at night, as I was coming from work.

Coroner Did you expect her home? I expected her home half an hour afterwards. I subsequently ascertained that she had been in and had gone out again, and I did not see her again alive.

Coroner Can you account for her sudden disappearance? Was she the worse for drink when you last saw her? She was perfectly sober.

Coroner you can assign no reason whatever for her going away so suddenly? She would occasionally go away.

Coroner Oh, she has left you before? During the three years I have known her she has been away from me about five months altogether.

Coroner: Without any reason? Not to my knowledge. I treated her the same as I would a wife.

Coroner: Do you know whether she had picked up with any one? I have seen the address of the brother of the gentleman with whom she lived as a servant, somewhere near Hyde Park, but I cannot find it now.

Coroner: Did she have any reason for going away? It was drink that made her go on previous occasions. She always came back again. I think she liked me better than any other man. I do not believe she left me on Tuesday to take up with any other man.

Coroner: Had she any money? I do not think she was without a shilling when she left me. From what I used to give her I fancy she must either have had money or spent it in drink.

Coroner: you know of nobody whom she was likely to have complications with or fall foul of? No, but I think the police authorities are very much to blame, or they would have got the man who murdered her. At Leman Street Police station, on Monday night, I asked for a detective to give information to get the man.

Coroner: what information had you? I could give information that would enable the detectives to discover the man at any time.

Coroner: then will you give us your information now? I told the inspector on duty at the police station that I could give information provided he would let me have a young, strange detective to act on it, and he would not give me one.

Coroner What do you think should be inquired into? I might have given information that would have led to a great deal if I had been provided with a strange young detective.

Inspector Reid: When you went to Leman Street and saw the inspector on duty, were you intoxicated?

Yes; I asked for a young detective, and he would not let me have one, and I told him that he was uncivil. (Laughter.)

Coroner you have been in the army, and I believe have a good pension? Only the reserve.

A Juror: Have you got any information for a detective? - I am a great lover of discipline, sir. (Laughter.)

Coroner: Had you any information that required the service of a detective?

Yes. I thought that if I had one, privately, he could get more information than I could myself. The parties I obtained my information from knew me, and I thought someone else would be able to derive more from them.

Inspector Reid: Will you give me the information directly, if you will not give it to the coroner? I believe I could catch the man if I had a detective under my command.

Coroner: You cannot expect that. I have had over a hundred letters making suggestions, and I dare say all the writers would like to have a detective at their service. (Laughter.)

Witness: I have information which I think might be of use to the police.

Coroner: You had better give it, then.

Witness: I believe that, if I could place the policeman myself, the man would be captured.

Coroner: You must know that the police would not be placed at the disposal of a man the worse for drink.

Witness: If I were at liberty to place 100 men about this city the murderer would be caught in the act.

Inspector Reid: But you have no information to give to the police?

Witness: No, I will keep it to myself.

A Juror: Do you know of any sister who gave money to the deceased? No. On Monday I saw Mrs. Malcolm, who said the deceased was her sister. She is very like the deceased.

Coroner did the deceased have a child by you? No.

Coroner Or by a policeman?

She told me that a policeman used to court her when she was at Hyde Park, before she was married to Stride. Stride and the policeman courted her at the same time, but I never heard of her having a child by the policeman. She said she was the mother of nine children, two of whom were drowned with her husband in the Princess Alice, and the remainder were either in a school belonging to the Swedish Church on the other side of London Bridge, or with the husband's friends. I thought she was telling the truth when she spoke of Swedish people. I understood that the deceased and her husband were employed on the Princess Alice.

Mr. Edward Johnson: I live at 100, Commercial Road, and I am assistant to Drs. Kaye and Blackwell. On Sunday morning last, at a few minutes past one o'clock, I received a call from Constable 436 H. after informing Dr. Blackwell, who was in bed, of the case. I accompanied the officer to Berner Street, and in a courtyard adjoining No. 40 I was shown the figure of a woman lying on her left side.

Coroner: Were there many people about? There was a crowd in the yard.

Coroner And police? Yes.

Coroner was any one touching the deceased? No.

Coroner was there much light? Very little.

Coroner what light there was, where did it come from? From the policeman's lantern. I examined the woman and found an incision in the throat.

Coroner was blood coming from the wound? No, it had stopped bleeding. I felt the body and found all warm except the hands, which were quite cold.

Coroner Did you undo the dress? The dress was not undone when I came. I undid it to see if the chest was warm.

Coroner Did you move the head at all? I left the body precisely as I found it. There was a stream of blood down to the gutter; it was all clotted. There was very little blood near the neck; it had all run away. I did not notice at the time that one of the hands was smeared with blood. The left arm was bent, away from the body. The right arm was also bent, and across the body.

Coroner Can you say whether any one had stepped into the stream of blood? There was no mark of it.

Coroner Did you look for any? Yes. I had no watch with me, but Dr. Blackwell looked at his when he arrived, and the time was 1.16 a.m. I preceded him by three or four minutes. The bonnet of the deceased was lying three or four inches beyond the head on the ground. The outer gates were closed shortly after I came.

Thomas Coram: I live at No. 67, Plummer's Road, and work for a coconut dealer. On Monday shortly after midnight I left a friend's house in Bath Gardens, Brady Street. I walked straight down Brady Street and into Whitechapel Road towards Aldgate. I first walked on the right side of Whitechapel Road, and afterwards crossed over to the left, and when opposite No. 253 I saw a knife lying on the doorstep.

Coroner what is No. 253?

Witness: A laundry. There were two steps to the front door, and the knife was on the bottom step. The production of the knife created some sensation, its discovery not having been generally known. It was a knife such as would be used by a baker in his trade, it being flat at the top instead of pointed, as a butcher's knife would be. The blade, which was discoloured with something resembling blood, was quite a foot long and an inch broad, whilst the black handle was six inches in length, and strongly riveted in three places. There was a handkerchief round the handle of the knife, the handkerchief having been first folded and then twisted round the blade. A policeman coming towards me, I called his attention to the knife, which I did not touch.

Coroner Did the policeman take the knife away? **Witness:** Yes, to the Leman Street station, I accompanying him.

Coroner Were there many people passing at the time? Very few. I do not think I passed more than a dozen from Brady Street to where I found the knife. The weapon could easily be seen; it was light there.

Coroner Did you pass any policeman between Brady Street and where the knife was? I passed three policemen.

Constable Joseph Drage, 282 H Division: On Monday morning at halfpast twelve o'clock I was on fixed point duty opposite Brady street, Whitechapel road, when I saw the last witness stooping down to pick up something about twenty yards from me. As I went towards him he beckoned with his finger, and said, "Policeman, there is a knife lying here." I then saw a long-bladed knife on the doorstep. I picked up the knife, and found it was smothered with blood.

Coroner was it wet?

Dry. A handkerchief, which was also bloodstained, was bound round the handle and tied with a string. I asked the lad how he came to see it, and he said, "I was just looking around, and I saw something white." I asked him what he did out so late, and he replied, "I have been to a friend's in Bath gardens." I took down his name and address, and he went to the police station with me. The knife and handkerchief are those produced. The boy was sober, and his manner natural. He said that the knife made his blood run cold, adding, "We hear of such funny things nowadays." I had passed the step a quarter of an hour before. I could not be positive, but I do not think the knife was there then. About an hour earlier I stood near the door, and saw the landlady let out a woman. The knife was not there then. I handed the knife and handkerchief to Dr. Phillips on Monday afternoon.

Mr. George Baxter Phillips: I live at No. 2, Spital square, and am surgeon of the H Division of police. I was called on Sunday morning last at twenty past one to Leman-street Police station, and was sent on to Berner street, to a yard at the side of what proved to be a club-house. I found Inspector Pinhorn and Acting-Superintendent West in possession of a body, which had already been seen by Dr. Blackwell, who had arrived some time before me. The body was lying on its left side, the face being turned towards the wall, the head towards the yard, and the feet toward the street. The left arm was extended from elbow, and a packet of cachous was in the hand. Similar ones were in the gutter. I took them from the hand and gave them to Dr. Blackwell. The right arm was lying over the body, and the back of the hand and wrist had on them clotted blood. The legs were drawn up, feet close to wall, body still warm, face warm, hands cold, legs quite warm, silk handkerchief round throat, slightly torn (so is my note, but I since find it is cut). I produce the handkerchief. This corresponded to the right angle of the jaw. The throat was deeply gashed, and there was an abrasion of the skin, about an inch and a quarter in diameter, under the right clavicle. On Oct. 1, at three p.m., at St. George's Mortuary, present Dr. Blackwell and for part of the time Dr. Reigate and Dr. Blackwell's assistant; temperature being about 55 degrees, Dr. Blackwell and I made a post-mortem examination, Dr. Blackwell kindly consenting to make the dissection, and I took the following note: "Rigor mortis still firmly marked. Mud on face and left side of the head. Matted on the hair and left side. We removed the clothes. We found the body fairly nourished. Over both shoulders, especially the right, from the front aspect under collarbones and in front of chest there is a bluish discoloration, which I have watched and seen on two occasions since. On neck, from left to right, there is a clean cut incision six inches in length; incision commencing two and a half inches in a straight line below the angle of the jaw. Three-quarters of an inch over undivided muscle, then becoming deeper, about an inch dividing sheath and the vessels, ascending a little, and then grazing the muscle outside the cartilage's on the left side of the neck. The carotid artery on the left side and the other vessels contained in the sheath were all cut through, save the posterior portion of the carotid, to a line about 1-12th of an inch in extent, which prevented the separation of the upper and lower portion of the artery. The cut through the tissues on the right side of the cartilages is more superficial, and tails off to about two inches below the right angle of the jaw. It is evident that the haemorrhage, which produced death, was caused through the partial severance of the left carotid artery. There is a deformity in the lower fifth of the bones of the right leg, which are not straight, but bow forward; there is a thickening above the left ankle. The bones are here straighter. No recent external injuries save to neck. The lower lobe of the ear was torn, as if by the forcible removing or wearing through of an earring, but it was thoroughly healed. The right ear was pierced for an earring, but had not been so injured, and the earring was wanting. On removing the scalp there was no sign of bruising or extravasation of blood between it and the skullcap. The skull was about one-sixth of an inch in thickness, and dense in texture. The brain was fairly normal. Both lungs were unusually pale. The heart was small; left ventricle firmly contracted, right less so. Right ventricles full of dark clot; left absolutely empty. Partly digested food, apparently consisting of cheese, potato, and farinaceous edibles. Teeth on left lower jaw absent." On Tuesday, at the mortuary, I found the total circumference of the neck 12« inches. I found in the pocket of the underskirt of the deceased a key, as of a padlock. A small piece of lead pencil, a comb, a broken piece of comb, a metal spoon, half a dozen large and one small button, a hook, as if off a dress, a piece of muslin, and one or two small pieces of paper. Examining her jacket I found that although there was a slight amount of mud on the right side, the left was well plastered with mud.

A Juror: You have not mentioned anything about the roof of the mouth. One witness said part of the roof of the mouth was gone.

Witness: That was not noticed.

Coroner: What was the cause of death? Undoubtedly the loss of blood from the left carotid artery and the division of the windpipe.

Coroner Did you examine the blood at Berner Street carefully, as to its direction and so forth? Yes.

Coroner The blood near to the neck and a few inches to the left side was well clotted, and it had run down the waterway to within a few inches of the side entrance to the club-house.

Coroner Were there any spots of blood anywhere else? I could trace none except that which I considered had been transplanted if I may use the term from the original flow from the neck. Roughly estimating it, I should say there was an unusual flow of blood, considering the stature and the nourishment of the body.

By a Juror: I did notice a black mark on one of the legs of the deceased, but could not say that it was due to an adder bite.

Before the witness had concluded his evidence the inquiry was adjourned until Friday, at two o'clock.

Day 4, Monday, October 5, 1888
(*The Daily Telegraph*, Saturday, October 6, 1888, Page 3)

Yesterday [5 Oct] afternoon at the Vestry Hall of St. George in the East, Cable Street, Mr. Wynne E. Baxter, coroner for East Middlesex, resumed the inquiry concerning the death of the woman who was found early on Sunday last with her throat cut, in a yard adjoining the International Working Men's Club, Berner Street, Commercial Road East.

Dr. Phillips, surgeon of the H Division of police, being recalled. On the last occasion I was requested to make a re-examination of the body of the deceased, especially with regard to the palate, and I have since done so at the mortuary, along with Dr. Blackwell and Dr. Gordon Brown. I did not find any injury to, or absence of, any part of either the hard or the soft palate. The Coroner also desired me to examine the two handkerchiefs, which were found on the deceased. I did not discover any blood on them, and I believe that the stains on the larger handkerchief are those of fruit. Neither on the hands nor about the body of the deceased did I find grapes, or connection with them. I am convinced that the deceased had not swallowed either the skin or seed of a grape within many hours of her death. I have stated that the neckerchief, which she had on, was not torn, but cut. The abrasion which I spoke of on the right side of the neck was only apparently an abrasion, for on washing it it was removed, and the skin found to be uninjured. The knife produced on the last occasion was delivered to me, properly secured, by a constable, and on examination I found it to be such a knife as is used in a chandler's shop, and is called a slicing knife. It has blood upon it, which has characteristics similar to the blood of a human being. It has been recently blunted, and its edge apparently turned by rubbing on a stone such as a kerbstone. It evidently was before a very sharp knife.

Coroner: Is it such as knife as could have caused the injuries, which were inflicted upon the deceased? Such a knife could have produced the incision and injuries to the neck, but it is not such a weapon as I should have fixed upon as having caused the injuries in this case; and if my opinion as regards the position of the body is correct, the knife in question would become an improbable instrument as having caused the incision.

Coroner what is your idea as to the position the body was in when the crime was committed? I have come to a conclusion as to the position of both the murderer and the victim, and I opine that the latter was seized by the shoulders and placed on the ground, and that the murderer was on her right side when he inflicted the cut. I am of opinion that the cut was made from the left to the right side of the deceased, and taking into account the position of the incision it is unlikely that such a long knife inflicted the wound in the neck.

Coroner the knife produced on the last occasion was not sharp pointed, was it? No, it was rounded at the tip, which was about an inch across. The blade was wider at the base.

Coroner was there anything to indicate that the cut on the neck of the deceased was made with a pointed knife? Nothing.

Coroner Have you formed any opinion as to the manner in which the deceased's right hand became stained with blood? It is a mystery. There were small oblong clots on the back of the hand. I may say that I am taking it as a fact that after death the hand always remained in the position in which I found it - across the body.

Coroner How long had the woman been dead when you arrived at the scene of the murder, do you think? Within an hour she had been alive.

Coroner Would the injury take long to inflict? Only a few seconds - it might be done in two seconds.

Coroner Does the presence of the cachous in the left hand indicate that the murder was committed very suddenly and without any struggle? Some of the cachous were scattered about the yard.

Foreman: Do you not think that the woman would have dropped the packet of cachous altogether if she had been thrown to the ground before the injuries were inflicted?

That is an inference, which the jury would be perfectly entitled to draw. **Coroner:** I assume that the injuries were not self-inflicted? I have seen several self-inflicted wounds more extensive than this one, but then they have not usually involved the carotid artery. In this case, as in some others, there seems to have been some knowledge where to cut the throat to cause a fatal result.

Coroner is there any similarity between this case and Annie Chapman's case? There is very great dissimilarity between the two. In Chapman's case the neck was severed all round down to the vertebral column, the vertebral bones being marked with two sharp cuts, and there had been an evident attempt to separate the bones.

Coroner From the position you assume the perpetrator to have been in, would he have been likely to get bloodstained?

Not necessarily, for the commencement of the wound and the injury to the vessels would be away from him, and the stream of blood for stream it was would be directed away from him, and towards the gutter in the yard. **Coroner** was there any appearance of an opiate or any smell of chloroform? There was no perceptible trace of any anaesthetic or narcotic. The absence of noise is a difficult question under the circumstances of this case to account for, but it must not be taken for granted that there was not any noise. If there was an absence of noise I cannot account for it.

The Foreman: That means that the woman might cry out after the cut? Not after the cut.

Coroner But why did she not cry out while she was being put on the ground? She was in a yard, and in a locality where she might cry out very loudly and no notice be taken of her. It was possible for the woman to draw up her legs after the wound, but she could not have turned over. The wound was inflicted by drawing the knife across the throat. A short knife, such as a shoemaker's well-ground knife, would do the same thing. My reason for believing that deceased was injured when on the ground was partly on account of the absence of blood anywhere on the left side of the body and between it and the wall.

A Juror: Was there any trace of malt liquor in the stomach? There was no trace.

Dr. Blackwell [recalled] (who assisted in making the post-mortem examination) said: I can confirm Dr. Phillips as to the appearances at the mortuary. I may add that I removed the cachous from the left hand of the deceased, which was nearly open. The packet was lodged between the thumb and the first finger, and was partially hidden from view. It was I who spilt them in removing them from the hand. My impression is that the hand gradually relaxed while the woman was dying, she dying in a fainting condition from the loss of blood. I do not think that I made myself quite clear as to whether it was possible for this to have been a case of suicide. What I meant to say was that, taking all the facts into consideration, more especially the absence of any instrument in the hand, it was impossible to have been a suicide. I have myself seen many equally severe wounds self-inflicted. With respect to the knife, which was found, I should like to say that I concur with Dr. Phillips in his opinion that, although it might possibly have inflicted the injury, it is an extremely unlikely instrument to have been used. It appears to me that a murderer, in using a round-pointed instrument, would seriously handicap himself, as he would be only able to use it in one particular way. I am told that slaughterers always use a sharp-pointed instrument.

The Coroner: No one has suggested that this crime was committed by a slaughterer.

Witness: I simply intended to point out the inconvenience that might arise from using a blunt-pointed weapon.

Foreman: Did you notice any marks or bruises about the shoulders?

They were what we call pressure marks. At first they were very obscure, but subsequently they became very evident. They were not what are ordinarily called bruises; neither is there any abrasion. Each shoulder was about equally marked.

A Juror: How recently might the marks have been caused? That is rather difficult to say.

Coroner Did you perceive any grapes near the body in the yard? No.

Coroner Did you hear any person say that they had seen grapes there? I did not.

Mr. Sven Ollsen deposed: I live at No. 23, Prince's Square, St. George's in the East, and am clerk of the Swedish Church there. I have examined the body of the deceased at the mortuary. I have seen her before.

Coroner: Often? Yes.

Coroner For how many years? Seventeen.

Coroner Was she a Swede? Yes.

Coroner What was her name? Her name was Elizabeth Stride, and she was the wife of John Thomas Stride, carpenter. Her maiden name was Elizabeth Gustafdotter. She was born at Torlands, near Gothenburg, on Nov. 27, 1843.

Coroner How do you get these facts? From the register at our church. Do you keep a register of all the members of your church?

Coroner Of course. We register those who come into this country bringing a certificate and desiring to be registered.

Coroner when was she registered? Her registry is dated July 10, 1866, and she was then registered as an unmarried woman.

Coroner was she married at your church? No.

Coroner Then how do you know she was the wife of John Thomas Stride? In the registry I find a memorandum, undated, in the handwriting of the Rev. Mr, Palmayer, in Swedish, that she was married to an Englishman named John Thos. Stride. This registry is a new one, and copied from an older book. I have seen the original, and Mr. Frost, our pastor wrote it, until two years ago. I know the Swedish hymnbook produced dated 1821. I gave it to the deceased.

Coroner When? Last winter, I think.

Coroner Do you know when she was married to Stride? I think it was in 1869.

Coroner Do you know when he died? No. She told me about the time the Princess Alice went down that her husband was drowned in that vessel.

Coroner was she in good circumstances then? - She was very poor.

Coroner Then she would have been glad of any assistance? Yes.

Coroner Did you give her some? I did about that time.

Coroner Do you remember that there was a subscription raised for the relatives of the sufferers by the Princess Alice? No.

Coroner I can tell you that there was, and I can tell you another thing - that no person of the name of Stride made any application. If her story had been true, don't you think she would have applied? I do not know.

Coroner Have you any schools connected with the Swedish Church? No, not in London.

Coroner did not ever hear that this woman had any children? I do not remember.

Coroner Did you ever see her husband? No.

Coroner Did your church ever assist her before her husband died? Yes, I think so; just before he died.

Coroner where has she been living lately? I have nothing to show. Two years ago she gave her address as Devonshire Street, Commercial Road.

Coroner Did she then explain what she was doing? Pretty well.

Coroner Do you know when she came to England? I believe a little before the register was made, in 1866.

William Marshall, examined by the Coroner, said: I reside at No. 64, Berner Street, and am a labourer at an indigo warehouse. I have seen the body at the mortuary. I saw the deceased on Saturday night last.

Coroner Where? In our street, three doors from my house, about a quarter to twelve o'clock. She was on the pavement, opposite No. 58, between Fairclough Street and Boyd Street.

Coroner What was she doing? She was standing talking to a man.

Coroner how do you know this was the same woman? I recognise her both by her face and dress. She did not then have a flower in her breast.

Coroner Were the man and woman whom you saw talking quietly? They were talking together.

Coroner Can you describe the man at all? There was no gas-lamp near. The nearest was at the corner, about twenty feet off. I did not see the face of the man distinctly.

Coroner Did you notice how he was dressed? In a black cut-away coat and dark trousers.

Coroner was he young or old? Middle-aged he seemed to be.

Coroner was he wearing a hat? No, a cap.

Coroner What sort of a cap? A round cap, with a small peak. It was something like what a sailor would About 5ft. 6in.

Coroner Was he thin or stout? Rather stout.

Coroner Did he look well dressed? Decently dressed.

Coroner What class of man did he appear to be? I should say he was in business, and did nothing like hard work.

Coroner not like a dock labourer? No.

Coroner Nor a sailor? No.

Coroner Nor a butcher? No.

Coroner A clerk? He had more the appearance of a clerk.

Coroner is that the best suggestion you can make? It is.

Coroner you did not see his face. Had he any whiskers? I cannot say. I do not think he had.

Coroner was he wearing gloves? No.

Coroner was he carrying a stick or umbrella in his hands? He had nothing in his hands that I am aware of.

Coroner you are quite sure that the deceased is the woman you saw? Quite. I did not take much notice whether she was carrying anything in her hands.

Coroner What first attracted your attention to the couple? By their standing there for some time, and he was kissing her.

Coroner Did you overhear anything they said? I heard him say, "You would say anything but your prayers."

Coroner Different people talk in a different tone and in a different way. Did his voice give you the idea of a clerk? Yes, he was mild speaking.

Coroner Did he speak like an educated man? I thought so. I did not hear them say anything more. They went away after that. I did not hear the woman say anything, but after the man made that observation she laughed. They went away down the street, towards Ellen-street. They would not then pass No. 40 (the club).

Coroner how was the woman dressed? In a black jacket and skirt.

Coroner was either the worse for drink? No, I thought not.

Coroner When did you go indoors? About twelve o'clock.

Coroner Did you hear anything more that night? - Not till I heard that the murder had taken place, just after one o'clock. While I was standing at my door, from half-past eleven to twelve, there was no rain at all. The deceased had on a small black bonnet. The couple was standing between my house and the club for about ten minutes.

Detective-Inspector Reid: Then they passed you? Yes.

A Juror: Did you not see the man's face as he passed? No; he was looking towards the woman, and had his arm round her neck. There is a gas lamp at the corner of Boyd Street. It was not closing time when they passed me.

James Brown: I live in Fairclough Street, and am a dock labourer. I have seen the body in the mortuary. I did not know deceased, but I saw her about a quarter to one on Sunday morning last.

Coroner: Where were you? I was going from my house to the chandler's shop at the corner of the Berner Street and Fairclough Street, to get some supper. I stayed there three or four minutes, and then went back home, when I saw a man and woman standing at the corner of the Board School. I was in the road just by the kerb, and they were near the wall.
Coroner Did you see enough to make you certain that the deceased was the woman? I am almost certain.
Coroner Did you notice any flower in her dress? No.
Coroner What were they doing? He was standing with his arm against the wall; she was inclined towards his arm and with her back to the wall.
Coroner Did you notice the man? I saw that he had a long dark coat on.
Coroner An overcoat? Yes; it seemed so.
Coroner Had he a hat or a cap on? I cannot say.
Coroner you are sure it was not her dress that you chiefly noticed? Yes. I saw nothing light in colour about either of them.

Coroner was it raining at the time? No. I went on.
Coroner Did you hear anything more? When I had nearly finished my supper I heard screams of "Murder" and "Police." This was a quarter of an hour after I had got home. I did not look at any clock at the chandler's shop. I arrived home first at ten minutes past twelve o'clock, and I believe it was not raining then.
Coroner Did you notice the height of the man? I should think he was 5ft. 7in.
Coroner Was he thin or stout? He was of average build.
Coroner Did either of them seem the worse for drink? No.
Coroner Did you notice whether either spoke with a foreign accent? I did not notice any. When I heard screams I opened my window, but could not

see anybody. The cries were of moving people going in the direction of Grove Street. Shortly afterwards I saw a policeman standing at the corner of Christian Street, and a man called him to Berner Street.

William Smith, 452 H Division: On Saturday last I went on duty at ten p.m. My beat was past Berner Street, and would take me twenty-five minutes or half an hour to go round. I was in Berner Street about half-past twelve or twenty-five minutes to one o'clock, and having gone round my beat, was at the Commercial Road corner of Berner Street again at one o'clock. I was not called. I saw a crowd outside the gates of No. 40, Berner Street. I heard no cries of "Police." When I came to the spot two constables had already arrived. The gates at the side of the club were not then closed. I do not remember that I passed any person on my way down. I saw that the woman was dead, and I went to the police station for the ambulance, leaving the other constables in charge of the body. Dr. Blackwell's assistant arrived just as I was going away.

Coroner: Had you noticed any man or woman in Berner Street when you were there before? Yes, talking together.

Coroner was the woman anything like the deceased? Yes. I saw her face, and I think the body at the mortuary is that of the same woman.

Coroner Are you certain? I feel certain. She stood on the pavement a few yards from where the body was found, but on the opposite side of the street.

Coroner Did you look at the man at all? Yes.

Coroner What did you notice about him? He had a parcel wrapped in a newspaper in his hand. The parcel was about 18in. Long and 6in. to 8in. broad.

Coroner Did you notice his height? He was about 5ft. 7in.

Coroner His hat? He wore a dark felt deerstalker's hat.

Coroner Clothes? His clothes were dark. The coat was a cutaway coat.

Coroner Did you overhear any conversation? No.

Coroner Did they seem to be sober? Yes, both.

Coroner Did you see the man's face?

He had no whiskers, but I did not notice him much. I should say he was twenty-eight years of age. He was of respectable appearance, but I could not state what he was. The woman had a flower in her breast. It rained very little after eleven o'clock. There were but few about in the bye streets. When I saw the body at the mortuary I recognised it at once.

Michael Kidney, the man with whom the deceased last lived, being recalled stated: I recognise the Swedish hymnbook produced as one belonging to the deceased. She used to have it at my place. I found it in the next room to the one I occupy in Mrs. Smith's room. Mrs Smith said deceased gave it to her when she left last Tuesday not as a gift, but to take care of. When deceased and I lived together I put a padlock on the door when we left the house. I had the key, but deceased has got in and out when I have been away. I found she had been there during my absence on Wednesday of last week - the day after she left - and taken some things.

Coroner what made you think there was anything the matter with the roof of her mouth? She told me so.

Coroner Have you ever examined it? No.

Coroner Well, the doctors say there is nothing the matter with it? Well, I only know what she told me.

Philip Krantz (who affirmed) deposed: I live at 40, Berner Street, and am editor of the Hebrew paper called "The Worker's Friend." I work in a room forming part of the printing office at the back of the International Working Men's Club. Last Saturday night I was in my room from nine o'clock until one of the members of the club came and told me that there was a woman lying in the yard.

Coroner Had you heard any sound up to that time? No.

Coroner any cry? No.

Coroner Or scream? No.

Coroner Or anything unusual? No.

Coroner was your window or door open? No.

Coroner supposing a woman had screamed, would you have heard it? They were singing in the club, so I might not have heard. When I heard the alarm I went out and saw the deceased, but did not observe any stranger there.

Coroner Did you look to see if anybody was about anybody who might have committed the murder? I did look. I went out to the gates, and found that some members of the club had gone for the police.

Coroner Do you think it possible that any stranger escaped from the yard while you were there? No, but he might have done so before I came. I was afterwards searched and examined at the club.

Constable Albert Collins, 12 H. R., stated that by order of the doctors, he, at half-past five o'clock on Sunday morning, washed away the blood caused by the murder.

Detective-Inspector Reid said: I received a telegram at 1.25 on Sunday morning last at Commercial Street Police office. I at once proceeded to No. 40, Berner Street, where I saw several police officers, Drs. Phillips and Blackwell, and a number of residents in the yard and persons who had come there and been shut in by the police. At that time Drs. Phillips and Blackwell were examining the throat of the deceased. A thorough search was made by the police of the yard and the houses in it, but no trace could be found of any person who might have committed the murder. As soon as the search was over the whole of the persons who had come into the yard and the members of the club were interrogated, their names and addresses taken, their pockets searched by the police, and their clothes and hands examined by the doctors. The people were twenty-eight in number. Each was dealt with separately, and they properly accounted for themselves. The houses were inspected a second time and the occupants examined and there rooms searched. A loft close by was searched, but no trace could be found of the murderer. A description was taken of the body, and circulated by wire around the stations. Inquiries were made at the different houses in the street, but no person could be found who had heard screams or disturbance during the night. I examined the wall near where the body was found, but could detect no spots of blood. About half-past four the body was removed to the mortuary. Having given information of the murder to the coroner I returned to the yard and made another examination and found that the blood had been removed. It being daylight I searched the walls thoroughly, but could discover no marks of their having been scaled. I then went to the mortuary and took a description of the deceased and her clothing as follows: Aged forty-two; length 5ft. 2in; complexion pale; hair dark brown and curly; eyes light grey; front upper teeth gone. The deceased had on an old black skirt, dark-brown velvet body, a long black jacket trimmed with black fur, fastened on the right side, with a red rose backed by a maidenhair fern. She had two light serge petticoats, white stockings, and white chemise with insertion, side-spring boots, and black crape bonnet. In her jacket pocket were two handkerchiefs, a thimble, and a piece of wool on a card. That description was circulated. Since then the police have made a house-to-house inquiry in the immediate neighbourhood, with the result that we have been able to produce the witnesses who have appeared before the Court. The investigation is still going on. Every endeavour is being made to arrest the assassin, but up to the present without success.

The inquiry was adjourned to Tuesday fortnight, at two o'clock.

Day 5, Tuesday, October 23, 1888
(*The Times*, October 24, 1888)

Yesterday afternoon [23 Oct] Mr. Wynne E. Baxter, Coroner for the South Eastern Division of Middlesex, resumed his adjourned inquiry at the Vestry-hall, Cable Street, St. George's in the East, respecting the death of Elizabeth Stride, who was found murdered in Berner Street, St. George's, on the 30th ult.

Detective-Inspector Reid, H Division, watched the case on behalf of the Criminal Investigation Department.

Detective-Inspector Edmund Reid, recalled, said, - I have examined the books of the Poplar and Stepney Sick Asylum, and find therein the entry of the death of John Thomas William Stride, a carpenter, of Poplar. His death took place on the 24th day of October, 1884. Witness then said that he had found Mrs. Watts, who would give evidence.

Constable Walter Stride stated that he recognised the deceased by the photograph as the person who married his uncle, John Thomas Stride, in 1872 or 1873. His uncle was a carpenter, and the last time witness saw him he was living in the East India Dock Road, Poplar.

Elizabeth Stokes, 5, Charles Street, Tottenham, said, - My husband's name is Joseph Stokes, and he is a brickmaker. My first husband's name was Watts, a wine merchant of Bath. Mrs. Mary Malcolm, of 15, Eagle Street, Red Lion Square, Holborn, is my sister. I have received an anonymous letter from Shepton Mallet, saying my first husband is alive. I want to clear my character. My sister I have not seen for years. She has given me a dreadful character. Her evidence is all false. I have five brothers and sisters.
A Juryman. Perhaps she refers to another sister.
Inspector Reid. - She identified the deceased person as her sister, and said she had a crippled foot. This witness has a crippled foot.
Witness. This has put me to a dreadful trouble and trial. I have only a poor crippled husband, who is now outside. It is a shame my sister should say what she has said about me, and that the innocent should suffer for the guilty.
Coroner. Is Mrs. Malcolm here?
Inspector Reid. No, Sir.

Coroner, in summing up, said the jury would probably agree with him that it would be unreasonable to adjourn this inquiry again on the chance of something further being ascertained to elucidate the mysterious case on which they had devoted so much time. The first difficulty which presented itself was the identification of the deceased. That was not an unimportant matter. Their trouble was principally occasioned by Mrs. Malcolm, who, after some hesitation, and after having had two further opportunities of viewing again the body, positively swore that the deceased was her sister Mrs. Elizabeth Watts, of Bath. It had since been clearly proved that she was mistaken, notwithstanding the visions which were simultaneously vouchsafed at the hour of the death to her and her husband. If her evidence was correct, there were points of resemblance between the deceased and Elizabeth Watts which almost reminded one of the Comedy of Errors. Both had been courted by policemen; they both bore the same Christian name, and were of the same age; both lived with sailors; both at one time kept coffee-houses at Poplar; both were nick-named "Long Liz;" both were said to have had children in charge of their husbands' friends; both were given to drink; both lived in East-end common lodging houses; both had been charged at the Thames Police court; both had escaped punishment on the ground that they were subject to epileptic fits, although the friends of both were certain that this was a fraud; both had lost their front teeth, and both had been leading very questionable lives. Whatever might be the true explanation of this marvellous similarity, it appeared to be pretty satisfactorily proved that the deceased was Elizabeth Stride, and that about the year 1869 she was married to a carpenter named John Thomas Stride. Unlike the other victims in the series of crimes in this neighbourhood a district teeming with representatives of all nations she was not an Englishwoman. She was born in Sweden in the year 1843, but, having resided in this country for upwards of 22 years, she could speak English fluently and without much foreign accent. At one time the deceased and her husband kept a coffee-house in Poplar. At another time she was staying in Devonshire-street, Commercial-road, supporting herself, it was said, by sewing and charring. On and off for the last six years she lived in a common lodging-house in the notorious lane called Flower and Dean Street. She was there known only by the nickname of "Long Liz," and often told a tale, which might have been apocryphal, of her husband and children having gone down with the Princess Alice. The deputy of the lodging-house stated that while with her she was a quiet and sober woman, although she used at times to stay out late at night - an offence very venial, he suspected, among those who frequented the establishment. For the last two years the deceased had been living at a common lodging-house in Dorset Street, Spitalfields, with Michael Kidney, a waterside labourer, belonging to the Army Reserve. But at intervals during that period, amounting altogether to about five months, she left him without any apparent reason, except a desire to be free from the restraint even of that connection, and to obtain greater opportunity of indulging her drinking habits. She was last seen alive by Kidney in Commercial Street on the evening of Tuesday, September 25. She was sober, but never returned home that night. She alleged that she had some words with her paramour, but this he denied. The next day she called during his absence, and took away some things, but, with this exception, they did not know what became of her until the following Thursday, when she made her appearance at her old quarters in Flower and Dean Street. Here she remained until Saturday, September 29. On that day she cleaned the deputy's rooms, and received a small remuneration for her trouble. Between 6 and 7 o'clock on that evening she was in the kitchen wearing the jacket, bonnet, and striped silk neckerchief which were afterwards found on her. She had at least 6d. in her possession, which was possibly spent during the evening. Before leaving she gave a piece of velvet to a friend to take care of until her return, but she said neither where she was going nor when she would return. She had not paid for her lodgings, although she was in a position to do so. They knew nothing of her movements during the next four or five hours at least - possibly not till the finding of her lifeless body. But three witnesses spoke to having seen a woman that they identified as the deceased with more or less certainty, and at times within an hour and a-quarter of the period when, and at places within 100 yards of the spot where she was ultimately found. William Marshall, who lived at 64, Berner Street, was standing at his doorway from half-past 11 till midnight. About a quarter to 12 o'clock he saw the deceased talking to a man between Fairclough-Street and Boyd Street. There was every demonstration of affection by the man during the ten minutes they stood together, and when last seen, strolling down the road towards Ellen Street, his arms were round her neck. At 12 30 p.m. the constable on the beat (William Smith) saw the deceased in Berner Street standing on the pavement a few yards from Commercial Street, and he observed she was wearing a flower in her dress. A quarter of an hour afterwards James Brown, of Fairclough Street, passed the deceased close to the Board school. A man was at her side leaning against the wall, and the deceased was heard to say, "Not to-night, but some other night." Now, if this evidence was to be relied on, it would appear that the deceased was in the company of a man for upwards of an hour immediately before her death, and that within a quarter of an hour of her being found a corpse she was refusing her companion something in the immediate neighbourhood of where she met her death. But was this the deceased? And even if it were, was it one and the same man who was seen in her company on three different occasions? With regard to the identity of the woman, Marshall had the opportunity of watching her for ten minutes while standing talking in the street at a short distance from him and she afterwards passed close to him. The constable feels certain that the woman he observed was the deceased, and when he afterwards was called to the scene of the crime he at once recognised her and made a statement; while Brown was almost certain that the deceased was the woman to whom his attention was attracted. It might be thought that the frequency of the occurrence of men and women being seen together under similar circumstances might have led to mistaken identity; but the police stated, and several of the witnesses corroborated the statement, that although many couples are to be seen at night in the Commercial Road, it was exceptional to meet them in Berner Street. With regard to the man seen, there were many points of similarity, but some of dissimilarity, in the descriptions of the three witnesses; but these discrepancies did not conclusively prove that there was more than one man in the company of the deceased, for every day's experience showed how facts were differently observed and differently described by honest and intelligent witnesses. Brown, who saw least in consequence of the darkness of the spot at which the two were standing, agreed with Smith that his clothes were dark and that his height was about 5ft. 7in., but he appeared to him to be wearing an overcoat nearly down to his heels; while the description of Marshall accorded with that of Smith in every respect but two. They agreed that he was respectably dressed in a black cut away coat and dark trousers, and that he was of middle age and without whiskers. On the other hand, they differed with regard to what he was wearing on his head. Smith stated he wore a hard felt deerstalker of dark colour; Marshall that he was wearing a round cap with a small peak, like a sailor's. They also differed as to whether he had anything in his hand. Marshall stated that he observed nothing. Smith was very precise, and stated that he was carrying a parcel, done up in a newspaper, about 18in. in length and 6in. to 8in. in width. These differences suggested either that the woman was, during the evening, in the company of more than one man - a not very improbable supposition - or that the witness had been mistaken in detail. If they were correct in assuming that the man seen in the company of deceased by the three was one and the same person it followed that he must have spent much time and trouble to induce her to place herself in his diabolical clutches. They last saw her alive at the corner of Fairclough Street and Berner Street, saying "Not to-night, but some other night." Within a quarter of an hour her lifeless body was found at a spot only a few yards from where she was last seen alive. It was late, and there were few people about, but the place to which the two repaired could not have been selected on account of its being quiet or unfrequented. It had only the merit of darkness. It was the passageway leading into a court in which several families resided. Adjoining the passage and court there was a club of Socialists, who, having finished their debate, were singing and making merry. The deceased and her companion must have seen the lights of the clubroom, and the kitchen, and of the printing office. They must have heard the music and dancing, for the windows were open. There were persons in the yard but a short time previous to their arrival. At 40 minutes past 12, one of the members of the club, named Morris Eagle, passed the spot where the deceased drew her last breath, passing through the gateway to the back door, which opened into the yard. At 1 o'clock the body was found by the manager of the club. He had been out all day, and returned at the time. He was in a two-wheeled barrow drawn by a pony, and as he entered the gateway his pony shied at some object on his right. There was no lamp in the yard, and having just come out of the street it was too dark to see what the object was and he passed on further down the yard. He returned on foot, and on searching found the body of deceased with her throat cut. If he had not actually disturbed the wretch in the very act, at least he must have been close on his heels; possibly the man was alarmed by the sound of the approaching cart, for the death had only just taken place. He did not inspect the body himself with any care, but blood was flowing from the throat, even when Spooner reached the spot some few minutes afterwards, and although the bleeding had stopped when Dr. Blackwell's assistant arrived, the whole of her body and the limbs, except her hands, were warm, and even at 16 minutes past 1 a.m. Dr. Blackwell found her face slightly warm, and her chest and legs quite warm. In this case, as in other similar cases, which had occurred in this neighbourhood, no call for assistance was noticed. Although there might have been some noise in the club, it seemed very unlikely that any cry could have been raised without its being heard by some one of those near. The editor of a Socialist paper was quietly at work in a shed down the yard, which was used as a printing office. There were several families in the cottages in the court only a few yards distant, and there were 20 persons in the different rooms of the club. But if there was no cry, how did the deceased meet with her death? The appearance of the injury to her throat was not in itself inconsistent with that of a self-inflicted wound. Both Dr. Phillips and Dr. Blackwell have seen self- inflicted wounds more extensive and severe, but those have not usually involved the carotid artery. Had some sharp instrument been found near the right hand of the deceased this case might have had very much the appearance of a determined suicide. But no such instrument was found, and its absence made suicide an impossibility. The death was, therefore, one by homicide, and it seemed impossible to imagine circumstances which would fit in with the known facts of the case, and which would reduce the crime to manslaughter. There were no signs of any struggle; the clothes were neither torn nor disturbed. It was true that there were marks over both shoulders, produced by pressure of two hands, but the position of the body suggested either that she was willingly placed or placed herself where she was found. Only the soles of her boots were visible. She was still holding in her left hand a packet of cachous, and there was a bunch of flowers still pinned to her dress front. If she had been forcibly placed on the ground, as Dr. Phillips opines, it was difficult to understand how she failed to attract attention, as it was clear from the appearance of the blood on the ground that the throat was not cut until after she was actually on her back. There were no marks of gagging, no bruises on the face, and no trace of any anaesthetic or narcotic in the stomach; while the presence of the cachous in her hand showed that she did not make use of it in self-defence. Possibly the pressure marks may have had a less tragical origin, as Dr. Blackwell says it was difficult to say how recently they were produced. There was one particular, which was not easy to explain. When seen by Dr. Blackwell her right hand was lying on the chest, smeared inside and out with blood. Dr. Phillips was unable to make any suggestion how the hand became soiled. There was no injury to the hand, such as they would expect if it had been raised in self-defence while her throat was being cut. Was it done intentionally by her assassin, or accidentally by those who were early on the spot? The evidence afforded no clue. Unfortunately the murderer had disappeared without leaving the slightest trace. Even the cachous were wrapped up in unmarked paper, so that there was nothing to show where they were bought. The cut in the throat might have been effected in such a manner that bloodstains on the hands and clothes of the operator were avoided, while the domestic history of the deed suggested the strong probability that her destroyer was a stranger to her. There was no one among her associates to whom any suspicion had attached. They had not heard that she had had a quarrel with any one unless they magnified the fact that she had recently left the man with whom she generally cohabited; but this diversion was of so frequent an occurrence that neither a breach of the peace ensued, nor, so far as they knew, even hard words. There was therefore in the evidence no clue to the murderer and no suggested motive for the murder. The deceased was not in possession of any valuables. She was only known to have had a few pence in her pocket at the beginning of the evening. Those who knew her best were unaware of any one likely to injure her. She never accused any one of having threatened her. She never expressed any fear of anyone, and, although she had outbursts of drunkenness, she was generally a quiet woman. The ordinary motives of murder - revenge, jealousy, theft, and passion appeared, therefore, to be absent from this case; while it was clear from the accounts of all who saw her that night, as well as from the post-mortem examination, that she was not otherwise than sober at the time of her death. In the absence of motive, the age and class of woman selected as victim, and the place and time of the crime, there was a similarity between this case and those mysteries which had recently occurred in that neighbourhood. There had been no skilful mutilation as in the cases of Nichols and Chapman, and no unskilful injuries as in the case in Mitre Square possibly the work of an imitator; but there had been the same skill exhibited in the way in which the victim had been entrapped, and the injuries inflicted, so as to cause instant death and prevent blood from soiling the operator, and the same daring defiance of immediate detection, which, unfortunately for the peace of the inhabitants and trade of the neighbourhood, had hitherto been only too successful. He himself was sorry that the time and attention which the jury had given to the case had not produced a result that would be a perceptible relief to the metropolis the detection of the criminal; but he was sure that all had used their utmost effort to accomplish this object, and while he desired to thank the gentlemen of the jury for their kind assistance, he was bound to acknowledge the great attention which Inspector Reid and the police had given to the case. He left it to the jury to say, how, when, and by what means the deceased came by her death.

The jury, after a short deliberation, returned a verdict of "Willful murder against some person or persons unknown."

This is a copy of Elizabeth Stride's Death Certificate, identifying how she was killed.

Chapter 6

Catharine Eddowes

Catharine Eddowes was the fourth canonical ripper victim and was killed as the alleged second victim in the "double" event on September 30, 1888. She was the eldest Ripper victim at the age of forty-six. This age may not be contradicted by her sisters who thought Catharine was only forty-three at the time of her death. She was five feet tall with hazel eyes and dark auburn hair. She had a blue tattoo on her left arm that was a capital "T" and "C." These initials stood for Thomas Conway. Catharine was known as an intelligent woman, jolly, but had a fierce temper. The overall opinion of Catharine by the people who knew her was that she was well-liked, was often found singing, and that she was not a drunk. None of the people who knew her described her as an Unfortunate.

Catharine was born in 1842 in Wolverhampton. She was the daughter of a tinplate worker named George Eddowes. The Eddowes family moved to Bermondsey before she was two years old. She was educated at St. Johns Charity School, Potters Field, Tooley Street. In 1855 Catharine's mother, also named Catharine, died and most of her siblings entered the Bermondsey Workhouse and Industrial School. Exactly what happened to young Catharine at this time is not really known. According to the Wolverhampton Chronicle she went to live with an aunt in Briston Street, Wolverhampton. She carried on her education at a School called Downgate Charity School.

Between 1861 and 1863 Catharine left home with a pensioner named Thomas Conway; he was a member of the Eighteenth Irish Regiment. The name Conway used in this Regiment was Quinn and he was having his pension paid to him in that name. The couple lived in Birmingham and the Midlands selling the chapbooks that Conway wrote. Friends of Catharine said the couple had married but there is no evidence that a marriage ever took place. The couple did, however, have three children: two boys and a girl.

In 1880 the couple separated and Conway took custody of the boys and Catharine took custody of the girl, named Annie. There are many accounts as to why the separation took place. Annie said it was because of Catharine's habitual drinking and periodic absences. Catharine's sister Elizabeth Fisher said it was because of Conway's drinking and violence towards her sister.

In 1881 Catharine met an Irish Porter by the name of John Kelly (possibly the John Kelly she was still living with seven years later), while Catharine and Annie were living at lodgings at Flower and Dean Street.

Frederick Wilkinson the deputy of the lodging house said that the couple lived on very good terms. Like any other couple they had their spats, but never anything serious. He said Catharine only really argued when she was drunk. He believed Catharine earned her living by hawking about the streets and cleaning for the Jews. He also said Catherine was a very jolly woman.

The exact date that Annie married Louis Phillips is not known. He was a lampblack packer (lampblack is a pigment made from soot). Catherine, in 1887, nursed her daughter through a "confinement" (pregnancy) but because of Catharine's drinking and constant appeals for money, the couple spent the next few years constantly moving around Southwark and Bermondsey. Apparently, the couple never stayed at any address very long as Catharine constantly asked Annie for money.

In September, like many other impoverish people, Catharine and John Kelly went to Kent to work at picking hops that would be used in the making of malt liquor. It is estimated that between 50,000 and 60,000 people went for a paid holiday hop picking. Kelly later commented to the *Star* newspaper

"We didn't get on any to well and started to hoof it home. We came along in company with another man and woman who had worked in the same fields, but who parted from us. The woman said to Catharine "I have got a pawn ticket for a flannel shirt. I wish you'd take it, since you're going up to town (London) and it may fit your old man". So Catharine took it and the ticket was in the name of Emily Burrell. We did not have money enough to keep us going till we got to town, but we did get there and came straight to the lodging house at 55 Flower and Dean Street."

The couple moved back to London on September 1888 and had 6d between them, which John had earned that day. At the inquest, John stated he gave Catharine four pence on that Friday night and kept two pence for himself. He suggested to Catherine that she should take the four pence and go pay for a bed at a lodging house. He then told Catharine that he would stay at the Casual Ward that was situated in Mile End, but Catharine insisted that she would go to the Casual Ward and that John should stay at a lodging house. John Kelly did go to Cooney's Lodging House, 55 Flower and Dean Street, and it is assumed that Catharine went to the Casual Ward. Why didn't the couple just pay for a double bed for the night and stay together as they had done the Thursday night? Why did Catharine insist that she would go to the Mile End Casual Ward? I believe the reason Catharine was going to Mile End was for the purpose of trying to meet Dr Barnardo. While at this workhouse she told the superintendent:

"I have come back to earn the reward offered for the apprehension of the Whitechapel murderer, I think I know him."
The superintendent told Catharine she should be careful that she was not murdered herself, to which she replied:
"oh, no fear of that."
Did Catharine read the newspapers while in Kent and read something that made her realise that she knew who the Ripper was. In my opinion, the only clue she most likely derived from the press reports on Annie Chapman's murder, was that the killer had medical knowledge. She must have been very certain of her facts to have walked back to London for the specific reason of claiming the reward.
The next day (29th) Catharine arrived at Cooney's at around 8 a.m. after being turned out of the Shoe Lane Workhouse. The couple, having no money, decided they needed to pawn a pair of John Kelly's boots in a pawnshop on Church Street. Pawn shops were the last resort for the poor women who did not want to resort to prostitution. Pawn shops were in abundance in the East End. On Saturday, which was pay day, the poor would go to the pawn shop and buy back their pawned goods, usually some sort of clothing, but by Monday most of the poor were re-pawning the same item, starting the cycle all over again. The couple were given 2/6d (12 ½p) for the boots and the pawn ticket was made out in the name of Jane Kelly. Catharine then tucked the pawn ticket away with the pawn ticket given to her by Emily Burrell. These tickets would be used in trying to identify her later. They went and bought sugar, tea, and some food before returning to Cooney's and eating breakfast between 10 a.m. and 11 a.m.
2:00 p.m. The next thing we know about Catharine's movements was that the couple parted in Hounsditch. Catharine said she was going to Bermondsey to borrow some money from Annie, her daughter, and promised John that she would be back by 4 p.m. We know that Catharine did not see her daughter. When questioned at the inquest, her daughter stated she had not seen her mother for over two years. Although Catharine may have been an occasional Unfortunate, John Kelly testified that he was unaware of here ever being an Unfortunate. John Kelly and the Deputy of Cooney's, Frederick William Wilkinson, may have been careful not to give such information because Kelly could have been charged with living off immoral earnings and Wilkinson for keeping a Brothel. Whether they knew it or not, Catharine was seen with a strange man at a dark corner in Mitre Square, and also from her having no money at 2 p.m. to being arrested six hours later for being very drunk; she must have received some money from somewhere. Perhaps she wasn't a regular Unfortunate because she was generally known to be intimate only with Kelly. Dr.

Barnardo during visiting the lodging houses in the area must have heard rumours that Catharine was going to the police to claim the reward.

The fact that she did not go to the police straight after her arrival back in Whitechapel makes you think that she may have had another plan in mind. This plan could have been to blackmail Dr Barnardo, hence why she went to Mile End that evening rather than stay in the lodging house with Kelly. I believe that Catharine and

Dr Barnardo arranged to meet Catharine that same night and gave her some money to secure there meeting, even promising that he would give her some more money when they met. Where Catharine had been drinking that day is not known, but by the state she was in, you can only imagine it was not far from where she was arrested.

8:30 p.m. The next sighting of Catharine is when she was very drunk, imitating a fire engine. This had attracted a small crowd as she lay down on the pavement outside 29 Aldgate High Street. City of London Police Constable Louis Robinson, with the assistance of Police Constable George Simmons, took Catharine to Bishopsgate Police Station. Constable Robinson later recalled he noticed a group of people surrounding a woman who was drunk and lying on the footway. He asked the crowd if any of them knew the woman or where the woman lived but got no reply. He then picked her up and sat her against the shutters, but she then fell down sideways. It is no surprise that no one in the crowd, not even the officers arresting Catharine, recognised her because she had come from Whitechapel which was governed by Scotland Yard police. On arrival at the station she gave her name as *"nothing"* and Station Sergeant Byfield locked her up in a cell to sober up. Shortly afterwards, PC Robinson looked in the cell to find Catharine asleep smelling strongly of drink.

9:45 p.m. Police Constable George Hutt came on duty and checked the cells at regular intervals. He was asked at the inquest whether persons taken to the station in a state of inebriation were searched. He replied: *"No, but we take from them anything that might be dangerous."* He then stated that at some point he had loosened the things around Catharine's neck and had noticed a white wrapper and a red silk handkerchief.

12:15 a.m. Catharine was wide awake and singing quietly to herself. At about 12:30am she called out to PC Hutt asking him when she could be released. PC Hutt replied, *"When you are capable of taking care of yourself."* Her response was *"I can do that now."* PC Hutt waited until 1:00 a.m. to release her. When she asked him what time it was, he replied, *"Too late for you to get any more drink."* Apparently, Catharine then told PC Hutt *"I am in for a damn fine hiding when I get home."* PC Hutt responded, *"Serves you right, you have no right to get drunk."* Catharine then surrendered her name as Mary Ann Kelly and the address she gave was 6 Fashion Street. PC Hutt then showed her the way out of the Police station through the passage. On her way out, PC Hutt asked her to close the outer door behind her. Her last recorded words were *"all right and good night old cock."* PC Hutt noticed that Catharine then turned left heading towards Aldgate High Street where she had been arrested.

1:35 a.m. The next sighting was by Joseph Lawende, Joseph Hyman Levy, and Harry Harris. They saw her standing in the Duke's Place entrance to Church Passage. This was a covered walkway that led to Mitre Square. Catharine was in the company of a man and was standing with her hand resting on his chest. I believe this man was Dr Barnardo and Catharine was keeping him at arms length, by putting her outstretched arm between her and him. Although Levy and Lawende never saw Catharine's face, they stated they recognised her by the clothes she was wearing. The description of the man Catharine was with was given by Lawende and was one of the best to date. According to Lawende, the man was about thirty years of age. He was five foot seven inches tall and medium build. He had a fair complexion and a moustache. He was wearing a salt-and-pepper coloured jacket and a grey cloth cap with a peak of the same colour. He had a red handkerchief knotted around his neck. The police took Lawende statement very seriously. Seriously enough that even the *Evening News* reported on it;

> *They (the police) have no doubt themselves that this was the murdered woman and her murderer. And on the first blush of it the fact is borne out by the police having taken exclusive care of Mr Joseph Levander (Lawende) to a certain extent having sequestrated him and having imposed a pledge on him of secrecy. They are paying all his expenses, and one if not two detectives are taking him about. One of the two detectives is Foster (Detective Superintendent Alfred Lawrence). Henry (Harry) Harris of the two gentlemen our representative interviewed is the more communicative. He is of the opinion that neither Mr Levander nor Mr Levy saw anything more that he did, and that was only the back of the man. Mr Joseph Levy is absolutely obstinate and refuses to give the slightest information. He leaves one to infer that he knows something, but he is afraid to be called to the inquest. Hence he assumes a knowing air.*

This paper also reported that:

> *"The police are extraordinarily reticent with reference to the Mitre Square tragedy."*

The Yorkshire Post reported;

> *"The police apparently have strict orders to close all channels of information to members of the press."*

These were not the only newspapers to report on this. Even the *New York Times* criticised the way the investigation was carried out. They reported that the police seemed to *"devote their entire energies to preventing the press from getting at the facts. They deny to reporters a sight of the scene or bodies, and give them no information whatever."* Whatever information the police were trying to keep back is still not known. Did they know who the Ripper was and were focusing on trying to build up evidence against him? Often the media can compromise such investigations. While Lawende was answering questions at the inquest, the coroner asked the jury not to ask any questions about the man he saw with the deceased. This fact leads you to believe that the police did think that the man Lawende saw with Catharine Eddowes was the Ripper. However, it wasn't long before the police changed their normal stance of being uncooperative and actually started offering information to the press. The *Manchester Guardian* commented on the new cooperation between the authorities and the media:

"The barrier of reticence which has been set up on all occasions when the representatives of the newspaper press have been brought into contact with the police authorities for the purpose of obtaining information for the use of the public has been suddenly withdrawn, and instead of the customary stereotyped negatives and disclaimers of the officials, there has ensued a marked disposition to afford all necessary facilities for the publication of details and a increase courtesy towards the members of the press concerned."

Why the sudden change in the police's method?

1.35 a.m. Police Constable James Harvey testified that he walked along Duke's Place and down Church Passage on his beat. He indicated that he didn't see anybody in the square and did not hear anything coming from the direction of the square. He said he did not actually enter the square. Why did the officer not bother to enter the square if it was part of his beat? He may not have heard anything as Dr. Barnardo could have followed the police's idea of nailing rubber to his boots, to prevent anyone hearing his footsteps in the courts and passageways of Whitechapel. This idea would have come via his connections. Because of his very high ranking friends and Brethren brother in the Metropolitan Police, Dr Barnardo would have known about the way the police on the ground were conducting their investigations into catching him. Because of the regulation boots the Police Officers wore, it was necessary for them to come up with some way to prevent their approach being heard. Out of this necessity, the officers of the day came up with the idea of the "sneaker." The officers nailed strips of rubber to their boots to make their footsteps softer. I believe that Dr Barnardo also copied this idea whilst roaming the streets looking for what ever prey was his target that night, whether it was a destitute child or a victim of his alto ego Jack the Ripper.

1:45 a.m. Within ten minutes of Catharine's last sighting, Police Constable Edward Watkins entered from the other side of the square with his lantern lit. He found Catherine's body lying on the ground. He then went over to inspect the body that was lying in the Southwest corner of the square. He noticed at once that the woman's throat had been cut and that her clothes had been thrown upwards. He then saw that her stomach had been ripped open and that she was lying in a pool of her own blood. When giving a statement to the press he said;

"She was ripped up like a pig in the market. The murderer had inserted a knife just under the nose, cut the nose completely from the face, at the same time inflicting a dreadful gash down the right cheek to the angle of the jawbone. The nose was laid over on the cheek. A more dreadful sight I never saw; it quite knocked me over"

PC Watkins whilst giving evidence at the inquest stated he did not touch the body but immediately ran over to the door of Kearley and Tonge, a tea warehouse in Mitre Square. He pounded on the door and summoned the assistance of George Morris a night watchman who was sweeping the floor. PC Watkins *said "For God sake mate, come to my assistance!"* Morris asked the officer to wait till he fetched his lamp and inquired what was wrong. The constable then said *"Here is another woman cut to pieces."* The pair returned to the square and Morris turned his lamp on and saw the deceased. Morris then ran out into Mitre Street and into Aldgate, where he quickly found Police Constable Holland and PC James Jarvis. PC Jarvis asked Morris what was wrong. Morris replied that there was a woman who had been ripped up in Mitre Square. The two officers then returned with Morris to the square and saw PC Watkins at the side of the body. PC Holland went to fetch Dr. Sequeira from Jewry Street and a bystander was sent for more officers.

1:45 a.m. Dr. George William Sequeira arrived at the crime scene. He was the first doctor to examine Catharine's body. At the scene he pronounced the woman as dead but did not make any detailed examination. He waited until Dr. Gordon Brown arrived.

1:55 a.m. Station Inspector Edward Collard was on duty at Bishopsgate Police Station when the finding was reported. The report was then telegraphed to headquarters. Inspector Collard sent for Police Surgeon Dr. F. Gordon Brown to attend the murder scene.

2:03 a.m. Inspector Collard arrived in Mitre Square, quickly followed by Dr. Brown. They were joined by Superintendent McWilliam and Sergeant Foster, and some time later by Major Henry Smith (Acting Commissioner, City of London Police). Detective Constable Daniel Halse arrived at the murder scene and immediately ordered the neighbourhood searched. He wanted everybody in the area stopped and examined. A few men were stopped and questioned and even searched in the street, but to no avail. At twenty past two, he went through Goulston Street and on to the mortuary, where he said that he noticed that the deceased woman had a piece of her apron missing.

Sargeant Jones found a number of items beside the body and immediately gave these items to Inspector Collard. Sergeant Jones described these items at the inquest:

- **3 boot buttons**
- **A thimble**
- **There was a mustard tin containing pawn tickets for Emily Birrell's man's shirt and Kelly's boots. These tickets were used to establish Catharine's identity.**

Catharine's body was taken to Golden Lane Mortuary where it was stripped by Mr. Davis the mortuary keeper in front of the doctors and Inspector Collard. The police listed her clothes and possessions:

- **A black straw bonnet with trimming of green and black velvet. On the bonnet were black beads and black strings**
- **A black jacket, with fur trims around the collar and sleeves. The two outer pockets were also trimmed with black silk braid**
- **A Chintz skirt, which had three, flounces and had brown buttons on the waistband**
- **A brown Lindsey dress bodice that had a black velvet collar and brown metal buttons down the front**
- **A grey petticoat with a white waistband**
- **A very old green Alpaca skirt**
- **A very old ragged blue shirt with red flounce and light twill lining**
- **A white calico chemise**
- **A man's white vest with two outside pockets and buttons to match**
- **There were no drawers or stays**
- **A pair of men's lace-up boots. The right one had been repaired at some time with red thread. The laces were of Mohair**
- **Found on Eddowes's neck was a piece of red gauze silk**
- **1 large white handkerchief**
- **2 unbleached Calico pockets**

- **1 blue stripe bed ticking pocket, waistband and strings**
- **1 white cotton handkerchief with red and white Birdseye border**
- **1 pair of brown ribbed stockings with white mending on the feet**
- **12 pieces of white rag some had bloodstains on**
- **1 piece of white coarse linen**
- **1 piece of blue and white shirting (three cornered)**
- **2 small blue bed ticking bags**
- **2 short clay pipes (black)**
- **1 tin box containing tea**
- **1 tin box containing sugar**
- **1 piece of flannel and 6 pieces of soap**
- **1 small toothcomb**
- **1 white-handled table knife**
- **1 metal teaspoon**
- **1 red leather cigarette case with white metal fittings**
- **1 tin matchbox empty**
- **1 piece of red flannel containing needles and pins**
- **1 ball of hemp**
- **1 piece of old white apron**

2:55 a.m. Back in Whitechapel, Police Constable Alfred Long was on his beat in Goulston Street. He had walked through Goulston Street earlier and had not seen anything on the ground or noticed anything chalked on the wall. However forty-five minutes later, when he re-entered the street, he found a piece of torn white apron with blood and some faecal matter on it; this piece of apron was believed to have been used by the Ripper to wipe his hands as he was escaping. This meant the killer made his way back to Whitechapel after the murder. At the inquest, Constable Long **said *"the apron had recent stains of blood on it"*** We know the piece was from Catharine's apron; the one she was wearing when she was found butchered, as it was cross-matched with the apron found on the body. The piece of apron in question was found in the doorway of 108-119 Wentworth Model Dwellings, which was a mile away from the murder scene. The Wentworth Model Dwellings were erected the previous year and housed mainly Jewish people. On the wall directly above the piece of apron there was some writing. It had been done in chalk and would become known as the Goulston Street Graffito. PC Long confirmed that the piece of torn apron was not there at 2:20 a.m. when he walked Goulston Street on his rounds. He could not verify if the writing had been there earlier. PC Long recorded the wording as;

"The Juwes are the men that will not be blamed for nothing."

Detective Constable Halse of the City police, however, noted that the wording was slightly different. According to him the words were:

"The Juwes are *not* the men that will not be blamed for nothing."

The five lines were in a good schoolboy's round hand. The size of the capital letters was about three quarters of an inch and the other letters were in proportion.

After a search of the staircases, Constable Long left another officer at the scene while he took the bloody apron to the Commercial Street Police station. Superintendent Arnold who was now at the scene was most anxious to have the graffito erased, and had a sergeant with a wet sponge standing by waiting until Sir Charles Warren arrived and authorised the erasure of the graffito. Police Constable Halse of the City Police arrived after hearing about the find. Constable Halse stated at the inquest he thought that the writing was freshly done. He requested the writing be photographed, but at 5:30 a.m., but, on the authorisation of Sir Charles Warren, the writing was washed away. The alleged reasoning for the removal of the graffito was to stop anti-Semitism, as the area had a high Jewish population. There was already a lot of tension in London at the time as the local residents felt that the influx of immigrants was taking away their jobs and stopping them earning a living.

Could there have been a different reason? The word "Juwes" is a Masonic word used for the three men who murdered Hiram Abiff. Hiram Abiff was the Masonic Grand Master and the builder of Solomon's Temple. The men's names were Jubelo, Jubela, and Jubelum. When these three men were caught they were lamented:

Jubela. O that my throat had been cut across, my tongue be torn out and my body buried in the rough sands of the sea.

Jubelo. O that my left breast had been torn open, and my heart and vitals taken from hence and thrown over my left shoulder.

Jubelum. O that my body had been severed in two in the midst, and divided to the north and the south. My bowels burnt to ashes in the centre, and the ashes scattered by the four winds.

So, was the Ripper a Mason? If he was, he must have been of a high rank, or at least knew of the Masonic ways to have known about the three Juwes. This information and the secret signs and responses are part of the ceremony of introduction to the third or master degree of the Mason Order. Dr Barnardo had some very good friends that were high ranking Masons and could have learnt all about their history through these friends in the pretence of becoming a Mason.

Sir Charles Warren, the man who ordered the writing to be washed off, was a Mason and a very high ranking one. Perhaps this was the reason he wanted the writing washed off. He may have feared that other Masons would think about a Masonic connection to the killer, because of the word Juwes. If this was the reasoning behind his actions, why not have the notes that were written by the Police Officers at the scene destroyed so the spelling of the word Juwes was not recorded?

In my opinion, I do not think that these killings had anything to do with the Masons. I believe that Dr. Barnardo did write the graffito and was just pointing the finger at the organisation because so many influential men were members. Certainly the Masons as a whole would be very upset at a killer roaming the streets killing Unfortunates and then pointing the blame at them. I think the only reason Sir Charles Warren had the writing erased was because both he and Superintendent Arnold recognised the handwriting.

Because Elizabeth Stride was found outside a workers club the Jews in the area were mistrusted and threatened, causing mobs to attack Jewish businesses and homes It was only because of the large police presence that there were no riots. The press was quick to jump on the bandwagon, printing propaganda against the Jews.

In the Vienna *Times* it was reported that a Jew man named Ritter had been charged with the ritual murder of a Christian woman. The prosecution charged Ritter as having sexual intercourse with the woman, and Ritter believed that he was obliged by Jewish law to kill her. That Ritter was not found guilty did not help the matter. In response to the article, a Chief Rabbi at the time wrote,

> *"I can assert without hesitation that in no Jewish book is such a barbarity even hinted at. Nor is there any record in the criminal annals of any country of a Jew having been convicted of such a terrible atrocity...The tragedies enacted in the East End are sufficiently distressing without the revival of moribund fables and the importation of prejudices abhorrent to the English nation."*

The Chief Rabbi of the Spanish and Portuguese Jews also responded to the press reports:

> *"These are superstitions entertained against the Jews from which the Jews turn in horror and disgust"*

These letters did little to help change the way people saw and treated the Jews in the East End.

The Police did investigate the Jewish ritual slaughter man steeped in the Old Testament law. Brooding on the manifold Talmudic denunciations of harlots and harlotry, this may have lead to an impulse to kill "harlots." The Talmudic law says that stoning or strangulation was a way to punish harlots. The Police visited kosher abattoirs and two *Shochtim* were detained, but both were released without charge. The Police also asked Dr. Frederick Gordon Brown to examine the Khalef, the knife the Shochtim used. The Police wanted to know if this knife could have inflicted the wounds in the murders of the Ripper victims. Dr. Brown decided that the Khalef could not be the murder weapon as it was a single-edged knife and did not have a point. As we have seen, the knife used in the Ripper killings did have a point and was more likely the type of knife used in a dissecting room or a morgue rather than the type of knife used in a slaughter house. The *Jewish Chronicle* issued a statement about the weapon on October 12, 1888: "We are authorised by Dr. Gordon Brown to state, with reference to a suggestion that the City and Whitechapel murders were the work of a Jewish slaughterer that he had examined the knifes used by the Jewish slaughterers, and he is thoroughly satisfied that none of them could have been used."

Finding the piece of apron in Goulston Street was very important as it gave the police the murderer's escape route. This was from Mitre Square, in the direction of Northeast Whitechapel, Spitalfields, or even Mile End New Town. Dr. Barnardo lived on Mile End Road!

The day after Catharine's murder (Sunday), John Kelly got up at dawn and went to work. He recalled that he wandered through the crowds; everyone was talking about the two new murders. Kelly stated that he did not know that Catharine had been one of the women murdered that night until he read the *Star* newspaper and saw the headlines. Still, with the details in front of him, he was not sure that the murdered woman was Catharine, she may have lost some of her possessions and this woman could have found them. However, the agonizing truth presented itself when he read that the victim had the two initials "T" and "C" on her arm; then he knew it *was* his Catharine.

The autopsy was conducted by Dr. Frederick Gordon Brown, who was the surgeon for the City of London Police. It goes as follows:

The body was found lying on its back and the head turned to the left shoulder. The both arms were lying at there respective sides of the body, whilst the palms were upwards and the fingers slightly bent. The throat had been cut across to the extent of about six or seven inches. The intestines were drawn out to a large extent and placed over the right shoulder (comparable to Annie Chapman). They were smeared over with some feculent matter. A piece of about two feet was quite detached from the body and placed between the body and the left arm, apparently by design. The lobe and auricle of the right ear was cut obliquely through.

There was a quantity of clotted blood on the pavement on the left side of the neck round the shoulder and upper part of the arm, and fluid blood coloured serum which had flowed under the neck to the right shoulder, the pavement sloping in that direction.

The body was quite warm and there was no stiffening of death in the body. The victim had died within half an hour of being found. There were no superficial bruises. There was no blood on the abdomen and no secretion of any kind on the thighs. There was no spurting of blood on the bricks or the pavement around the body. There were no marks of blood below the middle part of the body. Several buttons were found in the clotted blood after the body had been removed. There was no blood on the front of the clothing.

When the body arrived at the Golden Lane Mortuary some of the blood was dispersed through the removal of the body to the mortuary. The clothing was removed very carefully and while this was being done a part of the victim's ear dropped from the clothing. At this stage the body was not cold but rigor mortis was well marked and there was a green discoloration over the abdomen.

After the body was washed a bruise was seen on the back of the left hand between the thumb and first finger it was recent and very red, it was the size of a sixpence. There were a few older bruises on the right shin. The hands and arms were bronzed and there were no bruises on the scalp or the back of the body or the elbows. Unfortunately he did not mention if there were any bruises on the front of the body. The face had been very mutilated and there was a cut about a quarter of an inch through the lower left eyelid, dividing the structures completely through. The upper eyelid on that side, there was a scratch through the skin on the left upper eyelid, near to the angle of the nose. The right eyelid was cut through to about half an inch.

There was a deep cut over the bridge of the nose, extending from the left border of the nasal bone, down near the angle of the jaw on the right side of the cheek. This cut went into the bone and divided all the structures of the cheek except the mucous membrane of the mouth. The tip of the nose was quite detached from the nose by an oblique cut from the bottom of the nasal bone to where the wing of the nose joins on to the face. A cut from this divided the upper lip and extended through the substance of the gum over the right upper lateral incisor tooth. About half an inch from the top of the nose was another oblique cut. There was a cut on the right angle of the mouth as if the cut of a point of a knife. The cut extended about an inch and a half, parallel with the lower lip. There was on each side of the cheek a cut, which peeled up the skin, forming a triangular flap about an inch and a half. On the left chin there were two abrasions of the epithelium…under the left ear. The throat was cut across to the extent of about six or seven inches. A superficial cut commenced at about an inch and a half below the lobe of the left ear and extended across the throat to about three inches below the lobe of the right ear. The big muscle across the throat was divided through on the left side. The large vessels on the left side of the neck were severed. The larynx was severed below the vocal chord. All the deep structures were severed to the bone, the knife marking intervertebral cartilages. The sheath of the vessel on the right side was just opened. The carotid artery had a fine hole opening. The internal jugular vein was open a inch and a half - not divided. The blood vessels contained clot. All these injuries were performed by a sharp instrument like a knife, and pointed. The cause of death was haemorrhage from the left common carotid artery. The death was immediate and all the mutilations were inflicted after death.

We examined the abdomen. The front wall was lid open from the breastbone to the pubes. The cut commenced opposite the enciform cartilage. The incision went upwards, not penetrating the skin that was over the sternum. It then divided the enciform cartilage. The knife must have cut obliquely at the expense of the front surface of that cartilage. Behind this the liver was stabbed as if by the point of a sharp instrument. Below this was another incision into the liver of about two and a half inches and below this to the left lobe of the liver was slit through by a vertical cut. Two cuts were shewn by a jagging of the skin on the left side.

The abdominal walls were divided in the middle line to a quarter of an inch of the navel. The cut then took a horizontal course for two inches and a half to the right side. It then divided around the navel on the left side, and made a parallel incision to the former horizontal incision, leaving the navel on a tongue of skin. Attached to the navel was two and a half inches of the lower part of the rectus muscle on the left side of the abdomen. The incision then took an oblique direction to the right and was shelving. The

213

incision then went down the right side of the vagina and rectum for half an inch behind the rectum.

There was a stab of about an inch on the left groin. A pointed instrument did this. Below this was a cut of three inches going through all tissues making a wound of the peritoneum about the same extent.

An inch below the crease of the thigh was a cut extending from the anterior spine of the ileum obliquely down the inner side of the left thigh and separating the left labium, forming a flap of skin up to the groin. The left rectus muscle was not detached. There was a flap of skin formed from the right thigh, attaching the right labium, and extending up to the spine of the ilium. The muscles on the right side inserted into the frontal ligaments were cut through. The skin was retracted through the whole cut in the abdomen, but the vessels were not clotted. Nor had there any appreciable bleeding from the vessels. I draw the conclusion that the cut was made after death, and there would not be much blood on the murderer. The cut was made by someone standing on the right side of the body, kneeling below the middle of the body. I removed the contents of the stomach and placed it in a jar for further investigation. There was very little in the way of food or fluid in the stomach, but partially digested food had escaped through the cut end of the stomach.

The intestines were largely detached and about two feet of the colon was also cut away. The right kidney was pale and bloodless with slight congestion at the base of the pyramid. The liver was healthy and had a number of incisions in it. The spleen was still attached by only half an inch to the peritoneum. The gallbladder was in tact but the pancreas was cut through on the left side.

The person who removed the kidney from the victim must have had some considerable knowledge of the positions of the organs and how to remove them. It takes a great deal of medical knowledge to be able to remove the kidney in such a dexterous way and to know where it was situated. Both the uterus and the kidney were never found at the crime scene. The membrane of the uterus was cut through and so was the womb whilst the vagina and cervix of the womb was left uninjured again showing the killer had some medical skill. The bladder was healthy and uninjured. When asked at the inquest if any of the body parts were missing, Dr. Brown replied, *"Yes, the uterus was cut away with the exception of a small portion, and the left kidney was also cut out. Both of these organs have not been found."* Dr. Brown also stated that the killer must have had a good deal of knowledge as to the position of the abdominal organs and how to remove them. The removal of the kidney would require special knowledge of its position because it is apt to be overlooked, being covered by a membrane.

On October 8, 1888 Catharine's funeral cortege made its way through streets that were crowded by people crying and men taking their caps off in a sign of respect. She was laid to rest in an unmarked grave in Ilford. All of the funeral expenses were paid by a Mr Hawkes. The Mr. Hawkes in question could have been either Samuel Hawkes of Finsbury or George Hawkes of St Luke's.

Catharine was killed on Scotland Yard territory and Commissioner Smith assigned many men to the Ripper case. A total of 15,000 constables manned the streets and 1,500 undercover detectives prowled the docks and Covent Gardens. Even the Director of the Bank of England was disguised as a common labourer and walked the streets in hope of catching the Ripper. The investigation was being dealt with by two divisions and the lower ranking officers were liaising very well. However, the same was not true of the higher level officers. They weren't able to cooperate effectively and allowed their differences to prevent them for executing an effective investigation. One could even make the argument that all the internal fighting among the authorities helped Dr. Barnardo remain undetected until this day.

At the same time, 4,500 East End women had signed a very impassioned letter and sent it to the Queen. The letter was penned to show their concern over the number of Brothels in the East End and about all the drinking establishments. In a Scotland Yard file dated October 25, 1888, there were 62 known brothels, and 233 common lodging houses (also used by the Unfortunates). In the same files it was estimated there were 1,200 Unfortunates (prostitutes) in the East End area. It is reported that the women of the West End started to fear for their safety. All of this panic led to vigilante groups being formed in the East End; they would arrest people on the street and drag them to the police station without any proof of the person ever committing a crime, let alone a murder.

September 10, 1888 George Akin Lusk was elected President of the newly formed vigilante group called the Whitechapel Vigilante Committee. This election had taken place in the Crown pub situated on the Mile End Road. Was Dr. Barnardo in the pub during this meeting? It was common for him to be in public houses in the course of his work. He also lived in Mile End Road so he would have known about these meetings. I believe that Dr Barnardo did at least know of Lusk and would later use Lusk in his campaign by sending him what would be known as the 'Lusk Kidney'.(See October 16th 1888 below)

October 4 and 11, 1888 The Coroner Samuel Frederick Langham conducted Catharine's inquest at Golden Lane Mortuary, where Catharine's body was lying. Eliza Gold, Catharine's sister, was called as a witness. She told the court that the deceased woman was her sister Catharine Eddowes. She was also a little confused as to when she last saw her sister alive. First, she said that she had not seen her sister for three to four months, and then she said it was actually only three to four weeks.

When Catharine's partner John Kelly testified at the inquest, he confirmed that he and Catharine had been living as a couple. At the end of day, Mr. Crawford gladly announced that the Corporation had unanimously approved the offer by the Lord Mayor of a reward of five hundred pounds for the discovery of the murderer.

Mr. William Sedgwick Saunders, a medical officer for the City of London, told the inquest that he had received the stomach of the deceased from Dr. Brown. He said that he had checked the stomach for drugs of the narcotic class, but his tests proved negative.

Constable Richard Pearce was called to the inquest not as an officer involved in the case but because his bedroom window overlooked the spot where the body was found. He stated that he and his family had heard nothing out of the ordinary that night, and they had not been disturbed in any way at all.

October 15, 1888 a man walks into a shop on Mile End Road and asked the shop girl if she knew where George Lusk lived. The shop girl gave the man the name of the street but not the house number.

October 16, 1888 at 8:00 p.m., Lusk received by post a three-inch-square cardboard box wrapped in brown paper. It was addressed without a house number. Inside the box was half a human kidney preserved in wine. This half a kidney was allegedly Catharine's. Inside the box was a crudely written letter allegedly from the Ripper. The postmark on the brown paper that covered the box was almost indecipherable but it possibly had the post mark of the East End. Lusk at first thought it to be a hoax, maybe an animal kidney. But he was persuaded to get the kidney examined. Dr. Openshaw was, at the time, the curator of the pathology museum situated at the London Hospital. He examined the kidney and stated that it was from a woman who was about 45 years of age. The woman would have been suffering from Bright's disease. He also reported that the kidney had not been removed from its body any longer than three weeks before.

The very next day, Dr. Openshaw stated he had only pointed out that the kidney was from a human and that it had been preserved in wine. He maintained that other people had added everything else he was supposed to have said. In Dr. Openshaw's defence, Dr. Sedgwick Saunders, the City Pathologist, spoke to the press and ascertained that the sex and age of a kidney could not be recognised without the rest of the body. He confirmed that the remaining kidney was still in Catharine's body was healthy and that the kidney that was removed from her body would also have been healthy. Because the kidney Lusk received was preserved, Saunders believed it was most likely sent by a medical student. He assumed the kidney had been obtained from an operating or dissecting theatre. This kidney has been mentioned in many memoirs since, but unfortunately no one really knows if the Lusk kidney was from Catharine's body at all. Inspector Anderson thought the kidney was a prank. There was also a postcard that was sent to the police, which is now known as the "Saucy Jack" post card.

The letter that came with the kidney is now known as the "From Hell" letter. The contents of the letter were as follows:

> **"From hell**
> **Mr Lusk**
> **Sor**
> *I send you half the kidne I took from one women prasarved it for you tother piece I fried and ate it was very nise I may send you the bloody knif that took it out if you only wate a whil longer*
> **Signed   catch me when**
> **You can**
> **Mishter Lusk"**

The writer of the "From Hell" letter was described by a graphologist as between the ages of twenty and forty-five. The writer would have had a rudimentary education. A more detailed analysis stated that the writer was semi-literate but was an English writer.

The effect of these murders in the East End did little to change much around the area. The *Star* newspaper reported on the October 3, 1888, that it asked an Unfortunate, "Aren't you afraid to be out at this time?" The woman's reply was "No; the murders are shocking, but we have no place to go, so we're compelled to be out looking for our lodgings." Another woman was asked the same question and her response was "Afraid? No. I'm armed. Look here [taking out a knife from her pocket]. I'm not the only one armed. There are plenty more carrying knifes now." The saddest statement of all was the answer another Unfortunate gave when asked if she was afraid that the murderer would get her. She replied, "I hope he does get me, I'm sick of this life."

After the double murders, Dr. Barnardo was taken to the Lime Street Police Station for questioning. He told the police that he had spent the evening at a fund raising dinner. Dr Barnardo used his police connection again to his advantage by saying that Superintendent Thomas Arnold head of the H Division (Whitechapel) and a brother Brethren attended the same dinner. We have no record of what time this dinner started or finished or even where it was held.

Police Constable Spicer later gave a statement to the *Daily Express* stating that he took a doctor to Lime Street Police Station that same night. He also went on to say that the doctor was not questioned or his bag even searched. Instead Spicer was not allowed to investigate the matter any further and was reprimanded for actually arresting this doctor. I do not think that two different doctors were taken to the same police station on the same night. I believe that the doctor whom PC Spicer took to Lime Street was Dr. Barnardo. I also think that when Barnardo was at the station he used his influential "friend's" to enable him to walk out of the station without being searched or investigated further.

I would like to finish this chapter with the very short summation by the coroner:

That being all the evidence forthcoming, the coroner considered an adjournment unnecessary. A better plan would be for the jury to return their verdict and then leave the matter in the hands of the police. It was not necessary for him to go through the testimony of the various witnesses in his summation. But, if the jury wanted their memories refreshed on any particular point he would assist them by referring to the evidence on that point. That the crime was a most fiendish one could not for a moment be doubted, for the miscreant, not satisfied with taking a defenceless woman's life, endeavoured so to mutilate the body as to render it unrecognisable. The coroner presumed the jury would return a verdict of wilful murder against some persons unknown and then the police could freely pursue their inquiries and follow up any clues they might obtain. A magnificent reward had been offered, and that might be the means of setting people on the track of bringing the creature that had committed this atrocious crime to speedy justice.

On reflection, perhaps it would be sufficient to return a verdict of wilful murder against some person unknown, in as much as the medical evidence conclusively demonstrated that only one person could be implicated. The jury then returned the verdict accordingly.

The coroner speaking for himself and the jury thanked Mr. Crawford and the police for all their assistance during the inquest.

Because the police ceased their inquiries, and because the coroner did not want any information on the man last seen with the victim before her death divulged, we can only speculate what was going on. I think that the police at this time had a suspect in mind. I also believe that the man last seen with

Catharine was the killer and that the police believed the same. The police had every confidence of catching the killer when he struck again. The methods of police investigation were advancing and they were beginning to understand the Ripper's MO. If it was not for the Brethren connections that Dr Barnardo had with Commissioner Anderson, and Superintendent Arnold, I honestly think the police would have caught him. I believe that either Anderson or Arnold or even both men spoke to their good friend Dr. Barnardo about how the investigation was progressing. Unfortunately, for the police who were patrolling the streets waiting for their man to strike, he was already two steps ahead of them. He knew he had to change his MO completely. And, this is exactly what he did do.

The next few pages follow the Inquest into the death of Catherine Eddowes, as recorded by the newspapers at the time, followed by a copy of the Death Certificate.

Inquests were very important in the 1800's and they give an insight into how people, spoke, behaved and thought.

The inquests make for great reading as part of the book or separately for research.

Day 1, Thursday, October 4, 1888
(As told by *The Daily Telegraph*, Friday, October 5, 1888,)

At the Coroner's Court, Golden-lane, yesterday [4 Oct], Mr. S. F. Langham, coroner for the City of London, opened the inquest into the death of Catherine Eddowes, or Conway, or Kelly, who was murdered in Mitre-court, Aldgate, about half-past one o'clock on Sunday morning last. The court was crowded, and much interest was taken in the proceedings, many people standing outside the building during the whole of the day.

Mr. Crawford, City solicitor appeared on behalf of the Corporation, as responsible for the police; Major Smith and Superintendent Forster represented the officers engaged in the inquiry.

After the jury had viewed the body, which was lying in the adjoining mortuary,
Mr. Crawford, addressing the coroner, said: I appear here as representing the City police in this matter, for the purpose of rendering you every possible assistance, and if I should consider it desirable, in the course of the inquiry, to put any questions to witnesses, probably I shall have your permission when you have finished with them.
Coroner: Oh, certainly.
The following evidence was then called

Eliza Gold deposed: I live at 6, Thrawl Street, Spitalfields. I have been married, but my husband is dead. I recognise the deceased as my poor sister (witness here commenced to weep very much, and for a few moments she was unable to proceed with her story). Her name was Catherine Eddowes. I cannot exactly tell where she was living. She was staying with a gentleman, but she was not married to him. Her age last birthday was about 43 years, as far as I can remember. She has been living for some years with Mr. Kelly. He is in court. I last saw her alive about four or five months ago. She used to go out hawking for a living, and was a woman of sober habits. Before she went to live with Kelly, she had lived with a man named Conway for several years, and had two children by him. I cannottell how many years she lived with Conway. I do not know whether Conway is still living. He was a pensioner from the army, and used to go out hawking also. I do not know on what terms he parted from my sister. I do not know whether she had ever seen him from the time they parted. I am quite certain that the body I have seen is my sister.

Mr. Crawford: I have not seen Conway for seven or eight years. I believe my sister was living with him then on friendly terms.

Coroner Was she living on friendly terms with Kelly? I cannot say. Three or four weeks ago I saw them together and they were then on happy terms. I cannot fix the time when I last saw them. They were living at 55, Flower and Dean Street a lodging house. My sister when staying there came to see me when I was very ill. From that time, until I saw her in the mortuary, I have not seen her.

A Juryman pointed out that witness previously said she had not seen her sister for three or four months, whilst later on she spoke of three or four weeks.

Coroner: You said your sister came to see you when you were ill, and that you had not seen her since. Was that three or four weeks ago?

Mrs. Gold: Yes.

Coroner So that you're saying three or four months was a mistake? Yes. I am so upset and confused. Witness commenced to cry again. As she could not write she had to affix her mark to the deposition.

John Kelly, a strong looking labourer, was then called and said: I live at a lodging house, 55, Flower and Dean Street. Have seen the deceased and recognise her as Catherine Conway. I have been living with her for seven years. She hawked a few things about the streets and lived with me at a common lodging house in Flower and Dean Street. The lodging house is known as Cooney's. I last saw her alive about two o'clock in the afternoon of Saturday in Houndsditch. We parted on very good terms. She told me she was going over to Bermondsey to try and find her daughter Annie. Those were the last words she spoke to me. Annie was a daughter whom I believe she had had by Conway. She promised me before we parted that she would be back by four o'clock, and no later. She did not return.

Coroner Did you make any inquiry after her? I heard she had been locked up at Bishopsgate Street on Saturday afternoon. An old woman who works in then lane told me she saw her in the hands of the police.

Coroner Did you make any inquiry into the truth of this? I made no further inquiries. I knew that she would be out on Sunday morning, being in the City.

Coroner Did you know why she was locked up? Yes, for drink; she had had a drop of drink, so I was told. I never knew she went out for any immoral purpose. She occasionally drank, but not to excess. When I left her she had no money about her. She went to see and find her daughter to get a trifle, so that I shouldn't see her walk about the streets at night.

Coroner What do you mean by "walking the streets? I mean that if we had no money to pay for our lodgings we would have to walk about all night. I was without money to pay for our lodgings at the time. I do not know that she was at variance with any one - not in the least. She had not seen Conway recently - not that I know of. I never saw him in my existence. I cannot say whether Conway is living. I know of no one who would be likely to injure her.

Foreman of the Jury: You say you heard the deceased was taken into custody. Did you ascertain, as a matter of fact, when she was discharged? No. I do not know when she was discharged.

Coroner What time was she in the habit of returning to her lodgings? Early.

Coroner What do you call early? About eight or nine o'clock.

Coroner When she did not return on this particular evening, did it not occur to you that it would be right to inquire whether she had been discharged or not? No, I did not inquire. I expected she would turn up on the Sunday morning.

Mr. Crawford: You say she had no money. Do you know with whom she had been drinking that afternoon? I cannot say.

Coroner Do you know any one who paid for drink for her? No.

Coroner Had she on a recent occasion absented herself from you at night?No.

Coroner This was the only time? Yes.

Coroner But had not she left you previously? Yes, a long time ago some months ago.

Coroner For what purpose? We had a few words, and she went away, but came back in a few hours.

Coroner Had you had any angry conversation with her on Saturday afternoon? No, not in the least.

Coroner No words about money? No.

Coroner Have you any idea where her daughter lives? She told me in King Street, Bermondsey, and that her name was Annie.

Coroner Had she been previously there for money? Yes, once last year.

Coroner How long have you been living in this lodging house together? Seven years, in the self-same house.

Coroner Previous to this Saturday had you been sleeping there each evening during the week? No; I slept there on Friday night, but she didn't.

Coroner Did she not sleep with you? No.

Coroner Was she walking the streets that night? She had the misfortune to go to Mile-end.

Coroner What happened there? She went into the casual ward.

Coroner What was the evening you two slept at the lodging-house during that week? Not one.

Coroner Where did you sleep? On Monday, Tuesday, and Wednesday we were down at the hop picking, and came back to London on Thursday. We had been unfortunate at the hop picking, and had no money. On Thursday night we both slept in the casual ward. On the Friday I earned 6d at a job, and I said, "Here, Kate, you take 4d and go to the lodging-house and I will go to Mile-end," but she said, "No, you go and have a bed and I will go to the casual ward," and she went. I saw her again on Saturday morning early.

Coroner At what time did you quit one another on Friday? I cannot tell, but I think it would be about three or four in the afternoon.

Coroner What did she leave you for? To go to Mile-end.

Coroner What for? To get a night's shelter in the casual ward.

Coroner When did you see her next morning? - About eight o'clock. I was surprised to see her so early. I know there was some tea and sugar found on her body. She bought that out of some boots we pawned at Jones's for 2s 6d. I think it was on Saturday morning that we pawned the boots. She was sober when she left me. We had been drinking together out of the 2s 6d. All of it was spent in drink and food. She left me quite sober to go to her daughter's. We parted without an angry word. I do not know why she left Conway. In the past seven years she only lived with me. I did not know of her going out for immoral purposes at night. She never brought me money in the morning after being out at night.

A Juryman: Is not eight o'clock a very early hour to be discharged from a casual ward? I do not know.

Juryman? There is some tasks - picking oakum - before you can be discharged. I know it was very early.

Mr. Crawford: Is it not the fact that the pawning took place on the Friday night? I do not know. It was either Friday night or Saturday morning. I am all muddled up. (The tickets were produced, and were dated the 28th, Friday.)

Crawford? She pawned the boots, did she not? - Yes; and I stood at the door in my bare feet.

Crawford? Seeing the date on the tickets, cannot you recollect when the pawning took place? I cannot say, I am so muddled up. It was either Friday or Saturday.

Coroner: Had you been drinking when the pawning took place? Yes.

Frederick William Wilkinson deposed: I am deputy of the lodging-house at Flower and Dean Street. I have known the deceased and Kelly during the last seven years. They passed as man and wife, and lived on very good terms. They had a quarrel now and then, but not violent. They sometimes had a few words when Kate was in drink, but they were not serious. I believe she got her living by hawking about the streets and cleaning amongst the Jews in Whitechapel. Kelly paid me pretty regularly. Kate was not often in drink. She was a very jolly woman, always singing. Kelly was not in the habit of drinking, and I never saw him the worse for drink. During the week the first time I saw the deceased at the lodging-house was on Friday afternoon. Kelly was not with her then. She went out and did not return until Saturday morning, when I saw her and Kelly in the kitchen together having breakfast. I did not see her go out, and I do not know whether Kelly went with her. I never saw her again.

Coroner Did you know she was in the habit of walking the streets at night?

No; she generally used to return between nine and ten o'clock. I never knew her to be intimate with any particular individual except Kelly; and never heard of such a thing. She use to say she was married to Conway; that her name was bought and paid for meaning that she was married. She was not at variance with any one that I know of. When I saw her last, on Saturday morning, between ten and eleven, she was quite sober. I first heard from Kelly on Saturday night that Kate was locked up, and he said he wanted a single bed. That was about 7.30 in the evening. A single bed is 4d, and a double 8d.

By a Juryman: I don't take the names of the lodgers, but I know my "regulars." If a man comes and takes a bed I put the number of the bed down in my book, but not his name. Of course I know the names of my regular customers.

Mr. Crawford: When was the last time Kelly and the deceased had slept together in your house previous to last week?

The last time the two slept at the lodging-house was five or six weeks ago, before they went to the hop picking. Kelly slept there on Friday and Saturday, but not Kate. I did not make any inquiry about her not being there on Friday. I could not say whether Kate went out with Kelly on Saturday, but I saw them having their breakfast together. I saw Kelly in the house about ten o'clock on Saturday night. I am positive he did not go out again. I cannot tell when he got up on Sunday. I saw him about dinnertime. I believe that on Saturday morning Kate was wearing an apron. Nothing unusual struck me about her dress. The distance between our place and the scene of the murder is about 500 yards.

Several Jurymen: Oh, more than that.
Mr. Crawford: Did any one come into your lodging-house and take a bed between one and two o'clock on the Sunday morning? No stranger came in then.
Crawford Did any one come into your lodging-house about that hour? No; two detectives came about three, and asked if I had any women out.
Crawford Did anyone come into your lodging-house about two o'clock on Sunday morning whom you did not recognise? I cannot say; I could tell by my book, which can soon be produced.
By a Juryman: Kelly and the deceased were at breakfast together between ten and eleven on Saturday morning. If they had told me the previous day that they had no money I would have trusted them. I trust all lodgers I know. The body was found half a mile from my lodging-house.
The deputy was dispatched for his book, with which after an interval he returned. It merely showed, however, that there were fifty-two beds occupied in the house on Saturday night. There were only six strangers. He could not say whether any one took a bed about two o'clock on Sunday morning. He had sometimes over 100 persons sleeping in the house at once. They paid for their beds, and were asked no questions. **Edward Watkin**, No. 881 of the City Police, said: I was on duty at Mitre Square on Saturday night. I have been in the force seventeen years. I went on duty at 9.45 upon my regular beat. That extends from Duke Street, Aldgate, through Heneage Lane, a portion of Bury Street, through Cree Lane, into Leadenhall Street, along eastward into Mitre Street, then into Mitre Square, round the square again into Mitre Street, then into King Street to St. James's Palace, round the place, then into Duke Street, where I started from. That beat takes twelve or fourteen minutes. I had been patrolling the beat continually from ten o'clock at night until one o'clock on Sunday morning.

Coroner Had anything excited your attention during those hours? No.
Coroner Or any person? No. I passed through Mitre Square at 1.30 on the Sunday morning. I had my lantern alight and on fixed to my belt. According to my usual practice, I looked at the different passages and corners.
Coroner At half-past one did anything excite your attention? No.

Coroner Did you see anyone about? No.

Coroner Could any people have been about that portion of the square without your seeing them? No. I next came into Mitre-square at 1.44, when I discovered the body lying on the right as I entered the Square. The woman was on her back, with her feet towards the square. Her clothes were thrown up. I saw her throat was cut and the stomach ripped open. She was lying in a pool of blood. I did not touch the body. I ran across to Kearley and Long's warehouse. The door was ajar, and I pushed it open, and called on the watchman Morris, who was inside. He came out. I remained with the body until the arrival of Police constable Holland. No one else was there before that but myself. Dr. Sequeira followed Holland. Inspector Collard arrived about two o'clock, and also Dr. Brown, surgeon to the police force.
Coroner When you first saw the body did you hear any footsteps as if anybody were running away? No. The door of the warehouse to which I went was ajar, because the watchman was working about. It was no unusual thing for the door to be ajar at that hour of the morning.
Mr. Crawford: I was continually patrolling my beat from ten o'clock up to half-past one. I noticed nothing unusual up till 1.44, when I saw the body.
Coroner: I did not sound an alarm?We do not carry whistles.
By a Juror: My beat is not a double but a single beat. No other policeman comes into Mitre Street.

Frederick William Foster, of 26, Old Jewry, architect and surveyor, produced a plan, which he had made of the place where the body was found, and the district. From Berner Street to Mitre Street is three-quarters of a mile, and a man could walk the distance in twelve minutes.

Inspector Collard, of the City Police, said: At five minutes before two o'clock on Sunday morning last I received information at Bishopsgate Street Police station that a woman had been murdered in Mitre Square. Information was at once telegraphed to headquarters. I dispatched a constable to Dr. Gordon Brown, informing him, and proceeded myself to Mitre Square, arriving there about two or three minutes past two. I there found Dr. Sequeira, two or three police officers, and the deceased person lying in the south-west corner of the Square, in the position described by Constable Watkins. The body was not touched until the arrival shortly afterwards of Dr. Brown. The medical gentlemen examined the body, and in my presence Sergeant Jones picked up from the foot way by the left side of the deceased, three small black buttons, such as are generally used for boots, a small metal button, a common metal thimble, and a small penny mustard tin containing two pawn-tickets. They were handed to me. The doctors remained until the arrival of the ambulance, and saw the body placed in the conveyance. It was then taken to the mortuary, and stripped by Mr. Davis, the mortuary keeper, in presence of the two doctors and myself. I have a list of articles of clothing more or less stained with blood and cut.

Coroner Was there any money about her? No; no money whatever was found. A piece of cloth was found in Goulston Street, corresponding with the apron worn by the deceased. When I got to the Square I took immediate steps to have the neighbourhood searched for the person who committed the murder. Mr. McWilliams, chief of the Detective Department, on arriving shortly afterwards sent men to search in all directions in Spitalfields, both in streets and lodging-houses. Several men were stopped and searched in the streets, without any good result. I have had a house-to-house inquiry made in the vicinity of Mitre Square as to any noises or whether persons were seen in the place; but I have not been able to find any beyond the witnesses who saw a man and woman talking together.

Mr. Crawford: When you arrived was the deceased in a pool of blood? The head, neck, and, I imagine, the shoulders were lying in a pool of blood when she was first found, but there was no blood in front. I did not touch the body myself, but the doctor said it was warm.

Crawford? Was there any sign of a struggle having taken place?

None whatever. I made a careful inspection of the ground all round. There was no trace whatever of any struggle. There was nothing in the appearance of the woman, or of the clothes, to lead to the idea that there had been any struggle. From the fact that the blood was in a liquid state I conjectured that the murder had not been long previously committed. In my opinion the body had not been there more than a quarter of an hour. I endeavoured to trace footsteps, but could find no trace whatever. The backs of the empty houses adjoining were searched, but nothing was found.

Dr. Frederick Gordon Brown was then called, and deposed: I am surgeon to the City of London Police. I was called shortly after two o'clock on Sunday morning, and reached the place of the murder about twenty minutes past two. My attention was directed to the body of the deceased. It was lying in the position described by Watkins, on its back, the head turned to the left shoulder, the arms by the side of the body, as if they had fallen there. Both palms were upwards, the fingers slightly bent. A thimble was lying near. The clothes were thrown up. The bonnet was at the back of the head. There was great disfigurement of the face. The throat was cut across. Below the cut was a neckerchief. The upper part of the dress had been torn open. The body had been mutilated, and was quite warm - no rigor mortis. The crime must have been committed within half an hour, or certainly within forty minutes from the time when I saw the body. There were no stains of blood on the bricks or pavement around.

Mr. Crawford: There was no blood on the front of the clothes. There was not a speck of blood on the front of the jacket.

Coroner: Before we removed the body Dr. Phillips was sent for, as I wished him to see the wounds, he having been engaged in a case of a similar kind previously. He saw the body at the mortuary. The clothes were removed from the deceased carefully. I made a post-mortem examination on Sunday afternoon. There was a bruise on the back of the left hand, and one on the right shin, but this had nothing to do with the crime. There were no bruises on the elbows or the back of the head. The face was very much mutilated, the eyelids, the nose, the jaw, the cheeks, the lips, and the mouth all bore cuts. There were abrasions under the left ear. The throat was cut across to the extent of six or seven inches.

Coroner Can you tell us what was the cause of death? The cause of death was haemorrhage from the throat. Death must have been immediate.

Coroner There were other wounds on the lower part of the body? Yes; deep wounds, which were inflicted after death.

(Witness here described in detail the terrible mutilation of the deceased's body.)

Mr. Crawford: I understand that you found certain portions of the body removed? Yes. The uterus was cut away with the exception of a small portion, and the left kidney was also cut out. Both these organs were absent, and have not been found.

Coroner Have you any opinion as to what position the woman was in when the wounds were inflicted? In my opinion the woman must have been lying down. The way in which the kidney was cut out showed that it was done by somebody who knew what he was about.

Coroner Does the nature of the wounds lead you to any conclusion as to the instrument that was used? It must have been a sharp-pointed knife, and I should say at least 6 in. long.

Coroner Would you consider that the person who inflicted the wounds possessed anatomical skill? He must have had a good deal of knowledge as to the position of the abdominal organs, and the way to remove them.

Coroner Would the parts removed be of any use for professional purposes? None whatever.

Coroner Would the removal of the kidney, for example, require special knowledge? It would require a good deal of knowledge as to its position, because it is apt to be overlooked, being covered by a membrane.

Coroner Would such knowledge be likely to be possessed by some one accustomed to cutting up animals? Yes.

Coroner Have you been able to form any opinion as to whether the perpetrator of this act was disturbed? I think he had sufficient time, but it was in all probability done in a hurry.

Coroner How long would it take to make the wounds? It might be done in five minutes. It might take him longer; but that is the least time it could be done in.

Coroner Can you, as a professional man, ascribe any reason for the taking away of the parts you have mentioned? I cannot give any reason whatever.

Coroner Have you any doubt in your own mind whether there was a struggle? I feel sure there was no struggle. I see no reason to doubt that it was the work of one man.

Coroner Would any noise be heard, do you think? I presume the throat was instantly severed, in which case there would not be time to emit any sound.

Coroner Does it surprise you that no sound was heard? No.

Coroner Would you expect to find much blood on the person inflicting these wounds? No, I should not. I should say that a person kneeling at the right side of the body inflicted the abdominal wounds. The wounds could not possibly have been self-inflicted.

Coroner Was your attention called to the portion of the apron that was found in Goulston Street? Yes, I fitted that portion which was spotted with blood to the remaining portion, which was still attached by the strings to the body.

Coroner Have you formed any opinion as to the motive for the mutilation of the face? It was to disfigure the corpse, I should imagine.

A Juror: Was there any evidence of a drug having been used? I have not examined the stomach as to that. The contents of the stomach have been preserved for analysis. Mr. Crawford said he was glad to announce that the Corporation had unanimously approved the offer by the Lord Mayor of a reward of £500 for the discovery of the murderer.

Several jurymen expressed their satisfaction at the promptness with which the offer was made.

The inquest was then adjourned until next Thursday.

Day 2, Thursday, October 11, 1888
(*The Daily Telegraph*, October 12, 1888, Page 2)

Yesterday [11 Oct], at the City Coroner's Court, Golden-lane, Mr. S.
F. Langham resumed the inquest respecting the death of Catherine
Eddowes, who was found murdered and mutilated in Mitre Square,
Aldgate, early on the morning of Sunday, Sept. 30.

Mr. Crawford, City Solicitor again watched the case on behalf of the
police.

Dr. G. W. Sequeira, surgeon, of No. 34, Jewry Street, Aldgate, deposed:
On the morning of Sept. 30 I was called to Mitre Square, and I arrived at
five minutes to two o'clock, being the first medical man on the scene of the
murder. I saw the position of the body, and I entirely agree with the
evidence of Dr. Gordon Brown in that respect.
By Mr. Crawford: I am well acquainted with the locality and the position
of the lamps in the square. Where the murder was committed was probably
the darkest part of the square, but there was sufficient light to enable the
miscreant to perpetrate the deed. I think that the murderer had no design on
any particular organ of the body. He was not possessed of any great
anatomical skill.
Coroner Can you account for the absence of noise? The death must have
been instantaneous after the severance of the windpipe and the blood
vessels.
Coroner Would you have expected the murderer to be bespattered with
blood? Not necessarily.
Coroner How long do you believe life had been extinct when you arrived?
Very few minutes - probably not more than a quarter of an hour.

Mr. William Sedgwick Saunders, medical officer of health for the City,
said: I received the stomach of the deceased from Dr. Gordon Brown,
carefully sealed, and I made an analysis of the contents, which had not
been interfered with in any way. I looked more particularly for poisons of
the narcotic class, but with negative results, there being not the faintest
trace of any of those or any other poisons.

Annie Phillips stated: I reside at No. 12, Dilston Road, Southwark Park
Road, and am married, my husband being a lamp-black packer. I am
daughter of the deceased, who formerly lived with my father. She always
told me that she was married to him, but I have never seen the marriage
lines. My father's name was Thomas Conway.

Coroner: Have you seen him lately? Not for the last fifteen or eighteen months.

Coroner Where was he living then? He was living with me and my husband, at No. 15, Acre Street, Southwark Park Road.

Coroner What calling did he follow? That of a hawker.

Coroner What became of him? I do not know.

Coroner Did he leave on good terms with you? Not on very good terms.

Coroner Did he say that he would never see you again, or anything of that sort? No.

Coroner Was he a sober man? He was a teetotaller.

Coroner Did he live on bad terms with your mother? Yes, because she used to drink.

Coroner Have you any idea where Conway is now? Not the least. He ceased to live with Eddowes entirely on account of her drinking habits.

Coroner Your father was in the 18th Royal Irish Regiment? So I have been told. He had been a pensioner ever since I was eight years old. I am twenty-three now. They parted about seven or eight years ago.

Coroner Did your mother ever apply to you for money? Yes.

Coroner When did you last see her? Two years and one month ago.

Coroner Where did you live when you last saw her? Two brothers.

Coroner Where are they living? In London.

Coroner Did your mother know where to find either of you? No.

Coroner Were your addresses purposely kept from her? Yes.

Coroner To prevent her applying for money?

The Foreman: Was your father aware when he left you that your mother was living with Kelly? –Yes.

Mr. Crawford: Are you quite certain that your father was a pensioner of the 18th Royal Irish? I was told so, but I am not sure whether it was the 18th or the Connaught Rangers. It may have been the latter.

Coroner: That is the 88th I do not know.

Mr. Crawford: That is so. It so happens that there is a pensioner of the name of Conway belonging to the Royal Irish, but that is not the man.

To witness: When did your mother last receive money from you?

Witness: Just over two years ago. She waited upon me in my confinement, and I paid her for it.

Coroner Did you ever get a letter from her? No.

Coroner Do you know anything about Kelly? I have seen him two or three times at the lodging-house in Flower and Dean Street, with my mother.

Coroner When did you last see them together? About three years and a half ago.

Coroner You knew they were living together as man and wife? Yes.

Coroner Is it the fact that your father is living with your two brothers? He was.

Coroner Where are your brothers residing now? I do not know.

Coroner He was always with them. One was fifteen and the other eighteen years of age.

Coroner When did you last see them? About eighteen months ago. I have not seen them since.

Coroner Are we to understand that you had lost all trace of your mother, father, and two brothers for at least eighteen months? That is so.

Detective-Sergeant John Mitchell, of the City police, said: I have, under instructions, and with other officers, made every endeavour to find the father and brothers of the last witness, but without success up to the present.

Coroner: Have you found a pensioner named Conway belonging to the 18th Royal Irish? I have. He has not been identified as the husband of the deceased. **Detective Baxter Hunt:** Acting under instructions, I discovered the pensioner, Conway, of the Royal Irish, and have confronted him with two sisters of the deceased, who, however, failed to recognise him as the man who used to live with the deceased. I have made every endeavour to trace the Thomas Conway in question and the brothers of Annie Phillips, but without success.

A Juror: Why did you not confront this Conway with the daughter of the deceased, Annie Phillips? That witness had not been found then.

Mr. Crawford: The theory has been put forward that it was possible for the deceased to have been murdered elsewhere, and her body brought to where it was found. I should like to ask Dr. Gordon Brown, who is present, what his opinion is about that?

Dr. Gordon Brown: I do not think there is any foundation for such a theory. The blood on the left side was clotted, and must have fallen at the time the throat was cut. I do not think that the deceased moved the least bit after that.

Coroner: The body could not have been carried to where it was found?Oh, no.

City-constable Lewis Robinson, 931, deposed: At half-past eight, on the night of Saturday, Sept. 29, while on duty in High Street, Aldgate, I saw a crowd of persons outside No. 29, surrounding a woman whom I have since recognised as the deceased.

Coroner: What state was she in? Drunk. Lying on the footway? Yes. I asked the crowd if any of them knew her or where she lived, but got no answer. I then picked her up and sat her against the shutters, but she fell down sideways. With the aid of a fellow-constable I took her to Bishopsgate Police Station. There she was asked her name, and she replied "Nothing." She was then put into a cell.

Coroner Did any one appear to be in her company when you found her? No one in particular.

Mr. Crawford: Did any one appear to know her? No. The apron being produced, torn and discolored with blood, the witness said that to the best of his knowledge it was the apron the deceased was wearing.

The Foreman: What guided you in determining whether the woman was drunk or not?

Witness: Her appearance.

The Foreman: I ask you because I know of a case in which a person was arrested for being drunk who had not tasted anything intoxicating for eight or nine hours.

Coroner You are quite sure this woman was drunk? She smelt very strongly of drink.

Sergeant James Byfield, of the City Police: I remember the deceased being brought to the Bishopsgate Station at a quarter to nine o'clock on the night of Saturday, Sept. 29.

Coroner In what condition was she? Very drunk. She was brought in supported by two constables and placed in a cell, where she remained until one o'clock the next morning, when she had got sober. I then discharged her, after she had given her name and address.

Coroner What name and address did she gives? Mary Ann Kelly, No. 6, Fashion Street, Spitalfields.

Coroner Did she say where she had been, or what she had been doing? She stated that she had been hopping.

Constable George Henry Hutt, 968, City Police: I am gaoler at Bishopsgate station. On the night of Saturday, Sept. 29, at a quarter to ten o'clock, I took over our prisoners, among them the deceased. I visited her several times until five minutes to one on Sunday morning. The inspector, being out visiting, I was directed by Sergeant Byfield to see if any of the prisoners were fit to be discharged. I found the deceased sober, and after she had given her name and address, she was allowed to leave. I pushed open the swing-door leading to the passage, and said, "This way, missus." She passed along the passage to the outer door. I said to her, "Please, pull it to." She replied, "All right. Good night, old cock."

(Laughter.) She pulled the door to within a foot of being close, and I saw her turn to the left.

Coroner: That was leading towards Houndsditch? Yes.

The Foreman: Is it left to you to decide when a prisoner is sober enough to be released or not? Not to me, but to the inspector or acting inspector on duty.

Coroner Is it usual to discharge prisoners who have been locked up for being drunk at all hours of the night? Certainly.

Coroner How often did you visit the prisoners? About every half-hour. At first the deceased remained asleep; but at a quarter to twelve she was awake, and singing a song to herself, as it were. I went to her again at half-past twelve, and she then asked when she would be able to get out. I replied: "Shortly." She said, "I am capable of taking care of myself now."

Mr. Crawford: Did she tell you where she was going? No. About two minutes to one o'clock, when I was taking her out of the cell, she asked me what time it was. I answered, "Too late for you to get any more drink." She said, "Well, what time is it?" I replied, "Just on one." Thereupon she said, "I shall get a ---- fine hiding when I get home, then."

Coroner Was that her parting remark? That was in the station yard? I said, "Serve you right; you have no right to get drunk."

Coroner You supposed she was going home? I did.

Coroner In your opinion is that the apron the deceased was wearing? To the best of my belief it is.

Coroner What is the distance from Mitre Square to your station? About 400 yards.

Coroner Do you know the direct route to Flower and Dean Street? No.

A Juror: Do you search persons who are brought in for drunkenness? No, but we take from them anything that might be dangerous. I loosened the things round the deceased's neck, and I then saw a white wrapper and a red silk handkerchief.

George James Morris, night watchman at Messrs. Kearley and Tonge's tea warehouse, Mitre Square, deposed: On Saturday, Sept. 29, I went on duty at seven o'clock in the evening. I occupied most of my time in cleaning the offices and looking about the warehouse.

Coroner: What happened about a quarter to two in the morning? Constable Watkins, who was on the Mitre-square beat, knocked at my door, which was slightly ajar at the time. I was then sweeping the steps down towards the door. The door was pushed when I was about two yards off. I turned round and opened the door wide. The constable said, "For

God's sake, mate, come to my assistance." I said, "Stop till I get my lamp. What is the matter?" "Oh, dear," he exclaimed, "here is another woman cut to pieces." I asked where, and he replied, "In the corner." I went into the corner of the Square and turned my light on the body. I agree with the previous witnesses as to the position of the body. I ran up Mitre Street into Aldgate, blowing my whistle all the while.

Coroner Did you see any suspicious persons about? No. Two constables came up and asked what was the matter. I told them to go down to Mitre Square, as there was another terrible murder. They went, and I followed and took charge of my own premises again.

Coroner Before being called by Constable Watkins, had you heard any noise in the square? No.

Coroner If there had been any cry of distress, would you have heard it from where you were? Yes. I was in the warehouse facing the corner of the square.

Before being called I had no occasion to go into the square. I did not go there between one and two o'clock; of that I am certain. There was nothing unusual in my door being open and my being at work at so late an hour. I had not seen Watkins before during the night. I do not think my door had been ajar more than two or three minutes when he knocked.

James Harvey, City constable, 964: On the night of Saturday, Sept. 29, I was on duty in the neighbourhood of Houndsditch and Aldgate. I was there at the time of the murder, but did not see any one nor hear any cry. When I got into Aldgate, returning towards Duke Street, I heard a whistle and saw the witness Morris with a lamp. I asked him what was the matter, and he told me that a woman had been ripped up in Mitre Square. Together with Constable Hollins (Holland) I went to Mitre Square, where Watkins was by the side of the body of the deceased. Hollins went for Dr. Sequeira, and a private individual was despatched for other constables, who arrived almost immediately, having heard the whistle. I waited with Watkins, and information was sent to the inspector.

Coroner At what time previous to that were you in Aldgate? At twenty-eight minutes past one o'clock I passed the post-office clock.

George Clapp, caretaker at No. 5, Mitre Street, deposed: The back part of the house looks into Mitre Square. On the night of Saturday week last I retired to rest in the back room on the second floor about eleven o'clock.

Coroner: During the night did you hear any disturbance in the square? No.

Coroner When did you first learn that a murder had been perpetrated? Between five and six o'clock in the morning.

Mr. Crawford: A nurse, who was in attendance upon my wife, was sleeping at the top of the house. No person slept either on the ground floor or the first floor.

Constable Richard Pearce, 922 City: I reside at No. 3, Mitre- Square. There are only two private houses in the Square. I retired to rest at twenty minutes past twelve on the morning of last Sunday week.

Coroner Did you hear any noise in the square? None at all.

Coroner When did you first hear of the murder? At twenty past two, when I was called by a constable.

Coroner From your bedroom window could you see the spot where the murder was committed? Yes, quite plainly. My wife and family were in no way disturbed during the night.

Joseph Lawende: I reside at No. 45, Norfolk Road, Dalston and am a commercial traveller. On the night of Sept. 29, I was at the Imperial Club, Duke Street, together with Mr. Joseph Levy and Mr. Harry Harris. It was raining, and we sat in the club till half-past one o'clock, when we left. I observed a man and woman together at the corner of Church Passage, Duke Street, leading to Mitre Square.

Coroner: Were they talking? The woman was standing with her face towards the man, and I only saw her back. She had one hand on his breast. He was the taller. She had on a black jacket and bonnet. I have seen the articles at the police station, and believe them to be those the deceased was wearing.

Coroner What sort of man was this? He had on a cloth cap with a peak of the same.

Mr. Crawford: Unless the jury wishes it, I do not think further particulars should be given as to the appearance of this man.

The Foreman: The jury does not desire it.

Mr. Crawford (to witness): You have given a description of the man to the police? Yes.

Coroner Would you know him again? I doubt it. The man and woman were about nine or ten feet away from me. I have no doubt it was half-past one o'clock when we rose to leave the club, so that it would be twenty-five minutes to two o'clock when we passed the man and woman.

Coroner Did you overhear anything that either said? No.

Coroner Did either appear in an angry mood? No.

Coroner Did anything about their movements attract your attention? No. The man looked rather rough and shabby.

Coroner When the woman placed her hand on the man's breast, did she do it as if to push him away? No it was done very quietly.

Coroner You were not curious enough to look back and see where they went? No.

Mr Joseph Hyam Levy. The butcher in Hutchinson Street, Aldgate. I was with the last witness at the Imperial Club on Saturday night, Sept. 29. We got up to leave at half-past one on Sunday morning, and came out three or four minutes later. I saw a man and woman standing at the corner of Church Passage, but I did not take any notice of them. I passed on, thinking they were up to no good at so late an hour.

Coroner What height was the man? I should think he was three inches taller than the woman, who was, perhaps, 5ft high. I cannot give any further description of them. I went down Duke Street into Aldgate, leaving them still talking together.

By the Jury: The point in the passage where the man and woman were standing was not well lighted? On the contrary, I think it was badly lighted then, but the light is much better now. Nothing in what I saw excited my suspicion as to the intentions of the man. I did not hear a word that he uttered to the woman.

Coroner Your fear was rather about yourself? Not exactly. (Laughter.)

Constable Alfred Long, 254 A, Metropolitan police: I was on duty in Goulston Street, Whitechapel, on Sunday morning, Sept. 30, and about five minutes to three o'clock I found a portion of a white apron (produced). There were recent stains of blood on it. The apron was lying in the passage leading to the staircase of Nos. 106 to 119, a model dwelling house. Above on the wall was written in chalk, "The Jews are the men that will not be blamed for nothing." I at once searched the staircase and areas of the building, but did not find anything else. I took the apron to Commercial Road Police station and reported to the inspector on duty.

Coroner Had you been past that spot previously to your discovering the apron? I passed about twenty minutes past two o'clock.

Coroner Are you able to say whether the apron was there then? It was not.

Mr. Crawford: As to the writing on the wall, have you not put a "not" in the wrong place? Were not the words, "The Jews are not the men that will be blamed for nothing"?I believe the words were as I have stated.

Coroner Was not the word "Jews" spelt "Juwes?" It may have been.

Coroner Yet you did not tell us that in the first place. Did you make an entry of the words at the time? Yes, in my pocket book.**Coroner** Is it possible that you have put the "not" in the wrong place? It is possible, but I do not think that I have.

Coroner Which did you notice first, the piece of apron or the writing on the wall? The piece of apron, one corner of which was wet with blood.

Coroner How came you to observe the writing on the wall?I saw it while trying to discover whether there were any marks of blood about.

Coroner Did the writing appear to have been recently done? I could not form an opinion.

Coroner Do I understand that you made a search in the model dwelling house? I went into the staircases.

Coroner Did you not make inquiries in the house itself? No.

The Foreman: Where is the pocket book in which you made the entry of the writing? At Westminster.

Coroner Is it possible to get it at once? I dare say.

Mr. Crawford: I will ask the coroner to direct that the book be fetched.

Coroner: Let that be done.

Daniel Halse, Detective Constable City police: On Saturday, Sept. 29, pursuant to instructions received at the central office in Old Jewry, I directed a number of police in plain clothes to patrol the streets of the City all night. At two minutes to two o'clock on the Sunday morning, when near Aldgate Church, in company with Detectives Outram and Marriott, I heard that a woman had been found murdered in Mitre Square. We ran to the spot and I at once gave instructions for the neighbourhood to be searched and every man stopped and examined. I myself went by way of Middlesex street into Wentworth Street, where I stopped two men, who, however, gave a satisfactory account of themselves. I came through Goulston Street about twenty minutes past two, and then returned to Mitre Square, subsequently going to the mortuary. I saw the deceased, and noticed that a portion of her apron was missing. I accompanied Major Smith back to Mitre Square, when we heard that a piece of apron had been found in Goulston Street. After visiting Leman Street police station, I proceeded to Goulston Street, where I saw some chalk writing on the black fascia of the wall. Instructions were given to have the writing photographed. Before it could be done the Metropolitan police stated that they thought the writing might cause a riot or outbreak against the Jews, and it was decided to have it rubbed out, as the people were already bringing out their stalls into the street. When Detective Hunt returned inquiry was made at every door of every tenement of the model dwelling house, but we gained no tidings of any one who was likely to have been the murderer. At twenty minutes past two o'clock I passed over the spot where the piece of apron was found, but did not notice anything then. I should not necessarily have seen the piece of apron.

Coroner As to the writing on the wall, did you hear anybody suggest that the word "Jews" should be rubbed out and the other words left? I did. The fear on the part of the Metropolitan police that the writing might cause riot was the sole reason why it was rubbed out. I took a copy of it, and what I wrote down was as follows: "The Juwes are not the men who will be blamed for nothing."

Coroner Did the writing have the appearance of having been recently done? Yes. It was written with white chalk on a black fascia.

Foreman: Why was the writing really rubbed out? **Witness:** The Metropolitan police said it might create a riot, and it was their ground.

Mr. Crawford: I am obliged to ask this question. Did you protest against the writing being rubbed out? **Witness:** I did. I asked that it might, at all events, be allowed to remain until Major Smith had seen it. **Mr Crawford** Why do you say that it seemed to have been recently written?

Witness It looked fresh, and if it had been done long before it would have been rubbed out by the people passing. I did not notice whether there was any powdered chalk on the ground, though I did look about to see if a knife could be found. There were three lines of writing in a good schoolboy's round hand. The size of the capital letters would be about 3/4 in, and the other letters were in proportion. The writing was on the black bricks, which formed a kind of Daido, the bricks above being white.

Mr. Crawford: With the exception of a few questions to Long, the Metropolitan constable, that is the whole of the evidence I have to offer at the present moment on the part of the City police. But if any point occurs to the coroner or the jury I shall be happy to endeavour to have it cleared up.

A Juror: It seems surprising that a policeman should have found the piece of apron in the passage of the buildings, and yet made no inquiries in the buildings themselves. There was a clue up to that point, and then it was altogether lost.

Mr. Crawford: As to the premises being searched, I have in court members of the City police who did make diligent search in every part of the tenements the moment the matter came to their knowledge. But unfortunately it did not come to their knowledge until two hours after. There was thus delay, and the man who discovered the piece of apron is a member of the Metropolitan police.

A Juror: It is the man belonging to the Metropolitan police that I am complaining of.

At this point Constable Long returned, and produced the pocket book containing the entry, which he made at the time concerning the discovery of the writing on the wall.

Mr. Crawford: What is the entry? **Witness:** The words are, "The Jews are the men that will not be blamed for nothing." **Coroner** Both here and in your inspector's report the word "Jews" is spelt correctly? **Witness** Yes; but the inspector remarked that the word was spelt "Juwes."

Coroner Why did you write "Jews" then? I made my entry before the inspector made the remark.

Coroner But why did the inspector write "Jews"? I cannot say.

Coroner At all events, there is a discrepancy? It would seem so.

Coroner What did you do when you found the piece of apron? I at once searched the staircases leading to the buildings.

Coroner Did you make inquiry in any of the tenements of the buildings? No.

Coroner How many staircases are there? Six or seven.

Coroner And you searched every staircase? Every staircase to the top.

Coroner You found no trace of blood or of recent footmarks? No.

Coroner About what time was that? Three o'clock.

Coroner Having examined the staircases, what did you next do? I proceeded to the station.

Coroner Before going did you hear that a murder had been committed? Yes. It is common knowledge that two murders have been perpetrated.

Coroner Which did you hear of? I heard of the murder in the City. There were rumours of another, but not certain.

Coroner When you went away did you leave anybody in charge? Yes; the constable on the next beat 190, H Division but I do not know his name.

Coroner Did you give him instructions as to what he was to do? I told him to keep observation on the dwelling house, and see if any one entered or left.

Coroner When did you return? About five o'clock.

Coroner Had the writing been rubbed out then? No, it was rubbed out in my presence at half-past five.

Coroner Did you hear any one object to its being rubbed out? No. It was nearly daylight when it was rubbed out.

A Juror: Having examined the apron and the writing, did it not occur to you that it would be wise to search the dwelling? I did what I thought was right under the circumstances.

The Juror: I do not wish to say anything to reflect upon you, because I consider that altogether the evidence of the police redounds to their credit; but it does seem strange that this clue was not followed up.

Witness: I thought the best thing to do was to proceed to the station and report to the inspector on duty.

The Juror: I am sure you did what you deemed best.

Mr. Crawford: I suppose you thought it more likely to find the body there than the murderer?

Witness: Yes, and I felt that the inspector would be better able to deal with the matter than I was.

Foreman: Was there any possibility of a stranger escaping from the house? Not from the front.

Coroner Did you not know about the back? No, that was the first time I had been on duty there.

That being all the evidence forthcoming, the coroner said he considered a further adjournment unnecessary, and the better plan would be for the jury to return their verdict and then leave the matter in the hands of the police.

In summing up it would not be at all necessary for him to go through the testimony of the various witnesses, but if the jury wanted their memories refreshed on any particular point he would assist them by referring to the evidence on that point. That the crime was a most fiendish one could not for a moment be doubted, for the miscreant, not satisfied with taking a defenceless woman's life, endeavoured so to mutilate the body as to render it unrecognisable.

The **Coroner** presumed that the jury would return a verdict of wilful murder against some person or persons unknown, and then the police could freely pursue their inquiries and follow up any clue they might obtain. A magnificent reward had been offered, and that might be the means of setting people on the track and bringing to speedy justice the creature that had committed this atrocious crime.

On reflection, perhaps it would be sufficient to return a verdict of wilful murder against some person unknown, inasmuch as the medical evidence conclusively demonstrated that only one person could be implicated.

The jury at once returned a verdict accordingly.

The coroner, for himself and the jury, thanked Mr. Crawford and the police for the assistance they had rendered in the inquiry.

Mr. Crawford: The police have simply done their duty.

The Coroner: I am quite sure of that.

The jury having presented their fees to Annie Phillips, daughter of the deceased, the proceedings terminated.

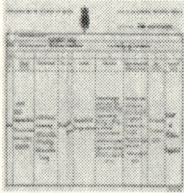

A copy of the Death Certificate of Catharine Eddowes.

Chapter 7

Mary Jane Kelly

On November 9, the last **canonical** victim was to meet her fate.

She was the youngest of the women killed by the Ripper, at only 25 years old. She stood five foot seven inches tall. She was stout and had a fair complexion with blue eyes and blond hair. She was attractive and was spotlessly clean. This poor Unfortunate was called Mary Jane Kelly or Marie Jeanette Kelly. The pseudonyms for Mary were "Black Mary," "Fair Emma," and "Ginger," which makes you wonder what colour hair Mary actually had. Could she have been a strawberry blond, which would account for "Ginger" and "Fair Emma" but would not explain "Black Mary." Apparently she loved to sing and was a friendly, happy woman.

Mary's background is as mysterious as the Ripper's true identity. She was born in Limerick around 1863, but the family moved to Wales when she was very young. It has been said that Mary could speak fluent welsh. Mary was the second daughter of John Kelly an ironworker. Mary may have married a man called Davis who died in a pit fall. There is no evidence that any children came from this marriage. Following this accident, Mary moved to Cardiff to stay with her cousin. This is where Mary was introduced to prostitution, maybe by her cousin but we do not know. What we do know is that venereal disease followed. Mary spent a long time in an infirmary because of an unknown illness.

1884

Mary moved to London and went to work in a very high-class brothel, possibly in Knightsbridge. How she came by this job is, again, not known. It is alleged that Mary left the brothel to go and live in France with a gentleman, but she returned to London a few weeks later because she disliked France. At the inquest, Joseph Barnett stated he did not know whether it was the place or the purpose Mary did not like about France. I believe at this point she was "shipped" to France as part of the trafficking of young English girls in brothels over there. She would not have been alone, there would have been young girls with her who were still children being shipped out there for the same purpose. Up to the year 1850 the age of consent was 12, and then in 1850 it increased to 13.

When she returned to London, Mary went to live with a woman called Mrs. Buki in St George's Street. From there she moved in with Mrs. Carthy in Breezers Hill. Here, Mary started drinking, which made her very unpopular and led to her decline to the East End. These women may have been brothel keepers or Madam's as they were and still are called.

1886

Mary left Mrs. Carthy. She went to live with two other men before she met Joseph Barnett in 1887. One of these men was called Morganstone who lived some where near Stepney Gas Works. The other was Joseph Flemming who lived in Bethnal Green. Flemming was a Stone Mason or a mason's plasterer. Mary was supposed to have been very fond of a man named Joe who often visited and gave her money.

1887

Mary was living in Cooley's common lodging house in Thrawl Street when she met Joseph Barnett on Good Friday, April 8.

Joseph Barnett was a Market Porter and was licensed to work at Billingsgate Fish Market. He was born in London but was of Irish decent. Julia Van Turney said Barnett was a good man who was kind to Mary and gave her money. After two dates, the couple decided to move in together. Their first home was in George Street, then Paternoster Row in Dorset Street. They were evicted for drunkenness and not paying their rent. They moved to Brick Lane, and finally to 13 Millers Court off Dorset Street.

Dorset Street ran east to west between Commercial Street and Crispin Street. It was well known for its crime and poverty. It was flanked by old brick buildings whose doors opened directly into the street. At the eastern end of the street stood the Britannia public house and at the western end sat the Horn of Plenty. Millers Court was one of three alleyways that run off Dorset Street. It was situated between numbers twenty-six and twenty-seven Dorset Street, and was entered through a three-foot-wide opening. These two properties were owned by Mary's landlord and local grocer John McCarthy. He lived at number twenty-seven and has his shop on the ground floor of the building. Number twenty-six was used as a storeroom. Directly opposite the entrance to Millers Court was Crossingham's lodging house, home to Annie Chapman—one of the Ripper's earlier victims.

Thirteen Millers Court was the back room of twenty-six Dorset Street. It had been partitioned off from the rest of the building and was reached through what would have been the back door of the property via Millers Court. This Court was situated off Dorset Street and had a narrow thoroughfare leading into it. The Court was about 130 yards long. Number 13 was the first door on the right as you entered Millers Court. Anyone entering or leaving this Court would have to pass Mary's room. The rent for this room was 4 to 6d a week. It was a small room about twelve-foot-square, containing two tables and a chair. The fireplace had a print above it called "The Fisherman's Widow." There were two small windows in the room; one window that was very close to the door had broken panes which Mary broke during an argument with Barnett. Because Mary had lost her door key she would put her arm through the open pane and unbolt the front door.

In 1888, the person who held the key to a property was the tenant; Mary had lost her key but had not informed her Landlord because he could have changed the lock and she could have done nothing about it. Because she owed him rent would have also made her not want to tell the landlord about the missing item.

A pilot's coat hung at the window instead of a curtain to keep the cold out. In a small cupboard there was some stale bread and some cheap crockery. Sometimes the payment for her *services* was not necessarily money but sustenance in the form of stale loaf of bread. There were also empty ginger beer bottles in the room. The bed was situated against the partition wall. In the crime scene photographs, it looks like a tin bath was under the bed. This was not listed as an item in the room when the crime scene was detailed. Barnett lost his job during the summer. Although he did not want Mary to walk the streets, she had to do something in order to live.

November 8, 1888 Mary and Barnett had quarrelled over how Mary kept letting other Unfortunates share their room. Barnett decided to leave, but would go and visit her every day taking to her any money he could. Barnett is quoted as saying that Mary only let the "Unfortunates" stay as she was too kind hearted, and did not like to refuse them shelter on cold bitter nights.

7:30-7:45 p.m. Barnett visited Mary in Millers Court. He said another woman was with Mary when he arrived that evening. The other woman also lived in the Court. It was probably Lizzie Albrook who lived at number 2 Millers Court. Albrook worked at a nearby lodging house. She remembered Mary's last comments to her: *"Whatever you do don't you do wrong and turn out as I did."* Albrook said that Mary often warned her against going on the streets. Mary also expressed feeling heartily sick of the life she was leading and wished she had enough money to go back to Ireland where she said her people lived.

8:00 p.m. Barnett left Millers Court and went back to Buller's Boarding house where he played cards past midnight, and then went to bed. Exactly what Mary did between 8:00 p.m. and 11:00 p.m. is a mystery. There is an unconfirmed story that Mary was drinking in either The Britannia or the Ten Bells public house with a woman named Elizabeth Foster.

11:00 p.m. Mary was seen drinking in The Britannia Pub with a very respectable looking young man with a dark moustache, and she appeared to be very drunk.

11:45 p.m. A woman named Mary Ann Cox, a widow living at 5 Millers Court, was returning home to warm her as the night was cold. Cox claimed she had just entered Dorset Street from Commercial Street when she saw Mary ahead of her. She says she saw Mary with a scruffy looking stout man wearing a *Billycock hat* and a long overcoat. In his hand the man was carrying a pale of Beer. The man is described as between the age of 35 and 36 with a carroty moustache and small side-whiskers and a blotchy complexion. Cox followed the couple into Millers Court, where they stopped outside Mary's room. At the inquest Cox was asked by the coroner *"did the mans heels on his boots sound heavy"* to which she replied that *"there was no sound as he went up the court"*. Then the coroner asked her if she thought that maybe the man's heels on his boots might have been worn down, she again replied that the man made no sound when walking. Passing the couple Cox said *"Goodnight"* to which a very drunk Mary replied *"Goodnight, I am going to sing"* A few minutes later Cox heard her singing a song called A Violet From Mothers Grave. Mary was still singing this song when Cox left her home again at midnight. It is thought that at this time Mary ate a meal of potatoes and fish.

9th November 1888 After the demands from the radical press for the resignation of Sir Charles Warren, this was the day that his resignation would be announced.

12.30 a.m. Catherine Picket was going to go down stairs to complain to Mary after she had disturbed her with her singing. Picket did not go as her husband told her *"to leave the poor girl alone"*.

1 a.m. It had started raining so Cox returned home to get warm again. She heard Mary still singing and there was also light in Mary's room when Cox came into Millers Court

1 a.m. A woman called Elizabeth Prater who lived at number 20 Millers Court stated that she was standing at the entrance to Millers Court, waiting for a man who she lived with. She had stood there for about half an hour and he did not show so she went into McCarthy's shop to have a chat. Elizabeth Prater stated she saw no one leave or enter Millers Court whilst she was waiting there. She also stated that she did not hear any singing coming from the court. Prater, who was drunk, then went home where she put two chairs behind the door, got into bed fully dressed and went to sleep. Number 20 Millers Court was the room immediately above Mary's room.

2 a.m. George Hutchinson states he saw Mary on his return from Romford. As he walked along Commercial Street, he noticed a man standing on the corner of Thrawl Street, but did not pay a lot of attention to him. He carried on walking and when he reached Flower and Dean Street he met Mary. Hutchinson claims that Mary asked him to lend her some money, to which he replied no, as he had spent it, all in Romford. Hutchinson then states Mary bid him Good Morning, saying she needed money and set off towards Thrawl Street. *I think Hutchinson was Mary's pimp, and the conversation was probably the other way round, Hutchinson was demanding money from Mary so she would not get hurt.*

Mary walked away and stops and talks to the man Hutchinson had passed earlier in the street. The man puts his arm on Mary's shoulder and says something that makes the couple laugh. Hutchinson then hears Mary say *"all right"* and the man replies *"you will be all right for what I have told you"* The couple then set off towards Dorset Street. Hutchinson noticed the man was carrying a small parcel in his left hand.

As the couple walked pass Hutchinson, he made a point of looking at the man closely; the description Hutchinson gave of this man is as follows;

- **He is about 5' 6" to 5' 7" tall.**
- **Aged about 35 to 36 years of age.**
- **Jewish looking, with a dark complexion.**
- **Dark eyes and bushy eyebrows.**
- **A thick dark moustache that curled up at the ends.**
- **He was wearing a long dark coat that had astrakhan trimming.**
- **A soft felt hat that was pulled down over his eyes.**
- **A white collar and a black necktie that was fastened with a horse shoe pin.**
- **A waistcoat that had a large gold chain that connected to a large seal with a red stone hanging from it.**
- **Dark spats over light button over boots.**
- **He carried kid gloves in his right hand and a small parcel in his left hand.**

The couple then crossed Commercial Street and went down Dorset Street. **Why had Hutchinson decided to follow them? The only conclusion could be that he was waiting to get some money off Mary?** The couple stopped outside Millers Court for a short time talking. Hutchinson heard Mary say *"alright my dear, come along, you will be comfortable"* The man then puts his arm around Mary and she kisses him. Mary tells the man she had lost her handkerchief. In response the man pulls out *a red one* and gives it to Mary. The couple make their way down Millers Court to Mary's room and Hutchinson waits outside Millers Court till 3 a.m. before leaving.

Dr. Barnardo went out late at night doing his **work** in disguise to enable him to enter the common lodging houses. He would wear a tattered coat and trousers with a Billy-Cock hat and a red handkerchief. Is this purely coincidence that the man seen with Kelly had a Billy-Cock hat and a red handkerchief? I do not think so I believe the man Hutchinson saw go home with Mary was Dr Barnardo. Apart from Mary all the previous victims used common lodging houses, so at any time would have come across Dr Barnardo during his regular visits of these houses.

I believe that Dr Barnardo had noticed Mary on one of his visits to a Ragged School that was cited only a few yards from her home. So when the need to change his MO arisen, Mary would have been an obvious choice. She was far younger than the other victims and because of visiting the school he would have known she had her own room. So whilst the officers on the beat were waiting for the killer to talk to a middle aged woman and go off with her into some dark place to conduct her business, the Ripper was again one step ahead.

3 a.m. Mrs Cox returns home again and it is still raining hard. She noticed that there was no light or sound coming from Mary's room as she turned into the Court this time. Cox does not go out again, but does not go straight to bed either. Cox also stated that during the night she heard men going in and out of the court, and at a quarter to six she heard someone leave the court but did not know where they came from as Cox never heard a door shut.

4 a.m. Elizabeth Prater is woken by her kitten Diddles walking across her and states that she heard a faint cry of murder. Prater stated at the inquest that she did not wake again till 5a.m. when she went down stairs and saw some men harnessing horses. By a quarter to six she was sat in the Ten Bells public house. She then returned home and slept till 11a.m. Another woman staying with friends in number 2, Millers Court was called Sarah Lewis, she later testified to hearing the same cry as Elizabeth Prater. The cry of *"murder"* was so common place in Whitechapel and neither woman took any notice. Sarah Lewis could have been the same woman the papers interviewed and called Mrs Kennedy. Both these women said that they had seen a man leaning against the wall of a lodging house on the opposite side of Dorset Street. They described the man as wearing a wide a wake hat, he was not tall but stout. ***This was probably Hutchinson waiting to get some money from Mary.*** Sarah Lewis stayed in Millers Court till 5.30p.m as the police would not let anyone leave the court. At the inquest the coroner asked Sarah Lewis if she had seen any one acting suspicious recently. She recalled an incident that had happened to her the Wednesday before Mary's death. She said that she was walking along Bethnal Green road with another woman. The time was about 8 o'clock and a gentleman followed the women before approaching them. He asked the women to follow him into an entry (alley). The man had a shiny leather bag in his hand. When asked by the coroner did the man want both women to go with him, Lewis replied *"no, only one of us"* Lewis refused to go with the man who then walked away. He then returned and said *"that he would treat them"* He put his bag down only to pick it up again and asked the women *"what are you frightened about? Do you think I've got anything in the bag?"* The women ran away because they were afraid. Lewis also stated that she had seen this man again on the Friday morning about half past two a.m., when she was on her way to Millers Court. She saw the man with a woman in Commercial Street near The Britannia public house. When asked by the coroner was the couple quarrelling? She replied *"no"* She did not know if the man recognised her as she passed him. She noted that he had the same bag with him. Again this man I believe was Dr Barnardo he had the effrontery to carry on approaching the Unfortunate's in the area without apprehension.

8a.m.-8.30a.m A Caroline Maxwell allegedly saw Mary alive. Caroline Maxwell stated at the inquest that she saw Mary standing on the corner of Millers Court. This was several hours after the estimated time of her death. Caroline Maxwell said she had known Mary for about four months, but had only spoken to her twice. She goes on to say that she had a conversation with Mary who told her she was feeling unwell and her condition was, she *"had the horrors of drink upon her"* Maxwell told Mary to have another drink to *"steady herself"* to which, Mary replied,*" I have already done that and brought it back up"*. Maxwell then replied *"I pity your condition."* She states she again saw Mary again an hour later with a stout man wearing a plaid coat standing outside the Britannia public house. When questioned by the coroner Maxwell did not change her statement. Maxwell said she knew the time and date was correct as she was returning some china her husband had borrowed from a neighbour across the road. Maxwell describes Mary as wearing a green bodice, dark skirt, and a maroon crossover shawl, the same clothes that Mary had worn the previous night. This description was the same description a Mary Ann Cox had stated seeing Mary wearing the night before. **10a.m.** Lewis Maurice a tailor who lived in Dorset Street told the press that he had known Mary for five years. He stated that he saw Mary in The Britannia public house the morning of her death. (If his timing was correct this would have been several hours after Mary's death). I believe that like Maxwell he was mistaken with the days, rather than the time he saw Mary. *In the 1880's East End people rarely drank the water, due to the cholera outbreak and lack of sanitation. Alcohol was the safest form of liquid refreshment at the time, apart from ginger beer this would have made* *the people in the East End constantly in a state of intoxication of some degree. So it is quite possible that Maxwell and Maurice had got there days mixed up. Unfortunately there was no detailed description taken by the Police at the crime scene of the clothes that were found folded up in Mary's room.*

Referring back to Maxwell and Mary's conversation, what did Maxwell mean by her condition? It has been suggested that Mary may have been pregnant at the time of her death; is that what Maxwell meant? Some authors believe this to be true and have used this word condition in their theories. I think it just meant that Maxwell felt pity for Mary having a hangover? The fact that Maxwell stated that she saw Mary several hours after her supposed death has again been used by authors in their theories that it was not Mary found butchered in Millers Court but another "Unfortunate".

If it was another Unfortunate then this then leads us to ask some obvious questions e.g.

1: who was this Unfortunate and why did nobody notice she was missing?

2: why was she killed in Mary's Room? Was it a case of mistaken identity?

3: did Mary return to her room in the early morning and to find the body and that is why she was unwell and vomited?

It was alleged that Mary may have rented her room to other "Unfortunates" to use while she was out. Mary wouldn't let others use her room if Mary herself was working and would need to take her clients back there. Barnett's statement will indicate that he left because another girl was staying with Mary. If it was not Mary that was slaughtered in that room, how could then she just disappear without a trace? I believe it was Mary who was killed that night in Millers Court. The fact that two people stated they saw Mary hours after her death, could lead you wrongly to believe that the murderer may have worn Mary's clothing to escape in. Could it therefore,(now the plot thickens) have been the murderer Maxwell spoke to instead of Mary dressed in her clothes? **I don't think so!** I don't think the murderer would have stopped to have a conversation with Maxwell and hang around talking to another man whilst wearing women's clothing. You may have your own conclusion to this theory.

It must be noted that after being summoned by the coroner on 12th November, four days after the event; Joseph Barnett could only identify Mary by her ear and eyes. It must have been very hard for him to identify her considering the condition her body and face must have been in.

10.45 a.m. This was supposed to have been a day of celebration in London as it was the day of the Lord Mayors Parade.

A Thomas Bowyer discovered Mary's body. He had gone to Mary's room to collect the rent arrears of 30 shillings that she owed to the owner of the building, John McCarthy. When Bowyer arrived at 13 Millers Court he knocked on the door but could not get an answer. As the door seemed locked he peered through a broken part of the window, moving the curtain and a coat that was hanging over the window to get a better view. The sight that greeted him would haunt him for the rest of his life. He recalled at the inquest that when he pulled back the curtain he saw two pieces of flesh lying on the table in front of the bed. The second time he looked he saw the deceased remains lying on the bed and blood on the floor. He then quickly returned to 27 Dorset Street where McCarthy ran his grocer shop and told him what he had seen back in Millers Court. Both men then went to Millers Court. When they arrived at Millers Court McCarthy looked into Mary's window just to satisfy him self. McCarthy initially sent Bowyer to Commercial Street Police Station, then followed swiftly on behind. Inspector Walter Beck and Detective Walter Drew returned with Bowyer to Millers Court. McCarthy recollections of the events given at the inquest are;

I sent my man Bowyer to "room thirteen to call for rent. He came back in five minutes saying "Guv'nor I knocked at the door and could not make anyone answer. I looked through the window and saw a lot of blood" McCarthy then told how he accompanied Bowyer back to Miller Court, and looked through the window, where he saw the victim and a lot of blood. He then said he could not speak for a few seconds, obviously shocked by the sight he had just seen.

11 a.m. At the scene of the crime the Police officers took it in turn to look through the broken window of Mary's room, more help was then immediately sent for.

11.15 a.m. Dr. Thomas Bond and Dr. George Bagster Phillips arrived at the crime scene in Millers Court. After looking through the broken pane Dr. Phillips decided that the mutilated cadaver had no need for urgent medical attention. The Drs waited till 1.30p.m for the door to be forced open. Dr. Phillips recalled that the door struck the table that was at the left side of the bed when opened. In his report Dr. Thomas Bond said:

"that he thought that the corner of the sheet to the right of the woman's head was to a large extent cut and saturated in blood, indicating that the face may have been covered with the sheet at the time of the attack."

In the same report he stated ;

"The murderer must have been a man of great coolness and daring."

Dr. Bond also gave his opinion of the killer's appearance as,

"A quiet inoffensive looking man probably middle-aged man. He would be respectfully dressed and in the habit of wearing a cloak or overcoat to cover any blood stains he may have had. He would most likely be eccentric in his habits. He is most likely not to have a regular occupation but living on some small income or pension. He probably lives among respectable people."

Dr. Phillips commented at the inquest that he thought that Mary's body had been moved away from the wooden partition after the initial, fatal wound to the throat was carried out. He reported that the severance of the right carotid artery was the immediate cause of death.

11.30 a.m. Inspector Abberline who was in charge of the investigation arrived at the scene. He told the police officers the bloodhounds named Barnaby and Burgho had been sent for, and they must not to enter the room until the dogs had arrived. *Two hours later* Superintendent Arnold arrived in Millers Court. He announced that the order in regard to the bloodhounds had been countermanded and the dogs were not coming. McCarthy was asked by Superintendent Arnold to break open Mary's door. McCarthy later gave unsympathetic interview to the press saying the crime scene was very disturbing and because of this murder it had led him to lose some tenants.

The Times newspaper reported McCarthy as saying;

"The sight we saw I cannot drive away from my mind. It looked more the work of a devil than of a man. The poor woman's body was lying on the bed, undressed. She had been completely disembowelled, and her entrails had been taken out and placed on the table. It was those that I seen when I looked through the window and took to be lumps of flesh. The woman's nose had been cut off, and her face gashed beyond recognition. Both her breasts too had been cut clean away and placed by the side of her liver and other entrails on the table. I had heard a great deal about the Whitechapel murders, but I declare to god I had never expected to see such a sight as this. The body was, of course, covered with blood, and so was the bed. The whole scene is more than I can describe. I hope I may never see such a sight again. It is most extraordinary that nothing should have been heard by the neighbours, as there are people passing backwards and forwards at all hours of the night, but no one heard so much as a scream".

Although most the details of the body parts were incorrect, he did capture the horror that greeted the men that entered Mary's room that day.

The first person to enter Mary's room was Dr. Bond. The room consisted of a bed, an old table, and a chair where Mary had put her folded clothes on when going to bed. Her boots were in front of the fire. Inspector

Abberline agreed with the inventory of Mary's room, but added that there had been a large fire in the grate of the room. He said it was so fierce that it had melted the spout of a kettle. He also stated that he and the Drs returned to the crime scene and went through the ashes in this grate and found the remnants of clothing and a brim of a hat as well as pieces of a skirt. When asked why he thought this fire had been lit? he replied that it could have been used for light for the purpose of the killer being able to see what he was doing, as the was only a small candle in the room.

Dr. Thomas Bonds report was lost or stolen until 1987 when it was returned anonymously to Scotland Yard.

The official crime scene report was written by Dr. Thomas Bond and was as follows;

The murder scene

"The body was found lying in the middle of the bed only wearing the remains of a chemise. At the right hand side of the bed it was noted the bedding was saturated in blood and under the bed in the same position was a pool of blood measuring two feet square. On the wall sited to the right of the bed and directly inline with the neck were bloodstains that had hit the wall by a number of separate splashes. On the right of the bed was a small table, which had a small candle and large lumps of flesh later, found to be the skin removed from the thighs and abdomen. Although the body was lying in the middle of the bed it was inclined more to the left. The victim was lying flat on her back and her shoulders were flat. The victim had her head turned to the left resting on the left cheek. The right arm was lying flat on the bed with the elbow bent, the right hand was clenched and there were cuts to the hand. The left arm was lying across the abdomen with the forearm flexed at a right angle; both arms were mutilated by many jagged wounds. The victim's legs were spread wide open and the left thigh was totally stripped of skin, fascia and muscles down to the knee. The left calf had a long slit that pierced the skin and tissue this slit extended from the knee to five inches above the ankle The whole surface of the abdomen had been removed and as stated earlier was placed on the table at the side of the victim's bed. The abdominal cavity had also been removed, the breasts were also detached from the body, The breasts had been removed in a circular incision and the muscles down to the ribs were still attached to the breasts. One of the breasts was found lying by the right foot, the other was found with the uterus and kidneys laying under the victims head. Placed between the left and right feet was the liver and at the right hand side of the body were the intestines whilst the spleen lay on the left-hand side of the body. The throat had been cut and the tissues of the neck were severed all around and down to the vertebra and the fifth and sixth

vertebra being deeply notched. The victims face and the air passage was cut was slashed beyond any recognition the nose, cheeks, eyebrows and ears being partly removed. The lips had cuts in several places running down the chin. When examining the thorax it was noted that the lower part of the right lung was missing and the left lung was intact. The heart had been removed but not found at the scene."

One thing to remember about this murder is that Mary was in bed and apart from a chemise she was naked; this may lead us to believe that she felt comfortable with her last client! So comfortable in fact that she fell asleep in his company. Or does it? Let's take another look at this. It's November! Mary's room had broken windowpanes which she had put a coat over to keep the drafts out. Taking into account the time of year, and the fact that women in Victorian England kept there bodies covered, as nudity was classed as obscene. So why was Mary almost naked? Could it have been the fact that she was stripped after she was strangled? We know there were signs of strangulation as her fists were clenched when her body was discovered. There were signs of clothing being burnt in the grate. This was not a common practice for women of Mary's standing, as they often only had the clothes they stood up in. If they were lucky enough to own a second set of clothing they certainly would not burn them.

The question is why was clothing burnt in the grate? One theory that has been suggested is that it provided light for the murderer to perform the mutilations. This theory does not stand up, as there was a candle at the side of the bed that was only burnt half way down. This would have meant the murderer would have to either have given Mary the clothes at an earlier date or carried them with him on the night of the murder. I honestly don't think the killer was walking about Whitechapel with women's clothes as well as the murder weapon do you? Again the question has to be asked why the clothes were burnt. One point that is clear is the fact that these clothes were burnt. Could these clothes have given the police a clue to the murderer? If so what clue?

Maybe the clothes had been labelled by a charitable organisation. As you probably already know from earlier, the workhouses in the area labelled their clothing. Indeed, because of this, one of the earlier Ripper victims was identified. Maybe the workhouses were not the only organisation to do this. Others organisations did the same and the clothes burnt in the grate in Mary's room may have bore a mark that would have led the police to Dr Barnardo. Destroying the clothing so this mark would not be recognised would have been his only option.

4 p.m. Mary's body was removed from Millers Court to the Shoreditch Mortuary. The police boarded up the windows of Mary's room and padlocked the door. Police officers stood guard at the scene. Inspector

Abberline returned to the crime scene the next day with the doctors to sift through the burnt ashes in the grate. The theory is they were looking for any burnt human remains.

It has been said that Mary's heart was missing, if this is the case, and the murderer burnt it, I am not sure if there would be any part of it left for the Doctors to see.

Today with all our forensic science the whole procedure would have been carried out very differently and DNA would have been searched for. But his was 1888 and they did not have this technology, so they could only use the human eye. Even in 1888 Doctors must have known that the heart was only soft tissue and muscle and would burn without leaving anything behind. So was it her heart they were really looking for?

The full Post-Mortem examination report was as follows;

The face was cut in all directions. The eyebrows, nose cheeks and the ears had been partly removed and the lips had been cut through with gashes running down the chin. The throat had been cut down to the 5th and 6th vertebrae these had been deeply notched, the cuts in the front of the neck showed signs of ecchymosis. At the lower part of the larynx the air passage had been cut through Proceeding downwards it was noted that the breasts has been removed by a circular motion and the chest muscled down to the ribs were still connected to the breasts. The intercostals between the 4th 5th and 6th ribs had been cut through and the contents of the thorax could be clearly seen. When the thorax was opened it was noted that the right lung was minimally adherent by old firm adhesions, but the lower part of this lung was torn and broken away. The left lung was found to be totally intact except a few adhesions over the side. The substances of the left lung had nodules of consolidation. The pericardium was open below and it was noted that the heart was missing and was never found. In the remains of the stomach that was still attached to the intestines partly digested food was found to be the same as in the abdominal cavity it was believed to have been fish and potatoes."

It is important to note that the way the heart was removed through the severed diaphragm may suggest some medical knowledge. It was never reported in the press that Mary's heart was missing, the chiefs of police kept this information secret. The fact that Mary's uterus was found seemed for some reason not to have been known by Inspector Abberline. There have been many stories either printed or told by word of mouth that this poor woman's remains were hanging on nails protruding out of the walls, this is nonsense; there was nothing of Mary's body hanging anywhere.

Dr. Bond also states the time of the murder was around 1 a.m. to 2 a.m. Dr. Bond worked his theory by the time rigor mortis had started to set in, so he thought that Mary had died about twelve hours before. Then he also said that he thought that she had died 3 to 4 hours after eating her last meal. It should also be noted that Dr. Bond thought that the killer of all the five women was the same person.

Dr Bond's opinion in all the cases was there were no signs of a struggle and the attacks were so quick that the women would not have had time to cry out. It has been suggested that the Ripper may have been lying on the bed next to Mary and threw a sheet over her head before slitting her throat. The question you have to ask yourself is why? Why would he cover Mary's face when he never made any attempt's to cover any of the other of his victim's faces? What was so different about Kelly? Could it have been that the Ripper knew Mary personally and she wasn't just any streetwalker he picked up? Or could it have been that Mary was so young?

The accounts of these injuries were not made public either in the press or at the inquest.

10[Th] **November 1888** a reward for the capture of the killer was still being denied by the Home Secretary Henry Mathews. The government was feeling the pressure so a compromise had to be reached. So on this day carrying Sir Charles Warren's signature on it a document was released by the government and went as follows;

MURDER-PARDON.

Whereas on November 8 or 9, in Millers Court, Dorset Street, Spitalfields, Mary Janet Kelly was murdered by some persons unknown: the secretary of State will advise the grant of Her Majesty's gracious pardon to any accomplice, not being the person who contrived or actually committed the murder, who shall give such information and evidence as shall lead to the discovery and conviction of the persons who committed the murder.

12th November. The inquest was held at Shoreditch Town Hall. This inquest was the shortest of all the Ripper victims, lasting only one day. Dr. Roderick MacDonald surgeon of K Division of the Metropolitan Police conducted the inquest. He only gave the jury the basic facts and his summing up goes as follows;

"The question is whether you will adjourn for further evidence. My own opinion is that it is very unnecessary for two courts to deal with these cases, and go through the same evidence time after time, which only causes expense and trouble. If the coroners jury can come to a decision as to the cause of death, then that is all that they have to do. They have nothing to do with the prosecuting a man and saying what amount of penalty he is to get. It is quite sufficient if they find out what

the cause of death was. It is for the police authorities to deal with the case and satisfy themselves as to any person who may be suspected later on. I do not want to take it out of your hands. It is for you to say whether at an adjournment you will hear minutiae of the evidence. Or whether you will think it is a matter to be dealt with in the police courts Later on, and that, this woman having met with her death by the carotid artery having been cut, you will be satisfied to return a verdict to that effect. From what I have learnt the police are content to take the future conduct of the case. It is for you to say whether you will close the inquiry to day. If not we shall adjourn for a week or a fortnight, to hear the evidence that you may desire. After consulting with the rest of the jury the foreman stated that the jury felt that they had enough evidence put before them on which to make a verdict. the coroner then asked the foreman what was the decision reached by the jury, to which he answered "Wilful murder against person or persons unknown."

The coroner decided that some evidence should not be used as he thought it would not be in the public's best interest. Why did he choose to do this? Was it in sympathy for the deceased? Perhaps he felt that having the extent of her injuries printed in every newspaper was not necessary. One odd thing was that the coroner MacDonald did not sign the certificate of findings, why?

At this inquest a juror strongly protested, he said, *"I do not see why jury from the Shoreditch district was dealing with a Spitalfield murder".* Dr. Roderick MacDonald thought that he should have done the inquest of Annie Chapman and overruled the juror's protestations.

Jury's normally sat at the inquests of deaths or murders in their own area. Not for murders that have been committed in other areas.

Dr. MacDonald stated Annie Chapman had died in his area and that her body having been taken to a mortuary in Dr. Baxter's area; it was right that Dr Baxter should have sat on Annie Chapman's case. As Mary Kelly was lying in a mortuary in his district it was his duty to perform the inquest. It has been suggested that Dr. Macdonald was used for the inquest, because he would not have conducted it as thoroughly as Dr. Baxter would have done if he had dealt with it.

A few hours after Mary's Inquest, George Hutchinson went to the Commercial Street Police Station. He gave a statement of what he saw on the night that Mary died. **(It has to be noted that the press does give altered reports of what he said for example the press changed Jewish looking to foreign looking, this could have been inspired by the police who were worried about anti- Semitism.)**

Hutchinson claimed in his statement which follows:

"About 2 a.m. he was walking by Thrawl Street and Commercial Street. Before he reached Flower and Dean Street he says he met Mary who had asked him to lend her sixpence, to which he replied that he could not, as he had spent all his money going to Romford. With that she bid him good morning, and then said she would go in search of some money and walked off towards Thrawl Street. He states that a man walking in the opposite direction to Mary tapped her on the shoulder and said something to her which started them both laughing. Hutchinson stated that Mary said all right to the man who replied "you will be alright, for what I have told you" the man then placed his right arm around Mary's shoulders. Hutchinson claims he was leaning against a lamppost outside the Queens Head Public House and watched Mary and the man come towards him. Hutchinson reported that as the pair walked past him the man bowed his head so his hat covered his eyes, Hutchinson stooped down to see the man's face. The man looked at Hutchinson very sternly. Hutchinson states he saw the man carrying a small parcel with a strap around it. Hutchinson followed the couple into Dorset Street where the couple stopped at the corner of the square and chatted for about three minutes. He heard Mary say to the man "all right my dear come along you will be comfortable". The man then placed his hand on her shoulder and then Mary gave the man a kiss. Hutchinson heard Mary say that she had lost her handkerchief; the man pulled a red handkerchief out of his pocket and gave it to Mary. The couple walked up the court together. Hutchinson went into Millers Court but could not see the couple. He waited three quarters of an hour. He did not see either of them come out, during this time, so he left the court."

As in the case Of Elizabeth Stride, when Packer stated he had seen the man who was with Elizabeth the night she died, still walking around the streets of Whitechapel.

Hutchinson also stated the man he saw with Mary was the same man he saw in Petticoat Lane on 11th November 1888, three days after the event. The question is if Hutchinson was right about the sighting, it means the murderer was <u>still</u> walking around Whitechapel without any fear of being caught. Why was this? Maybe he was still in the area because he had no choice; perhaps he lived in the area and could not afford to move away. Maybe it was because he worked in the streets of Whitechapel and would have brought too much attention to himself if he suddenly stopped working in the area. I believe it was the latter. Dr. Barnardo could not suddenly stop doing his work, not that he would have wanted to any way.

Mary was laid to rest at Walthamstow Roman Catholic Cemetery on the 19th November. None of her family members attended her funeral despite the massive media attention these killings had attracted. Joseph Barnett could not pay for Mary's funeral so the expense was incurred by H Wilton the Sexton attached to the Shoreditch Church. He provided the funeral as a mark of sincere sympathy with the poor people of the neighbourhood in whose welfare he is deeply interested. A report of the funeral that was printed in the *East London Advertiser* and read as follows;

The polished elm and oak coffin was carried in a open car drawn by two horses and taken to the Roman Catholic Cemetery at Leystone for interment, Amidst a scene of turbulent excitement. The bell of St. Leonard's began tolling at noon, and the signal appeared to draw all the residents in the neighbourhood together. There was an enormous preponderance of women in the crowd. As the coffin appeared borne on the shoulders of four men, at the principal gate of the church, the crowd appeared greatly affected. Round the open car in which it was to be placed, men and women struggled desperately to get to touch the coffin. Women with faces streaming with tears cried out, *"God, forgive her!"* and every man's head was bared in token of sympathy. The sight was quite remarkable, and the emotion natural and unconstrained."

Many years later in 1986 a John Morrison, Author of the book *"Jimmy Kelly's Year of the Ripper Murders 1888",* marked Mary's unmarked grave by erecting a large white stone. Sadly the stone marked the wrong grave and was later removed. In the 1990's the Superintendent of the graveyard marked the grave with a very simple memorial.

Mary's murder sent alarm bells ringing all over the world. Newspapers as far away as the United States were reporting on the killings. Queen Victoria sent a telegraph to the Prime Minister Lord Salisbury telling him that things had to change in the East End; Courts must be lit and the detectives improved. On the day of Mary's murder Sir Charles Warren resigned due to the radical and conservative press demanding his resignation. The press accused Warren of introducing mindless militarism in the police force and had demoralised the CID. He came under fire about letting the blood hounds trace him and not a lower ranking officer through Regents Park, during the trails the hounds were going through to see if they would be an asset to the police.

Warren's resignation was not only the direct result of the press but also over his position as head of CID. Warren and Assistant Commissioner James Monro both thought they were head of CID. Commissioner Monro was like Inspector Anderson and Superintendent Arnold were all of the same religious beliefs. When they had an argument over this, both decided to offer The Right Honourable Henry Matthews their resignation. Henry Matthews was the Home Secretary and the first Roman Catholic Minister of cabinet rank since the reign of Queen Elizabeth. Matthews was not a very good minister and was very unpopular. However Prime Minister Lord

Salisbury did not want to lose the Catholic Minister and force a risky by-election. This was the only reason Matthews remained Home Secretary. Matthews accepted Monro's resignation, and then swiftly reinstated him with an office in Whitehall as the head of the secret department; at Monro's request his new title was Head of the Detective Service.

Exactly how many women were true victims of the Ripper has been argued throughout the last hundred years. Some Ripperologists say five, others think only four. No one knows how many were killed and no one will actually be able to prove it, we just have to make up our own minds.

The question is not; how many were actually killed? But, why the murders really happened and why they suddenly stopped?

Shortly after the death of Mary Kelly it is claimed that Dr. Barnardo had an accident which left him quite deaf. Could this be the reason the killing spree stopped, as he could no longer hear if someone was approaching? I think not - the killings stopped because Dr. Barnardo had reached his goal.

Whilst the killings were taking place the police and the newspapers received hundreds of letters from the *supposed murderer* and as you have already read, many were fakes. I believe Dr. Barnardo was responsible for at least one of these letters. He often wrote his sermons in red or purple ink and would underline anything he felt was important. The *"Dear Boss"* letter was written in red ink and words are underlined. I am sure if you compare this letter with a sample of his handwriting you would agree with me that there is a similarity. Dr. Barnardo spent some time as a freelance journalist and he would know just where to send the letters so they would get noticed. He would have had an excellent knowledge of how the police conducted murder investigations from his visit in 1884 to the United States. He spent time with detectives working in New York, Boston and Chicago. This experience would have equipped him with a good understanding of the British Police system. During his stay in America he would have heard many Americanisms such as "Boss".

The letter dated 5th October 1888 addressed to the Central News Agency contained the words "dear old boss". It was sent from a location close to Dr. Barnardo's editorial office. His address at the time was 279 The Strand. You need to ask why he wrote these letters.

As a committed philanthropist he wanted to draw attention to these murders. His message via the letters was to inform readers about the deprivation of the East End. The fact the letters contained threats was to put fear into the Unfortunates in Whitechapel, to stop their immoral ways and to keep them off the streets.

The letters worked, the newspapers were full of the murders. *The Star* reported;

"you could walk Whitechapel at night without even bumping into a female. Neither prostitute nor respectable women would walk the streets in fear of being attacked by Jack the Ripper".

I personally don't believe *The Star's* report; these Unfortunates had nowhere to go, so they would still have to be on the streets plying their trade. He sent a letter, mocking the police saying; *"They think I am a doctor_ha ha."* (Underlining was something Dr. Barnardo did to make a point). He thought by sending this letter the police and everyone would think that the murderer was *not* a doctor maybe he was right, as he was never caught.

You can only imagine how much Dr. Barnardo abused his connection with Assistant Commissioner Robert Anderson, Superintendent Arnold and even Assistant Commissioner Monro all of the Metropolitan CID. These men would have regarded Dr. Barnardo as a friend and a religious brother from as far back as their first meeting. However, I feel that Dr. Barnardo abused this friendship. Superintendent Arnold would help raising funds, and Robert Anderson became involved with the Dr. Barnardo homes, being an active member of the committee. He filled his obligations of visiting the homes and regularly attending meetings. Through these friendships Dr. Barnardo would have learnt everything about the way the investigation was being carried out in total confidence.

You may ask why Dr. Barnardo killed these women and then got further involved in the investigation foe example writing to the newspapers. Surely he should have kept a low profile. Serial killers have a need to get involved in their murder investigation. It could be to find out if they are close to getting caught, or the thrill of being hunted with the police not realising that the killer is right under their noses. Either way Dr. Barnardo is not the only killer to get involved in his own murder investigations. During the writing of this book a man murdered two little girls. He immediately became involved in the murder inquiry and 'pretended' to help the police search for the girls. He was filmed by the television news, and gave statements to the papers. Exactly why he and other serial killers feel the need to get involved we may never know, all we know is that they follow a blueprint. Whether it is helping the police directly or writing to the papers or even keeping a dairy, research into many serial killers has proved that this need to be involved does exist.

It has been perceived that Dr. Barnardo hated the Catholic faith with as much passion as he hated the Unfortunates. Dr. Barnardo hated Catholicism so much he would break the law to stop them having the children of there faith that he had rescued. In one case he thought he was going to lose his fight over one child, as the Catholic Church wanted the child to be sent to them, so the child could be cared for in the Catholic faith. Dr. Barnardo was not having the Catholic Church telling him what he could do or not do. In a very typical bombastic and I would say spiteful act he sent the child abroad rather than hand the child back to the Catholic faith.

This again shows what his personality was like; he thought he could control anything and anyone he wanted. Another way Dr. Barnardo could feel power and control over people, was when an Unfortunate brought their child to one of his homes, he would tell the poor woman that she had to sign an agreement letting Dr. Barnardo change the child's religion and be taught the word of God as he chose fit. Dr. Barnardo knew that the parent would sign the release document because it was a choice of the child staying a Catholic and going to one of the many workhouses, or having an education, security and comfort in one of Dr. Barnardo's homes. Dr. Barnardo knew that in many cases the parent could not read or write, so did not understand all if any of the conditions set down by him.

It is important to note that an Alfred Dyer, a publisher who specialised in books and pamphlets on the cause of *"social purity"* produced evidence about girl trafficking from England to brothels in Belgium, Holland and France.

This could be what happened to Mary Kelly when she first arrived in London?

Dr. Barnardo's work with destitute children is still today unsurpassed. He saw these killings as a means to an end using his alter-ego 'Jack' to fulfil his mission. You may ask wasn't there another way this could have been done without committing murder? In response, I don't know of anything else he could have done that would have grabbed the worlds attention so quickly. Because of what 'Jack' did, the man totally succeeded in his mission. What 'Jack' did caused thousands of lives to be saved and improved.

One hundred years on the legacy of his work survives. There are no longer any homes, but the modern day 'Barnardos' believes that a child's life should be free of "poverty, abuse and discrimination"

Dr. Barnardo would be proud of the organisation he founded. Today it spends over £158 million on the welfare of children and their families.

Today in the East End there are also charities like U-Turn who attempt to look after the moral and physical well being of today's prostitutes (Unfortunates).

It would appear from recent articles that *'slumming'* has become as popular today in high society as it was in 1888.

Sir Robert Anderson went on to state several times in writing that the identity of the Ripper was known to the police. In *Criminals and Crime* (1907) Sir Anderson said;

"For I may say at once that undiscovered murders are rare in London, and the Jack the Ripper crimes are not in that category."

Sir Anderson in his memoirs called *The Lighter Side of My Official Life.* (1910)
Wrote;

"In saying that he (Ripper) was a polish Jew I am merely stating a definite ascertained fact, and my words are meant to specify race, not religion, and that his remarks were founded on fact, not speculation."

Sir Anderson's last statement on the Ripper was printed in an introduction to *H.L Adams Police Encyclopaedia. Anderson wrote;*

"So, again with the Whitechapel Murders of 1888; despite the lucubration's of many an amateur Sherlock Holmes, there was no doubt whatever as to the identity of the criminal, and if our London Detectives possessed the power, and might have recourse to the methods of foreign police forces, he (Ripper) would have been brought to justice. But the guilty sometimes escape."

H.L. Adams in Volume IV of the Police Encyclopaedia wrote;

"A great deal of mystery still hangs about these horrible Ripper outrages, although in a letter which I have just received from Sir Robert Anderson, he intimates that the police knew well enough at the time who the miscreant was, although unfortunately, they had not sufficient, legal evidence to warrant them laying hands upon him."

At the time of the murders Robert Anderson had the report from Dr Phillips who was the Police Surgeon of H Division, who thought the killer has shown that he had some anatomical or surgical knowledge. So why then did he ask Dr Bond the Police Surgeon of A division to review the report by Dr Phillips? Dr Bond disagreed with Dr Phillips verdict and thought that the killer did not have any anatomical or surgical knowledge.

This action seemed that either Anderson did not trust Dr Phillips opinion, or Anderson was trying to play the medical connection.

In the *Evening News* (Portsmouth) dated July 4th 1894 there was a copy of an interview that an American reporter had done with Arthur Conan Doyle. Arthur Conan Doyle explained hoe Sherlock Holmes would have dealt with the 'Dear Boss' letter. The Article reads as follows; Dr Conan Doyle, in a interview with an American journalist, has explained how 'Sherlock Holmes' would have set about the work of tracking the notorious Whitechapel miscreant, He says:--

I am not in the least degree either a sharp or an observant man myself. I try to get inside the skin of a sharp man and see how things would strike him. I remember going to the Scotland Yard museum and looking at the letter which was received by the police, and which purported to come from the Ripper. Of course, it may have been a hoax, but there were reasons to think it genuine, and in any case it was well to find out who wrote it. It was written in red ink in a clerkly hand. I tried to think how Holmes might have deduced the writer of that letter. The most obvious point was that the letter was written by someone who had been in America. It began, 'Dear Boss,' and contained the phrase, 'fix it up' and several others which are not usual with the 'Britishers'. Then we have the quality of the paper and the handwriting, which indicated that the letters were not written by a toiler. It was good paper, and a round, easy, clerkly hand. He was therefore, a man accustomed to the use of a pen.

Having determined that much, we can avoid in inference that there must be somewhere letters which this man had written in his own name, or documents or accounts that could be readily traced to him. Oddly enough, the police did not, as far as I know, think of that, and so they failed to accomplish anything. Holmes's plan would have been to reproduce the letters in facsimile and on each plate indicate briefly the peculiarities of the handwriting. Then publish these facsimiles in the leading newspapers of Great Britain and America and in connection with them offer a reward to anyone who could show a letter or any specimen of the same handwriting. Such course would have enlisted millions of people as detectives in the case.

I would like to finish this chapter by Quoting A.E. Williams from his book Barnardo of Stepney:

"Dr. Barnardo was not satisfied merely to rescue the homeless child. In his magazine and in his public utterances he was ever drawing attention to many evils pressing upon the neglected child-life of the nation, and striving to create such a public opinion on the subject as would ultimately do away with these evils".

The next few pages follow the Inquest into

'Mary Jane Kelly'

As recorded by the newspapers at the time, followed by a copy of the death certificate.

This is the shortest recorded Inquest

This is a copy of the original Death Certificate for Mary Kelly.

The Coroners Report

12th November. The inquest was held at Shoreditch Town Hall. This inquest was the shortest of all the Ripper victims, lasting one day. Dr Roderick MacDonald surgeon of K Division of the Metropolitan Police conducted the inquest. He only gave the jury the basic facts and his summing up goes as follows;

"The question is whether you will adjourn for further evidence. My own opinion is that it is very unnecessary for two courts to deal with these cases, and go through the same evidence time after time, which only causes expense and trouble. If the coroners jury can come to a decision as to the cause of death, then that is all that they have to do. They have nothing to do with the prosecuting a man and saying what amount of penalty he is to get. It is quite sufficient if they find out what the cause of death was. It is for the police authorities to deal with the case and satisfy themselves as to any person who may be suspected later on. I do not want to take it out of your hands. It is for you to say whether at an adjournment you will hear minutiae of the evidence. Or whether you will think it is a matter to be dealt with in the police courts Later on, and that, this woman having met with her death by the carotid artery having been cut, you will be satisfied to return a verdict to that effect. From what I have learnt the police are content to take the future conduct of the case. It is for you to say whether you will close the inquiry to day. If not we shall adjourn for a week or a fortnight, to hear the evidence that you may desire. After consulting with the rest of the jury the foreman stated that the jury felt that they had enough evidence put before them on which to make a verdict. The coroner then asked the foreman what was the decision reached by the jury, to which he answered "Willful murder against person or persons unknown".

Chapter 8

Summing up the Evidence

Firstly let me say that when I started researching Jack the Ripper seriously over fourteen years ago (this does not include all the years I spent reading and watching everything I could get my hand on about the murders.), I never intended my findings to end up as a book, it has just evolved that way. In the beginning I needed to satisfy my own inquisitiveness as to who could have been '*Jack.*' Before writing this book, I had not read anything on Jack the Ripper and concurred with the author's theory. Then again there has never been one suspect that everyone agrees on, me included. I would not call myself a *"Ripperologist"* or even an *expert* on the case. I am merely a person who has taken the facts available studied them, and came to my conclusion as to who I think Jack the Ripper really was.

I am no relative of Dr. Barnardo or in any way a descendent of his, so I do not know of any family secrets. I started my research where any newcomer to this case would; by ploughing through the vast amount of evidence available. Even though these murders had been committed over a hundred years ago a lot of the evidence has survived. Not having a suspect in mind I decided that I would look at all the previously named suspects, and decide what it was about that suspect I did not agree on, if of course I did disagree with them.

After careful consideration, I soon started to dismiss them one by one, as I felt that the case against them, for me personally, was not strong enough, or believable enough. I felt that the killer had to be known by these women especially after the first killing. These women were hardened street walkers and knew the area and the type of residents so well, that if anyone acting strangely started to speak to one of these Unfortunates they would have been put on there guard. This was proven when Sarah Lewis and a companion were approached by a man carrying a black leather bag. The man wanted one of the two women to go into the entry (alley) with him. The women became frightened by his odd behaviour and ran away.

I decided that a number of questions were needed to be answered in order to narrow down the list of suspect's. These questions had to not only be answered but be plausible, before I could believe that the person I was researching was actually Jack the Ripper.

The most pertinent questions had to be:

- **Who could walk the streets of Whitechapel at all times of the day and night and not be a cause for suspicion by the Unfortunates or locals?**

- **Who would have the medical knowledge to carry out the post mortem mutilations that was performed on these women?**
- **Who would be able to walk straight past a policeman on any occasion, including some of the nights that a Ripper murder had occurred and fail to be noticed?**
- **Who knew the East End well enough that he could just "disappear" when necessary, but then also had the confidence to walk the streets again days after committing these murders?**
- **Who could have known the exact plans of the police, e.g. flooding the streets with extra police officers dressed as women, and also been able to know when he needed to change his M.O. (Mary Kelly)?**
- **Who would have the financial means to buy a hat for Polly Nichols, supply drugs to Annie Chapman, and give Elizabeth Stride a piece of velvet ?**
- **What reasons if any would this person have for committing these murders?**

My Jack the Ripper's name leapt out at me from the pages I was reading, very late one night whilst researching the case. His name although mentioned briefly in some other Ripper books had never been a serious suspect, until now. My next step was to research this mans life and work. (I quickly realised that although his raison d'etre could not be doubted, although his personality had many flaws.)

I soon discovered that the deeper I searched the more the answers to my to my own questions became apparent.

This man had very good reason for being on the streets of Whitechapel any time of the day or night. His reasons were two-fold;

Firstly was his never ending search for desolate children. This was his life's work and he lived only to save these poor mites. Secondly was his hatred of the Unfortunates who lived in and worked this area. You have already read that one of these Unfortunates was the reason for a campaign against him that would last for a number of years. This woman's "story" nearly ruined his reputation completely and probably caused problems in his marriage. His wife not only had to accept the fact that her husband was walking the streets of the East End at all hours of the night spending time with Unfortunates, she also had to tolerate the fact that her husband was being accused of having an affair with one. So you can see why Dr. Barnardo must have felt a strong revulsion towards these women.

His revenge was again two-fold; firstly he felt he exerted power over them by taking their children away. He felt they did not deserve to have children. Secondly was his darker plan, using his alter ego (Jack) to eradicate some of these Unfortunates to enlighten the world to the deprivation he felt these women were causing.

•   This man had studied medicine at the London Hospital. He was trained as a Doctor, but spent most of his time in the dissecting rooms of the hospital. He excelled in post-mortem techniques. After qualifying as a Doctor then went on to do a Gynaecology course. This action seems rather strange as he never intended, and never did, use his medical training as his employment. Dr. Barnardo could have carried out with great ease and coolness, any of the post mortem mutilations that were performed on the Ripper victims.

•   Dr. Barnardo was very well known by the policemen of the area, as well as being personal friends with the leading men of the Metropolitan CID. He would see and talk to the beat officers every single day he was on the streets looking for children. These officers would not think it was strange to see him wandering around the streets at very early hours of the morning, or even see him talking to an Unfortunate. A local police officer would often have to go to Dr. Barnardo's rescue if he was being attacked. Most of these attacks were usually done by an Unfortunate trying to stop Dr. Barnardo taking her children away from her. Please don't think for one minute these women were fighting to save their children because they did not want to be separated from them. In actual fact, these women were attacking Dr. Barnardo because the child was worth money. This financial gain could have come from the child begging or if it was a young girl she could have been an Unfortunate herself. So you can see that Dr. Barnardo's work was very important, and these children desperately needed to receive some help.

•   Because of his work this man knew the Whitechapel area like the back of his hand. He had lived in the area at one time. Working the streets every day looking for children to "rescue", as well as preaching in the area. Through his work at the Ragged School's he became aware of the children's hiding places (known then as lays.) The children used these lays to hide away and sleep. These "Lays" were often roof tops, disserted buildings, or even openings into anything that was big enough to hide somebody well enough without being seen. Because of this information I believe Dr. Barnardo knew where to hide in the streets better that any policeman who walked them on there beats.

•   Police Commissioner Robert Anderson, Superintendent Arnold and Assistant Commissioner Monro all heads of Metropolitan CID were good friend of Dr. Barnardo. I believe that Dr. Barnardo used this friendship to secure the information he needed about this case. He not only knew about the police movements, he also used this information to keep one step ahead of the police at all times. This fact was proved when he decided to change the location for his last victim. This killing was the only one that took place indoors, also the age of the victim changed. Before Kelly, all the other victims had been killed in the streets they worked. Also the other victims were in there thirties/forties; Kelly was only in her twenties. I believe that Dr. Barnardo knew what the policemen on the streets were expecting the killer to do, e.g. talk to a "Unfortunate" who would be of middle aged and go down a dark alley or into a quiet street with her.

• Because Dr. Barnardo raised charitable donations, he felt he was not accountable to anyone financially. All the donations were paid directly to him and he assumed he should be able to spend the money where he saw fit, even thought he now wasn't in total control of the financial running of the homes, and was reduced to receiving a £600 pound per year salary from the trustees. This in turn meant that he could have bought a hat or a piece of material quite easily without anybody asking any questions. The fact that he was a married man also gave him an alibi when buying these items as they could have been for his wife.

• I believe the reason for these killing was to bring the situation that existed in Whitechapel to the world's attention. I have never believed that these killings were done by a mad man or during a sexual frenzy. I believe that these victims were only used as a means to an end. A man, who believed that by performing these murders would lead to a reform in the living conditions of the East end, performed these murders. I feel that it was a terrible shame that so drastic a measure had to be taken to make the people in power sit up and take notice.

Soon after answering these questions I started to find what I call the "links" that these women may have had with Dr. Barnardo. These links are as follows;

Mary Ann (Polly) Nichols

As you have already read Polly went to work for a couple who both worked for the police. Because of his connection with both religious groups and his connection with the police force, I believe that Dr. Barnardo placed Polly with them through his employment agency in good faith that she would stop drinking, as the couple was teetotal. Having this employment would also mean that Polly would not have to be an Unfortunate any more, and walk the streets looking for clients. Sadly Polly's employment was not to last very long, before she left the couples home with clothing she had stolen from them. This situation would not have looked good for Dr. Barnardo, as the couple must have trusted his word about this woman.

Exactly why Dr. Barnardo chose such a drastic measure to bring the plight of the East End into the public's eye, I do not know. All I know is that his plan worked.

I believe that Dr. Barnardo chose Polly as his first victim, and that it was he who gave Polly the new hat she was proudly showing off on the evening she died. The reasoning behind this action was to lure her into a false sense of security. He had arranged to meet Polly later that same night with the intention of killing her.

The 'Unidentified' man seen in Buck's Row shortly after the murder of Polly was in fact Dr. Barnardo making his escape.

I don't think at this point Dr. Barnardo knew exactly how many women he would go on to murder in order to reach his aim. I do however think that at this stage he had already planned to use the newspapers to his full advantage in his cause.

Annie Chapman

Through the witness statements we know that Annie had been complaining that she had been unwell. Again through the Doctor's statements at Annie's inquest we know that she was suffering from an advanced disease of the lungs (tuberculosis), as well as the membranes of the brain. These symptoms may also have been caused by syphilis.

Annie was receiving and taking medicine on a fairly regular basis. We know this because a bottle of medicine was found in the room she regularly slept in at the lodging house after her death. Also when her body was discovered she had two tablets in her possession in a torn piece of envelope. Sadly we do not know what the medicine was or even what the tablets were used for. Who was supplying Annie with this medication? The answer to this question was Dr. Barnardo; he was supplying her with these drugs, and again doing this as a favour to lure her in a false sense of security. Then there is the site that Annie's murder took place. The yard at the back of 29 Hanbury Street was not a place that Unfortunates regularly used for their 'business'. One of the residents of this building stated that the gate was always bolted, so you need to ask your self why was Annie found in the back yard of 29 Hanbury Street. I believe the answer to this question again lies with Dr. Barnardo. The back room of 29 Hanbury Street was used for weekly prayer meetings. At some point if not regularly Dr. Barnardo may have attended these meetings, and because of this fact he knew the seclusion of the back yard. Dr. Barnardo took Annie to the yard under false pretences. He had decided that this yard was a safe enough place to carry out the post mortem mutilations that he felt he needed to do.

Dr. Barnardo visited the lodging house that Annie stayed at on a regular basis, and it was on some of these visits he supplied Annie with medicines.

Dr. Barnardo may have chosen Annie as his next victim as he knew she was seriously ill and would die soon. His reasoning for picking this woman as his next victim could have been that this act would also be a mercy killing. His justification for the killings would be for the greater good of the children and to highlight the East Ends plight. He did not do this for self gratification.

Elizabeth Stride

Remembering that Elizabeth Stride was a woman of no means, and needed to sell herself just to earn a few pence to eat, it seems difficult to believe that she would have been in the position to buy herself a piece of velvet.

Dr. Barnardo gave Elizabeth the velvet on one of his many visits to the lodging houses frequented by these women, where he obviously met Elizabeth. Exactly when Dr. Barnardo chose Elizabeth to be his next intended victim, I cannot say. He did unto Elizabeth as he did Polly, giving a false sense of security and arranging to meet her later that same night. Dr. Barnardo did not actually kill Elizabeth that night, but I am sure that she was to be one of his intended victims. Dr. Barnardo wrote to the papers stating he had seen Elizabeth in the lodging house the day she was murdered.

On the evening of Elizabeth's death she asked a fellow lodger to take care of the material. Another lodger stated that Elizabeth asked him to lend her a clothes brush, which he did not, prior to Elizabeth leaving the lodging house. He also said that she seemed *'all dressed up'* as if she was going to meet someone; possibly Dr. Barnardo.

The couple did meet up that night, but I certainly do not believe that Elizabeth was killed by Dr. Barnardo.

Why she was murdered when she was, I do not know or by whom. She could have been a victim of one of the many gangs that roamed around the area terrorising the Unfortunates. One of these gang members may have demanded money from her, and when she could not pay them they killed her. The killer may have stolen any money that she may have had. This killing could have been a message to the other Unfortunates who could not pay when the money was demanded from them. This I believe is what happened to Martha Tabram before the Ripper killings started. Martha was stabbed 39 times with a pen knife and subsequently died.

Even though I do not believe that Elizabeth was killed by the Ripper, this murder was the first of two that would take place that same night. These two murders would go on to be known as "the double event".

Dr. Barnardo *was* questioned at Lime Street police station on the same night as the "double event". The alibi he gave was that he had spent the evening fund raising with Superintendent Thomas Arnold. Today I think this alibi would have been investigated further. It was unlikely that this fund raising event would have gone on into the early hours of the morning. Dr. Barnardo's connection with the police had yet again helped him out of a very sticky situation. I can almost imagine his face when he left the police station, it must have had a look of superior satisfaction on it.

Catharine Eddowes

Catharine was picked as the next victim purely because of what she thought she knew. She stated that she had returned to London from hop picking in Kent and was going to claim the reward offered in the newspapers to catch the Ripper.

The same day as she was murdered she told the Superintendent at Cooney's lodging house that she thought she knew who the Ripper was. Later that day she used the name Jane Kelly for pawning a pair of boots, then in the evening when she was arrested for being drunk she used the name of Mary Kelly. These women often called themselves by other names when they were arrested. So it is not strange that she chose to give a false name, it's just coincidental that she chose the name of a future Ripper victim. It could have been that Dr. Barnardo was visiting Cooney's lodging house when Catharine was talking about claiming the reward. Alternatively he could have heard a rumour whilst visiting another lodging house that Catharine was about to go to the police, and claim her reward. Dr. Barnardo could not risk being uncovered and at some point in the day he had managed to make arrangements to meet Catharine later that night.

After being arrested for being drunk Catherine was incarcerated until the officer in charge thought she was fit to leave. As she was released from the police station at 1 a.m. Catharine did not go straight to the lodging house but instead was seen at 1.35 a.m. by three men standing in the Duke's Place entrance that led to Church Passage, which in turn led into Mitre Square. The men stated Catharine and a man were talking very amicably. They also stated that she had her hand on the man's chest. She was not arguing with him but I feel she was holding him 'at arms length' in the knowledge that she was in danger. It may have been her intention to blackmail him and make it worth her while to keep his secret.

Dr. Barnardo's aim was to try and find out exactly what Catharine knew. After killing Catharine Dr. Barnardo placed her intestines over her shoulder, and cut two v shapes in either cheek, could this have been an attempt to point the finger at the Masons. On his escape route he was passing through Goulston Street and could not stop himself trying to point the finger at the Masons yet again. He probably aimed this at the Masons, as he felt they could do more than they were doing to help his plight. If the wording is correct and he did spell the word "juwes" whilst chalking on the wall in Goulston Street; this was directly pointed at the Masons, as he knew only a high ranking Mason would have understood it.

The Masons had nothing to do with these killings. Dr. Barnardo may have felt that by pointing the finger at the Masons and using some of their history (Juwes) and some of their rituals (intestines) he may have caused a stirring in a hornets nest.

It was as though he had created a smokescreen for his actions. The message would have possibly created great unrest and fear if it had been left to daylight before being washed off.

Mary Jane Kelly

The night Mary Kelly died Dr. Barnardo had decided to totally change his M.O.

We have to ask ourselves why?

Dr. Barnardo would have known because of his friend's in the CID that extra police officers had flooded the streets. He would have also known that some of these officers had been disguised as women. If you look at photographs taken of police officers in 1888, you would have to have had a very good imagination to be able to picture one of these officers in a dress convincing anyone that he was a woman.

This information alone made Dr. Barnardo realise that he could not kill on the streets again. He now needed to find an "Unfortunate" who had, or at least had use of a room for her business. Dr. Barnardo changed his M.O. to avoid capture. He chose Mary Kelly who was only in her twenties, where as his other victims had been middle aged. Dr. Barnardo probably met Mary at some point whilst visiting on of the many Ragged Schools. This particular School was only a few doors away from where she lived in Millers Court. As before Dr. Barnardo had arranged to meet Mary on the day she was murdered. There is another difference in the killing of Mary to the other murders; he covered her face with a part of a sheet. The Ripper could have covered any of the other victim's faces during the murders either by placing a handkerchief over the victims face, or by pulling the skirt high enough to cover the face. Why he only chose to cover Mary's face, he could only answer.

It has been alleged that Mary may have sold clothes for someone that worked in the mortuary of the London Hospital. This person may have been Dr. Barnardo during his time as a medical student, trying to raise some money for one of his many causes he had to fund. In *Jack the Ripper the Myth*, by A P Wolf the Author says that the post mortem mutilations that Mary had suffered was a ritual that is described in the bible. A P Wolf states that Moses had laid down.

"The cutting off the breasts and the right thigh and the fat covering it, the liver and both the kidneys are removed and burnt".

If this statement is true could this have been what Dr. Barnardo did to Mary? We know that there had been a fire in Mary's room that night and some clothing had been burnt in the grate. Dr. Barnardo may have given Kelly these clothes earlier in the day as a favour, again to put her in a false sense of security. Then he may have used them to burn the body parts later. If Moses words were being followed, then the killer had to be very familiar with the teachings of the bible and the way it dealt with Unfortunates. Dr. Barnardo was a very religious man and took the word of God and the Lords teachings very seriously. Why he chose to totally destroy Mary in the way he did, I can not say, it may be because he knew she would be his last and wanted a grotesque finale. What ever his reason was all we know is that he completely eradicated this woman. Thankfully Mary was to be the Rippers last victim.

The lodging houses in Flower and Dean Street where Dr. Barnardo stated he had spoken to Elizabeth Stride was also used from time to time by both Catharine Eddowes and Polly (Mary Ann) Nichols. One can only assume that these women must have met Dr. Barnardo whilst carrying out his work visiting the lodging houses looking for children; it also leads you to believe that these women must have also known each other.

The clothing Dr Barnardo wore and his overall appearance coincides with the witness statements given to the police. They describe a <u>foreign looking</u> man wearing a Billycock hat and a using a <u>red handkerchief</u>. As you have already read these corresponds with Dr Barnardo's disguise.

I think the red handkerchief may have been used as a calling card by Dr. Barnardo, to identify himself to the police, maybe if he was stopped he just pulled it slightly out of his pocket and the officer involved would recognise him and let him go about his business. It must be noted that in Victorian times handkerchiefs were usually white. A red one was not common for the times.

Dr. Barnardo's alter ego was Jack the Ripper. He was led to commit these murders through his calling to save the children of the East End's Unfortunates. His faith gave him the sense of urgency required to carry out Gods work. I strongly feel that he was not capable of harming anyone else. He was driven by circumstance, belief and a form of revenge; after all he was a human being.

You may not agree with the actions of his alter ego, but for the first time in history you will understand the need for the Ripper. He gave the wider world an understanding of real life in Whitechapel. It was shocking enough for the Queen and Government to intervene and improve living conditions in the East End, including the tightening of controls on brothels and lodging houses.

I don't expect many people who read this book will wholly agree with my theory. Then again as I have already said there has never been a suspect that many people agree on and Dr. Barnardo won't be any different.

There have been numerous suspects over the years ranging from a Royal Surgeon to a Barrister. Lewis Carroll has even been mentioned as a suspect. Here are just a few;

Charles Lutwidge Dodson (Lewis Carroll) was born in 1832. Although he was a religious man he decided to become a photographer. In 1856 a new dean arrived at the church and brought along with him his wife and children including his daughter called Alice. Dodson would take Alice and her two sisters on picnics and in 1862 started outlining his first Alice book. He was begged by Alice to write this book and in 1865 *Alice's Adventures in Wonderland* was published under the pen name of Lewis Carroll .In 1996 Richard Wallace published a book called *Jack the Ripper, light Hearted Friend.* In this book Wallace speculates that Carroll and a friend of Carroll's carried out the Ripper murders. He said his evidence was the supposed anagrams that Carroll had put into his work. Wallace believed these anagrams were relay Carroll's confessions of his crimes. I will leave you to make your own mind up about this theory. I know what I think about it.

Next in the suspect line is *Prince Albert Victor Christian Edward,* also known as Eddy. He was Queen Victoria's grandson and was born in 1864. There have been different versions of this theory. Firstly the basic's of these versions are the same and goes as follows; Eddy met a Catholic shop girl whilst learning to paint. Her name was Annie Crook and Eddy was so smitten by her, the couple secretly married and had a daughter called Alice Crook. Supposedly Queen Victoria found out about the matter. The problem was that not only was Annie a commoner, she was also a Catholic. Queen Victoria is alleged to have asked her Prime Minister Lord Salisbury for help. He in turn asked Royal Surgeon Sir William Gull for assistance in solving this problem. The story goes that Gull sent some men to the home of Annie and kidnapped her. She was then taken to a hospital, where they operated on her to make her seem insane. It is alleged that Mary Kelly was Alice's nanny and escaped unharmed with her. Mary is alleged to have told the other Ripper victims the story of Annie and the Prince and jointly they decided to blackmail the Government. I don't think that the word of an East End "Unfortunate" would have been taken seriously by anyone in Government. This story originated from the word of Joseph Sickert. Joseph Sickert said that his father Walter Sickert the painter actually married Alice Crook, and was Josephs mother.

How ironic can this get as in 2003 Patricia Cornwell wrote a book called *Portrait of a killer, Jack the Ripper- Case Closed.* In this book Cornwell states that Jack the Ripper is actually *Walter Sickert.* She used forensic science to prove that Sickert had links to some of the Ripper letters. This may have been the case as many hoax letters were received by both the newspapers and the police. But the fact that he may have written a few hoax letters does not make him the Ripper. Cornwell's other theory is that Sickert's guilt is highlighted in some of his paintings, and he changed some of the titles to Ripper related subjects. Well I would think that any struggling artist would have changed the names of paintings in order to sell them easily. A number of Ripperologists believe that at the time the murders were committed Sickert was not even in England.

Then the next suspect is *Montague John Druitt.* Druitt was considered the top suspect by Assistant Chief Constable Melville Macnaghten. In response to an article the *Sun* newspaper run Macnaghten wrote what is now regarded as an important document in the Jack the Ripper case. The document goes as follows;

"A Mr J Druitt, said to be a doctor and of good family- who disappeared at the same time of the Millers Court murder, and whose body which is said to have been upwards of a month in the water was found in the Thames on the 31st December, or about seven weeks after that murder. He was sexually insane and from private information I have little doubt but that his own family believed him to have been the murderer."

Druitt's mother had been committed for mental illness. Because of this he feared that he would end up the same as his mother and decided to commit suicide by throwing himself in the Thames.

In the 1990s the Maybrick Diary was found. *James Maybrick* was a Liverpool cotton merchant who had an addiction for arsenic. His addiction caused him to be paranoid and delusional. He married a woman called Florence and they had children together. Maybrick is alleged to have had a second wife who lived in Whitechapel. The killings are alleged to have started because Maybrick thought that Florence was having an affair. In the diary Maybrick calls his wife 'the whore' and her lover 'the whore master'. The thought of the lovers are meant to have driven him insane and turned him into a killer. Maybrick died by an overdose of arsenic. His wife Florence was arrested and found guilty of his murder and served fifteen years in prison before being released.

Despite the fact that the whole scenario of the couple discovering this diary seems bizarre, the fact that the male of the couple has since admitted more than once that he and his wife forged the diary doesn't seem to matter, and Maybrick is still the top suspect to many people.

During the writing of this book I have spoken to a Graphologist in England who was requested to analyse the Maybrick Diary and he told me he found them to be a crude hoax. So it is not surprising that this Graphologists report was never made public and another Graphologist was found.

A bizarre suspect is *Joseph Barnett.* He was the partner and lover of Mary Kelly. He was interviewed by the police who were satisfied with his alibi. The theory is that he killed the other Unfortunates to frighten Mary, so she would not walk the streets plying her trade. When he realised that Mary was still walking the streets he killed her. I really do not think that this theory has any credibility. Why kill other women to stop your lover doing what she had to do to live? She had a choice of how she lived.

Another suspect in the case is *Severin Klosowski* alias George Chapman. He was born in Poland in 1865. Between 1880 and 1885 he studied to become a surgeon. He had worked in London as a hairdresser's assistant in a barber shop. He got married and the couple went to live in New Jersey in the USA. Whilst in the States Chapman tried to kill his wife by holding her down on the bed and pressing his face against her mouth to stop her screaming. Luckily for her a customer entered the shop and Chapman stopped and attended to the customer. The woman noticed that under the pillow was a knife, which it is alleged he told her he intended to use to 'cut her head off'. Scared and pregnant his wife fled back to London. Chapman soon followed his wife's footsteps and was back in London by the winter of 1893. He then married and poisoned at least three women and was executed for these murders on the 7th April 1903. Inspector Abberline thought that Chapman was Jack the Ripper. He could not see that there was a problem with a mass murder changing his M.O from cutting his victims throats and mutilating them to just administering poison. Abberline is to have remarked;

"A man who could watch his wives being slowly tortured to death by poison, as he did, was capable of anything; and the fact that he should have attempted, in such a cold-blooded manner to murder his first wife with a knife in New Jersey, makes one more inclined to believe in the theory that he was mixed up in the two series of crimes."

I don't believe that mass murderers change there M.O from performing savage killings to poisoning their victims.

Another suspect is *Francis Tumblety.* Tumblety was an American who travelled around selling herbal remedies. He arrived in Liverpool in June 1888. On the 7th November he was arrested and charged with homosexual activities with four men between the 27th July and the 2nd November. He fled the country and got aboard a steamer bound for New York. It is alleged that police officers from London followed Tumblety to the States but lost track of him. It is thought that Tumblety travelled around the States living under false identities. Tumblety died in 1903. Amongst his belongings were some copper rings similar to the ones that Annie Chapman wore.

Lastly in this extensive line up, is the latest suspect *Sir John Williams*. His descendent Tony Williams has recently released a book Called *Uncle Jack*. Williams tells the reader how his uncle worked as a physician in many colleges and Hospitals in London. He states his uncle killed the women for their organs for use in his research. His research according to Tony Williams was infertility in women, something his wife suffered from. I do not believe that this man was Jack the Ripper. He may have been researching infertility, but I don't think that is a good enough reason for him to commit murder. In addition the general description of the Ripper does not match Sir John at all. He was forty eight years old at the time of the murders and a photograph of him taken at that time shows a clean shaven ***English looking*** gentleman. I do not believe that anybody could stretch their imagination enough to think that Sir John looked **'foreign'**.

In my opinion, Dr. Barnardo was not a sex maniac who killed these women for sexual gratification, or a mad man. He did not kill these women with the intention to sell their body parts, or use them in for any research purposes. These murders were not part of some satanic ritual performed by a devil worshiper, as some would have you believe. These murders were not performed by a Mason in the tradition of their ritual history as implied in the case of Annie Chapman (by the placing of the intestines over the woman's shoulder).

Once chosen by Dr. Barnardo these women were sacrificed for a greater cause; granted not a cause they personally chose to die for. *But* sometimes *very* desperate situations called for *very* desperate measures. An intelligent, calculating and extremely methodical man carried out these murders.

You will have read in this book that the medical profession of the day thought the killer had shown some medical knowledge. I would like to reiterate that there was nothing frenzied about these murders, they were performed in places that Dr. Barnardo felt safe enough to carry out the post mortem mutilations on these women.

I do not believe for one moment that any CID members had anything to do with these murders. In my opinion amongst close friends and fellow church members, Anderson, Arnold or Monro may have spoke in detail about there work with the confidence that it would have gone no further. Unfortunately for them Dr. Barnardo listened with great interest.

No one would be spared in his wrath; the Police, Jews and even the Masons would be targeted by using some of their rituals and words (Goulston Street Graffito).

This deed had to go down in history as the deed that cleaned up the East End, and in reality that is exactly what it did do.

As a direct result of this fact the Police force went on to be better trained and more men patrolled the streets. There was more lighting placed in the streets and in the courts. The area as a whole was cleaned up. New landlords bought the run down properties including Dr Barnardo and refurbished them into cheap but clean places for the poor to rent. The police became stricter over the whole issue of prostitution. Brothels were closed down and owners were fined for keeping illicit houses. Prostitution was not as blatant as it had been before, especially on the streets. I cannot say prostitution was totally abolished, as I would be lying. Even today you could find a prostitute in the East End just as easily as you could find one anywhere in the world. Today you probably would not find her drunk and starving to death, or down a dark alley doing her business. Today you certainly would not get her services for four pence or a stale loaf of bread.

You may think that Polly Nichols murder was not that brutal, so why was it reported in the papers if other similar murders of Unfortunates were never reported? *The simple answer is that previous murders were not committed by a serial killer, who had decided that even his first victim's murder would make the headlines.*

The letter Dr Barnardo wrote to The Times caused excitement and panic, leading to many other Ripper letters being sent to both the Police and the Newspapers. Unfortunately as in this murder case and in many other to follow there are people who send hoax letters about the case to the police and to the press.

In my opinion the Dear Boss letter is actually written by Dr Barnardo. There are a number of similarities to the letter and his style of writing. By this I refer to the underlining of words and the red ink used to pen the letters.

Opposite you will see a copy of the Dear Boss letter as featured earlier in the book and a picture of Dr Barnardo including a copy of his signature.

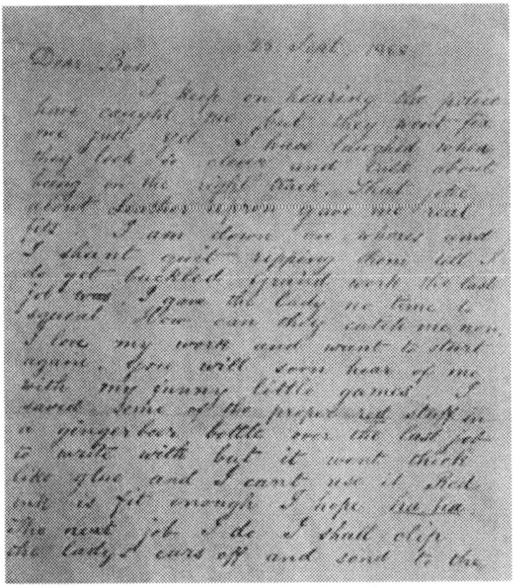

25 Sept. 1888.

Dear Boss

I keep on hearing the police have caught me but they wont fix me just yet. I have laughed when they look so clever and talk about being on the right track. That joke about Leather Apron gave me real fits. I am down on whores and I shant quit ripping them till I do get buckled. Grand work the last job was. I gave the lady no time to squeal. How can they catch me now. I love my work and want to start again. You will soon hear of me with my funny little games. I saved some of the proper red stuff in a ginger beer bottle over the last job to write with but it went thick like glue and I cant use it. Red ink is fit enough I hope ha. ha. The next job I do I shall clip the ladys ears off and send to the

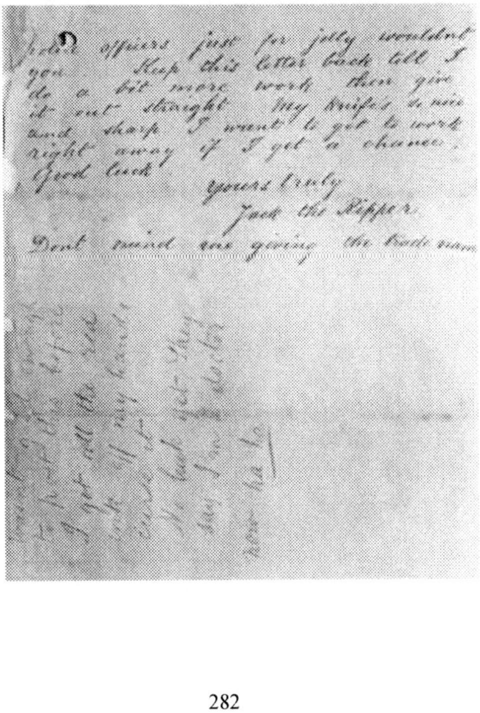

police officers just for jolly wouldnt you. Keep this letter back till I do a bit more work then give it out straight. My knifes so nice and sharp I want to get to work right away if I get a chance. Good luck.

Yours truly

Jack the Ripper

Dont mind me giving the trade name

got all the red ink off my hands curse it No luck yet. They say I'm a doctor now ha ha

From a photograph taken shortly before his death

The Yorkshire Ripper in the 1970s case is a prime example. The police in this case broadcast the playing of an audio cassette, in which a man's voice could be heard talking about the killings. The police officers wasted a lot of valuable time thinking that the man on the tape was the Yorkshire Ripper only to find out later it was a hoax. As each murder in 1888 became more horrific, public interest and panic ensued. At some murder sites a crowd would quickly gather; residents would charge anyone interested a few pence to see where the woman was butchered. Even the International workers educational club charged a fee to anyone who wanted to enter the yard where Elizabeth Strides body had been discovered.

The murders caused vigilante groups to be formed including the one run by George Lusk. Lusk was elected President of the Whitechapel Vigilance committee on September 10th 1888. Lusk went on to receive a hoax parcel from the Ripper which contained a human kidney. These vigilante groups also caused panic; anyone acting even a little strangely could be seen being dragged of to one of the Police stations followed by an angry mob. Jews would have there windows smashed by frightened residents who believed that because the description of the killer that had been given by a witness was that of a foreign looking man.

Even today the story of Jack the Ripper still has an impact on anyone who reads about him or watches a film about him or even goes on one of the interesting Ripper walks around the East End. There is something enigmatic about the Victorian period as a whole. The fact that a man could brutally kill women on the streets of London and get away with it completely is the stuff of fiction, surely.

Today Jack the Ripper is now a part of the school curriculum, only recently a friend's son asked me to help him do his homework on Jack the Ripper. I have since done talks at secondary schools on this very subject.
It is a great shame that this name, invented out of need, is still a legend today. There have been numerous films and documentaries on this subject, and equally as many books written.

If you go on to read one other book on Jack the Ripper may I suggest that you read 'Jack the Ripper A to Z', by Paul Begg, Martin Fido and Keith Skinner. Also The Complete Jack the Ripper by Donald Rumbelow.

To anyone like me who has a great interest in the case these good books would be a very valuable source to use to check facts, correct spelling of names and are fascinating book's to just absorb. I can only say that during my research of the case, the Jack the Ripper A to Z book became my Ripper Bible (no pun intended).

There is a fantastic web site dedicated to Jack the Ripper and should be looked at by anyone with an interest in the case. This web site is full of all the facts on the case and is constantly updated. This website is www.casebook.org

If there is only one undying fact about the case that everyone who writes about it would agree on, it has to be that Jack the Ripper will never be brought to justice.

I found this letter to The Times written by Dr John Thomas Barnardo, in which he makes his feelings clear on the subject of deprivation in the East End.

"THOS. J. BARNARDO.

18 to 26, Stepney-causeway.   **October 6th.**

Sir,

Stimulated by the recently revealed Whitechapel horrors many voices are daily heard suggesting as many different schemes to remedy degraded social conditions, all of which doubtless contain some practical elements. I trust you will allow one other voice to be raised on behalf of the children. For the saddest feature of the common lodging-houses in Whitechapel and other parts of London is that so many of their inmates are children. Indeed, it is impossible to describe the state in which myriads of young people live who were brought up in these abodes of poverty and of crime.

I and others are at work almost day and night rescuing boys and girls from the foul contamination of these human sewers; but while the law permits children to herd in these places, there is little that can be done except to snatch a few here and there from ruin and await patiently those slower changes which many have advocated. Meanwhile, a new generation is actually growing up in them. We want to make it illegal for the keepers of licensed lodging-houses to which adults resort to admit young children upon any pretext whatever. It is also desirable that the existing laws relating to the custody and companionship of the children should be more rigidly enforced. At the same time some provision is urgently required for the shelter of young children of the casual or tramp class, something between the casual wards of the workhouse and the lodging-house itself, places where only young people under 16 would be admitted, where they would be free to enter and as free to depart, and which could be made self-supporting, or nearly so. A few enterprising efforts to open lodging-houses of this class for the young only would do immense good.

Only four days before the recent murders I visited No. 32, Flower and Dean-street, the house in which the unhappy woman Stride occasionally lodged. I had been examining many of the common lodging-houses in Bethnal-green that night, endeavouring to elicit from the inmates their opinions upon a certain aspect of the subject. In the kitchen of No. 32 there were many persons, some of them being girls and women of the same unhappy class as that to which poor Elizabeth Stride belonged. The company soon recognized me, and the conversation turned upon the previous murders. The female inmates of the kitchen seemed thoroughly frightened at the dangers to which they were presumably exposed. In an explanatory fashion I put before them the scheme which had suggested itself to my mind, by which children at all events could be saved from the contamination of the common lodging-houses and the streets, and so to some extent the supply cut off which feeds the vast ocean of misery in this great city.

The pathetic part of my story is that my remarks were manifestly followed with deep interest by all the women. Not a single scoffing voice was raised in ridicule or opposition. One poor creature, who had evidently been drinking, exclaimed somewhat bitterly to the following effect:- "We're all up to no good, and no one cares what becomes of us. Perhaps some of us will be killed next!" And then she added, "If anybody had helped the likes of us long ago we would never have come to this!"

Impressed by the unusual manner of the people, I could not help noticing their appearance somewhat closely, and I saw how evidently some of them were moved. I have since visited the mortuary in which were lying the remains of the poor woman Stride, and I at once recognized her as one of those who stood around me in the kitchen of the common lodging-house on the occasion of my visit last Wednesday week.

In all the wretched dens where such unhappy creatures live are to be found hundreds, if not thousands, of poor children who breathe from their very birth an atmosphere fatal to all goodness. They are so heavily handicapped at the start in the race of life that the future is to most of them absolutely hopeless. They are continually surrounded by influences so vile that decency is outraged and virtue becomes impossible.

Surely the awful revelations consequent upon the recent tragedies should stir the whole community up to action and to the resolve to deliver the children of to-day who will be the men and women of to-morrow from so evil an environment.

I am, Sir, your obedient servant,
THOS. J. BARNARDO.”

Quote

"Are we as Christian men, always under all circumstances to be governed by English Law? Is judicial law always to be co-extensive with moral law? Does a period never arise when a higher law may compel a man to take a step, which the law of the land would possibly condemn?"

Dr John Thomas Barnardo 1888

Bibliography

Jack the Ripper, the final solution
Stephen Knight (Grafton Books 1976)
Jack the Ripper – sunning up and a verdict
Colin Wilson and Robin Odell (Corgi Books 1988)
Jack the Ripper the Final Chapter
Paul H Feldman (Virgin Books 1998)
Jack the Ripper the uncensored facts
Paul Begg (Robson Books 1988)
The Mammoth book of Jack the Ripper
Maxim Jakubowsk and Nathan Braund
Jack the Ripper an Encyclopaedia
John J Eddleston (Metro Publishing 2002)
Jack the Ripper a Psychic Investigation
Pamela Ball (Arcturus Publishing 1998)
The many faces of Jack the Ripper
MJ Trow (Summersdale Publishers 1998)
The Complete Jack the Ripper
Donald Rumbelow (W H Allen 1975)
The Diary of Jack the Ripper
Shirley Harrison (Blake Publishing 1998)
The Ripper File
Elwyn Jones and John Lloyd (Futura Publications 1975)
A Casebook on Jack the Ripper
Richard Whittington-Egan (Wildy & Sons Limited 1975)
Jack the Ripper
William Stewart (The Camelot Press 1939)
Hidden Evidence
David Owen
Psychic Detectives
Jenny Randles and Peter Hough (Silverdale Books 2001)
Crimes and Victims
Frank Smyth (Abbeydale Press 2003)
The Harlot Killer. The story of Jack the Ripper
Allan Barnard
Jack the Ripper the first American serial killer
Stewart Evans and Keith Skinner
Jack the Ripper Letters from Hell
Keith Skinner and Stewart Evans
Jack the Ripper
Dan Farson

Bibliography

The Crimes, detection and death of Jack the Ripper
Martin Fido
Sickert and the Ripper Crimes
Jean Overton Fuller
Jack the Ripper the bloody truth. The Ripper File.
The true face of Jack the Ripper
Melvin Harris
Jack the Ripper a bibliography and review of the literature
Alexander Kelly and David Sharp
Ripper Diary
Seth Linder and Caroline Morris and Keith Skinner
The people of the Abyss.
Jack London
The Mystery of Jack the Ripper
Leonard Matters.
Jack the Ripper in fact and fiction
Robin Odell
Jack the Ripper the simple truth
Bruce Paley (Headline Books 1996)
Jack the Ripper "light hearted friend"
Richard Wallace
Murder "whatduneit"
JHH Gaute and Robin Odell (Harrap Limited 1982)
The identity of Jack the Ripper
Donald McCormic (ArrowBooks 1970)
The Complete History of Jack the Ripper
Phillip Sugden (Robinson Publishing 1995)
Portrait of a Killer
Patricia Cornwell (Time Warner 2003)
The Last Victim
Anne E Graham and Carol Emmas
Jack the Ripper the Definitive History
Paul Begg (Pearson Press 2004)
The Complete Jack the Ripper
Donald Rumbelow
Father to nobody's children
David E Fessenden
Dr Barnardo as I knew him
A R Neuman

Bibliography

Dr Barnardo
J W Bready
Barnardo
Gillian Wagner
Barnardo of Stepney
A E Williams
The Trail of George Chapman
H L Adam
The Jack the Ripper A – Z
Paul Begg, Martin Fido, and Keith Skinner
(Headline Book Publishers 1991)
The Autumn of Terror
Tom Cullen
Uncle Jack
Tony Williams & Humphrey Price (Orion Books 2005)
Directories
The Medical Directory
The Medical Registers
Journals
Daily Express
Daily News
Daily Telegraph
East London Advertiser
Evening News
The Criminologist
North London Press
The Observer
Pall Mall Gazette
The People
The Star
The Sun
The Times
Documents
Scotland Yard Files, relating to the Whitechapel Murders
Home Office Files, relating to the Whitechapel Murders
Internet
Jack the Ripper Casebook

Printed in the United Kingdom
by Lightning Source UK Ltd.
135906UK00002B/5/A